LINDSAY BUROKER'S

For ged in Blood

II

A HIGH FANTASY NOVEL IN AN ERA OF STEAM

D1729144

FOREWORD

Welcome, good reader, to the conclusion of the Emperor's Edge series. I've had fun creating these characters and writing their adventures, and I'd like to thank you for sticking with me through seven books. I've appreciated the positive reviews, the nice emails, the fan fiction and fan art, and just knowing that people enjoy spending time in this world.

I'd like to also thank my fabulous beta readers, Kendra Highley and Becca Andre, who've stuck with me since Book 1. They've made a lot of great suggestions along the way, and I know these are better stories due to their advice. I've also been fortunate enough to have a great team of people who have helped get these books ready to publish. Thank you to Shelley Holloway, my editor, Glendon Haddix, my cover designer, and Ted Risk, my ebook formatter.

Now I better let you get into the story, as I seem to remember leaving a cliffhanger at the end of Part 1...

CHAPTER 1

AMARANTHE WASN'T DEAD. AT LEAST, SHE DIDN'T THINK so. Dead people probably didn't hurt all over. The flying lifeboat had insulated them from the crash somehow, though her head had connected with a couple more walls before the craft stopped bouncing.

"Books?" she asked into the darkness. "Akstyr? I hope one of you is alive, because I have no idea how to open that door and get out of this thing."

A deep, pained sigh came from underneath her—she'd tumbled back on top of the men again during the landing. Amaranthe crawled to the side, though there wasn't much open space in the cramped cabin.

"One of you?" Books repeated. "You have no preference as to whom your survivor is, nor a belief that one of us would be more equal to the task of opening a door secured by ancient unfathomable technology, or of deciphering instructions written in an inscrutable alien tongue?"

He must not be wounded horribly if he could utter all that.

"You saw instructions?" Amaranthe asked.

"Well, no, but it was hard to get a good look in the dark. And while we were being shot at."

"We still have the darkness problem," Amaranthe pointed out. The viewport that had appeared while they were in flight had disappeared before the crash, leaving the inside of their lifeboat utterly black. "Akstyr?" Amaranthe patted about, finding his back, then following it up to his neck so she could check his pulse. She hadn't heard from him since he'd hurled

himself into the craft, dodging the incendiary beams of those indestructible cubes.

He mumbled something at her touch on his neck.

"What?" Amaranthe breathed a sigh of relief. They might be a thousand miles from the capital, but at least they were all alive.

"Wanna rest," he slurred. He lay facedown, his mouth pressed into the floor. "But some muddy's knee is up my buss."

"I think he's referring to your body part," Amaranthe told Books mildly, fairly certain she wasn't sitting on anyone anymore. Though she couldn't be sure what a "buss" was.

"Ah." Books shifted. "I'd wondered why that section of the floor was so bony."

"Ma buss not bony," Akstyr slurred.

Maybe more than his positioning accounted for the mangled words. Amaranthe prodded his scalp and found a lump. He must have hit his head, among other things. He'd also been wearier than a long-distance runner after a race when he'd stumbled into the lifeboat. Out of curiosity, Amaranthe investigated her own scalp. She snorted when she found three lumps. Maybe her words were coming out slurred too.

Books groaned as he stood up. "I'll see if I can find the—"

The door slid up, the material disappearing into the hull. Starlight, freezing air, and the scent of snow-covered pine trees entered. The cold air slithered through Amaranthe's leggings, and she tugged her dress down as far as it would go. A chunk of blonde hair tumbled into her eyes. She shoved it behind her ear and wished for a beaver fur hat. She had a feeling her Suan costume wasn't going to be suitable for this next adventure. Not to mention that ridiculous underwear she'd let Maldynado pick out. One slip down an icy slope, and she'd have snow all the way up her—

She sighed. At least the fur boots were practical.

"Good work, Books." Amaranthe patted around, finding two of their rifles. The cartridge ammunition littered the floor, and she scooped up as much as she could. Who knew what they'd

face out there? The craft could have plopped them down into grimbal or makarovi territory.

"Uhm, yes. Except I didn't do anything. Perhaps it sensed that we've landed and is ready to spew us forth into the world of its own accord."

"That's fine," Amaranthe said. "I'm ready to be spewed."

"Think I was already spewed," Akstyr muttered and curled his legs up to his chest. "It's cold. I wanna stay here and sleep. Be warm."

"If the door closes again," Books said, "you may be stuck inside forever, because I don't know how to open it."

Akstyr lurched to his feet and stumbled out into the snow. "Never mind. I'm ready."

He barely made it through the threshold before slumping against the hull.

"Why don't you stay here," Amaranthe suggested, "and try to make a fire? Books and I will figure out where we are."

When she stepped outside, shivering at the wind scouring the mountainside, her optimism floundered. A few pines, the bases half buried by drifts, dotted the slope below them. They'd landed above the tree line and, she feared, far from any towns. Not good. They weren't prepared for winter wilderness survival conditions.

Books stepped out beside her and surveyed their dark surroundings. "Hm."

"Does that mean you don't know where we are either?" Amaranthe wished she had an idea of how far they'd flown and in which direction. Were they fifty miles from the capital? Or five hundred? Though she'd been out of Stumps more times in the last year than in her entire life prior to meeting Sicarius and the others, she didn't exactly qualify as a world explorer yet.

"That may be a pass over there," Books mused. "And those four peaks in a row remind me of the Scarlet Sisters, though there are arrangements like that in other mountain ranges, too, I'm certain. We don't seem to have left the climate zone, albeit we're at a higher and, ah, chillier altitude. The stars are familiar."

"That was a yes, right? You don't know where we are?"

Books grumped something that might have been agreement.

"I hear a train," Akstyr said from where he still leaned against the lifeboat hull, his eyes closed, his arms wrapped tightly about himself and the rumpled guard uniform he'd acquired on the way down to the *Behemoth*.

Amaranthe perked up. He was right. She caught the distant chuffing of an engine working hard to pull its load up an incline.

"Oh!" Books said. "Those *are* the Scarlet Sisters then. That'll be the East-West Line, and that train is either traveling to or from Stumps."

Given the chaos the *Behemoth's* appearance must have caused—Amaranthe had no idea if it'd sunken back down into the lake or taken off for some distant destination, but people would have witnessed it either way—she thought traveling *from* was the more likely scenario. Or *fleeing* from perhaps. Still... "Let's see if we can get to the rails before it's gone. If it's going to the city—"

"It could be our ride home," Books finished.

"Does this mean no fire?" Akstyr asked.

"Sorry." Amaranthe grabbed his arm. They'd have to hurry to have any chance of scrambling down the mountain in time.

"You can sleep on the way back to the city," Books said. "We're over one hundred and fifty miles from Stumps."

Amaranthe's mind boggled at the idea that they'd traveled that far in a couple of minutes, but she was more concerned about getting back now. She handed Books the other rifle and led the way down the mountainside, plowing through snow that enveloped her legs up to her knees with every step. It didn't take long for sweat to break out on her brow and weariness to slow her limbs. Her newly acquired bruises and lumps further protested this unasked-for workout, and she wasn't altogether upset when Akstyr announced he was too tired to go on. They stopped to rest, huddling beneath the boughs of a tree for protection from the wind. The chugs of the train faded from hearing.

"I believe that one was heading away from the capital," Books said.

Amaranthe doubted he could tell—with the mountain walls, canyons, and crevasses distorting sound, *she* couldn't—but she could understand the desire for optimism. Especially when her toes were freezing in her boots. Once again, she was glad she'd ignored Maldynado's suggestion to wear sandals to the yacht club.

"Anyone have any food?" Akstyr asked when they started out again.

"Not unless Amaranthe's purse contains more than glue for her fake nose," Books said.

"Actually, I have some of Sicarius's dried meat-and-fat bars in here," Amaranthe said.

"I'd rather eat the nose glue," Akstyr said.

"You may change your mind after another day out here."

Akstyr's grumbled response was too low to make out.

They continued their trudge, cold and miserable and unequipped for the terrain, though traveling downhill took some of the anguish out of the trek. As dawn broke over the mountains, the clear sky untouched by smog and impressive in its gradated pinks and oranges, they reached the pass. The cleared tracks, snow piled high to either side, wound through the treacherous terrain, a black snake navigating boulders and slopes.

Amaranthe angled toward a bridge, the support structure towering well over the tracks. It'd be an opportune place—or rather the *only* place—to jump onto a moving train, and the team had practiced such maneuvers before.

That didn't keep Books from groaning as they approached. "Why am I certain of what's in your mind and certain it'll be dangerous?"

"Really, Books, we've been chased by man-incinerating machines, flung from an aircraft so alien our science can't begin to fathom it, and hurtled hundreds of miles to crash on a mountainside. You're going to complain about something as benign as hopping onto a train?"

"She's got a point, you know," Akstyr said. "It's freezing out here. I'd do just about anything to get off this mountain."

Books's harrumphed.

Amaranthe nudged Akstyr. "He's just complaining out of habit now. It's what men do when they get old."

"I am *not* old," Books said. "I probably wouldn't even have any gray hair yet if I weren't traipsing around after you all the time. This last year has been enough to age a man ten."

"That's a lie. You had gray temples when I met you."

"Fine, these last *two* years have been enough to age a man ten."

They'd reached the base of the bridge, frothy white water frozen into ridges of ice far below, and Amaranthe stopped teasing Books. She didn't wish to remind him of the death of his son and the difficult times he'd faced before joining her team. Granted, he was right that the last year hadn't been without difficulties either. But it'd all end soon. One way or another.

This time, Amaranthe heard the train first, the distant chugs coming from the west. "It's heading to the capital. This is our opportunity." She waved for them to climb halfway up one of the towers rising from the suspension bridge. "It's still dark enough that, if we're lucky, the engineer won't notice us crouching up there."

"We're due some luck," Books said.

"Let's be happy there are trains coming through and that we didn't have to wait for days out here." The East-West Line was a busy one, taking passengers and freight from Stumps to the various ports on the west coast and back, but Amaranthe hadn't known what to expect with the capital locked down. She did know the train would be stopped and searched before being allowed into the city. Best to worry about getting on first. "Akstyr, can you make the climb?" she asked.

Books was shimmying up the steel supports, but Akstyr stood at the base, staring upward, his eyes sunken and his body slumped.

"Yes," he sighed and started climbing. "But promise me I can curl up in a corner and sleep the rest of the way back to the city."

"It'd probably be best to stay on the roof," Books called

down, "so they don't know we've sneaked aboard. You can sleep up there."

"Sounds cold."

Amaranthe secured her rifle across her back and climbed up after them without commenting, though she agreed the roof might be best. That way, they could jump off the train as it was pulling into the checkpoint, before any soldiers climbed aboard to search.

By the time she joined the men on a ledge halfway up the tower, the train was lumbering into view, its pace slow as it wound its way up the mountainside and into the pass.

"Dead ancestors with caltrops," Amaranthe said when she spotted black-painted cars with golden imperial army logos on the sides. Those cars, dozens of them, would be filled with soldiers. More troops to support Flintcrest? Or Heroncrest? Or even Ravido? Whoever's men they were, they wouldn't be coming to join Sespian.

"*Definitely* best to stay on the roof," Books said, "or avoid getting on altogether. How do you feel about waiting for the next train?"

Akstyr groaned, doubtlessly displeased at the idea of climbing back down, then having to climb back up again later. And then there was the cold and the limited food supply. Amaranthe flexed her numbed fingers within mittens made to ward off the chill during a quick outing into the city, not to protect digits from sub-zero mountain temperatures. Thanks to the wind, she already couldn't feel her nose, and white crystals had frozen her lashes together. Now that they'd stopped moving, the chill was more noticeable. The sun might bring a reprieve, but another storm could come in that day too.

"We have no idea how long we'd be waiting," she said, "and the next train might be more of the same. Someone ought to block the pass so all these reinforcements can't continue to trickle in."

"*No*," Books said, sounding like Sicarius for a moment, he being the only one of the men who blatantly naysayed her.

Amaranthe had simply been musing aloud, so she wasn't affronted by his vehemence. Their priority should be getting back to the city, not attacking supply lines, and she knew it. Yet... she had a hard time dropping the idea now that it'd formed.

"We don't have any explosives," Akstyr said. "And I'm too tired to make a landslide."

"We wouldn't necessarily need anything so permanent. What if we jumped on behind the locomotive, and decoupled the rest of the cars, the same as the last time we hopped a train? The soldiers would be stranded, and the railway into the city would be blocked until someone got another locomotive out to move the cars."

Books was staring at her. "Can't you ever take the easy route? Why can't we catch a ride into the city and leave it at that?"

"You disagree that it'd be wise to deny reinforcements to the generals competing with Sespian for the throne?"

"No, but why do *we* always have to do these things?" Books sounded tired and frazzled. They'd all been up for too long without sleep.

"Who else will?" Amaranthe asked.

He growled. "Maybe we should stand back, let them all fight each other until they're tired of it, then come in and offer a less bloodthirsty system of government to the survivors."

"You think it would be that easy?"

Books sighed and leaned his head against the steel beam. "No."

"It's going to be here in a second." Akstyr pointed at the oncoming train, the black locomotive leading the way, its grill guard like a wolf's snarling face, full of sharp fangs.

Amaranthe shifted her weight on the ledge, readying herself to jump. "Coal car," she instructed.

Books didn't look pleased, but he didn't resume the argument.

The pass was flat compared to the terrain the train had finished climbing, and it picked up speed as it bore down on the bridge. They'd have to time their jump carefully. None of them were fresh.

Judging the approach in her head, listening to the clicketyclack of the wheels rolling over rail segments, Amaranthe said, "Now!" and dropped from the tower. Wind roared in her ears, then faded as her feet hit the coal.

Elbows jostled her as she turned the landing into a roll, Akstyr and Books doing the same. They couldn't have dropped in any closer to each other if they'd held hands. She banged someone with her rifle, and the coal scraped her fake nose off, but that was the worst of their injuries. As one, they rose into low crouches, careful to keep their heads down. If someone in the first troop car had seen them drop, or noticed them now... She was all too aware that Sicarius, Maldynado, and Basilard weren't with her this time. As much as her ego wanted to reject the notion, she, Books, and Akstyr were the weakest fighters on the team. When she'd been separating everyone into neat parties, she hadn't planned on combat for her half. Naive, that. She hoped Sespian was finding her men useful in Fort Urgot.

Books pointed to the locomotive and signed, *Do we take it first? Or try to decouple the rest of the train?*

The last time the team had decoupled cars on a moving train, Sicarius had been the one to do it. Even though she'd suggested it, the idea of attempting the maneuver herself daunted Amaranthe. She didn't know how much physical strength it would take. At least nobody was shooting at them this time. Yet.

She eyed the route ahead. The locomotive had sped off the bridge and was on a downhill slope, picking up speed as it went. More snowy peaks loomed ahead, so there'd be more uphill swings.

Let's wait to do that, Amaranthe signed and waved at the rest of the cars, *until we slow for another climb. It'll be less dangerous then. Besides, the engineer and fireman will be alert and ready for trouble if we try to take over after the majority of their train wanders off of its own accord.*

Agreed, Books signed.

We'll take care of those men first. She pointed at the locomotive.

Books grimaced, but didn't argue. Akstyr yawned. Such heartening support.

On a military train, the men in the locomotive would be trained fighters, a soldier and an officer shoveling coal and working the controls. Knowing the transport was heading into trouble, its commander might have placed guards up front as well.

I'll go left, Amaranthe signed, *and you go right, Books. With luck, there'll only be two of them, and we can stick our rifles in their backs and convince them to tie themselves up.*

Akstyr, Books signed, *you can usually tell how many people there are in a room. Is it just two?*

Akstyr closed his eyes, winced, and shook his head. "I can't right now, sorry." He didn't bother with hand signs, and Amaranthe struggled to hear him over the wind and the grinding of wheels on rails. "When I try to summon mental energy, my head hurts like there's a knife stabbing into the backs of my eyeballs."

Old-fashioned way then, she signed. *Akstyr, you come in after me and help out if there's more than two people, or there's trouble.*

Akstyr tossed a lump of coal. "When is there *not* trouble?"

The odds suggest something will go easily for us eventually. Amaranthe winked. It was more bravado than belief, but she tried to use the thought to bolster herself. Rifle in hand, she clambered down the side of the coal car, the wind tearing at the hem of her dress—ridiculous outfit to hijack a train in—and pulled her way along the ledge toward the locomotive.

On the other side, Books was doing the same. Amaranthe trusted they'd make the same progress, but paused to peer in the window next to the cab door before jumping inside. The two men in black military fatigues with engineering patches were as she'd expected, a sergeant leaning on a shovel by the furnace and a lieutenant standing behind the seat overlooking the long cylindrical boiler and the tracks beyond. What she *didn't* expect were the two kids in civilian clothing. A boy and a girl, both appearing to be about fifteen years old, shared the cab with the two men. From the rear side window, Amaranthe couldn't see much of their faces, but the girl had a pair of brown pigtails and sat in the engineer's seat, pointing at various gauges and speaking, asking questions perhaps. The boy stood shoulder-to-shoulder with the sergeant, a book of schematics open in his hands as the fireman pointed things out inside an open panel.

"What is this?" Amaranthe muttered. "A private tutoring lesson?" She'd be less mystified if this were a civilian transport; she could imagine some warrior-caste lord on a family vacation arranging for special access for his privileged offspring, but what could children be doing on a military train? Was one of the invading generals, having realized he'd be in the capital for some time, having his family brought in? She couldn't fathom it. Even if there wasn't much outright fighting in the streets—or hadn't been when she left—who would bring kids into a volatile situation?

At the other window, on the opposite side of the cabin, Books's nose and eyes were visible, he too wearing a perplexed expression.

Amaranthe tilted her head, indicating they should go ahead with their plan. They still needed control of the locomotive. The sergeant and officer wore their standard-issue utility knives, and there were flintlock rifles mounted within reach above the cab doors, but the men were otherwise unarmed. Neither of the youths had weapons, as far as Amaranthe could tell, though in examining them, she took a closer look at their clothing and grew even more confused. Beneath parkas suitable for the cold weather, they wore homespun garments of light colors and materials, the styles foreign, though Amaranthe wasn't worldly enough to put a finger on their origin. She only knew the children weren't wearing the typical factory-made clothing or styles currently common around the capital.

Books was moving, so she ended her musings. A second before Amaranthe opened the cab door, the boy glanced in her direction. She hadn't thought she'd made a noise, but she must

have. Books opened his own door and jumped inside, rifle at the ready. Amaranthe entered as well, raising her firearm to her shoulder, aiming at the lieutenant's head. The weapon wasn't ideal in the tight space, but she had enough room. When the officer spun around, his eyes crossed as he found himself staring at the muzzle.

The sergeant's hand twitched toward his knife, but Books prodded his arm with his own rifle, and the man scowled and desisted. The youths—siblings, Amaranthe decided, as soon as she saw their faces and the gray-blue eyes they shared—spread their arms to their sides, calmly opening their hands to show they held no weapons. That calm was surprising in people too young to have had military training, and she made a note to watch them, though the soldiers were more of an immediate threat.

"Who are you people?" the lieutenant asked, glancing out the door, as if to assure himself that yes indeed the train was still moving. Rapidly. He also shifted his stance so that he stood in front of the girl. The sergeant shifted so he stood in front of the boy, though his glances were toward the rifles above the door.

"My apologies for hopping onto your train without a boarding pass. We found ourselves lost in the mountains and need a ride to Stumps." Amaranthe eased forward a couple of inches so Akstyr could squeeze in behind her. "Get their weapons," she told him without taking her eyes from the soldiers.

"Hijacking an imperial train is punishable by death," the lieutenant said, glowering as Akstyr removed his knife and patted him down for hidden items.

"Is it?" Amaranthe asked. "Then I probably shouldn't tell you it's not our first. Search the children for weapons, too, Akstyr."

"*Children?*" the girl whispered to her brother. She had a grown woman's curves, even if the pigtails made her look young, and Amaranthe probably could have used a different word. Indeed, the speculative consideration Akstyr gave her as he searched her suggested she was plenty old enough by his teenaged reckoning. Amaranthe was thankful his pat down was professional.

"She's talking about you, naturally," the brother responded.

They were speaking in Turgonian, but with a faint accent. Again, Amaranthe couldn't place it. She wondered if Books had a better idea.

"Oh, yes," the sister said, "I'm certain the three minutes longer you've had in the world than I grants you scads of wisdom and maturity."

"Mother does say I was born with a book in my hands. I imagine that gave me a head start."

The lieutenant exchanged glances with the sergeant, and the two men lunged, one toward Amaranthe, and one toward the door behind her. She reacted instantly, ramming the muzzle of the rifle into the officer's sternum, the blow accurate enough to halt his charge. She tried to whip the weapon around to crack him in the head with the butt, but it caught on the doorjamb, and she settled for stomping on his instep. In the same movement, she brought her knee up to catch the soldier angling for the exit. By that point, he was stumbling for the exit, since Books had slammed the butt of his own weapon into the sergeant's back. Amaranthe lowered her rifle, tapping the side of the lieutenant's head with the muzzle. He'd bent over under her attack, and didn't straighten, not with the cool kiss of metal against his temple.

"Next time, we'll shoot." Amaranthe hoped they wouldn't know she was lying.

Akstyr had a knife out and was keeping an eye on the siblings, who were exchanging looks of their own. Amaranthe thought she read an oh-well-we-tried quality in their expressions. They'd been hoping to divert their attackers' attention with their arguing? Hm.

"Slag off," the sergeant snarled. Sort of. His cheek was smashed into the textured metal floor, and the endearment lacked clarity.

"Akstyr, tie everyone up, please. The sooner we get to phase two of our plan, the better." Amaranthe peeked out the door toward the coal car and the rest of the train. As long as everything

was attached, anyone could amble up front and cause trouble. For all she knew, shift change was three minutes away.

The girl murmured a question to her brother, not in Turgonian this time. He nodded back.

Amaranthe met Books's eyes, sure he'd have an answer as to the language.

Kyattese, he signed.

Kyattese? Emperor's warts, now what? It was bad enough the Nurians were tangled up in this vying for the throne—did the Kyattese want some part of it too?

Amaranthe signed, *Any idea who they might be?*

She was aware of the siblings watching her, noticing the finger twitches, though she was positive they wouldn't understand Basilard's hand code. Even his own Mangdorian people were hard pressed to follow it, given how much he'd added to the lexicon over the last year.

"I'm out of rope and belts." Akstyr had tied the lieutenant, but not the sergeant yet. He gave Amaranthe an aggravated look.

"Get creative," she told him.

"My head hurts too much for creativity. I—" Akstyr stood abruptly. "Sci—" He switched to code: *Science.*

What? Amaranthe stepped toward the siblings. She knew it wasn't the soldiers, so that only left—was that one of those I'm-about-to-fling-magic looks of concentration on the boy's face? Though she was reluctant to aim her rifle at a youth, Amaranthe prodded him in the chest with the barrel, hoping to distract him.

Something popped on the furnace, and black smoke poured into the cabin. Amaranthe cursed, left with little choice but to club the kid. As she drew back the rifle to swing, the girl reached into her coat, toward a pocket or perhaps a belt pouch.

"Books," Amaranthe barked.

"I can't—ergh."

Someone grabbed Amaranthe from behind, yanking her away from the siblings and propelling her into the rear of the cab with jaw-cracking force. Though she threw an elbow back, trying to catch her attacker in the ribs, the person evaded the blow. Her rifle was torn from her fingers. She didn't know if it was the same someone or someone else. Men in black uniforms moved in her peripheral vision, and soon the cabin was so crowded with bodies, she couldn't have unpinned herself even if someone *didn't* have a forearm rammed against her spine. Now it was her face that was smashed against something, her eyes meeting Books's—he was in a mirror position two feet from her. It was neither the familiar sergeant nor the lieutenant who had him pinned, a cutlass prodding his back, but a grim-faced captain. Strong, calloused fingers tightened around the back of Amaranthe's neck. She couldn't see her own attacker, but he spoke from right behind her.

"Captain," he asked in a rich baritone, that of an older but obviously not—as the grip pinning her proved—infirm man, "is hijacking a train still a capital punishment in the empire?"

"Yes, my lord. It is. In addition," the captain said, his tone icy, "it is also quite illegal to attack warrior-caste children."

Amaranthe blinked. It was all the movement she could manage at the moment. Warrior-caste children that muttered to each other in Kyattese? Just who in all the abandoned mines in the empire was standing behind her? Another general charging in to make a claim on the throne?

Books, with his head turned sideways toward her, must have had a better view of the man behind her, or he was simply more adept at assembling the pieces of this particular puzzle, for his mouth dropped open in... Amaranthe was sure that was recognition.

"Enlighten me," she whispered to him.

"I... I could be mistaken," Books whispered back, "since I've never met the man nor even seen him in person, military history not being my favorite subject in the least, but—"

The captain jostled Books, probably to discourage him from talking. Amaranthe wished the jostle would *en*courage him to get to the point.

"*Who?*" she mouthed, wanting the name, not an explanation.

The captain was discussing what to do with "these interlopers"

with a third man, another officer. Take them to the capital to face the magistrate or simply hurl them from the train and let the mountain—and the high-speed fall—handle the matter?

"That one is a criminal with a bounty on her head." A finger jabbed toward Amaranthe's nose. "The others may very well be too."

Books finally mouthed a response to Amaranthe's question. "Fleet Admiral Starcrest."

Amaranthe sagged insomuch as the iron grip holding her would allow.

One of the empire's greatest war heroes. And her just outed as a criminal. Oh, yes, this was sure to go well.

* * *

The air smelled of musty tent canvas, coal smoke, and the pungent scent of sandalwood incense. That aroma was popular amongst Nurian practitioners; they believed it focused the mind. An odd odor to find in a Turgonian army tent, but not a surprising one.

Few sounds came from within the canvas enclosure—only the soft hiss of the fire—but outside, men moved about. Some spoke, some grunted and grumbled as they carried gear, and others simply walked past, their boots crunching on snow and ice.

Sicarius opened his eyes. He shouldn't have. Wakefulness brought awareness.

And memory. And pain.

Finding the former too depressing to contemplate, he examined the latter, assessing his fitness. Though the aches that emanated from his calf, shoulder, and abdomen were not trivial, the physical pain wasn't as intense as he would have expected. He recalled being shot multiple times, and before that, the soul construct had torn a chunk out of his leg. He grew aware of bandages around the wounds, stiff after being saturated with blood that had since dried. All of his digits responded to orders to move, and he flexed his muscles without untoward discomfort.

The mental pain...

Sicarius closed his eyes again. His son was dead. Amaranthe was dead. The rest of her team was likely dead as well—at the least Basilard and Maldynado would have fallen, just as Sespian had, crushed beneath that monstrous artifact from the past.

Footsteps crunched outside the tent. A moment later, the flap lifted, and cold air flowed inside.

A white-haired general with thick spectacles strode in, followed by two Nurians, one the silver-haired practitioner who'd created the soul construct and the other, a younger fellow with a limp. Enemies, Sicarius's instincts cried, and he sat up, a hand going to his waist, where his black dagger usually hung. It wasn't there. None of his knives were. He'd been stripped of shirt and shoes as well. He might have attacked the Nurians anyway, but a strange tingle throbbed at his temple. He found himself lying down on his back again, his muscles operating of their own accord—no, of the *practitioner's* accord. In a final humiliation, his hands betrayed him by folding across his abdomen, fingers laced. His face tilted attentively toward the newcomers.

Flintcrest was eying him through those thick spectacles, chomping on a cigar as if he wished he were chomping on Sicarius. "It's not a good idea, Kor Nas. Safest to kill him right now, if you can."

"Of course I can," the silver-haired man said smoothly, his accent barely distinguishable. "But I wouldn't have brought my associate to continue healing his wounds if I intended to do that."

"This man isn't some soldier," Flintcrest said. "He's an ancestors-cursed assassin, a notorious one. He's killed dozens of high-ranking Turgonians, including one of my fellow satrap governors."

"I know precisely who he's killed. The Nurians have also suffered at his hands. But he can be made to work for us now, as surely as my soul construct did. Perhaps one of his first tasks will be to figure out a way to retrieve my pet from the bottom of

the lake." The Nurian's dark eyes glittered, the almond shapes narrowing further as they oozed menace toward Sicarius.

As far out into the lake as he'd hurled the creature's trap, Sicarius would drown trying to swim down and open it. Perhaps that was a way to escape this. Better to be dead than enslaved, especially now when there was nothing to live for, nothing waiting for him if he fought and escaped. One way or another, these people would send him to his death eventually. He cared little what happened in the meantime.

"Well, get him fixed up and out of my camp," Flintcrest said. "My men will welcome him even less than that beast of yours."

"That is the plan, General. After which target should I send him first?"

Flintcrest grimaced. "You want me to make use of an assassin?"

"You were willing to make use of my beast, as you call it."

"I... don't remember agreeing to that exactly either."

"So long as you agree to my people's requests for favorable trade agreements," spoke a third man as he pushed aside the tent flap and walked inside. In his early thirties, with shoulder-length black hair swept into a topknot, he wore a feathered flute and a long *rek rek* pipe across his back as others would wear a sword. The items were the symbols of a Nurian diplomat.

Kor Nas waved to the healer. "Finish repairing my new minion."

"Yes, *saison*."

Saison, the Nurian word didn't mean "master" precisely, more like a term of respect for a high-ranking practitioner, often a teacher, but it might as well have meant it in this case. He'd be loyal to the older man and do as told.

"I have not forgotten, *He shu*," Flintcrest told the diplomat. "The trade agreements will be created as promised."

He shu, that was an address for a male who shared blood with a great chief, close blood usually. After all the missions Sicarius had undertaken for Emperor Raumesys, ensuring Nuria wouldn't gain a toehold in the empire, it irked him to know

that the Nurians might have found a way in anyway. He didn't know whether they'd be worse than this Forge outfit or not. He decided he didn't care—what could he do about it at this point anyway?—though he did admit that it bothered him that everything he had endured in his life had been for naught.

The healer laid a hand on Sicarius's bandaged abdomen and warmth spread from the fingertips. Weariness seeped in as well. He didn't bother seeking a meditative state, didn't bother with trying to control his sleep—or his dreams. He simply sank into oblivion.

CHAPTER 2

MARANTHE, BOOKS, AND AKSTYR SAT AGAINST THE back of the locomotive cab, their wrists tied behind them and rifles aimed at their chests. This wasn't quite how Amaranthe had imagined the hijacking going. Judging by the scowls Books and Akstyr were shooting her, they thought the team should have remained in the coal car for the rest of the ride.

The fireman and engineer had returned to their duties, while a captain and colonel stood in a cluster with Starcrest, discussing the situation. In the confined space, one couldn't have squeezed in any more men, so the captain had been elected to hold the rifle on the prisoners. A redundant security measure, since Amaranthe's ankles were tied as well as her wrists, with her legs folded beneath her. She couldn't have started a brawl if she'd tried with all her might. In addition to Starcrest and the army men, the two siblings remained in the cramped cabin; they were standing in the doorway, probably hoping their presence wouldn't be noticed and they wouldn't be ordered to go back to the passenger cars. The captain glanced at them a few times, as if he wished to give precisely that order, but he refocused on Starcrest and said nothing.

Amaranthe considered the legendary man, not surprised that he could command the respect of officers twenty years after his exile, but impressed. One might have expected a softness in someone who'd spent so long on the Kyatt Islands, but he appeared lean and powerful, even in his civilian clothing, a mix of browns and forest greens beneath a fur-trimmed parka.

Beneath his beaver cap, his silver hair was short and thick, a regulation military cut. His height and broad shoulders surely lent him authority—he had to duck his head to keep it from bumping the ceiling of the cab—but Maldynado possessed the same physical dimensions, and people didn't stare raptly at him, awaiting an opportunity to please—unless they were women of course. Starcrest probably had a few admirers of that sex too. His face, not so angular as Sicarius's but of a similar vein, was weathered and creased from the sun, with an old scar bisecting one eyebrow, but he'd still fit any woman's definition of handsome. Amaranthe could easily imagine him as a rock-solid admiral, commanding his troops in the heat of battle, though his brown eyes lacked the cold intensity she associated with so many of the senior military officers she'd met; rather, there was a hint of warmth in them, or even mischievousness, as he chatted with the men, as if now that the threat to his children had been nullified, he appreciated this break from the monotony of cross-country train travel.

So, Amaranthe mused, how do I get a legend to join our team?

Unfortunately, she feared he was heading in to join one of the other candidates, Ravido most likely, given Forge's connection to the ancient technology and Starcrest's history with it. Though his *wife* was the expert at deciphering it, wasn't she? If the children were along, did that mean she'd come on the trip too?

After all Amaranthe had done to ensure Forge didn't have anyone left who could control the *Behemoth*—she winced, remembering Retta's horrible death—here came someone who had a better mastery of the technology than anybody else in the world.

"Lord Admiral Starcrest," Amaranthe said during a lull in the men's conversation, "I..." She grew uncharacteristically shy as every set of eyes in the cab swiveled toward her—even those of the engineer. Shouldn't he be studying the snow-covered trees and bends in the tracks ahead? Amaranthe cleared her throat and pushed on. "I must apologize for any harm you perceived we meant to do to your children. We didn't know they

were up here and that they were… gifted enough to impact our, uhm, results." Right, reminding them that she'd meant to take over the train probably wasn't wise. She shifted to, "What the captain says about my comrades and me is true. We're outlaws, but we're wrongfully accused outlaws and seek to clear our names. We also seek to put the rightful emperor back on the throne, Sespian Savarsin."

"You thought to do this by hijacking our train?" Starcrest asked, his voice mild. Deceptively so? There might have been an edge beneath it. Amaranthe had heard foreigners call the Turgonian language guttural and harsh, but his accent had been polished smooth by so many years away from the empire.

Books nudged her and whispered out of the side of his mouth, "Sespian wasn't born yet when he was last in the empire. He might not care about him."

"It's not a good idea to remind your captors of their advanced age when they're holding firearms on you," Starcrest told him.

Amaranthe thought it had been a joke, but Books's eyes widened with concern. "Urp?" he announced.

Akstyr snorted. He was doing his best to look tough and surly, a hard image to convey when hunched in a ball on the floor. In addition, his sneer faded every time he glanced at the girl.

Amaranthe was on the verge of deciding Starcrest's humor might be a sign that they weren't in as much trouble as she'd thought, but his tone grew cooler for his next question, "Why did you seek to commandeer the train?"

"It wasn't the original plan. We were…" Amaranthe tilted her chin skyward, then caught herself—explaining a flying lifeboat that traveled hundreds of miles in minutes seemed a daunting task—and shifted her chin tilt toward the back of the train, toward the mountains they were leaving. "We were stranded in the pass and needed to get back to the city as quickly as possible—Fort Urgot was under siege, and there may be full-on war in the streets by now."

Starcrest's jaw tightened, and he glanced at the children. As

one, they blinked innocently, clasped their hands behind their backs, and pretended to study the ceiling. Amaranthe imagined some past argument about whether they should be allowed to come or not.

"Sespian needs us," she continued. "We've been helping him with—I don't know what you've heard, but there's been a business coalition trying to control him from within the Imperial Barracks for the last year, and before that, Hollowcrest was drugging him, and... well, he hasn't had a chance yet to prove what he can do for the empire. He hired us to help him." Technically true, though he'd only wanted to be kidnapped, and they'd succeeded at that task several weeks earlier.

"Sespian is dead," the colonel snapped. "My lord, you can't accept any of this woman's words as truth. She's a criminal, and I sincerely doubt she's 'wrongfully accused.' She runs with that assassin, Sicarius, after all."

Starcrest's face grew closed, masked. "Does she?" he said neutrally.

Cursed ancestors, of all the times for him to hide his thoughts... He and Sicarius had met in those tunnels, twenty years earlier, she knew that, but had they been working together? Or against each other? Sicarius would have been doing the emperor's bidding—quite loyally at that age, she imagined— and Starcrest had gone his own way afterward. Had they parted as enemies? Allies? Agreed not to kill each other this time, but with no promises for the future? She knew Sicarius respected Starcrest—one might almost say idolized, though that was a strong word to attribute to someone so cool and aloof as he. What had Starcrest thought of *him*?

"Where is the assassin now?" Starcrest asked.

"I haven't seen him in a couple of days," Amaranthe said, "but I can take you to him once we return to the city if you want to talk to him. I understand you had an adventure together once." She raised her eyebrows, inviting him to elaborate.

He didn't. His face grew colder.

Amaranthe couldn't tell if that was a warning or a threat in

his eyes. "He should be with Sespian right now. I *know* Sespian would like to see you." Belatedly, she added, "My lord." She wasn't sure *what* his status was, as Emperor Raumesys had been the one to send him into exile and Raumesys was years dead now. The military men were "my lord"ing him, though, so she better do it too.

"If Sespian has been alive all this time," the colonel said, "why'd he let all of this come to pass? Why isn't he on the throne now?"

"Forge ushered him out of the city on that months-long inspection of the border forts," Amaranthe said. "They tried to arrange his death on the train ride back, only, with the help of some plucky outlaws, he refused to die in the fiery explosion that lit up the night." She decided not to mention that the plucky outlaws had been responsible for the explosion. The *Behemoth* had been on its way with plans to annihilate the train anyway.

"My lord," the colonel said in an exasperated you're-not-believing-any-of-this-rubbish-are-you voice.

"Let's secure them in one of the freight cars," Starcrest said. "I've kept in touch with General Ridgecrest over the years, and my understanding is that he's currently commanding Fort Urgot." When the colonel nodded, Starcrest finished with, "I'll get the latest intelligence from him."

"He doesn't *know* the latest intelligence, my lord," Amaranthe said. "He might only have the version that's been in the newspapers. Very few know what's really going on, that Forge has been angling to run the empire, *more* than the empire, from the beginning. They own Ravido Marblecrest. They—erk."

The captain had grabbed her arm, hauling her to her feet. With her ankles bound, she had to concentrate on not tripping over Starcrest's boots—that seemed a faux pas an exoneration-seeking outlaw should avoid—instead of speaking. Books and Akstyr were similarly hoisted. Akstyr did trip and would have planted his nose in the metal decking right in front of Starcrest's daughter, except someone caught him by the collar, like a mother wolf picking up a pup by the scruff of its neck.

This save didn't keep Akstyr from blushing with indignation, perhaps embarrassment.

"Sergeant," someone yelled out the doorway.

Were there reinforcements waiting in the coal car? There must be, for mere seconds passed before three burly men swung inside, crowding the already crowded cab further. Amaranthe got a face full of someone's back, then a meaty arm wrapped around her waist, hoisting her into the air. She landed with an "oomph" on someone's shoulder.

Her captor swung out of the cab and climbed along the narrow ledge back to the other cars. Icy wind clawed at them, and tree branches whipped past, all too close for comfort, but neither the threat of a fall nor his burden slowed him down. Amaranthe decided not to wriggle or attempt any sort of escape at that moment.

Not until she, Akstyr, and Books had been paraded through five cars of troops—more than one man hissed at her with recognition in his eyes, half-rising from a seat, a hand reaching for a dagger—and dumped in a freight car did she start considering escape plans again. Crates were piled all about them; surely she could find something to facilitate rope freeing. Although, given the overpowering smell of turnips and potatoes, that wasn't a guarantee. The two armed soldiers stationed on either side of the door provided a further obstacle to freedom.

"Did I not say we should ride back to town and forgo the hijacking attempt?" Books asked.

Alas, the soldiers had not thought to gag anyone. Well, that could be to her advantage. Perhaps she could plant some suggestions in their captors' minds.

"You did say that," Amaranthe agreed. "But if we had, we wouldn't know that Fleet Admiral Starcrest has returned to the empire, and we couldn't have begun the process of wooing him to our side."

One of the guards grunted with disbelief while the other rolled his eyes. Books and Akstyr's expressions weren't much more supportive.

"He didn't look wooed," Akstyr said, "and didn't we agree to stop using that sissy word?"

"Maldynado mocked it, but we didn't discuss removing it from our collective vocabulary." Books dropped his head, looking much like a man who would be pinching his nose and rubbing his temples if his hands weren't bound. "Are you suggesting that this is all going according to plan, Amaranthe?"

"No." She made eye contact with Akstyr, silently urging him to do something to loosen their bonds. "I'm only suggesting that the plan could be modified to incorporate these new circumstances."

"New circumstances such as us being trussed up like a leg of lamb about to go in the oven?" Books asked.

"Among other things." Amaranthe shifted so she could gaze serenely at the door guards. "Who are you fellows working for, anyway?"

The younger of the two, a gangly private who had more growing to do, opened his mouth. The other, a corporal with a few years on him, stopped him with a glare and a, "Sh, don't talk to them."

"Why not? I'm sure it's been a long, boring train ride." Amaranthe assumed they'd come from the west coast, if they'd been toting Admiral Starcrest all the way. "We're probably the most interesting thing to happen in weeks."

"She's got a point," the private muttered. The nametag sewn onto his parka read Gettle.

"We'll be in Stumps soon," his comrade said. His name, Moglivakarani, must have challenged the seamstress who'd sewn the tag, shrinking the letters to fit. "Ignore them."

"You're not wearing any armbands," Amaranthe observed. "Does that mean you haven't sworn allegiance to anyone yet? You're not working for Admiral Starcrest, are you? He's not an officer any more, or even an imperial citizen right now, is he?"

"Not as I understand the situation," Books said.

"We're Colonel Fencrest's men. That's all that you need to know." Moglivakarani squinted at her. "What armbands?"

A tickling sensation, like a kiss of air, brushed the hairs on Amaranthe's wrists. Something plucked at the knot on her ropes. She struggled to keep any hint of discomfort off her face, though it was an eerie sensation, knowing her bindings were being untied without anyone being near her. "Flintcrest, Ridgecrest, and Marblecrest's men are all wearing different color armbands on their fatigue sleeves. Someone asked Sespian if we should adopt a color for the troops he's gathering to his side, but he objected, saying let the less legitimate parties change their uniforms. We are in the right here." Actually, Amaranthe had said that when Yara asked, but Sespian, after hesitating over the "in the right" comment, had nodded.

"*Sespian*?" Moglivakarani asked.

"*Emperor* Sespian?" Gettle asked. "But he's dead. That's why all this… this." His wave encompassed the train.

"The newspapers reported him dead, but I assure you, he's quite alive." Or was when she'd last seen him two days before. Or was it three now? Amaranthe needed a full night's sleep. All the crazy events were blurring together, the days seeming unending. "My team is serving him. By detaining us, you place obstacles in front of him. He seeks to reclaim the throne even as we speak."

The ropes fell away from her hands, and the ones on her ankles loosened as well. With her wrists behind her back, she doubted the guards could see, but she did her best to scoop the slack ropes in close anyway. Akstyr had his chin to his chest, hiding his eyes and the concentration on his face from the guards. Books gave her a slight nod. He was either free or would be shortly.

Several feet separated her from the men and the door. Since she was on her knees, with ropes tangled about her ankles, it was conceivable, no, probable, that the guards would be able to pull out their weapons before she could cross the distance and attack them. A distraction would be good.

"You could be telling us any sorts of lies," Moglivakarani said, "thinking it'd improve your position."

Akstyr sat up straighter, met Amaranthe's eyes, and gave the barest hint of a nod.

"That's true, Corporal." She tilted her head. "I do have a letter in my pocket with his signature on it if you want to take a look. It's dated so you'll know it's from this past week."

Books gave her a curious look. She gazed blandly back at him.

"Which pocket?" Moglivakarani took a wary step toward her.

Belatedly, Amaranthe remembered she wasn't dressed in her usual pocket-filled fatigues. Though the prosthetic nose had fallen off, she still wore her Suan costume, complete with blonde hair and a pocket-free dress. Oh, well. Improvise. The letter wasn't real either, after all.

"It's an inside pocket." Amaranthe lowered her chin, eyes toward her bosom.

"I'll get it," Gettle blurted and hustled forward.

Moglivakarani lunged after him, grabbing his arm. "Private, you're not going to grope the—"

Books and Akstyr leaped to their feet, each barreling into a separate man, as if they'd somehow coordinated their attack ahead of time. It didn't take Amaranthe much longer to rise, but she needn't have hurried. Akstyr and Books were both kneeling on the backs of their men, pinning arms behind backs and mashing faces into the worn floorboards. She gave them nods, admiring how efficient they'd grown in the last year, then collected the soldiers' weapons.

"Perhaps I should wear dresses more often," Amaranthe said. "That ruse doesn't work as effectively when I'm in those figure-shrouding army fatigues."

"Ruse?" Gettle muttered. "Does that mean there was no letter?"

"No pockets either," Amaranthe said.

"Idiot," Moglivakarani said.

"How was I supposed to know their hands were free? *How* were their hands free?"

"Tie them up, please," Amaranthe told Books and Akstyr.

She didn't want to encourage the private's line of thought.

The clacks of the wheels on the rails seemed to be slowing. Wondering if they were reaching the lake and the capital, Amaranthe clambered onto a crate and peered through a slat in the wall. They'd come out of the mountains, but were passing through white rolling hills rather than the farmlands west of the lake. "Willow Pond," she guessed, naming the last stop before Stumps.

"Perhaps we should get out here and catch the next train," Books said.

"And let a legendary war hero go without making a solid attempt to win him to our side?" Amaranthe asked.

"We did attempt that," Akstyr said, "and we got thrown in here. We—"

The metal rollers of the sliding door squeaked, and light flooded the car. Amaranthe spun, raising her new army pistol. She halted, however, when she spotted a similar weapon already pointed at her chest. The hand holding it belonged to Starcrest. Books and Akstyr had finished tying the soldiers, and they, too, spun toward the door, crouching, fists curled into loose fists, ready for a fight.

"Interesting," Starcrest said, taking them in, as well as the prone soldiers.

They groaned when they heard his voice, more in embarrassment than pain, Amaranthe guessed.

She lowered her pistol. Starcrest was the only one standing in the doorway as the train slowed, icicle-bedecked buildings passing behind him, but she couldn't be certain there weren't ten more soldiers lined up to either side of him. She didn't want to fight with him anyway.

"We like to think so." Amaranthe propped an elbow on a crate. "Won't you come in? We'd love to discuss things with you."

"That is what I had in mind." Starcrest eyed her pistol.

Since he had the advantage anyway, his weapon still trained on her chest, Amaranthe set her firearm on the floor. If there was a chance she could earn his trust, she'd happily make the

first concession. Besides, she always had Akstyr's secret skills
to draw upon if needed, so long as Starcrest didn't bring his
children in. They obviously had some mental sciences training
and might sniff out Akstyr's gift. For all she knew, they'd sensed
him untying the ropes and that had been what drew Starcrest
back here to start with. But, no, it must be more than that, or
he'd simply have sent soldiers. If he'd come alone, he must
want to talk to them about something. Maybe he'd believed
what she said in the cab.

Books kicked aside the other firearm they'd taken from the
fallen men. The train rolled to a stop, and Starcrest nodded and
waved to someone out of Amaranthe's sight.

That made her nervous until he holstered the pistol and
stepped inside. "Mind if we let these two go?" He spread a hand
toward the soldiers.

"Won't they go off and tell that colonel that you're in here
alone, being suborned by outlaws?" Amaranthe asked.

"Suborned?" Starcrest's eyebrows rose.

"I was going to say wooed, but I've been told that word is
'sissy.'" She glanced at Akstyr.

"Well, it is," he muttered.

"I simply wish to have a private discussion with you,"
Starcrest said. "I've already expressed this desire to Colonel
Fencrest, and he's already expressed his vehement disapproval
over the notion. What these two report back will matter little
in regard to our ability to converse privately until we reach
Stumps, which is, if I recall correctly, less than a half an hour
away." He stepped inside and sat on a crate. "We'll be departing
shortly, as nobody's boarding here in Willow Pond and only two
passengers have departed."

Two fifteen-year-old siblings too young for the dangers
of the capital? There was a north-south train that ran through
Willow Pond, heading to numerous quiet rural towns along the
way. Maybe Starcrest had relatives in the area, or his own lands
might be nearby too, if he still had lands.

Amaranthe used one of the soldiers' purloined knives to sever

their bonds. Shoulders slumped, heads bowed, they shuffled for the door.

"My lord," the corporal said, avoiding Starcrest's eyes, "we... we were tricked. They—"

"I'm not in command of anything here, Corporal." Starcrest said *Corporal* in the same tone a father might say *son*. "I suggest you report to your superior for orders."

"Yes, my lord." The corporal shambled the last two steps to the door, but paused again. "My lord, are you going to tell Sergeant Nastor... uhm."

"I doubt I'll have time to tell your sergeant anything before we arrive in the capital."

"Oh." The corporal exchanged glances with his private, who shrugged back at him. "Thank you, my lord," he said with more spirit upon realizing that he wasn't going to be outed for his inability to keep the prisoners secured.

They hopped from the car and jogged out of sight. A whistle blew outside.

Before the train chugged into motion again, a woman climbed up to the doorway and hesitated on the threshold until she spotted Starcrest sitting on the crate. Her thick blonde-gray hair fell in a braid down her back, spectacles framed her blue eyes, and freckles splashed cheeks that Amaranthe would consider pale, despite the tanned skin. She wore a soft gray felt dress with wool leggings and heavy boots to thwart the cold.

"Have a seat, love." Starcrest gestured to a crate next to his. "These are the outlaws I told you about, people who have unlikely knowledge about our first adventure together."

This must be Tikaya Komitopis, the Kyattese linguist and cryptographer. Amaranthe immediately wanted to pump her for information on the *Behemoth* and what she knew about Forge, specifically Suan and Retta. The sisters had both been to the Kyatt Islands on Forge's behalf, Retta to study the ancient language, and Suan to purchase submarines for her wealthy colleagues.

"Outlaws." Tikaya sat next to Starcrest on the crate. "And here I thought an excursion into the empire in your wake would

mean a chance to meet aristocrats and military leaders from the highest echelons of society."

"That might have happened if you'd married me when I was an upright young officer. These days... well, I don't think anyone has scribbled out the exile mark next to my name. These—" Starcrest spread a hand toward Amaranthe, Books, and Akstyr, "—should be precisely the sorts of people you expected."

"Should we be offended?" Akstyr muttered to Books.

"I believe so, yes," Books said. "Word of my sublime work mustn't have reached the Kyatt Islands yet." He sighed.

Amaranthe swatted him on the arm.

"I haven't been informed of their names yet," Starcrest said, "but they know Sicarius."

Tikaya grimaced. "Is that association as precipitous for them as it is for most people?"

Starcrest's eyes sharpened as he regarded Amaranthe. "I don't think so."

"It is for us." Akstyr pointed to his chest, then Books.

"Do you actually know what precipitous means?" Books asked him.

"Dangerous, right? You've used it before. You've even used it when talking about Sicarius."

"I didn't realize you'd listened." Books sounded pleased.

"Sometimes. If I'm not doing something more important."

Books's eyes narrowed, some of the pleasure fading.

Amaranthe shushed them and said, "My name is Amaranthe Lokdon, and this is Akstyr and Books, formerly Professor Marl Mugdildor."

Books's back straightened, and he glanced at Tikaya, as if hoping she'd heard of him. She merely gazed back at the three of them with an expression of polite wariness. Outside, the train had started up, and Starcrest slid the rolling door shut before resuming a seat next to his wife. Enough light slanted through the slats in the walls that the two parties could see each other.

"You already know who I am," Starcrest said, "but you can call me Rias. This is my wife, Professor Tikaya Komitopis."

"Just Tikaya," she said.

Sure, like Amaranthe was going to be on a first-name basis with people out of the history books.

Starcrest slipped a hand into his jacket and withdrew an envelope. "Do you recognize this?"

Books and Akstyr shook their heads.

Amaranthe didn't. "Was it, by chance, postmarked from Markworth a few weeks ago?"

"It was indeed."

"Sicarius didn't tell me what was in it or who it was going to. I got the impression that he hoped for an answer, but didn't expect one."

Starcrest and Komitopis exchanged wry looks, and Amaranthe had the sense that there'd been quite a discussion as to whether to respond to that letter or not. "Can I see it?" she asked. "It doesn't mention me, does it?"

Starcrest's brows rose.

"I ask because there was a hasty postscript penned after I… ah, I was there when he wrote it. It's possible my plans had some influence on the information contained within."

"As in," Akstyr whispered to Books, "please help, Admiral, before my crazy girlfriend blows up the empire."

Long accustomed to their teasing, Amaranthe might not have flushed, but the topic—and the agreement implicit in Books's smirk—made her self-conscious. "It doesn't say *that*." She eyed Starcrest. "It doesn't, right?"

"Show her the letter, love," Komitopis said.

The pair exchanged looks again, and this time Amaranthe couldn't decipher the hidden meaning. For a moment, she allowed herself to wonder what it'd be like to be married to someone—not someone, *Sicarius*—long enough to understand each other so well that words weren't needed. She knew Sicarius better than most, but that wasn't saying much. It was rare for her to have a clue what was going on behind his facade.

Starcrest held out the crinkled envelope, distracting her from wistful thinking.

It was addressed in Sicarius's precise hand to Federias Starcrest at 17 View Ridge Loop, Eastern Plantation County, Kyatt.

"We weren't anywhere we had access to records." Amaranthe opened the envelope and pulled out the single page inside. "I wouldn't have guessed he knew your address."

"Nor I," Komitopis said. "I was alarmed to learn that."

Starcrest spread a hand. "It's not surprising. The emperor has surely kept track of me over the years, and he was the emperor's man."

"*Hench*man."

Amaranthe's lips flattened. She was glad Starcrest didn't share his wife's unveiled rancor toward Sicarius.

When she lowered her gaze to the page, she stared blankly at it for a moment. The words were gibberish. No, a code. Sicarius must have assumed other eyes would read any mail addressed to Starcrest from the empire. She imagined some Kyattese intelligence analyst pawing over letters to the kids from their Turgonian grandparents.

"The translation is on the back," Komitopis said. "He used an old key, one employed during, as your people call it, the Western Sea Conflict."

"Nothing wrong with the man's memory then," Amaranthe said, remembering that they'd been out in the woods when Sicarius penned the note. There were a few lines on the back, a signature, and a postscript.

"He was a bright boy," Starcrest said. "I thought it was a shame what the emperor molded him into."

"Oh, that's right." Amaranthe lowered the letter, distracted by a new thought. "You knew his father. Did you know about... more? His upbringing?" She wasn't sure how she'd feel about the man if it turned out he had known about it and had ignored the cruelties being perpetrated in the name of creating a perfect assassin.

But Starcrest's mouth had dropped open. "*I* knew his father? I wasn't aware of Sicarius's existence until..." His gaze skimmed

over Amaranthe, Books, and Akstyr, as if he was wondering how much of those classified times he should be sharing, even at this late date. "He was fifteen when our paths first crossed."

"According to Hollowcrest's records, his father was… Books, what was the name?"

"Sergeant Paloic."

Starcrest sank back on the crate, bracing himself with his palms. "I remember him. He died—"

"He committed suicide," Amaranthe said. "After being ordered—coerced—into impregnating the woman they'd chosen to bear Sicarius. A Kyattese woman." She glanced at Tikaya. The professor's eyes widened, but she didn't say anything. "According to Hollowcrest's files," Amaranthe continued, "Paloic's name first came to his attention after you recommended the sergeant for a promotion."

"I see," Starcrest whispered. "I'd… never known."

It was a harsh thing to bring up—it wasn't as if Starcrest had been to blame—but she didn't regret laying the tiles on the table. If he felt guilty, he might be more inclined to work with them. He'd already come at the behest of the letter, but that didn't mean he meant to join forces with them. She didn't think so anyway. Maybe she should read the translation before forming conclusions.

> *Lord Admiral Starcrest,*
>
> *Emperor Sespian has been ousted from the throne, and numerous men with blood ties to the Savarsin line are marching armies into the city. A business coalition named Forge seeks control of the empire through a Marblecrest figurehead. Forge possesses the technology we saw on our mission twenty years ago. Among other things, they have a great flying craft from that ancient race and can use it to force their candidate onto the throne. A student of Professor Komitopis's has mastered its flight and at least some of its many weapons. I've seen them. They are devastating, and the whole world is in danger. You and your wife may be the*

only ones who can bring about a peaceful solution. If you still care anything for the empire, you must come.

Sicarius

Postscript: Sespian is alive and in hiding, but it is unlikely anyone will be able to bring about a solution that doesn't involve much bloodshed. The people and the military will listen to you.

Amaranthe lowered the letter and handed it to Books. Akstyr peered over his shoulder to read it as well.

"Our foremost reason for coming is to deal with the alien technology," Starcrest said. "As for the rest... at this late date, I'm less certain than Sicarius that my influence over people or troops would be great."

Truly? Someone had given him command of a train full of men...

"What we *didn't* understand," Starcrest said, "is why Sespian was ousted in the first place. And why he isn't marching on the city to reclaim the throne. You say this Forge outfit has been imposing their will upon him?"

"As it turns out, Sespian isn't Raumesys's son," Amaranthe said. "Forge has learned this. It's possible the whole city will learn it soon, if it hasn't already. We haven't seen a paper in a couple of days."

"Sespian is a bastard?" Professor Komitopis asked.

"Not exactly." Given that Sicarius had personally written Starcrest and pleaded—or as close to pleading as he'd ever get—for assistance, Amaranthe didn't think he'd mind sharing secrets. "He's Sicarius's son. Princess Marathi, after going through all the typical bedroom adventures one is expected to have with one's husband, failed to produce an heir. She assumed the problem was Raumesys, and it turns out she was correct. Not wanting to suffer the fate of a previous wife who failed to produce, Marathi found someone suitable to lend his, ah, essence."

"Essence?" Akstyr choked.

Books tried to elbow him, but they weren't standing closely enough together.

"I didn't think any of you Turgonian men fired blunt arrows," Komitopis said. "You being such a hale and hearty people, prolific enough to populate a massive continent in a couple hundred years."

Her words stirred Starcrest from whatever dark thoughts had devoured him, and he managed a half smile. "Given how many relatives *you* have, I don't think you can accuse *us* of being overly prolific."

"Yes, but we have a bountiful supply of sun, surf, and those fertility-boosting oysters I've mentioned. Your people manage it in a much harsher land, with nothing except those dreadful tooth dullers to fuel your gonads."

Amaranthe blinked at the blunt term, but she'd heard that the Kyattese had a habit of saying things by their proper scientific names. Either that or "love apples" weren't a common crop on the islands.

"The field rations *are* dreadful," Starcrest agreed. "Or they were twenty years ago."

"You should try one of Sicarius's dried organ bars," Akstyr grumbled.

Amaranthe leaned against one of the crates, eyeing the white fields passing beyond the slits in the walls. She didn't know what to make of the professor's derailment of the conversation. She supposed this talk of covert organizations, militant politics, and deflowered secrets was all academic to Komitopis. What did she truly care about the empire?

A banging at the door surprised Amaranthe. The train was still in motion, though the white flatlands outside had grown familiar. They had to be close to the lake, if it wasn't already passing by on the other side of the car.

"Enter," Starcrest called over the noise of the train.

The door slid aside, and Colonel Fencrest stood on the ledge, his face ashen. He gulped. "My lord." He didn't seem to

notice that Amaranthe, Books, and Akstyr were no longer tied. He didn't notice them at all.

Starcrest rose. "What is it?"

The colonel's mouth opened and closed, but he couldn't find words. He pointed past Amaranthe, toward the slats allowing glimpses of the countryside.

She climbed onto a crate for a better view as everyone else came to that side of the car. She leaned her temple against the cold wood, trying to see what lay ahead of the train, though she had a guess. They ought to be closing on Fort Urgot. If that army was still camped around it, that would certainly alarm someone coming into the situation new.

But it wasn't an army that came into sight. It was...

"No," Amaranthe whispered. Overwhelming horror swallowed her, weakening her limbs and invading her stomach like a poison. If she'd been standing, her knees would have given out, dumping her on the floor. She would have deserved it.

"Dear Akahe," Komitopis whispered at her side.

The unmistakable black dome shape of the *Behemoth* towered over the landscape—what was left of it. Felled trees and flattened tents littered the white fields, along with one corner of collapsed rubble, of...

Amaranthe shook her head slowly, not believing, not wanting to believe. Never in her worst nightmares had she imagined the massive craft would crash into—*onto*—Fort Urgot. It had annihilated the walls, the building, everything. The *people*, she admitted though her mind shied away from the awfulness of that thought.

"How could we have..." Books whispered. "How could it have possibly landed in that one spot? The odds..."

Amaranthe thumped her forehead against the slats. The odds didn't matter. What mattered were the thousands of people that had been in that fort. They couldn't have seen it coming, not in time. They couldn't have escaped. And if Sicarius, Sespian, Maldynado, and Basilard had still been within those walls...

Where else would they have been? She'd sent them there.

Amaranthe climbed—*fell*—off the crate and shambled to— she didn't know where. A corner, she had in mind, but didn't make it. She dropped to her knees and vomited.

CHAPTER 3

A MARANTHE DIDN'T NOTICE ANYTHING ABOUT THE REST of the train ride or the trip back to the factory. If a bounty hunter had stepped out of the shadows and raised a crossbow at her, she wouldn't have ducked. She probably wouldn't have even flinched, not until the quarrel burrowed into her chest.

Thousands dead. Her team. Her... Sicarius. Because of her. Because she'd presumed to try and control that... that... monster craft. It was a force of nature, not a machine. She might as well have tried to direct a tornado or an avalanche.

"This is it." Books pointed past the large four-story molasses tanks dominating the front of the lot and toward the entrance to the factory.

He'd taken charge when Amaranthe hadn't, offering their hideout for Starcrest and the train full of soldiers until they figured out somewhere more amenable. Starcrest *had* been heading toward Fort Urgot. Not now.

Night had come by the time they breached the city boundaries, and nobody stepped out to harass the squads of soldiers marching along the waterfront. The usual patrols weren't about. Everyone was probably too stunned by what had happened to think about fighting, at least this day.

"Did you see how many people are out there staring at that thing?" Akstyr had asked, pointing out the crowds as the train chugged past the fort's remains. "Half the city is out there gawking. It's sure not going to be a secret any more."

Nobody had answered him. Starcrest and Tikaya were as

grim as everybody else, maybe grimmer, their easy banter of before wiped from memory, their faces older and more lined without the humor to brighten them.

Amaranthe supposed she should be relieved that Books wasn't among the stunned or gawking, unlike her. But then, he hadn't directed the mission. Those people weren't dead because of him.

On the trek from the train station to the factory, Books had looked at her often, touching her arm a couple of times in silent questions. They might have been, "Do you want to take over?" or "Are you all right?" Amaranthe didn't know. She couldn't meet his eyes, couldn't lift her gaze from her boots.

Nobody had pointed at her or spoken a word of condemnation, but she hadn't confessed either. Akstyr and Books were the only ones who knew she was guilty of... dear ancestors, manslaughter. On a massive scale. Had Admiral Starcrest himself been responsible for as many deaths in his entire twenty-year military career? If he had, those had been the *enemies*, not his own people.

"Halt," called out a guard beside the door, the suborned Private Rudev, "and identify, er..."

The sheer number of men marching out of the darkness must have intimidated him. Perfectly understandable. They were five-hundred strong, not a huge number in comparison to all the troops in the city, but enough people to make a young private quake, especially one who'd defected from his unit to join with mercenaries. For all Rudev knew, these were some of Ravido's men, coming to fetch him.

"Is that an example of the kind of security your outfit runs?" Colonel Fencrest asked.

When Amaranthe didn't answer, Books spoke. "He's a new recruit. We actually lifted him from the army. Sicarius's men are trained better, even the least robust among them."

"I saw you glance at me," Akstyr whispered. "You're no born athlete either."

"So are we going to get shot if we go in, or what?" Fencrest asked. He waved to one of his captains, and the man ordered the sergeants to bring the troops to a halt, forming them up into companies and platoons, then picking a few scouts to keep an eye out at the closest intersections.

"No," Books said, after glancing at Amaranthe again, no doubt wondering if she'd speak first, "but I better go in and brief everyone."

"Whoever's left alive in there," Amaranthe muttered.

Books paused, maybe thinking she'd take over—it was the first thing she'd said in hours—but she shook her head mutely. Didn't he understand? She couldn't lead anyone now, maybe not ever again. Not after that. Her orders were death.

"Go with him, Lieutenant," Fencrest said, waving to another of his men. "We don't want any surprises."

Right, the soldiers had no reason to trust Amaranthe and her team. Quite the opposite. If it weren't for Starcrest, who'd liked the idea of a waterfront location since it meant they wouldn't have to march their troops through the city, they wouldn't have come at all. But where else might they have gone? Ravido wouldn't be inviting unknown soldiers into the Barracks, and Fort Urgot was certainly no longer an option. Amaranthe knew they'd brought supplies on that train, food and ammunition at least, but didn't know if they had gear for setting up a camp in sub-freezing temperatures.

She waited, numb and cold, while Books and the lieutenant went inside. She should go in, too, and disappear into her office, locking the door, and hiding in there until... Until what? Someone needed her for a mission? She didn't know. Would anyone need her at all? With Starcrest and trained military men here, who would want the advice of an outlaw?

Starcrest was standing to the side, conferring with his wife. Their voices were soft, and they'd switched to Kyattese.

The door banged open, and someone hustled outside, someone with a limp and a cane. Deret Mancrest gaped at the troops, his gaze raking over them, looking for someone. Several people fingered weapons, but nobody drew. They wouldn't

unless the sergeants standing at the heads of the companies ordered them to.

Deret's search halted when he spotted Amaranthe. He walked over briskly, though not so briskly that it might alarm anyone with a gun. One hand gripped his swordstick, but he kept his other arm out, his palm open so people would see he didn't have a weapon.

"Amaranthe," he whispered, "I need to talk to you."

She was tempted to direct him to Books, but maybe he'd already talked to Books. "Yes?"

"In private."

The colonel was watching them from a few paces away.

"I'm not certain I'm allowed to wander off," Amaranthe said. "We were prisoners at one point. Now we're..."

"Hosts is what Books said."

"That's so, but it may not preclude the prisoner status."

Deret's mouth formed a silent, "Oh." After a thoughtful moment, he turned slightly so his back was to the colonel. He shifted his weight onto his good leg, letting the swordstick lean against his side, and used both hands to sign. *Yara and I kidnapped the sister. She's tied up inside. That might not look good if hundreds of soldiers are suddenly roaming around.*

Amaranthe closed her eyes. The last person she wanted to see was Suan Curlev. She'd have to explain... or choose *not* to explain... how she'd caused Retta's death. No, Suan was a Forge founder, an enemy. She didn't have to explain anything to her. Except somehow she didn't think her guilt would allow her to treat the woman poorly.

Amaranthe? Deret prompted. *Shall I take her somewhere?*

Let her go, Amaranthe thought. They didn't need her now. But Suan knew where their hideout was. Of course it wouldn't be a hideout much longer, not with five hundred men going in and out of the area.

"Leave her," she said quietly. "I'll explain her to the soldiers if they ask. She's a Forge founder. Questioning her could be valuable."

"Questioning, *how*? With the use of your—" Deret must have remembered they were being observed for he lowered his voice to finish, "—assassin?"

Amaranthe could only imagine how bleak her expression was when she said, "I don't think he'll be questioning anybody any time soon." Her voice cracked on the last word. She needed rest, a break, something. You need to have not survived when half of your team is dead, the voice in her head whispered. No, she didn't know for sure that they'd been in the fort when the *Behemoth* had crashed. Maybe they'd been out fighting on the field, or infiltrating the enemy camp, or... She rubbed her face. Did it matter, given how many soldiers had died? Not everybody could have escaped.

"Amaranthe," Deret prodded.

"I don't know. I'll figure it out later."

"You should talk to her. She's not a raving sycophant. She's intelligent and seems reasonable."

Because she wants to get you to let her go, Amaranthe thought. "Good," she said aloud. "But tonight I need to be... left alone." She walked toward the door, not caring whether the colonel tried to stop her or not. She avoided Starcrest's eyes, everyone's eyes.

No one stepped into her path. She made it inside and stumbled up the stairs to her office. Once the army moved in, she probably wouldn't be able to keep it. Would her people be allowed to join in with whatever planning Starcrest started? Did she care at this point?

Amaranthe dropped onto her blankets, lamenting the cold seeping up through the floor, and flung her arm over her eyes.

She couldn't remember the last time she'd gotten more than a couple of hours of sleep—wait, yes, she did... with Sicarius keeping watch from her blankets. But tonight, as weary as she was, it eluded her. There was too much noise in the factory. Barked orders, hundreds of boots thudding on the floors and catwalks, the thumps, clanks, and grunts of people settling in... Then conversations started up in the office next to hers.

She ignored it all until someone knocked at her door. Maybe if she didn't respond, the person would go away. It was dark in her office, after all.

The door creaked open, and a lantern's light probed the room. That would teach her for not throwing the lock. Maybe if she kept her back to the door and ignored—

Thunk!

The light flickered. Either the lantern had been slammed down on the desk with maximum force, or the ceiling was falling.

Reluctantly, Amaranthe rolled over and faced the intruder.

Sergeant Yara stood beside the desk, her face flushed, her eyes puffy, her lips peeled back in a snarl. "Were you responsible?"

Amaranthe didn't have to ask for what. She wished she could disappear beneath the blankets.

"Were you?" Yara demanded, her voice breaking on the "you." "Was it your ludicrous scheme that—that—" She thrust an arm toward the wall, no, toward the north end of the lake beyond the wall. "He's *dead*. They *all* are."

"I know," Amaranthe whispered.

"How am I supposed to—*you're* the one who encouraged me to care about that dumb oaf, curse your ancestors. And then you—" Yara's voice broke again, and her fists clenched.

Amaranthe wished she could muster the indignation to do more than say, "It wasn't intentional, Yara." She'd known Maldynado longer, and Basilard, and Sespian, and she'd loved Sicarius longer than Yara had known Maldynado existed. But she knew it was all her fault, that one of her plans had finally gotten her teammates killed—along with thousands of others.

"It wasn't intentional? Oh, that makes it dandy, doesn't it?" Yara's fists clenched and unclenched at her sides.

Would she lunge forward and strike? If she did, would Amaranthe bother defending herself? No...

"You talked me into joining your team, into following you on this fool's mission, because... You made it sound noble and honorable. Stop Forge, save the empire. But you've killed more people than any of them have, you know that, don't you?"

"I didn't singlehandedly kill everybody," Amaranthe said. "I couldn't foresee that the *Behemoth* would crash. Emperor's warts, I wasn't steering it into the fort."

"It was damaged and crashed as a result of your plan, didn't it?"

Amaranthe opened her mouth, though she didn't know what she'd say. "Not exactly" didn't have the ring of expiation she needed.

"If you hadn't gone down there, they'd all still be alive, wouldn't they?" Yara asked. "*Wouldn't* they?"

Technically, there was no way to know that... The fort had been under siege, after all. Yara didn't want a debate though, and Amaranthe was already blaming herself, so why bother arguing?

"Yes, it's my fault, Yara. I'm sorry you lost someone you cared about. I cared about Maldynado too." And Sicarius, curse it all. Fresh tears stabbed at the corners of her eyes.

"I'm sorry I ever saw you on that mountainside, you and your bungling team of miscreants." Yara stalked outside, slamming the door so hard that a nail flew out of a wall and fell to the floor with an insignificant clink.

Amaranthe wished Yara had taken the lantern. She preferred the darkness. It was too much effort, though, to stand up and cut it out. She rolled onto her side, putting her back to the door—and the world—again.

* * *

Sicarius's injuries were healed. Someone had repaired the rips in his clothes and retrieved most of the daggers and throwing knives he'd hurled during his illogical and ill-considered storming of the *Behemoth*. Now, he stood next to the entrance flap inside the Nurian tent, his hands clasped behind his back, his face devoid of emotion. In the center of a rug that kept people from having to walk on the frozen ground, General Flintcrest and Kor Nas sat on crates, speaking in low murmurs as a third man knelt, his eyes closed. A ledger, an elegant gold pen, and a couple of pieces of clothing rested before the kneeling man. A checkered scarf dangled from his fingers.

Though no one had introduced him to Sicarius, this new Nurian was clearly a seer, one talented at finding people. He must have been the one who'd figured out Sespian was still alive and suggested the creation of a soul construct to hunt him.

On that suspicion alone, Sicarius might have killed him. If he could.

The opal embedded in the flesh at his temple hummed softly in his mind, its warm tendrils of energy not painful but always present. He'd found that he could leave his cot and even the tent, but he couldn't raise a hand toward anyone in the camp. Not the soldiers, and most certainly not the Nurians. He'd tried a few times to trick his body into responding in such a way that might hurl a dagger into Kor Nas's chest, but it was the mind the artifact controlled, and he couldn't trick his own mind.

"This one is living on top of that hill." Without opening his eyes, the seer waved vaguely toward the city.

"We'll need something *slightly* more precise." Flintcrest tossed a notepad into the man's lap. "Write down an address."

Kor Nas's jaw tightened at the disrespectful treatment of his fellow Nurian. The seer opened his eyes, a bewildered expression on his face. "An address? This is not—" His faced tilted toward Kor Nas, and he switched to the Nurian language. "*Saison,* have you not explained it to this... man?" He clearly wanted to use a different noun, but glanced warily at the general, perhaps fearing he understood Nurian.

"Write down some landmarks. My new pet seems bright enough to follow such instructions." Kor Nas smiled at Sicarius, a strange caress in his eyes, like a man gazing fondly at some treasured prize won in a contest of skills.

After a lifetime of hiding his thoughts, Sicarius had no trouble keeping his face expressionless. He didn't know if the opal shared what lay in his mind with the practitioner, but doubted it mattered. Kor Nas could surely guess that his "new pet" would like to stick a dagger in his chest.

"Yes, *saison.*" The seer picked up the pen and bent over the notebook.

"Write down directions for other ones as well."

"Speak in Turgonian," Flintcrest snapped.

And thus the general answered the unspoken question, as to whether or not he understood the language. The seer winced at his tone, but kept his head bent, and scribbled furiously with the pen. As Sicarius waited to see what assignment they'd give him, he tried to decide if he cared. Not really. Maybe it'd be something ridiculously dangerous, something impossible to accomplish, something that would get him killed. If so, he'd have the end he'd expected in that aircraft. Perhaps he could manage it even if the task weren't *that* dangerous... Odd that the idea of displaying any sort of ineptitude still pushed his hairs in the wrong direction, but he didn't want to spend the next year—or decade—enslaved to this Nurian.

"Here." The seer unfolded from his kneeling posture, stood, and extended the notebook.

"Give it to him." Kor Nas pointed at Sicarius.

The seer licked his lips and eyed Sicarius for several long moments before creeping forward, his arm extended as far from his body as possible, as if he feared an electric shock—or worse. Sicarius would have ignored the offering, but his hand came up of its own volition. No, of the practitioner's volition. Inwardly, he sighed, but outwardly, he didn't let his expression change.

"Kill those five women tonight," Kor Nas said. "Get as much information as you can before you cut their throats. Then report back to me. I'll expect you by dawn."

Sicarius eyed the list. The directions were written in Nurian, landmarks to lead him to three residences, a hotel near the waterfront, and a sublet by the University. A surname was scribbled above each set of landmarks.

"You do read Nurian, do you not?" Kor Nas asked.

Sicarius wouldn't have answered, but, again, the response was plucked from his lips without his assent. "Yes."

"Thanks to my intelligence-gathering team, you've got three of the Forge founders on that list," Flintcrest said. "If you truly control him—" he eyed Sicarius like one might eye a rattlesnake

poised to escape its terrarium, "—and he gets rid of them, we'll be close to the end. Once Marblecrest's female allies have been disposed of, he'll have nothing except those fancy firearms, and we can take those from him. The man's a joke as a general and as a candidate for the throne. Even if nobody had heard of Forge, everyone would guess he'd been bought."

One of Kor Nas's silvery eyebrows rose, as if to remind Flintcrest that he, too, had been bought, or at least had a deal in place with an outside entity.

Flintcrest read the gesture clearly, for he glowered back at Kor Nas. A long moment passed, the men staring at each other. Surprisingly, it was the practitioner who broke eye contact first.

"If five assassinations will bring this organization to its knees," Kor Nas said, "it is not so formidable as my government thought."

"Oh, I'm sure its tendrils have slithered all over the world, but the founders are the ones we have to worry about. With them gone... it'll take time for them to reorganize. By then, the issue of the throne will be decided." Flintcrest's chin jerked up, and he thumped his chest.

"As you say." Kor Nas pointed at Sicarius. "You understand that note? Can you find those people?"

"I want their heads as proof of the deed done," Flintcrest said.

How like Raumesys and Hollowcrest. Truly, the empire would change little if Flintcrest found the throne, though Raumesys never would have dealt with the Nurians. What other concessions had he promised them?

"Understood," Sicarius found himself responding.

"I'll have my spies continue to research and get the rest of the founders' names," Flintcrest said.

"I don't think that will be necessary." Kor Nas smiled slightly. "I'm sure a trained assassin can extract the needed information before cutting the final throat."

"Yes," Sicarius heard himself saying.

The founders names. Amaranthe had known them, Sicarius recalled, though she hadn't shared them with him. Out of fear

that he'd take it upon himself to assassinate them. And he would have. To protect her and Sespian. It was too late for that now, but he'd kill them anyway, without fighting the practitioner. He hadn't thought it was within him to hate, to care enough about any one thing to have such a strong feeling, but loathing welled up in him now as he studied the names. Yes, he hated the Forge people for their role in Sespian's and Amaranthe's deaths.

He recognized one of the names on the list, the person staying in the hotel by the yacht club, and decided he'd take particular satisfaction in killing her. Neeth Worgavic.

CHAPTER 4

S LEEP CONTINUED TO ELUDE AMARANTHE, AND DAWN SAW her no better rested than the night before. It was just as well. Her nightmares were sure to take on a whole new vile bent now. For hours, the talk had continued in the office next door. She hadn't tried to make out any of it. She'd been busy with her own thoughts, though they'd stopped spinning so rapidly through her brain at some point. They were fewer and farther between now. For the last hour, whether or not she should get up to use the latrine had been foremost among them. She didn't want to go out there. Perhaps the trash bin in the corner of the room would suffice...

A feminine screech cut through the door, and Amaranthe bolted up. Who could that have been? Starcrest's wife? And had that been a cry of surprise? Or pain? Maybe their hideout had been discovered, and the factory was being attacked.

Amaranthe scrambled to the door, then out onto the landing. Every inch of floor space below was taken up by packs, hastily spread bedrolls, and weapons, everything from rifles to cutlasses and short swords to crossbows and longbows. She didn't see any sign that the factory was being attacked, though a few amused soldiers were gazing toward the door, where...

She stumbled forward and gripped the railing. Surprise and delight lifted her spirits, and she grinned like a fool. She couldn't imagine how it could be possible, but Maldynado stood a couple of paces from the threshold, or at least he was *trying* to remain standing. Yara had flung herself at him, wrapping her legs and arms around him, and her face was buried in his shoulder. That screech... had been her?

Maldynado's face was grimy and unshaven, his eyes weary with dark hollows beneath them, his clothing ripped and stained with dirt and blood, but he was undeniably standing and breathing. After a startled moment, he smiled and wrapped his arms around Yara in return.

Amaranthe thought to call out, to ask where he'd been and how he'd survived, but Yara was kissing him by then, showing more naked enthusiasm than Amaranthe had ever seen from the woman, and he probably wouldn't hear her.

Sespian and Basilard walked through the door, appearing equally battered and tired. Amaranthe started for the steps, intending to run down and grab them both in an embrace, but Basilard noticed her, and their eyes met from across the building. Something in those frank blue eyes made her halt, an uneasy premonition sinking into her stomach.

When no one else walked in behind them, Amaranthe signed, *Sicarius?*

Basilard hesitated, then shook his head.

She stumbled back to her door. How? How could the others have made it out and not Sicarius? She loved Maldynado and couldn't wish for anything but happiness between him and Yara, but cursed ancestors, why couldn't Sicarius have walked in so *she* could fling herself into his arms?

Wait, she told herself, wait to mourn until you know for certain. Maybe he was just... missing. Maybe nobody knew for sure.

Thumps and grunts came from the bottom of the stairs. Maldynado, with Yara still latched to him, was fumbling his way up the steps at the same time as he accepted a barrage of kisses. How he reached the top when he couldn't see where he was going, Amaranthe didn't know. She said nothing, having a hard time finding joy in her heart for their reunion. Not when...

Well, she hadn't spoken to anyone yet. Maybe she could find hope in Basilard or Sespian's news.

"Hullo, boss," Maldynado managed when his lips were free. "Good to see—oooph."

Yara had grabbed his cheeks with her hands and kissed him. Maldynado turned a quick wave into a grab for the doorknob of the room he and Yara had been sharing.

Amaranthe lifted a hand, intending to warn them that it was occupied, but neither Maldynado nor Yara was paying attention to her. They barreled into the office, and voices inside halted.

Basilard and Sespian were halfway up the stairs, and Sespian smiled and lifted a hand toward her. He opened his mouth, but Maldynado and Yara stumbled out again before he could speak. Surely they'd find it easier to get from one place to the next if she put her legs down and walked of her own volition...

Maldynado peered about, wearing a bewildered expression, perhaps noticing all those soldiers for the first time. "Who are all these people?" he blurted.

"Admiral Starcrest and his advisers," Amaranthe said.

"Admiral Star..." Maldynado stared into the office.

From her position, Amaranthe couldn't tell if Starcrest or any of the others were staring back, but she imagined that'd be the case after having entwined lovers barge into their meeting.

"Erp?" Maldynado said.

"Downstairs," Yara said. She dropped her legs so she could stand, though she didn't let go of Maldynado's arms. She dragged him down the stairs, past Basilard and Sespian who parted for their speedy retreat. Amaranthe didn't know if the haste of that retreat was entirely due to sexual urgency.

"Admiral Starcrest is here?" Sespian asked when he reached the top of the landing.

Amaranthe extended a hand toward the open office door. "We ran into him west of the city and brought him back here."

"That's amazing." Sespian rushed forward and gripped her shoulders, glancing at the doorway on the way by. "How did you find him? What did you—"

"It was Sicarius's doing," Amaranthe rushed to say. She didn't want credit for any of this. It surely hadn't been any brilliance on her part that had resulted in Starcrest's arrival.

At the name, Sespian lowered his hands, the animation

draining from his face. Amaranthe feared she wasn't going to get any good news. "I'm glad you're well," he said. "You wouldn't believe what happened to us."

Amaranthe had no trouble believing. She would have said as much, but Sespian's gaze had been drawn to the doorway again. He seemed torn between wanting to check in with her and wanting to check in with Starcrest.

"I'm sure they've been waiting for you," Amaranthe said, making the decision for him.

Sespian squeezed her arm. "I'll talk to you later. I want to know everything that's happened."

Amaranthe wanted to know, too, but she merely nodded and waved for him to go inside. Someone shut the door as soon as he did.

"Basilard." Amaranthe gripped his arm even though he stood in front of her, and appeared ready to answer all of her questions. "How did you survive that... catastrophe? And Sicarius? Is he...?" She couldn't bring herself to say dead.

Basilard lifted his shoulders. *He was out hunting the soul construct. Nobody's seen him since he left.*

A wave of relief almost bore Amaranthe to her knees. She caught herself on the railing. He could still be dead, especially if he hadn't made it back yet, but for now, he was simply missing. He'd been missing before. He was the sort to stick to a mission until he completed it. She wouldn't give up on him.

"How did you, Sespian, and Maldynado escape?" Amaranthe asked.

We were in the tunnels. General Ridgecrest, too, though his family was inside when the Behemoth *crashed.* Basilard grimaced. *He's in shock. Only two hundred of his men made it out with us. Did you see the... site?*

Did she *see*? She'd caused it. She couldn't bring herself to voice the admission. "I saw." Amaranthe clawed her stray hair back into a fresh bun and tried to straighten her thoughts as well. She ought to see what Starcrest and all these soldiers were planning to do. After all this... anything except a solution that

was truly good for the empire would be unacceptable. She still wanted to curl up into a ball, luxuriating in self-pity, but she drew strength from Basilard's presence. At least her men had made it out. It would have been beyond horror if they'd given her their hard work and cooperation—and trust—this last year, only to die because of her negligence. "What tunnels are under Fort Urgot?"

Heroncrest's army brought tunnel-boring machines. While the surface troops distracted us, they were digging routes through the earth to come up in the housing section of the fort. About a half hour before the... crash, they broke through and soldiers ran out. It wasn't far from Ridgecrest's section of the wall, and he leaped down, personally leading the charge to kill them or drive them back. Maldynado, Sespian, and I followed him. We collapsed one of the tunnels, but were down in the other one, fighting our way to the borers. Sespian had an idea to destroy the machines so more passages couldn't be made. We were in the middle somewhere, between the fort and the camp, when... it felt like the world ended. Basilard rubbed his hand over the three days of growth on his head. With all the scars, it had come in patchy. *So much dirt and rubble poured down. We were buried and had to dig our way out. Down there, we couldn't tell what had happened, except that all of the sudden there was utter silence. The opposition disappeared. The tunnel exit wasn't guarded. We came out and saw... we saw it all.*

"Yes." What else was there to say?

Are Books and Akstyr all right? I haven't seen them.

"We're battered from our adventure, but we all escaped," Amaranthe said. "Akstyr has grown useful of late. We wouldn't have made it without him."

"Oh?" came Maldynado's voice from the stairs. "Maybe I should take him to the Pirate's Plunder as a reward. Do you think Yara would—" He glanced back down the stairs, but she wasn't in sight. Amaranthe was surprised she'd released him so soon.

"Yes, she'd mind if you went to a brothel," Amaranthe said. "Where'd she go?"

"To find soap and to heat water. After her initial pleasure at seeing me wore off—" he smiled at this memory, "—she insisted on bathing me before engaging in more amorous activities. Oh, and I wasn't going to ask if she minded if I went to a brothel. I was going to ask if you thought she'd like to come along."

"She'd mind that even more. I'm sure Akstyr would be fine with a celebratory pie." Though now that she knew of Curi's questionable allegiance, Amaranthe wouldn't be shopping for sweets there.

"Pie. Just when I think you know men fairly well, you say something like that." He met Basilard's eyes, giving him a women-are-surely-odd look.

Amaranthe tried to smile, but her soul felt so weary, so pitted and ravaged by guilt, she didn't manage it.

I should also seek a bath, Basilard signed.

"I wasn't going to comment on the matter," Maldynado said, crinkling his nose, "but, yes. Yes, you should."

"Before you go... does either of you know where Sicarius went to look for that soul construct?" Practically speaking, finding him shouldn't be her priority, especially when he preferred to hunt alone anyway, but Amaranthe would worry about him until she knew he was safe.

Both men shook their heads.

Maldynado waved vaguely in the direction of the lake. "Sespian was the last one to talk to him. You should ask him."

Basilard eyed the closed meeting door, then gave a parting wave and descended to the factory floor. Maybe he wasn't certain whether having this legendary Turgonian admiral show up was a good idea or not. Maldynado was giving the door a wary look, too, though perhaps for other reasons.

A one-eyed, gray-haired man with a fierce glower stomped up the stairs. He pushed past Maldynado and entered the meeting room without a word. Numerous raised voices flowed out before the door shut again.

"That's General Ridgecrest," Maldynado said. "I reckon the meeting will really be getting started now."

"I should join them," Amaranthe said, "if they'll let me."

She reached for the doorknob, but peeked in the window first and paused, intimidated by all the uniformed men sitting around a conference table comprised of several desks and bookcases that had been pushed together. Lanterns blazed, lighting up the room, and general's and colonel's ranks glinted on all the uniforms. Sespian sat amongst them, his clothes as grimy, ripped, and stained as Maldynado's, but he didn't appear daunted by the company, most of it gray-haired and stern of face. By his choice or theirs, he'd taken the head of the table. Starcrest, also in civilian clothes, albeit much cleaner ones, leaned against the wall to the side, his arms folded across his chest, his eyelids half drooped, listening rather than talking. Or *trying* to talk. Judging by the gesticulating and the raised voices, three people were speaking at once. Maybe Starcrest had decided to absorb information for now. After all, he couldn't be that current on events, if he'd been traveling for weeks. She could only guess at how much he'd kept up with Turgonian news in the years prior.

Amaranthe wondered where the professor was. She would have felt more comfortable walking in if there'd been another woman in the room—or if she didn't have that pesky bounty on her head. Or if Sicarius were at her side, glaring over her shoulder at anyone who belittled her.

She sighed. She wouldn't have relied on him so heavily in the past—when had she grown so gun shy?

"When everything started going wrong," she muttered.

"What's that?" Maldynado asked.

"Nothing."

"You're not afraid to go in, are you? I'm sure Sespian won't let anyone shoot you."

"Comforting, thank you."

Maldynado scratched an armpit, glanced back down the stairs, then met her eyes. "Want me to go in with you?"

"Do you *want* to go in with me?"

"Dear ancestors, no, those generals are intimidating."

Amaranthe snorted. "Who's afraid now?"

"Oh, that'd be me. I'm still disowned, you know. Those people are all... owned. They won't appreciate my irreverent charm. Besides Yara might have my water ready by now. I just wanted to check in with you and make sure... you're all right." He raised his eyebrows.

All right? Not even close.

"I'm fine," Amaranthe said. "You better not delay your bath. I can smell those armpits from here."

Maldynado was kind enough not to point out that *she* hadn't bathed recently either. He simply sniffed one of the offending pits, nodded in agreement, and wandered back down the stairs.

Amaranthe took a breath and slipped into the room. Hardly anyone noticed, as the officers were busy leaning on the tables, pointing sharply, and arguing with each other.

"The problem is his legitimacy," a general she didn't recognize was saying. "If we throw our men behind him and we're not successful, if Marblecrest or Flintcrest or someone else comes out on top, we'll be condemning every single one of our soldiers to the firing line."

"He who controls the capital can force the issue," said an earnest bald colonel with stubby sausage-like fingers that he waved about as he spoke. "It's no longer about legitimacy, it's about power."

"I'm not disagreeing with that," the general said. "I'm pointing out how meager our forces are in comparison with those that the other contenders command."

"Especially now," Ridgecrest growled. His single eye was bloodshot. He ought to be in a bunk somewhere, not staying up for this meeting. But then, with the nightmares he'd have, he'd probably rather work than sleep. Amaranthe understood that all too well. "But we do have an advantage that they don't." Ridgecrest lifted a hand toward Starcrest. "Even if he's forgotten all he knew of military strategy in the last twenty years, his name alone will cast doubt into our enemies' minds."

"Thank you, Dray," Starcrest said. "I see you're as much the flatterer as you always were."

"It's just that I don't know how useful a *naval* commander can be in a city siege. All those pesky buildings are wont to get in the way."

This conversation caused the rest of the room to drop to silence, most of the men gaping at Ridgecrest for his audacity. Amaranthe recognized the teasing for what it was and guessed the general and the admiral had gone to school together or otherwise known each other for a long time. Starcrest appeared a little younger, but a missing eye could certainly age a man prematurely.

"All of those pesky buildings seem to be confusing Marblecrest," the other general said—his tag simply read Wranz, making him one of the rare men to rise to such a rank without a warrior-caste surname. "Why is he bothering with the Imperial Barracks? The railways, river, and aqueducts will be the key to controlling the city, especially at this time of year with limited food stores within its boundaries."

"Because his soft backside prefers imperial suites to camp cots," Ridgecrest said. "Last I heard his priority was shopping for new uniforms for his troops, so they'll look good while they're parading around the city."

"That's a Marblecrest for you."

"Flintcrest has the two major railways," Colonel Fencrest said, "and Marblecrest does have the river mouth blockaded. I don't think anyone has considered the aqueducts yet. It's possible we could start with that. With the lake freezing over, the underground water supply will be all the more important. My lord?" the colonel asked, tilting his face toward Starcrest. "What are your thoughts on the situation? You haven't voiced them yet."

A dozen sets of eyes turned toward Starcrest. Amaranthe would have quailed beneath all those gazes, but Starcrest merely gazed back, hard to read. Something about his silence, and his position in the room, made her think he might consider the succession issue the secondary problem, at least for the moment. He'd had firsthand experience with that ancient technology and

must have a good idea exactly what the *Behemoth* could do. Amaranthe may have denied Forge its two foremost experts on it, but as long as it was sitting out there in the open, anyone could come and poke around.

"I'll want to see reports from your intelligence analysts before suggesting targets and troop placement strategies," Starcrest said, "but laying siege on the city... nobody wins there. Not when it's our own city. I'd guess the people are already restless and irritated at the martial law. Civilians will be starting to see uniformed men as enemies rather than allies. It wouldn't take much to uncork the bubble cider bottle and let the contents overflow."

Amaranthe nodded to herself. She, too, had thought the answer lay with the populace. The tens of thousands of soldiers out there seemed like a lot, but there were hundreds of thousands of civilians living in the city. If one could win *their* minds...

General Wranz shifted. "It's true. There have already been incidents."

"We don't want to try to turn the population against the army though," Ridgecrest said. "That would set a horrible precedent. Whoever takes the throne next would inherit a mess." He glanced at Sespian. "Though we haven't decided on an heir yet, I suppose."

"You make the job sound so appealing, General," Sespian murmured, then raised his voice, facing Starcrest. "It sounds like you think we need someone with the ability to charm people to his or her side."

He didn't look at Amaranthe, but her belly did a queasy flip, for she had an inkling of what was coming. The last thing she was qualified to do was to try and sweet talk an entire city, especially now.

"You think you're that person?" Ridgecrest asked Sespian.

"No, but I have a skilled diplomat on my team." He spread a hand toward Amaranthe.

Every head in the room swiveled toward her. She felt more like a deer caught on the railway with a locomotive barreling at her than some sort of smooth-talking diplomat.

"Diplomat?" Colonel Fencrest asked. "We tied her up on the train. She's an outlaw, Si—Sespian."

Amaranthe caught the slip. Out of habit, these men were still apt to think of Sespian as their leader. She hoped he could take advantage of that.

"Did she *stay* tied up?" Sespian asked.

"Yes," Fencrest said at the same time as Starcrest said, "No."

The colonel frowned at him.

"By the time I went back to question her, she'd freed herself."

Question her? That wasn't exactly what he'd been doing. Why did she have a feeling Ridgecrest, Fencrest, and the others weren't on the list of people who knew about Starcrest's mission to those tunnels? Or the tunnels' existence at all, for that matter.

"What are you— She'd only been back there five minutes, my lord," Fencrest said. "And they were all tied."

"Indeed. When I entered, the guards were smashed face-first into the floor, and her team... was not."

Sespian smiled at Amaranthe. "Had a chat with those guards, did you?"

Not sure what to say—after all, it'd been Akstyr's gift that had allowed them to get the best of those men—she only offered a weak return smile. Or a *bleak* return smile, perhaps. She didn't want this mission. She wanted... she didn't even know what. To find Sicarius and fade into the background. Let the experts finish this. "Given my outlaw status, Sire, I don't think I'd be the best person to give speeches." Oh, and the fact that she'd killed thousands of people the night before. Emperor's teeth, she wanted to throw up again.

"We have some work to do before we're ready for that regardless." Starcrest headed for the door. No, he was heading for *her*. "May I speak with you for a moment, Corporal Lokdon?"

Had she given him her rank? Her history as an enforcer? No, someone had filled him in.

"Yes, sir. I mean, my lord. Admiral." Erg, why was she fumbling her words in front of him? She was no military history fanatic with a zealous love for naval strategists. Maybe it was

the fact that he was the one man Sicarius openly respected.

Before her tongue could trip her up again, she ducked her head, and led the way onto the catwalk. She'd planned to take him to her office, but he walked the other way, to the one other private room up there. The last time she'd been in it, Akstyr and Books had been using it as a study.

Only one small desk remained, the others having been purloined for the conference table. Starcrest's wife sat at it, the contents of an upturned valise sprawled across the top: journals, pens, pencils, crinkled pages of hastily scrawled notes, and a fist-sized black sphere. Chin in hand, she was frowning down at a small notebook held open in the other hand. She obviously hadn't come to the empire with the intent to take up winter sports and get massages from the spas on Mokath Ridge.

Amaranthe's fingers twitched at the unorganized mess, wanting to bring order to the desk. She did allow herself to pick up a few slips of papers that had fallen to the floor. Indecipherable runes had been copied onto the pages. She recognized the style from the *Behemoth*.

Starcrest shut the door and touched Amaranthe's shoulder. "If we stand here and talk, she'll notice us in a few minutes."

Amaranthe glanced at him, certain he was joking. One corner of his mouth twitched upward in a wry half smile, but Professor Komitopis hadn't looked up yet. Maybe he *wasn't* joking.

"What shall we talk about?" she asked.

"I understand you've been in that ship."

Ship, was that how he thought of it? None of the words in her vocabulary seemed sufficient, though she supposed she couldn't think of it as simply an aircraft now, since it could go beneath lakes too. Or maybe it wasn't going anywhere else. Ever. It'd end up being a tourist attraction, like the pyramid in the middle of the city.

Starcrest was waiting for an answer, she reminded herself.

"Yes. Twice now, though the first time was as a prisoner rather than as a..." She thought about saying guest, but that wasn't apt. Besides, she didn't want anyone thinking *she* was aligned with Forge. "Spy."

"Hm. And you had something to do with it being placed in its current locale?"

In other words, had she crashed it? What a tactful way to put it. Maybe *he* should be the diplomat giving speeches. "It was on the bottom of the lake. In hindsight, that was a better spot for it. I had thought to have it flown to the South Pole where we could bury it in a glacier or at the bottom of some distant ocean trench. I wanted to get it out of Forge's hands. I've seen some of what that technology can do. No organization should control it. Forge is already close enough to owning the world as it is. If nobody stops them... Well, I've been trying to stop them. My team and I have, that is. For the last year." She was, she noted, doing a good job of *not* answering the question he'd asked. "As for its current locale, Retta, one of the Forge scholars of that technology, was trying to fly it for us. I talked her into helping us."

Starcrest's eyebrows rose. She needed to be careful how she phrased things or they *would* think she had a magic tongue. She'd end up in front of a podium, making a fool of herself as she stammered through an inept speech. That hadn't been one of her best classes in school.

"But there was opposition," Amaranthe said, "and the other woman on board who knew how to operate the *Behemoth*—that's my name for the thing, not theirs—tinkered with those black cubes and—er, are you familiar with them?"

"Yes," Starcrest said.

"She tinkered with them so they started attacking us, attacking *everything*."

"Isn't that their normal function?"

"I thought so, but Retta had apparently changed the ones on the craft to recognize humans as... something not to be incinerated."

"Did they?" Starcrest glanced at Komitopis, who was still puzzling over her notes. He walked around the table and nudged her.

The book twitched, and she blinked in surprise when she saw him and Amaranthe. "Hello. Meeting over?"

"No, but we're discussing that ship."

"Oh, yes. Good." Komitopis closed her journal and gazed attentively at them.

Amaranthe couldn't believe she truly hadn't noticed them walk in and start talking.

Starcrest nodded to her. "Go on, please."

"So the cubes had been modified to be less deadly, but they've been unmodified now. I don't know if it's possible that some of them have left the craft and escaped into the city, but... I've seen them outside of the *Behemoth* before."

"I'll instruct the soldiers on how to make a concoction that destroys them."

"There *is* such a thing?" Amaranthe asked.

"Through trial and error, I found something that works. A variation on royal water."

Huh. Amaranthe hadn't thought anything in the known world could put a dent in any of those relics. This new revelation comforted her an iota. "Anyway, the cubes started shooting holes into their own ship and did some damage to the engines or whatever's behind the walls in the control room. As I said, Retta was trying to raise us up from the lake and take us to the South Pole, but smoke started coming out of the walls, and Ms. Worgavic's shaman didn't help either. She... burned Retta alive. There was no chance of controlling the *Behemoth* at that point, and we went down. Books, Akstyr, and I escaped on a lifeboat—that's what Retta called them, though they fly instead of floating—and I didn't realize *where* the craft had crashed until we were coming back on the train, and..." She swallowed. No need to explain. They'd seen too.

Starcrest nodded to his wife. "Do you know a Retta?"

"Retta Curlev?" Komitopis asked.

"Yes," Amaranthe said.

"She was one of the imperial students in the archaeology program at the Polytechnic a few years ago. I wasn't on the island teaching at the time, but I think they put her into the secret program to study the technology." Komitopis touched the sphere on the table.

"Random people can simply sign up to study it?" Amaranthe asked.

"No. It's not spoken of with students and certainly not listed in the course catalogue, though information about the technology isn't as tightly ratcheted down in Kyatt as it was here. The program is entered by invitation only."

"So people with enough money could arrange an invitation?" Amaranthe didn't mean for her tone to sound accusing, but it came out that way. Why had the Kyattese allowed *any*one to study that technology? It should have been buried somewhere for another fifty thousand years. Except, she thought with an inward sigh, secrets had a way of becoming unburied whenever more than one person held them. There must have been dozens of people on that mission, and Forge might have found the *Behemoth* one way or another regardless.

"That *shouldn't* be a criteria," Komitopis said, "but I couldn't promise that it never has been. As soon as Rias and I returned to my homeland, our gear was searched and the artifacts I'd discovered taken. Though the Polytechnic has kept me as an adviser, and I've argued for a tight-lipped policy, I am not now, nor have I ever been, in charge of the study of that race and its relics."

"I had the tunnel entrances blown up before I left the Northern Frontier," Starcrest said, "and we never saw anything like that ship, but we've since learned there are other deposits of the technology in the world." He shared a look with his wife. Amaranthe remembered Retta mentioning an underwater laboratory they'd discovered. "Unfortunately, we've heard of a handful of the artifacts appearing on the black market. The only boon is that few of the people who acquire them know how to work them."

"Except Forge," Amaranthe said, "though now that..." She took a breath. Confession time again. "Retta and Mia are both dead. I believe they were the only Forge votaries who knew how to control the *Behemoth* fully. Fully enough to operate it anyway."

"They must have been quite bright," Komitopis said, "to learn even that much in a few short years. One could spend a dozen lifetimes studying that ancient race, its languages and technology, and not truly understand it." She waved to the sphere on the desk. "After twenty years, I haven't grasped everything in this little dictionary."

"More of an encyclopedia than a dictionary," Starcrest said at her self-deprecation. "And even that is a poor term to describe the depths of knowledge inside of it."

Komitopis wiggled her fingers in acknowledgment.

Starcrest faced Amaranthe again. "What you're saying is that your *Behemoth* is stuck exactly where it is until someone figures out how to fly it elsewhere?"

Her *Behemoth*. Amaranthe cringed at the notion of taking possession of it. "I believe so, yes."

"Anyone could enter it as long as it's right there," Komitopis said, "and they could be inside, gathering artifacts to sell or hold as keepsakes. Knowing what I know of that race, many of those devices will have the potential to be deadly. Few people know how to work them today, but someday, someone will publish books on the language, and..." She spread her hands helplessly.

"It must be moved," Starcrest said. "The South Pole might work. Or better, put it at the bottom of the Drellac Trench. It'll be a few generations, at least, before we develop our own technology to the point of making a subaquatic descent of over six miles in depth. By then, we can hope humans have forgotten about the ship." A twist to his lips suggested he didn't have much faith in that hope.

"Perhaps it'll be destroyed by dropping it in there," Komitopis said.

"Can anything destroy it?" Amaranthe asked. "We know it can survive on the bottom of the lake, and... if it can fly into outer space..."

"The lake is a few hundred feet deep, true," Starcrest said, "but six miles deep is a far greater order of pressure. At the bottom of the Drellac Trench, the water column above an object

would exert a pressure of 15,750 pounds per square inch, over a thousand times the standard atmospheric pressure imposed at sea level." He didn't pause as he spoke, and Amaranthe wondered if he was capable of making such calculations between one breath and the next or if he had the facts memorized. "As for outer space," Starcrest went on, waving skyward, "it's a vacuum, we believe, with pressure close to nonexistent. Quite a different environment than the depths of the ocean. It would pose its own challenges, but I wouldn't be surprised if we breach outer space before we roam about in the deepest seas. Of course, entering, or in our case reentering, the atmosphere would be problematic with the friction heat caused by the extreme speeds a craft would..." Starcraft glanced around at his audience, catching a knowing smile on his wife's lips. "Ah, I wandered off on a tangent, didn't I?"

"Yes, but an interesting one," Komitopis said. "I dare say you'd like to put that craft somewhere that *you* can study it."

"That *is* tempting, but I'd wish to publish anything I learned, and everyone's concerns are deathly real. The world isn't ready for this kind of power. It may never be, so long as humans walk upon its continents. Though I'd be lying if I said I wouldn't like to be proved wrong about that." He waved away his musings. "Yes, the trench, that may be the best bet. Corporal Lokdon, you have some men available here, don't you? Men who are capable fighters and loyal to you?"

"Ah?" Though they'd been including her in the conversation, Amaranthe had felt like an outsider and hadn't been imagining herself as being a part of the *Behemoth*-trench mission. "I mean, yes, I do."

"I'd appreciate it if you and a couple of your better fighters would go along to the ship and see what can be done. I imagine Tikaya will be able to find some map inside to show her around, but a guide could prove helpful."

A guide? Her? Amaranthe had accidentally wandered into her own torture chamber the last time she'd been looking for something in there.

"It may be dangerous over there—if they haven't already, people will soon stop gawking and will see that monstrosity as a prize to be claimed," Starcrest said, giving his wife a solemn nod.

She crossed her arms over her chest and arched her eyebrows. "Usually when you send me off into danger, you come along."

"Yes, but there's a room full of officers next door who have convinced themselves I'm the answer to all their woes. I'm not sure yet if they actually want my help, or simply want to toss my name at their enemies, but they might wet themselves if I were to wander off right now." Starcrest gave her a warm smile. "Regardless, I'm positive that you're more capable of independent competence."

Komitopis shook her head, her long blonde braid swaying, and told Amaranthe, "I should have known I was in trouble back on Kyatt, when he asked if I'd packed my bow."

To Amaranthe's eye, the professor appeared more motherly and academic than athletic, so the admission that she *had* a bow was surprising. How well did she use it?

"Yes," Amaranthe said, for Komitopis seemed to be expecting an answer. "That must have been a warning. I'm told men tell you to pack scented soaps and skimpy undergarments if they have romantic interludes in mind." Though, she admitted, Sicarius would doubtlessly prove an exception there. No doubt, he'd suggest that romantic interludes should be punctuated with obstacle courses and knife-throwing practices. Though perhaps she should launder the "skimpy undergarment" Maldynado had foisted on her for the Suan costume. If nothing else, it would amuse Sicarius, and that was something that happened rarely.

You have to *find* him before you can amuse him, she thought. This mission would delay that. True, she didn't know for certain that he was in trouble, or where to start looking for him, but if he *was* in trouble… she hated to abandon him.

"I fear the romantic interludes will have to wait a little longer," Starcrest said.

"Yes, we finally get the children old enough to send off on

their own—or to visit their Turgonian grandmother—and now you have five hundred soldiers toddling along after you."

"We're up to seven hundred now," Starcrest said brightly.

"My bow," Komitopis said. "Very well."

"If you can thwart man-eating plants from the Lariat Islands and convince cannibalistic aborigines to run off down the beach, their tails tucked between their legs, I'm certain a few Turgonians won't be any trouble."

The statement—and the amused smiles of remembrance the pair shared—made Amaranthe quite certain that any fireside stories they might share would be riveting.

"I'll ask Colonel Fencrest to send a couple of men with instructions that they follow your orders," Starcrest went on, "and you'll have Corporal Lokdon and whomever she's willing to bring as well."

Amaranthe was thinking about pointing out that she hadn't agreed to go anywhere near the *Behemoth* again, but when Starcrest added, "Her team strikes me as eclectic and capable," all thoughts of defying him evaporated.

"My team? You mean Books and Akstyr? Or have you met others?" And *who* that had impressed him so? Surely not Maldynado.

"A couple," Starcrest said. "But mostly I talked to Sespian before he sat down at the table." He waved at the wall—raised voices were audible through it. "As your comrade pointed out, he's too young for me to have met before I left the empire, so I was curious to speak with him. He recounted his experiences over the last year, and you figured prominently in them."

"Oh." Amaranthe would have been curious to listen in on *that* conversation.

"I understand, among other things, that Sicarius works for you and not the other way around."

Komitopis's mouth dropped a centimeter or two at that statement.

Amaranthe cleared her throat. "Well, I come up with schemes, and he mostly goes along with them, because... it's complicated, but he had his reasons."

"Hm." Another look passed between Starcrest and his wife.

Erg, Amaranthe had a feeling he was assigning her too much credit based on her command, if one could call it that—she wouldn't—of Sicarius. They couldn't know about all the tightrope walking she'd done in the last year to keep him going along with her schemes and how much of it had to do with Sespian.

"I don't know where he is right now," she felt compelled to add. "It's been days since I've seen him. I can't promise him as a guard for the professor."

"I'm sure you and whatever men you can spare will be sufficient," Starcrest said. "Tikaya can handle herself in a fight if need be, though I'd prefer she be allowed to study that ship without worrying about watching her back. She doesn't, ah..."

"Doesn't do both at once effectively," Komitopis supplied dryly. "At all."

Starcrest looked relieved that she'd said it so he wouldn't have to. Remembering the way the professor had *not* noticed her husband's entrance and subsequent conversation, Amaranthe could have guessed it on her own.

"With your team helping and protecting her, I'm certain you can take care of the ship," Starcrest said, giving Amaranthe a single firm nod, then met his wife's eyes. "And you should stop by the docks, too, and see if our other anticipated arrival has come in."

Amaranthe barely heard the added comment. She was dwelling on his request and the fact that she'd accepted it so easily. Yes, she knew in her mind that getting rid of the *Behemoth* had to be the priority, but her heart... she wanted to go after Sicarius. *He* wouldn't approve of her choosing him over Starcrest's mission, though, and she knew it. And, independent of Sicarius's theoretical wishes, she found herself wanting to prove that Starcrest was right, that she could take care of the professor and the ship. She wanted to earn the respect he'd thus far granted her, based wholly on what he remembered of Sicarius. And on whatever Sespian had said as well. How odd

that Starcrest's opinion should matter to her. *She* hadn't read his books as a child. He had no true power here and certainly couldn't offer her the exoneration she desired—earning his respect might be nice, but she shouldn't fling herself at his feet in an effort to win favor. She ought to bargain for something; this was an opportunity.

Amaranthe lifted her chin. "I will help your wife, my lord, because what you want in this matter is what I've also been fighting to achieve, but... I would ask a favor in return."

"Oh?" Starcrest did that unreadable expression well. Not so well as Sicarius, perhaps, but she wagered quite a few of his men had struggled to guess his thoughts in his command days. Or maybe they'd attributed great thoughts to him when he'd merely been contemplating lunch.

Professor Komitopis, on the other hand, had an open expressive face, and her lips quirked up at Amaranthe's proclamation.

"I want you to help Sespian," Amaranthe said.

Starcrest's face remained guarded. "To reclaim the throne? I have not had time to fully assess the situation here. Putting aside his now questionable right to rule, I..." His brown eyes flickered toward his wife. "We aren't certain a nineteen-year-old ruler would be best for Turgonia. When it was not my decision to make, and I was twenty years removed from the politics of the empire, I was content to let events unfold as they would, but if I am to have a hand in shaping the future, I should want to thoroughly consider where I place my support."

The honesty was both appealing and alarming. Amaranthe appreciated that he didn't have any interest in lying to her, but the notion that he might decide one of the lords general vying for the throne was a better candidate made her want to shout with frustration. Or maybe cry. Extemporizing, she said, "As it happens, I wasn't asking you for that promise, my lord. That would be... if nothing else, a little out of scale in proportion to what you're asking from me. But Sespian..." She glanced toward the door to make sure it was still closed, and nobody was standing at the window, staring in—Sespian might not appreciate her speaking so openly about him to a man who was, books and legends aside, a stranger. "It's my impression—and he's as much as confirmed it—that Raumesys was an indifferent and sometimes cruel father to Sespian. And Sicarius... who and what he is makes Sespian keep him at arm's distance. Besides, it's only been a couple of weeks since Sespian learned about that truth. What I'm saying is he has had people conspiring against him since he was born and very few friends or allies. I believe he's of two minds as to what he should be doing, going forward, and I think he'd very much appreciate some friendly advice from someone who is respected in the empire and experienced in the ways of the world. You also seem sage and serene in the face of all that's happening. Sespian could use some serenity in his life."

Amaranthe chomped down on her lip to keep from going on. She hadn't meant to act the flatterer. The man didn't fluster her quite as much as Sicarius, but she did feel off balance in his presence.

"Sage," Starcrest said. "Hm. Sespian told me he had you in mind for a diplomatic position, should he find his way back to the throne. I thought it was some sort of idealistic infatuation, but perhaps not."

"Oh, I don't think so," Komitopis said, her blue eyes crinkling at the corners, "she just called you old in the most lovely manner."

Amaranthe almost blurted a protest—she hadn't been thinking of his age at all, only of his reputation, and the fact that Sicarius, of all people, thought so highly of his achievements—but she caught herself in time, recognizing the teasing for what it was.

"Indeed," Starcrest said, his own eyes crinkling a touch. "Sage. I prefer that to the term Fencrest used. What was it? Ah, yes, *venerable*. Ancestors, help me."

Sensing that she'd won what she wished—or at least what she'd amended her wish to be—Amaranthe remained silent.

"Very well." Starcrest offered a small bow. "I shall speak

with the young man at greater length, though I confess I would have been pleased to do so in any event. You needn't have wheedled for it." The now-familiar half smile formed again, taking the sting out of the word wheedled.

"Now, now," the professor said, "I thought that was quite wise, no, sage of her. You would have talked to the boy, yes, but most likely of engineering. Or submarines. Or... I saw that gleam in your eye earlier. You're even now contemplating the chain of technological advances that would be required to send a rocket into outer space, aren't you?"

"Not... *right* now," Starcrest said.

"But your mind wandered at some point while she was talking, didn't it?"

"Really, dear, I don't think you should betray me thusly to people we've just met."

Watching their easy banter, Amaranthe again felt a wistful pang. I want this with Sicarius, she sighed to herself. The ease at least. Asking him to trade jibes back and forth might be a bit much, though perhaps in twenty years...

You'd better find him first, she thought grimly.

CHAPTER 5

MARANTHE EYED THE DIM SKY, THE CLOUDS HANGING low over the waterfront. It'd be dark in another hour, and they hadn't even left the city. Komitopis had some errand at the docks, and after that it'd be another five miles to Fort Urgot. Amaranthe wasn't enthused at the idea of reentering the *Behemoth* at night, but, as the professor had pointed out, the artificial lighting inside would make the windowless tunnels appear the same no matter what time of day it was. And, as Starcrest had said, the sooner the better, insofar as getting rid of the ship went.

She caught Komitopis frowning thoughtfully over her shoulder, not for the first time.

"He's a good fighter, Professor Komitopis," Amaranthe explained, certain what had the other woman's attention without looking. "Really."

"I don't disbelieve you—and please call me Tikaya; I was just wondering if that represented a fashion choice or if it had cultural significance. I study ancient cultures, of course, but am not abreast with current trends." Tikaya glanced over her shoulder again.

The four guards Colonel Fencrest had detached to her command wore pressed uniforms and clean parkas, their rifles nestled into their shoulders in an identical fashion as they marched in unison. And then there was Basilard and Maldynado. Clad in unassuming brown and beige utility clothing and a bear fur coat, *Basilard* wasn't a problem, but sometime during the hours that Amaranthe had been attempting to sleep, Maldynado

had been shopping again. His clothing was sedate enough—a mix of black, forest green, and velvety gray—but the newest hat... it had to have been a dare. Amaranthe had been inured to tassels, so that wasn't the problem, but the... she didn't know what to call them. Tentacles? Tendrils? The colorful fabric appendages danced and writhed about his head with every step. There were bells at the end of each tendril, though he'd stuffed something into them to muffle the noise.

"No cultural significance that I'm aware of," Amaranthe said, "though it does say he's big enough and strong enough to fight off any bullies who might want to beat him up on principle."

"Yara thought it was hideous," Maldynado said. She didn't know if he was close enough to have heard their quiet conversation, but he'd probably guessed at the significance of the glances.

"Thus you naturally purchased it." Amaranthe wondered how long that relationship would last. Maybe they'd surprise everyone and get married. And have children. *That* was hard to imagine, but Yara had been uncharacteristically pleased to have Maldynado return from the dead.

"Naturally the shopkeeper *gave* it to me," Maldynado corrected. "To model around town and drive sales."

"Drive them... *away?*" Tikaya murmured.

"I notice the shop's name isn't visible anywhere on the hat," Amaranthe replied. "Poor advertising if that's what it's meant as. Maybe it was some kind of... demonstration model that the proprietor wanted to get rid of."

"Very funny, Bas," Maldynado said.

Tikaya looked back again, this time studying Basilard's hand signs. Keeping an eye out for soldiers and enforcers, Amaranthe missed half of the quick comments, though she did catch something about Sicarius applying his knife to the hat much the way he had to Akstyr's hair.

Sicarius. Amaranthe shifted her focus from the streets around them to the lake and the fields and foothills in the distance on the other side. Was Sicarius out there somewhere, even now?

Still hunting the soul construct to ensure it couldn't harm Sespian? She couldn't help but feel he should have found it by now if he sought it, for it'd happily seek *him* with its claws and fangs blazing as soon as he drew close. If he was... still alive, he should have returned by now. What else could he be doing? Hunting the practitioner that had summoned the construct as well? A dangerous mission for one man, even one as formidable as he.

"What is that language?" Tikaya asked, walking backward now, watching Basilard's half of the continuing conversation. "It reminds me of the Mangdorian hunting code, but—" Her heel slipped on the slick cement street, and she stumbled, arms flailing.

Though startled, Amaranthe reacted reflexively, catching the professor's elbow and shifting her weight to keep her from hitting the ground. Barely. Arrows spilled from Tikaya's quiver, and her rucksack slid halfway off her back. Maldynado and Basilard rushed forward to help right her. The soldiers, no doubt under orders from Starcrest to keep his wife safe, rushed forward, too, and Amaranthe found herself pushed out of the way.

"I'm fine," Tikaya said, straightening her pack and waving away the small legion trying to help her. "Thank you." The freckles and pale skin did little to hide her reddening cheeks. "I believe I'll walk facing forward now."

"Always a good idea when visiting a foreign nation, my lady." Maldynado smiled at her and bowed, the felt tendrils flopping about his face.

More usefully, Basilard picked up her fallen arrows and handed them back to her.

"Thank you," Tikaya said again, returning them to the quiver. "Good advice, yes, though I can trip when I'm facing forward too. Rias is usually around to catch me, fortunately, and I've yet to break any bones. Though I imagine sprains are slow to heal here without the use of—are practitioners still forbidden here?"

"Not so much forbidden as hanged when spotted,"

Amaranthe said as they resumed walking. "Would you like me to carry anything?"

Thanks to the professor's six feet of height, the rucksack didn't seem oversized or unwieldy on her, but it *was* bulky and heavy, with jars or something similar pushing bumps into the canvas. In addition, the longbow and quiver were attached to it.

"I can handle it, thank you." Tikaya waved. "You have your own load."

"Just food and water and first aid supplies. You're right in that nobody here can fix a sprained ankle with his mind." Amaranthe thought of mentioning Akstyr, but he was still sleeping at the factory and hadn't come along. Amaranthe ought to be sleeping, too, but she'd woken from a nightmare during her attempt at an afternoon nap and had had no wish to return to her bed.

Basilard moved up to walk on Tikaya's other side, so she wouldn't have to crane her neck around to observe him. He signed, *Hunting code. Yes. With additions.* He raised his eyebrows. *You understand?*

"The original language, yes," Tikaya said. "Additions, interesting. Because you can't speak?"

Basilard touched the scar tissue at his throat and nodded.

"Ah, I'd be most curious to learn what you've done with the simple code. Has it been documented anywhere?"

Basilard shook his head. *It's all made up. Nothing real.*

"That's how *all* language starts," Tikaya said. "Words are born out of necessity to communicate."

But only a few of us speak it.

Tikaya couldn't know anything except the original terms, but she seemed to read between the lines—or the signs, as it were—and picked up the gist of Basilard's sentences now that she knew what she was looking for. "In the Pasas Unius Chain, there are only seven people left alive who speak the aboriginal tongue of D'skhmk Mk."

Amaranthe blinked at the name or word or whatever it had been. Had there been any vowels? She didn't think so.

"Even at the height of its power and population, four hundred years ago, the remote island tribe never had more than one hundred and fifty speakers. That does not make it any less of a language."

Basilard didn't look convinced, but was too polite to naysay her.

"You should make a lexicon," Tikaya went on. "Draw the gestures and write down what they mean. Surely, you are not the only mute Mangdorian in the world. You could pave the way for others of your people with a speech impediment."

At this, Basilard's mouth dropped open. *I... don't know how to draw.*

Amaranthe hadn't seen Basilard truly daunted very often. "I'm sure Sespian would help you once everything is settled."

"My daughter is skilled with a pen, too," Tikaya said, "though it'd be difficult to convince her to draw something without fur, scales, or antennae. Still, creating a simple lexicon shouldn't take long. And once you retire from—" Tikaya shrugged and waved at Basilard's pistol, short sword, and knives, "—your current job, you could return to your country with the book and find others to teach."

Basilard scratched his jaw. *I have... another quest, but perhaps someday. It is an interesting idea. Thank you.*

Tikaya nodded.

"Is your daughter the girl we met on the train?" Amaranthe could imagine the young woman in pigtails drawing fanciful images of winged flying lizards complete with human riders.

"Koanani is my daughter, yes, and you met Agarik, too, but I'm speaking of my eldest, Mahliki. She's the reason we've detoured in this direction. Oh, are these the private docks?" Tikaya peered around, as if she'd just noticed that they'd turned onto Waterfront Street. "Or... no, those are for fishing and canneries, aren't they?"

Amaranthe didn't point out that they'd been walking north along the street for four blocks. "We have a ways to go. We'll pass the yacht club—" she glowered to the north, where the

familiar docks and buildings hunkered beneath the darkening gray sky, "—and reach the private berths shortly."

"Why would your daughter be down by the docks?" Maldynado asked, thankfully not making a comment about the sorts of women one usually found loitering in such locales, at least in the warmer months.

"This is where she would have arrived." Tikaya produced a scrap of paper. "Rias's family owns a small berth here in the capital."

Amaranthe stopped. "Didn't anyone tell you? Soldiers are stopping all of the steamboats and ships coming up the river. They're searching the public transports and turning away private ones." She couldn't fathom why the Starcrests would have sent their daughter on a steamboat or some other ship when the rest of the family had come in on the train. Or had she sailed in on some private yacht? That sounded like a perilous voyage this time of year. Surely, the winter storms were tearing across the Western Sea.

"That shouldn't have been a problem." Tikaya smiled.

That smile conveyed much. "She's coming on a submarine?" Amaranthe asked.

"Indeed so. Rias wanted to stop on the coast to talk to an old comrade of his—he's the one who sent the train and the troops with us—but we decided it might be wise to have the submarine here in the capital, should we need to escape or, knowing him, launch some subaquatic attack at the enemy."

"How old is your daughter?"

"Seventeen," Tikaya said.

"And you sent her all this way by herself?" Amaranthe shuddered, remembering all the things that had gone wrong during her own underwater excursions. She wouldn't want to face a kraken, octopus, or even a particularly nettlesome snarl of seaweed down there on her own.

"She's quite able to pilot and maintain the craft," Tikaya said, "but her cousin Lonaeo came along to share the duties. Or—" her voice lowered, and Amaranthe almost missed the rest, "—distract her in such a way that they never arrive."

"Pardon?" Amaranthe's first thoughts were of a sexual nature, but surely the Kyatt Islands weren't *that* liberal, that cousins should openly, ah... Lonaeo, was that even a man's name?

"He's an entomologist and she's a biologist," Tikaya said. "They've been wandering off in the forest together to poke under rocks and in logs since they were children. Lonaeo is eight years older. He was *supposed* to be the babysitter, the mature one who kept her out of trouble, but she had this tendency to get *him* in trouble. Five years old and she somehow convinced him that they needed to capture a wasps' nest for study, and she had this marvelous plan for removing it without anyone being stung. *She* didn't get stung. Lonaeo still has scars. And that section of forest up in the mountains hasn't completely regrown. It's a wonder—well, I knew what I was getting into when I married a Turgonian. A terribly bright Turgonian at that."

From behind them, Maldynado made a sound somewhere between a snort and a chortle. "Sounds like your long-lost sister, boss. You two should get along famously."

"Er, maybe. Though I've never burned down a forest."

"Surely only because of the dearth of them in the city," Maldynado said. "You've blown up countless things though. Professor Komitopis, I know you're a learned lady, but I suggest you *not* visit the *Gazette* for a tour of the capital's oldest continuously publishing newspaper institution at this time."

"I... shall keep your suggestion in mind." Tikaya considered Amaranthe anew—wondering if she would be a bad influence on her daughter?

"*Thank* you, Lord Tour Guide Maldynado," Amaranthe hissed, trying a version of Sicarius's icy stop-talking-or-I'll-hurt-you glare.

"No problem, boss." Maldynado's cheery wink didn't show signs of concern.

She caught a smirk on Basilard's face too. Grumbling under her breath, she resumed walking, picking up the pace as they strode past the yacht club. It was chilly and getting darker every moment. No need to dawdle.

Perhaps she will grow out of finding trouble, Basilard signed to Tikaya. *Biology sounds like a sedate career.*

"Not the way Mahliki does it," Tikaya murmured. "Is this the spot?" She looked from a piece of paper in her hand to a plaque full of dock numbers.

"What's the address?" Amaranthe asked.

"1473. Yes, there it is." Tikaya tapped the second to last number on the plaque.

They had stopped at the head of a long dock with dozens of boathouses and berths to either side, all empty at this time of year. A layer of ice had finally formed, crusting around the pilings and stretching across the entire lake. It didn't appear thick, but it would be soon.

"When did they arrive?" Amaranthe asked as they started down the long dock.

"I'm not certain if they're here yet, but it wouldn't have been long ago if they are. They had to go around the Cutter Horn, through the Tiberian Gulf, and up the Goldar River, a much less direct route than our train trip through the heartland. If they're not here, I'll leave a note as to where they can find Rias."

Amaranthe chewed on her lip, not certain how she felt about leaving notes with directions to their hideout. But with hundreds of soldiers now occupying the factory, it wasn't going to remain a secret to their enemies for long anyway.

Maldynado tossed a snowball at an icicle hanging from the eaves of a small boathouse. It shivered and fell, shattering on the ice below. "Will they be able to come up through all that if they're in a submarine?"

Tikaya paused to peer over the side. "I'm not very familiar with ice—how thick is that? Can you tell?"

"Less than two inches," Amaranthe said. "I wouldn't walk on it yet."

"Ah, they can break through that then."

"And if it gets thicker before they get here?" Maldynado adjusted his hat and pushed a tendril out of his eyes. "Huge trucks drive out there in the winter, you know."

"Do they? That must be an interesting sight." Tikaya resumed her walk down the dock. They passed the structural remains of a boathouse that had succumbed to fire recently, its singed frame leaning precariously toward the lake. "I'm sure they'll figure out a way to break through. If nothing else, it being a Starcrestian design, there are weapons."

Amaranthe was imagining what sorts of weapons might work underwater when they passed the corner of the last boathouse along the dock and came face-to-face with two enforcers. The men were staring down at a jagged hole in the ice with a dark gray hatch visible in the middle of it. Before Amaranthe waved her men forward, Basilard and Maldynado were already in motion. She allowed herself a smidgeon of pride at the quickness with which they flattened the enforcers to the dock. Their crossbows and short swords skidded across the frosty boards to stop at her feet.

"Tie them, boss?" Maldynado asked.

"Yes, please."

The four soldiers assigned to Tikaya made a few choked noises and sent silent queries toward her. For them, enforcers weren't enemies, and they had to question this manhandling.

"I believe those are the uniforms and accoutrements of law enforcement officers," Tikaya said. "Is that correct?"

"Yes," Amaranthe said, "but I've found it easier to nullify them than to explain that we are indeed trying to help the city. For some odd reason, they rarely believe me."

Basilard finished tying his man and knelt back to sign, *Might have something to do with the number of wanted posters featuring your face.*

"Possibly." Amaranthe pointed toward the boathouse. "Put them in there, please."

The soldiers were shifting their weight and fingering their weapons. Amaranthe's response must not have mollified them.

"We'll leave their bonds loose enough that they can work themselves free shortly after we've gone," she told them, then pointed at the hatch and asked Tikaya, "Is that familiar?"

"It is." She seemed to be looking for a way to reach it. Though the submarine had come up in the 1473 berth, it was about four feet from the dock. Given the water and possibly ice that coated the concave hatch, landing on it without slipping off would prove a challenge.

"Basilard," Amaranthe said, "you're the most agile of us. I don't suppose you'd hop out there and... knock?"

Basilard nodded and shrugged off his pack.

Maldynado frowned. "I'm agile too."

"Yes, but I thought the hat might throw off your balance."

That drew a snort from one of the soldiers, though his comrades were quick to glare him to silence.

Basilard made the leap, landing lightly on the hatch, his fingers touching down to steady himself. He considered it for a moment, then, as Amaranthe had suggested, knocked politely. She wondered if the enforcers had already tried that. For that matter, what had drawn them out to investigate? The boom of a weapon being fired to break the ice?

"You may want to stand in view of the opening," Amaranthe told Tikaya, pointing her farther out on the dock. "In case they're the sort to come out armed, a familiar face could keep an incident from occurring."

"Yes, of course." Tikaya picked her way out along the icy arm of the dock.

The hatch didn't open though. Basilard spread his hands, asking what to try next.

"Is it possible they've arrived and gone into the city to explore?" Amaranthe asked, though if they'd broken through the surface with some weapon recently—as the enforcers standing around suggested—they shouldn't have had time to wander off to explore anything yet.

"It's possible," Tikaya said.

A crack sounded behind Basilard, and he whirled about. A metal pipe of some sort broke through the ice and shot up a foot. There was a perpendicular bend near the tip, and it rotated toward them, the opening at the end reminding Amaranthe of a firearm's muzzle.

She yanked out her pistol. "Is that a weapon?"

"No." Tikaya waved at the orifice. "A periscope."

Realizing the "muzzle" was glassed over, Amaranthe lowered her weapon.

"You may want to jump back, Mister Basilard," Tikaya said. "If they come out, they'll open the—"

A clank-thunk-clank sounded beneath Basilard's feet. Eyes widening, he leaped back to the dock. A moment later, the hatch swung open, and a young woman with long raven hair braided similarly to her mother's appeared in the opening. She had more of her father's coloring, with olive skin less prone to freckles, but the blue eyes were much like Tikaya's. It made for a striking combination, and Amaranthe wondered if she'd have to remind Maldynado that he was in a relationship, a monogamous one, insofar as she'd heard.

"Good to see you, dear," Tikaya said warmly, still speaking in Turgonian. "Is Lonaeo well too?"

"Yes," the girl, Mahliki, Amaranthe reminded herself, said. She didn't send her mother a greeting, rather she peered in all directions visible from the hatchway. "Is it gone?"

"It?" Amaranthe and Tikaya asked at the same time.

"That black cube."

Amaranthe rocked back on her heels. "You saw one? Out here?" Her mind spun. Maybe the girl meant something else. Something perfectly ordinary, like a… a… yes, what, Amaranthe?

"A *kelbhet*?" Tikaya asked. "You're sure?"

"It looked exactly like the ones in your drawings," Mahliki said.

"And it shot a red beam at us," came a male voice from within the submarine.

"Yes, that was the truly defining trait," Mahliki said dryly. Her rigid shoulders relaxed when she didn't see any sign of the deadly device. "It was hovering above the lake when we arrived. We popped out and it veered in this direction. It shot its beam and—ah, yes, there's the recipient of its damage." She pointed at the boathouse Amaranthe had assumed burned in a fire.

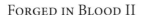

"Odd," Tikaya said. "The *kelbhet* are typically much tidier when they're incinerating something."

Yes, chillingly so, Amaranthe thought, picturing the guards she'd seen devoured by those crimson beams.

"You said they'd been modified?" Tikaya asked Amaranthe.

"Yes, by Retta's assistant," Amaranthe said. "The first modification changed them so they didn't target humans, but then she changed them again so that they did. The last I saw them, they were mowing down their own people."

"Not *their* people," Tikaya murmured.

"Well, Forge people." Amaranthe didn't want to imagine the "people" who had thought incendiary cleaning constructs were a good idea.

"If it's safe to come out..." Mahliki considered the thus-far mute soldiers, shrugged, and did something inside, near the lip of the hatchway.

A panel on the bottom side of the hatch popped open, and a thin metal square with hinges slid out. It unfolded in four segments, creating a gangplank that thudded down on the edge of the dock.

"I told you it would reach," Mahliki said into the submarine.

"Yes, yes, now get your big butt off the ladder so I can get out, will you?" came the cousin's voice from inside.

Mahliki rolled her eyes. "My butt isn't big. It's *contoured*."

"Please, everything you have is big. You're a giant, just like Aunt Tikaya."

"Not here, I'm not. Lots of Turgonian women are six feet tall, Father says, and the men are even taller, just like him." Mahliki considered Maldynado and the soldiers, a hint of appraisal in the gaze. It seemed more like a tourist examining the curious natives rather than anything with sexual undertones, but Maldynado naturally straightened and returned this appraisal with a yes-I-*am*-a-handsome-fellow-aren't-I smile.

"Stop dithering around, you two," Tikaya said. "We have a larger mission to complete tonight."

Amaranthe tapped a finger to her lips as she watched the

exchange. She wasn't sure what she'd expected, but the girl sounded like a normal teenager, rather than some precocious genius.

It'd been hard to judge height when only Mahliki's head and shoulders had been sticking through the hatchway, but on the dock, she stood even with her mother, maybe even a hair or two taller. Amaranthe could understand why someone from Kyatt would consider her a big woman, though neither her butt nor anything else was disproportionate, despite her cousin's teasing. Rather she had her mother's curves along with an easy athleticism that captured every man's attention as she climbed from submarine to gangplank to dock, catching herself quickly when her foot slid in a patch of ice.

Watching the soldiers puff their chests out, Amaranthe imagined her team of men starting brawls in their haste to gain the young woman's favor. For the sake of simplicity, she hoped Tikaya intended to send her off to stay with the same grandmother who was housing the other children.

Mahliki clanked as she walked down the dock to join her mother. Curious, Amaranthe eyed her for weapons—surely, she didn't have some knife collection beneath her jacket? Although with a Turgonian admiral for a father, perhaps it wouldn't be that strange. Though, upon consideration, what she'd first thought of as clanks were more like clinks, such as bumping glasses might make.

Mahliki returned the gaze, cocking an eyebrow.

"Sorry," Amaranthe said, "I was wondering why you were rattling."

"Ah." Mahliki unzipped her jacket and displayed rows of vials of various sizes secured to the inside flap, along with a few metal tools, and was that some sort of folded net?

"Dear," Tikaya said, "what samples are you expecting to find here? It's winter."

"Not all flora, fauna, and insects die off or hibernate, Mother, and I've read that the nymphs of Turgonian flies live in ponds and streams, often under the ice. They feed throughout the cold

months and emerge as adults in the spring. I've never had a chance to observe insects in a sub-freezing climate. I'm also terribly excited to find a dragonfly for my collection. We don't have them on the islands. I'll be curious to study them. They're vicious predators."

Tikaya pulled her parka closer, nodding and casting a wary eye toward the surrounding landscape, as if she expected the empire to be full of vicious predators.

"Those are for collecting insects?" Amaranthe asked, wondering if the girl knew she and her submarine had popped up in a war zone.

Mahliki waved a hand, as if guessing her thoughts. "Whenever there's time."

"And sometimes when there's not," Tikaya said. "She's faster with those specimen collection tools than your assassin friend is with his knives."

Mahliki smiled, not disagreeing.

The gangly man who climbed out in her wake was more of what Amaranthe imagined typical Kyattese citizens looked like. More bone than brawn, he had shaggy blond hair that hung into blue-gray eyes half hidden behind a pair of spectacles, and while he didn't trip clambering through the hatchway and onto the gangplank, it was close. An equally shaggy tuft of hair dangled from his chin, the classification somewhere between beard, goatee, and flower gone to seed.

He paused on the gangplank, chomping down on his lip as he considered the soldiers lined up on the dock. His attention snagged on their swords and rifles, and he didn't seem to notice that they were too busy pretending not to watch Mahliki to know he existed.

"Lonaeo," Tikaya said, "can you secure the *Explorer*, please? We won't be back tonight, perhaps not for a few days. If you have any food and water rations easily accessible in there, you may want to grab them too. We aren't going to the city. We're going to deal with... a problem."

"A *problem*?" Maldynado asked, his eyes devoid of humor.

"I assure you it's more than that. I was there when it landed."

Tikaya nodded in acknowledgment. She probably hadn't wanted to alarm her daughter, who was, it seemed, being invited along.

"A bigger problem than those cubes?" Mahliki asked.

"By a billion times," Maldynado said.

"I thought we were going to visit Uncle Rias's mother and cousins up north," Lonaeo said.

"That was the plan, but we may need your help in the ship." Tikaya caught Amaranthe's dubious gaze. "Though they didn't choose to study archaeology or linguistics for their careers, they grew up around my work, and they've both proved useful in navigating other ruins before."

"How far is it?" Lonaeo asked.

"About five miles," Amaranthe said.

"We're walking?" Lonaeo peered toward the head of the dock. "No runabouts here?"

"There are steam carriages," Amaranthe said, "for those who can afford them. And trolleys, but that's for the city. Street skis and lots of bicycles, though the ground's a bit treacherous for that now. Actually..." She eyed the submarine. "Fort Urgot is—was—" she winced, "—a couple hundred meters from the lake. It has a dock, if that wasn't destroyed. Maybe we could..." She gestured toward the submarine.

"Boss," Maldynado hissed, "haven't we been underwater enough in this last year—" he caught Mahliki looking at him, and changed his complaint to, "—to develop a taste for that travel? Yes, indeed, I'd love to see that submarine."

Amaranthe rubbed her face. This was going to be a problem.

"I suppose there's room," Tikaya said, though she eyed the four soldiers dubiously.

"We'll have to squish," Mahliki said.

"We're fine with that," Maldynado said brightly. The soldiers were quick to nod as well.

Yara is going to pound you if you don't quit that, Amaranthe signed tersely to Maldynado.

He blinked. *What?*

For once, his innocence didn't seem feigned. Maybe it was some sort of reflex, and he truly didn't realize he was flirting.

"All right then," Mahliki said. She'd noticed the hand signs and crinkled a brow at her mother, but Tikaya waved it away as nothing. Good. "Everyone in, I guess."

"By the way," Amaranthe said, gesturing for the soldiers to cross the gangplank before her, "which way was that cube heading when you saw it last?"

"North, I think," Mahliki said. "It was hard to get a good look. We were busy diving back underwater and calculating the penetration speed and depth of those beams."

"*She* was doing that," Lonaeo said. "I was trying to figure out how to crawl under a seat that was bolted to the deck."

Mahliki swatted him. "Which way is this Fort Urgot?"

"North," Amaranthe said.

"Oh." Mahliki grimaced.

"Did you find a way to get under that seat?" Maldynado asked as he passed the scruffy young man.

"Sorry, no."

"A shame."

When Tikaya drew even with her, Amaranthe quietly asked, "Any idea how many of those cubes are likely to be on a ship the size of the *Behemoth*?"

Tikaya's met her eyes. "A lot."

"That's what I was afraid of."

* * *

In an alley behind the Clearview Hotel, one block up from the yacht club, Sicarius set a canvas bag into the snow behind a waste bin. Bloodstains had seeped through the fabric, but it was dark enough that he doubted anyone would notice it. The information he'd pried from the Forge operative's mouth before killing her had promised a meeting was taking place in Worgavic's suite tonight, should he arrive early enough to find the attendees still there. He'd postponed the other assassinations on the Ridge to detour down to the waterfront.

He eyed the rooftop of the five-story building, the eaves stretching into the alley above him, then listened without moving, his back to the wall, the shadows cloaking him. This early into the night, many sounds drifted from within the hotel, the clinks of glasses in the drinking room, the chatter of guests in the lounge, the chops of knives in the kitchen, and the moans of couples who had retired to their rooms for trysts.

It was early to stage an assassination, but given the duress he'd applied to the Forge woman, he knew she hadn't lied to him. He had experience enough to tell such things, even if he'd had little need to call upon it in the last year. Somewhere along the way, he'd stopped pointing out to Amaranthe the effectiveness of torture. Because she always rejected it, he'd assumed, but maybe there was more to it. This evening it had bothered him. It might simply be that he'd had no choice in the matter. Before he'd had more than a thought that he had enough information and could make a quick kill, Kor Nas's voice had sounded in his head, demanding he spend *time* with his victim before ending her life, productive time. He didn't know if the practitioner had known she had information or if he'd simply relished the idea of torturing someone through Sicarius.

A drunk couple walked past the front of the alley, supporting each other as they staggered off to their next destination. It reminded Sicarius to get to work. The meeting would allow him to kill several Forge people in one spot, but only if he arrived before they departed.

Would Kor Nas require another round of torture?

Sicarius lifted his fingers, sliding them beneath a black wool cap, and touched the smooth opal. The size of a robin's egg, it nestled against his skull. It'd grown into his flesh, and he couldn't feel a separation between stone and skin. Like a tumor. He didn't think it'd be possible to pull it out, but what if he tried to cut it out with his knife?

At the thought, a tendril of pain shot from the stone and into his brain. It wasn't agonizing, nothing to bring a man to his knees, or certainly not to bring him to *his* knees, but the

warning came through sharp and clear. Why fight this anyway? Hadn't he wished to kill these Forge people regardless?

Yes, he decided. He didn't know whether the thought was truly his or not, but he left the sack and climbed.

The building's drainpipes weren't sturdy enough to support a man's weight, but his fingers found sufficient handholds in the mortar gaps between the stones. He reached the eaves, gripped the edge of the roof, and pulled himself over the side. He trotted across the snowy tiles to the front of the building. According to the seer's notes, Worgavic's suite overlooked the lake and lay behind the third and fourth windows from the south side.

The hotel had an attic so there was a twelve-foot gap between the roof and the tops of those windows. He uncoiled a thin, strong cable from his waist and tied off one end. A trolley clanged below, coming to a stop in front of the hotel. People were still about on the street, entering and exiting the hotel. Sicarius would have to wait or choose his moment carefully.

Waiting would be more prudent, perhaps taking the role of sniper and killing the Forge women as they departed from their meeting, but a thought entered his mind: *Finish your task and return to me.*

Maybe Kor Nas had another list of people to be assassinated.

Sicarius pulled out a few clips and fashioned a rappelling setup that would allow him to descend headfirst. A minute later, when the street lay momentarily clear, he lowered himself over the edge. Gas lamps blazed at either side of the hotel's front door, leaving the stairs and the piles of cleared snow on either side of them well lit. He doubted anyone would see him in the shadows near the roof, but worked quickly regardless.

Lamps burned behind shutters in the room marked by the fourth window, so Sicarius chose the third. This one wasn't shuttered. When his eyes reached the top of the window he confirmed that it was dark inside. By the embers of a fire burning in a hearth, he could just make out a large canopied bed, the sheets turned down, waiting for its occupant.

With one hand holding his body weight above him on the

rope, he pulled out his black dagger with the other. It'd proven effective at cutting any number of materials in the past and had no problem scoring the window. He returned the blade to its sheath, pushed the glass circle free, and caught it before it dropped out of reach. He unlocked the window from within, pulled the larger pane open, and slithered inside.

Sicarius landed in a soundless crouch on the rug and paused, senses stretched out to verify that nobody occupied the room. It smelled of lavender perfume and freshly laundered linens, with a hint of tobacco smoke lingering in the air. Worgavic's vice? Or that of a lover? Amaranthe had seen her with the senior Lord Mancrest, he recalled.

Amaranthe. The thought of her caused a lump to swell in his throat. He'd been trying to keep her out of his mind, not wanting to be caught thinking of her, not when the practitioner could rifle through his thoughts like pages in a book. Amaranthe's memory was private, not something to be shared with an outsider.

Muffled voices came from the door between the rooms. He padded across a lush carpet to listen, detecting four, no five distinct voices. This close, he could make out snatches of conversations. Several of the speakers seemed to be standing, some with their backs to his door, and at least one was pacing. And drinking. The clink of ice cubes in a brandy glass sounded more than once.

"—crest can't figure out what to do next? He needs you to come up and hold his hand?"

"He's done what we asked, taken the Barracks."

"...*asked* him to deal with the Company of Lords."

"He said he would, but I think he had something bloody in mind."

"*Men*, ach. We'll deal with them. But do we buy them or force their votes?"

"Those old sods have lived too long not to have some tidbits that can be used in blackmail."

"Blackmail, Lorsa, really. You've grown so felonious of late."

Sicarius had heard Worgavic before, in that meeting beneath Lake Seventy-Three, and he thought one of the voices belonged to her, the one speaking of forcing or buying votes, but he couldn't be certain. Listening through a door made it difficult.

He intended to wait for an opportune moment to attack, or at least long enough to make sure there weren't six guards standing silently about the room, but Kor Nas's voice whispered in his mind.

No delays. Kill them all. Emotion came through the mind link as well as the words, an eager anticipation with a tinge of arousal in it. It reminded Sicarius of Emperor Raumesys. Hollowcrest had been dispassionate and logical, but Raumesys had darkly enjoyed having an assassin at his disposal, relishing ordering prisoners tortured and standing back to watch. Fortunately, Sicarius had never had to share a mind link with the man. Such emotions distracted one from one's work.

They are all enemies to your general Flintcrest, came Kor Nas's next words, a touch defensive perhaps.

All of the heads won't fit in that bag, Sicarius thought in return, not bothering to hide the sarcasm. Had he spoken, he would have swept it from his voice, but the practitioner was in his head anyway, so it hardly mattered.

Bring Worgavic's for your general to see. The others don't matter. No, wait. Bring them all, and leave a mess in the room. I want this story in the newspaper. I want Forge to know someone is hunting them and to be afraid.

Sicarius's sarcasm, his derision for the practitioner, might be misplaced. Hadn't he killed a number of the Forge people for the same reason? After he'd learned they intended Sespian's death? He'd done it to protect Sespian though, not simply to kill, not because he enjoyed it.

Yes, tell yourself that, my pet, Kor Nas purred. *We two, we are not so different. We serve our masters, but we enjoy our work, don't we? We could have found other work long ago if we did not.*

Not caring for the conversation, Sicarius pulled out his dagger.

Kill them all, Kor Nas repeated. *And leave your mark. I want them to know it was you.*

Sicarius paused, his hand on the door. *My mark? I have no mark.*

No? Too bad. Perhaps they'll figure it out on their own. I want the world to know we own you. A chuckle followed the words. *I want the world—your empire—to be afraid.*

For a long moment, Sicarius stared down at the dagger. A couple of quick movements would cut out the stone.

It'll kill you if you try to remove it.

Sicarius didn't doubt it. But wouldn't death be nobler than this slavery?

You want to kill that one anyway, Kor Nas thought, the words coming quickly. With a tinge of... desperation? No doubt he didn't want to lose his "pet." *Worgavic. She ordered the torture of your woman. Kill the others, too, for they are all of the same ilk. They enjoyed hearing about your woman's torture.*

Sicarius recognized the arguing, the bargaining, for what it was, but he couldn't do anything about it. He found his mind made up for him. Yes, he'd kill these women and add to the heads in the sack below.

Before turning the knob, however, a new thought arose. He remembered the female shaman he'd seen running out of the *Behemoth,* the one who might have been responsible for Amaranthe's death. If the woman at her side had been Worgavic, that shaman could be in the meeting room with the others. She'd be more of a concern than guards. The Forge women weren't likely to be capable fighters, but that shaman would be a different matter, especially if she had time to marshal her power.

If there is a practitioner, I will handle her. Again, emotion accompanied Kor Nas's words, this time conveying a sense of satisfaction at the notion of pitting himself against another.

Your powers will be diminished when channeled through me, Sicarius responded.

I am still strong enough to deal with one of those barefoot, tattooed Kendorians. They are uneducated, and their Science is weak.

Sicarius thought to point out the foolhardiness of arrogance, but what did Kor Nas care? If he failed, Sicarius might die, but the practitioner would remain safe in his tent. He might suffer the discomfort of a mental backlash, but nothing more damaging.

An image flashed into his mind then, a memory. He was back on Darkcrest Isle with the vengeful spirit of Azon Amar in his head, the incredibly powerful Nurian warrior mage who had assassinated Emperor Morvaktu. Before dying to a platoon of Hollowcrest's soldiers, Azon Amar had cursed the island, leaving his spirit to haunt it and aid any Nurians who stepped foot upon it. Though he'd been familiar with the story and the curse, Sicarius had followed Amaranthe out to Darkcrest Isle for a mission, and the spirit had taken over his body, forcing him to chase her, to try and kill her. She'd escaped, swimming back to the mainland. Compelled by Azon Amar, he'd given chase, but as he'd swum away from the island, the fount of the dead practitioner's power, the grip on his mind had faded and he'd broken away.

He'd reached the mainland before Amaranthe, but he'd hidden while she finished her swim, crouching in the bushes and catching his breath, terrified at what he'd almost done, horrified at the memory of the tender flesh of her neck beneath his hands. In that moment, he'd been fighting the powerful spirit with every ounce of his mental strength, using every trick he'd learned from the Nurian wizard hunter who'd been one of his tutors, yet he would have failed if not for Amaranthe's cleverness. He'd taken a moment to recover his equilibrium—and brush moisture from his eyes—before walking out to the dock to rejoin her. Her wariness—no, her outright fear—as he approached had made him want to fall to his knees in abject apology. He'd hugged her. He should have done more, but it'd been all he could manage at the time. More might have... he might have lost his composure and cried in front of her. He'd been a fool to think that would have been some world-ending failure on his part. The failure had been in being arrogant enough to go out to that island and in falling prey to the wizard in the first place. And now, he was in the thrall of another one.

One who isn't dead, Kor Nas whispered in his mind. *Do not accuse* me *of arrogance, and do not doubt my power over others. Or over you.*

You're no Azon Amar, Sicarius thought back mulishly. That Nurian had been so powerful people around the world had heard of him.

Perhaps not, but think about how much trouble he gave you from beyond the grave, his powers a mere fraction of what they were when he lived. Do not believe you can defy me; you will only harm yourself if you try.

The opal at Sicarius's temple throbbed, its light radiating through the wool cap, creating a bizarre yellowish-green pattern on the closest wall. With no other choice, Sicarius pulled out a throwing knife as well as his dagger. The throwing knife would be for the shaman. If she was in the room, she had to go down first.

He listened again before barging in, placing people by the distance and direction of their voices.

When someone on the far side of the room was in the middle of talking, Sicarius chose his moment; other people's focus should be toward the person, away from the door.

Silent as always, he'd entered and launched three throwing knives before the first startled shriek filled the room or before anyone leapt from her chair. The tattooed shaman wasn't there. His first blade took a guard by a fireplace in the throat. The next two hammered into the chests of security men stationed by the main door. They hadn't been prepared, hadn't expected an attack in this relaxed parlor.

With his throwing knives spent, Sicarius lunged after the next target, a familiar dark-haired woman with spectacles. Worgavic. She was running for the hallway door, a shout on her lips. Sicarius leaped a table and dropped behind her before her hand reached the knob. He gripped her shoulder, yanking her back, and sliced his black dagger across her neck, severing her arteries with the very technology she'd thought she'd controlled.

In seconds, Sicarius finished the other four women in the

room. He acted quickly, in part to ensure their prolonged screams wouldn't bring additional security, and in part so Kor Nas wouldn't have time to demand more torture.

Directed by the opal, he knelt to collect Worgavic's head. He glanced around the room as he worked. No one remained alive. No one had tested his abilities. Odd that he should find himself missing Amaranthe's crazy plans, the challenge inherent in them. In her insistence that they leave people alive, or suborn them to her side, she'd often made things difficult for him. And for herself. Too difficult in the end.

Grimly, he finished cutting and went to the next head. Sicarius felt nothing for the dead. There was no one left among the living whom he cared about.

As he stood there, amidst the blood and bodies, a new image flashed into his mind. This time he was standing with Amaranthe on a road outside of Markworth at the southern end of Lake Seventy-Three. He was penning a letter, dredging up a remembered military encryption key from two decades earlier to encode it for its recipient. Former Fleet Admiral Sashka Federias Starcrest.

He's rumored to be in the city, came Kor Nas's words in his mind. *We don't know where yet, but we will soon. He can't be allowed to help our enemies.*

CHAPTER 6

S QUISHED. WAS THAT THE WORD MAHLIKI HAD USED? AN apt word. Amaranthe could breathe, though she would have preferred not to. Her new soldier buddies hadn't visited the public baths in a while, and at least one had consumed sardines and fermented cabbage for dinner. In addition, an elbow was lodged in her stomach while a sword hilt jabbed into her kidney. There was plenty of room in the navigation area up front, where Tikaya and Mahliki sat with Lonaeo looking on, but the soldiers had, by some unspoken rule, decided not to crowd the Starcrest family. Too bad Amaranthe didn't have Sicarius with her—his forbidding presence always commanded plenty of space. Neither she nor Basilard could see much past the towering men surrounding them. Perhaps it was for the best. Amaranthe would have been tempted to clean and organize if she'd had a better view of the papers, books, specimen jars, and tools littering the interior. She'd thought there was a rule about unattached items needing to be secured on ships, due to their tendency to fly about in rough waters, but the calm waters of the Goldar River must have convinced the two young scientists that they could bring out their projects. *All* of their projects.

"We're almost there," Mahliki said, glancing apologetically at the packed crowd behind her.

"No hurry," Maldynado responded. "It's cozy and warm down here, not to mention devoid of flying cubes that want to incinerate people."

Amaranthe might have chosen dealing with the cubes over breathing the miasma of body odors clogging the air, but she

hoped they'd be able to avoid both once they climbed out. They'd go straight to the ship, figure out what needed to be done to get rid of it, and finish up as quickly as possible.

"Did Lord Admiral Starcrest build this submarine?" one of the soldiers asked. He touched the hull a couple of inches above his head, stroking the sleek metal.

"Yes," Tikaya said. "This is the third one he crafted for the family, and he's designed and helped construct a number of larger ones for the marine studies departments at the Polytechnic. He's published his work, making it available to all, and we're starting to see derivative models in the seas, though only nations willing to embrace... non-standard energy sources have made progress."

"He's been publishing? For everyone?" The aggrieved soldier sounded more betrayed by this than the implication that the boats required magic to run. "I thought he was *dead*. We *all* did."

"Just in exile," Tikaya said. "My understanding is that your last emperor wanted your people to believe he was dead rather than that he'd chosen not to follow criminal orders that would, uhm..." She glanced at her audience of hulking soldiers and decided to finish with, "I'm sure he would have returned to his homeland if he'd been allowed, at least to visit."

"It's too bad he never had a chance to work for Sespian," Amaranthe said.

"The world knows little of the boy," Tikaya said. "Most of what we heard in Kyatt was that he—"

A soft thunk reverberated through the submarine. An algae-coated dock piling floated into view.

"We're here," Mahliki said.

Amaranthe remained silent, curious to hear what the world thought of Sespian, but Tikaya didn't finish her statement. She and her daughter flipped a few switches, examined gauges, and finally pushed a lever. The submarine rose a few feet, then clunked against the ice.

"This mode of transportation won't be available to us much

longer," Mahliki said. "Give me a moment... We'll have to... Oh, I'll just use the auger." She slid out of her seat and headed for a hatch behind the soldiers. "Pardon me."

Amaranthe was elbowed and jostled as the men made room for her to pass.

"Auger?" Maldynado asked. "I thought we'd get to blow our way through the ice with some special underwater cannon."

"Torpedo," Tikaya said.

"What?"

"Rias calls them torpedoes. They're launched from tubes with charges contained within the shell. He has some that detonate on timers."

"They could blow through the ice?" Maldynado asked.

"They could blow up the whole dock and any ships moored there." Tikaya pursed her lips with faint disapproval.

"And we're not going to use one?" Maldynado asked.

"You needn't sound so distressed," Amaranthe said. "It's not as if they were going to invite you to flip the switch that launches them."

Maldynado digested that for a moment. "Well, you never know."

A grinding sound came from above them. Mahliki had disappeared into a small cabin behind the hatch, some sort of research area, Amaranthe guessed from the cabinets, shelves, and tools she glimpsed.

"Do you need any help?" Lonaeo asked.

"No, I'm already through," Mahliki called back. "I'll crack it a bit and... try surfacing now."

Tikaya's hands darted across the controls, a confusing array of gauges, levers, switches, and... Amaranthe didn't have words for some of the doohickeys. The submarine rose again. Snaps and cracks erupted above, almost like overzealous logs throwing off sparks in a hearth. They broke through, the buoyancy of the craft discernible beneath their feet as it bobbed.

Lonaeo squeezed past Maldynado and Basilard and hopped up, catching a beam near the hatch above them. For someone of

Starcrest's height, or even Tikaya's, it would have been easy to do while standing, but he had to dangle from one arm while he spun the wheel.

"Care for some help?" Maldynado tapped a ceiling beam with a finger.

"Nah," Lonaeo said, "I'm used to scrambling up trees and under shrubs to collect insects. This isn't much different." When the lock released, he pushed the hatch open, still dangling from one arm as he did so. He was stronger than his scrawny form would have suggested. He caught the lip and pulled himself out. "Come on out, boys," he called down. "Don't forget your fur coats. I think the temperature dropped a couple hundred more degrees in the last fifteen minutes."

The soldiers snorted.

"Foreign weaklings," one muttered, though not loud enough for Tikaya or Mahliki to hear.

"What kind of career is collecting bugs?" Maldynado asked while the soldiers clambered out ahead of him. "That doesn't sound very useful."

Mahliki stepped out of the hatchway behind him, a hurt frown on her face.

Hoping to alleviate any abraded feelings, Amaranthe asked, "Should you be questioning other people's life choices, considering what you were doing for a career when we first met?"

"What's wrong with bringing delight and pleasure to the lives of lonely women?"

"You were wearing a loincloth," Amaranthe said.

"I fail to see your point."

"They have loincloths in Turgonia?" Mahliki asked, securing the uppermost buttons on her jacket. "For... summer use?"

"For *decorative* use," Amaranthe said firmly, "by dandies."

"Really, boss." Maldynado sniffed.

He might be offended for the next thirty seconds, but at least Mahliki's frown had turned into a slight smile.

"I'm sure entomology is fascinating," Amaranthe said, then realized she didn't have much of a notion of what an entomologist *did*, so she voiced the one thing she knew about insects. "I'm told bugs are a superior source of protein and that it's a shame they're largely lacking in the Turgonian diet."

"Fifty ranmyas says I know who told her that," Maldynado muttered to Basilard.

"You wouldn't say that if you'd spent two weeks in the South Fernsils living on palm weevil larvae," Tikaya said. She'd finished at the controls and now stood beneath the hatch. A soldier lowered a hand, offering to help her up.

"I don't think we have those here," Amaranthe said. "But if you spend any time in the woods with Sicarius, he'll attempt to feed you cicadas, grasshoppers, and giant black ant eggs."

"I knew there was a reason I didn't care for that boy," Tikaya said, though she smiled while she spoke. She accepted the proffered hand and disappeared through the hatchway.

Her daughter followed without further comments on entomology or loincloths.

"Did she call Sicarius a *boy*?" Maldynado choked.

"He was when they met." Nobody lowered a hand to assist her, but Amaranthe managed the hatch without trouble.

"Yes," Maldynado said in response to some comment from Basilard, "it sounds like he was as charming as a youth as he is today."

The rest of the party was waiting on a wide dock buried beneath eight inches of snow. Full darkness had fallen, but it did nothing to cloak the fact that a giant dome-shaped craft had smashed Fort Urgot into oblivion. Most of the trees around the lake and the parade fields had been mowed down or hurled down by the force of the landing. Even the water tower, which hadn't been crushed, leaned to one side, the tank tilted precariously over the slope of the hill beneath it. Fresh snow had fallen since the... incident—no, carnage, Amaranthe told herself, utter devastation and carnage—but body-sized lumps remained on the field. Someone should burn funeral pyres for the dead, but that ominous black presence must have convinced the military to flee.

"What's the plan, boss?" Maldynado asked.

"We'll scout the area to determine if it's safe to approach," a sergeant, the highest-ranking soldier in the group, said after leveling a cool look at Maldynado. Amaranthe guessed that meant they weren't going to line up to take orders from her. "Lady Starcrest," the sergeant finished, "please wait here until we return."

With a couple of quick hand signs, he divided his team in half, and two soldiers jogged in each direction, their rifles at the ready.

"Return to me if you see any of the *kelbhet*," Tikaya called, then added, "cubes," for clarification. "I have a way to deal with them." She dropped her voice to say, "Lady Starcrest, how odd."

"Not the name you usually go by?" Amaranthe asked.

"No, and my understanding was that due to his exile status, Rias has no right to claim that name any more either."

"Who's left alive that knew he was exiled?" Amaranthe asked.

"I... don't know," Tikaya said. "Do you think it'd be terribly unwise to ignore their admonishment to stay here and get right to work?"

"Uh." Amaranthe had no problem going off on her own, but she hadn't guessed a fifty-year-old linguistics professor would be quite so bold.

"They didn't tell *us* to stay here," Mahliki said. "Just you, Mother."

"Oh, but staying here is nice," Lonaeo said. "You have a good view of anything inimical that might be approaching, and you can hop into the submarine and escape beneath the surface."

"You can stay if you wish, Lonaeo," Tikaya said. "Your mother won't be pleased with me if I get you killed. As I recall, she objected to you coming along in the first place, deciding for whatever reason that Turgonia was more dangerous than some of the islands full of spear-flinging, brain-eating cannibals we've visited."

Lonaeo tugged at his scruffy beard. "Was she wrong?"

"That… remains to be seen."

While waiting for them to decide who was staying and who was going, Amaranthe signed, *Do you two have any idea which direction Sicarius went when he left the fort?*

Basilard pointed to the western side of the lake.

Watch for signs of him or the soul construct while we're out here, please.

Understood.

"I haven't heard any yowls the last couple of nights," Maldynado said quietly. "That's promising, don't you think? Maybe he killed it somehow."

"Or led it out of the area." Amaranthe had a vision of Sicarius standing on the rear of a train, the giant fanged hound chasing after him.

"We're ready when you are." Tikaya had put on gloves and a fur cap in addition to her bow, quiver, and rucksack, and she'd lit a lantern. Her daughter stood at her side, similarly clothed for the cold weather, though she stomped her feet and had pulled her scarf up to her eyes. This weather must be quite shocking after the tropics. Lonaeo had disappeared back into the submarine, pulling the hatch down behind him. "Lonaeo will keep the *Explorer* ready in case we need to leave swiftly."

"What about the soldiers?" Amaranthe asked.

"If they can't find us, they aren't the scouts they think they are." Tikaya tilted her chin toward the *Behemoth*. "You've been in there twice, you said? Can you find one of the entrances?" She was bouncing in her boots, too, though Amaranthe wasn't certain if it had anything to do with the cold. There was an eager gleam of anticipation in her eyes. Dear ancestors, was she looking *forward* to climbing into that monstrosity? After all the death it had delivered?

And who are you to judge her, her mind asked. Especially now…

"I'll try." Amaranthe checked her weapons and readjusted her own pack, then led the way up the road she knew to be buried beneath the snow. It would take them past the jogging path and to what *had* been the front gates of the fort. "The hull is smooth, and I don't remember any markings. I wasn't given a lot of time to explore on my previous visits." Though she had a distinct memory of a close-up chance to study an interior wall, thanks to Pike smashing her face against it.

Amaranthe kept her eyes on the towering black hull as they approached, pointedly not looking too closely at the body-sized bumps beneath the snow. Tikaya reached the side of the ship first, took off a mitten, and rested a hand against the hull.

"I wouldn't recommend doing that with your tongue," Maldynado said.

Tikaya cocked her head curiously at him.

"Never mind. It's not that cold yet anyway."

"Why don't you and Basilard stand watch?" Amaranthe suggested.

Basilard had his neck craned back, staring up at the black dome towering over them. He stepped closer to a lantern to sign, *It must be a hundred stories tall. It's... unfathomable.*

Amaranthe didn't know if it was quite that high, but it might very well be. It certainly dwarfed the few trees left standing. If she remembered her city trivia, the tallest building in Stumps was sixteen stories high.

A firearm boomed somewhere to their left. The *Behemoth* blocked the area from view, but Amaranthe's hand dropped to her pistol.

"Our soldier friends?" Mahliki slid her own hand into her jacket, toward something at waist level—hopefully something more fearsome than a collection vial.

That was a pistol, Basilard signed. *The soldiers are carrying rifles.*

"We have company out here then," Amaranthe said. "Not surprising."

"The door?" Tikaya asked.

Amaranthe stared bleakly at the unmarked hull. "The wall grew translucent, and I walked through it, but it wasn't at ground level." She waved to a spot above their heads. "I slid down the curve ten or fifteen feet. That was when I escaped. When I entered, we went up a ramp that came out of nowhere, but the door—more of a big bay opening—was higher. When we escaped in the lifeboat... I have no idea where that came out of, but some sort of tube. We shot out and..." She shrugged. "It was before the crash."

"I understand," Tikaya said. "Let's walk around and see if we spot any clues. I don't see any writing or anything useful yet."

"I vote that we walk in the opposite direction from the shooting," Maldynado said. "Just in case they're shooting at some of those cubes."

"But it'd be acceptable if they were shooting at our soldier allies?" Amaranthe had been thinking they should check in that direction.

"Er."

"We don't have many soldiers on our side. We should try to keep the ones we do have alive." Pistol in hand, Amaranthe led off, following the base of the ship.

Tikaya strode behind her, though her focus was toward the *Behemoth*. Her daughter walked at her side, more like Amaranthe, watching the dark snowy fields. Amaranthe wondered if that signified less of a passion for the ancient technology or a more practical soul.

More shots fired, farther away this time. Maybe the soldiers were leading them—whoever them was—away from the ship. There weren't any other lights out on the field, and Amaranthe was conscious of their two lanterns, like beacons against the black hull.

Three more body-sized lumps in the snow waited ahead of them, and her stomach squirmed. They'd have to walk around them. She wasn't going to risk stepping on somebody, dead or not. Nor did she want a good look at them—they might have been cut in half by the edge of the *Behemoth*.

Except it didn't look like that, she admitted as they drew closer. The three bodies were crumpled, one half leaning against the hull. It was as if they'd died *after* the ship landed.

Tikaya and Mahliki veered to the side to walk around the spot—Amaranthe wondered if it occurred to them what those snow-blanketed bumps were. She started to step to the side, too, but halted.

"Wait," she blurted.

If these people had died *after* the ship landed, what had killed them? Injuries acquired jumping out of a door? Or maybe they'd been injured during the crash and had fled, but their wounds had been too bad to make it farther than the exit. Enh, that might make sense for one, but for all three?

"What is it?" The way Tikaya eyed the lumps suggested she'd twigged to what they were.

"People trying to escape, I think," Amaranthe said, "implying a door up there perhaps."

"Ah?" Tikaya lifted her lantern as high as she could to study the hull.

"Must be way up there," Maldynado said, "if they broke their necks falling out."

Broken necks? Would that explain it? Maybe they'd been running from some of those cubes—at the thought, Amaranthe gave their surroundings another quick check—and hadn't realized the door would be so high above ground level.

"No, I think I see the bottom edge there," Tikaya said, "about ten feet up. Can someone give me a boost? Maybe there are runes etched in the hull, something that would allow entry from outside."

"Allow me to offer my shoulders, my lady." Maldynado dipped to one knee and laced his fingers together, offering her a leg up.

As Tikaya removed some of her gear and prepared to scale Mount Maldynado, Basilard knelt next to the bodies and brushed away snow. Amaranthe had thought of doing the same thing, to figure out why these people had succumbed to the afterlife in that particular spot, but she hadn't wanted to stare into the accusing eyes of the dead.

Stop it, she told herself. She had to accept the blame for now and deal with the guilt later.

Basilard knelt back, his pale blue eyes finding hers, a message in them.

"What is it?" Amaranthe leaned closer.

A lot of snow still coated the bodies, but the yawning red canyon slashed into the neck of the frozen woman on top of the pile was hard to miss. Arteries severed. A quick death. One that hadn't been caused by the crash, and not one the cubes had inflicted either.

One of Basilard's gloved fingers made his throat-cutting sign, the one he used for Sicarius's name.

"I... don't know," Amaranthe said. "He's not the only one in the world who cuts throats."

"Just one of the best," Maldynado muttered then grunted as he hoisted the professor into the air.

Not the natural athlete her daughter promised to be, Tikaya struggled, slipping and thumping a knee into Maldynado's ear, but she did finally attain her perch atop his shoulders. "Light, please."

Mahliki handed the lantern up to her mother.

Basilard uncovered the other two bodies, pointing out that they—a man and a second woman—had also been killed by a knife and that none of the three had been appropriately dressed for the sub-freezing temperatures outside.

"If it *was* him," Amaranthe whispered, "what'd he do? Kill these people as they were coming out? Assume they were part of Forge and therefore enemies?"

Maybe he was looking for you, Basilard signed.

That was possible. If he'd seen the crash, he would have guessed that she'd be in the *Behemoth*. "So he killed these three and then ran inside, checking to see if Books, Akstyr, and I were still in there?"

Mostly you, I'd guess.

Amaranthe twitched her fingers, to wave that away. She reminded herself that they had no way to *know* Sicarius had killed these people. It could have been some private with a knife, determined to defend the capital from the invaders who had destroyed Fort Urgot.

"If he did go in there, looking for us, where is he now? It's been a couple of days, long enough to search even that massive craft." Assuming he hadn't gotten lost—somehow she doubted it. She'd never seen him lose his way in woods, tunnels, or anywhere else. "Why didn't he come back to the factory to see if we were there?"

Basilard hesitated, then shrugged.

Because he was injured or killed was probably what he thought, but wouldn't say. Not to Amaranthe. As if she didn't know how deadly some of the things inside the *Behemoth* were.

Her eyes widened as she spotted movement out on the field, or rather, floating *above* the field. There were, she reminded herself, deadly things out here too.

"Any luck with that door?" she asked, "because we may have a visitor coming."

Mahliki groaned. "Not again."

"I haven't found any writing up here," Tikaya said. "It's possible though... hm."

The black cube, blending with the dark night, wouldn't have been visible if not for the snow, but everyone spotted it easily against all that white. It hadn't turned toward them yet—it was drifting along, parallel to the hull of the *Behemoth*. It stopped here and there to shoot a crimson beam out, incinerating some stick or branch. It paused at one point and melted a hump of snow. At first, Amaranthe thought a body lay underneath it, but the cube simply seemed to be burning snow into water. Because it saw the white stuff as debris to be removed? Or because it was broken? Whatever Retta's assistant had done to change the cubes hadn't been that well thought out. Understandable, given the rush she'd been in....

"It's open. We can go in by thrusting ourselves through the membrane here." Tikaya pushed her hand through a section of the hull to demonstrate. "We just have to climb up."

Oh, right, Amaranthe should have mentioned that. She'd walked out a door like that during her escape.

"Let's get to climbing then," Maldynado said. "That black butt sniffer is getting closer."

Butt sniffer? Basilard signed.

"That's not *quite* how the original word translates." Tikaya's fingers disappeared into the hull as she gripped something behind the barrier—membrane, that's what she'd called it. "Give me a boost, please, Mister Maldynado."

"Yes, my lady." Maldynado grabbed the bottoms of her feet and hoisted her up, perhaps with more vigor than expected, for a startled squawk floated down.

Tikaya made it inside though, her body disappearing in segments as she squirmed over the ledge.

"That looks so odd," Maldynado said.

"Hoist her daughter up next," Amaranthe said. "We should—"

"My bow!" came Tikaya's voice from above. "Throw up my bow and my rucksack."

Mahliki hissed. Maldynado snatched the longbow from where it leaned against the hull, threw it at the membrane, then reached for the pack. But Mahliki had it between her knees as she pawed through the contents.

"Here, we'll throw the whole thing up." Maldynado reached for it.

"No." Mahliki pulled it back. "I know what she needs." She yanked out a ceramic jar. "Mother, I have it. Can you catch it?"

A beam of red streaked out of the hull, out of the door-membrane.

Mahliki spat a Kyattese curse.

Basilard grabbed the jar in one arm and scrambled up a surprised Maldynado, launching himself from the bigger man's shoulders. The force sent Maldynado tumbling backward into the snow, but Basilard reached the door and hauled himself inside.

"Me next," Amaranthe barked, waving for Maldynado to hurry up and stand so he could give her a boost. Though curved, the *Behemoth's* hull was too sheer for her to climb.

"Look out!" a man cried from the edge of the field. A rifle cracked.

Amaranthe crouched, her back to the *Behemoth*. She spotted two soldiers—two of the men who'd accompanied her team over here—one with a lantern, one holding a smoking rifle.

She assumed he was firing at the cube, but, no, it had drifted off to her left, toward the lake. There were more men in the shadows at the edge of the field, and something bulky with a—

"Down," Maldynado barked, grabbing her leg.

In the same second that he yanked her from her feet, a thunderous boom sounded. Something head-sized hammered into the hull a few feet above them. Not head-sized, Amaranthe realized, *cannonball*-sized. Some idiots were trying to blow their way into the *Behemoth*.

The cannonball clanged off with as much force as it'd struck, taking off at an angle and sailing toward the lake, landing with a distant crack-splash. Amaranthe rolled from her back to her belly, pulling out her pistol again.

Excited chatter came from the direction of what she now recognized as a mobile field cannon.

"...why'd you shoot, dolt... they found a way in."

"Can't let others get in first... treasure..."

"Watch out for the..."

The pair of soldiers were charging toward the people manning the cannon. The snow slowed them down, and they didn't cross the distance as quickly as they would have liked. A couple of the dark figures turned toward them. Nobody over there was holding a lamp, though someone held a burning brand, ready to load and light the cannon again. Amaranthe cut out their own remaining lantern and aimed her pistol at the brand. She didn't want to hit anyone, but she *did* want to keep them from shooting at her allies.

"Owph," Maldynado grunted, enduring a slap from Mahliki.

"Get up, and throw me up there. Mother's in trouble, and your friend too."

"Do it," Amaranthe said, though she didn't take her eye from her target. She fired.

The short-barreled pistol lacked the accuracy of the rifles, and there must have been fifty, sixty meters between them and the cannon, but the brand flew to the snow behind the shadowy figures. She'd either struck true or surprised the man enough for him to drop it.

Someone over there fired anyway, not at her, but at the approaching soldiers.

The two men dropped to their bellies in the snow. They were *controlled* drops, Amaranthe thought, not like one might see if a man received a rifle ball to the chest.

"Get rid of your lantern," she called to the soldiers. The light made them easy to target.

The soldiers must have been thinking the same thing, for the lantern was extinguished immediately.

Another shot fired from the group by the cannon—they'd crouched down and were now using the big artillery piece for cover. The bullet clanged off the hull high overhead. Maldynado swore. It must have come close to hitting him. He was standing, having lifted Mahliki into the ship.

Amaranthe pulled ammo and powder out of her belt pouches, wondering how she hadn't managed to retain any of Forge's repeating firearms for herself.

A shot boomed not far from her ear, Maldynado unleashing a round at the relic raiders or whatever they were. For all she knew, they were some of Ravido's soldiers, trying to recover tools or devices from within the *Behemoth* for his allies. No, the Forge people would have known enough to instruct those men on the proper way to enter the ship. A cannon. What idiots.

They continued to exchange fire with the pair of soldiers, who continued to shoot from their bellies. One of the men by the cannon cried out and flopped to his back. His fall didn't stop his comrades from shooting.

"We might want to find better cover, boss," Maldynado said, "if we're staying out here."

Amaranthe didn't *want* to stay out there. She wanted to fling herself into the *Behemoth* and help the others with what had to be more of those cubes, cubes that might not be as defective as the one roaming about out here. A cannon could kill her just as dead as a beam of energy though.

As if to remind her of the fact, someone fired in their direction. She ducked her head. The rifle ball skimmed across

the snow six inches to her right and ricocheted off the hull. She didn't know where it went, but heard it whistle by her ear. Far too close for her tastes.

"Cover, where?" Amaranthe tried to wriggle deeper into the snow. "There aren't any trees left around—there isn't any anything left around."

"Uhm—oh, those'll be frozen solid."

Without rising from his stomach, Maldynado grabbed one of the corpses and dragged it toward them. Amaranthe couldn't squelch her grimace—or her squeamish repulsion at the idea of using dead human beings for cover.

Less squeamish, Maldynado did the work, piling the three corpses up in front of them. Before he'd finished, a rifle ball slammed into one, proving his words true. Frozen solid, indeed.

"Gruesome, but effective," Maldynado said.

"I'll say. All we've bought ourselves is a stand-off though. Those people probably brought tons of ammo to lay siege to the ship."

"I could thump them all into the nearest snow drift if I could make it over there without being shot." Maldynado pounded a fist into his gloved hand for emphasis.

He probably *could* if given the opportunity to hurl himself into the middle of the pack.

"So you need a distraction," Amaranthe mused. "Where'd that cube go?"

Maldynado pointed far to their left, toward a couple of trees by the lake with the tops shorn off. "It's been incinerating the fallen needles, one at a time, around the base of that pine."

"Its job *is* to clean things, I understand."

"If we could arrange to lob a few tons of pine needles over to land on top of that cannon, it might drift over and pay those blokes a visit."

"Unfortunately, I forgot to pack my pine-needle-launcher," Amaranthe said.

"Mercenary leaders are supposed to be prepared for anything, you know."

"I'm failing on all sorts of levels lately." Amaranthe flicked a finger toward the cube. "I wonder if it'd get annoyed and come visit if you shot it."

"I'd think that would be a given, but why would you *want* it to visit?"

"I wouldn't, but maybe we could convince our enemies to shoot it."

"Uh, yes, and how do you plan to do that?"

"I noticed that the curving hull of the *Behemoth* causes projectiles to ricochet off at an angle," Amaranthe said. "In fact, that first cannonball landed not far from where the cube is now."

Maldynado stared at her. "You're not thinking…"

"It couldn't hurt to try. If one of their bullets comes anywhere close, and the cube notices, maybe it'll drift over there and say hello to them."

A long moment passed with Maldynado staring at her before he said, "There are times like this when I wish I'd gone to the military academy and joined the army."

"Why?"

"Because there's a soldier axiom about not sharing a foxhole with anyone crazier than yourself. If I'd actually joined, I'd be able to quote it precisely. That would be apt right now."

"Ha ha." Amaranthe considered the curving hull again, then pushed up to her hands and knees. "Don't worry. I think we need the bullet to strike a few meters in that direction if there's hope for it to land anywhere close to the cube. I won't draw fire to our foxhole, such as it is."

"I don't want you to draw fire at all." Maldynado reached for her.

Amaranthe sprang away from him—she didn't want his protectiveness to convince him to volunteer for the drawing-fire assignment. Utter foolery shouldn't be delegated; one should take the risk and accept the consequences oneself.

"Wait," Maldynado blurted as she ran from cover. "They've got the brand. They're going to light the—"

A cacophonous boom tore across the field, and Amaranthe flung herself into the snow. The cannonball didn't come anywhere close to hitting her—it wasn't a weapon meant to fire at a moving target—but it startled all the needles off her branches. Instead of landing in a controlled roll, she face-planted in the snow as the cannonball clanged off the hull. The reverberations thundering against her eardrums made her feel like the clapper in a clock tower bell.

Ignoring her pulsing eardrums, she jerked her head up, trying to see where the ball landed. It'd already struck its target. The tree next to the one the cube had been working around wobbled, then fell to the snow.

The cube, lacking any animal instincts, didn't draw back with a start, but its beam did wink out, and it paused, hovering in place.

A hand clamped around Amaranthe's ankle. "Get back here, you fool woman," Maldynado growled, hauling her back to the barrier of bodies.

The action sent a barrage of snow down her trousers and she would have cursed his ancestors if she could manage anything so coherent. As soon as he let her go, she scraped handfuls of the cold stuff out of her undergarments. "Not calling me 'boss,' anymore?"

"Not when you—emperor's teeth, Amaranthe, it's just as likely to think the attack came from here."

She'd thought of that and pointed toward the hull overhead. "We can flee inside if it heads this direction."

She lifted her head to see if it was going to head anywhere at all. It'd left its position by the pine tree, and it took her a moment to find it. The dark form was floating across the snow, not toward them but toward the cannon and clump of men around it.

Amaranthe refrained from a triumphant fist pump and a chortle, instead extending her arm, palm up toward the cube, as if showing off a particularly fine dish she'd delivered to the table.

"I see it," Maldynado grumbled. "That doesn't make you any less crazy."

No, probably not, Amaranthe thought, wondering if she'd take such risks if she weren't feeling like she herself deserved to die after all the carnage she'd wrought. Nonetheless, she took satisfaction in the startled cries and curses from the cannon men. The two soldiers took advantage of their distraction, firing fresh rounds into their midst. Maldynado had reloaded, and he fired again as well. A yelp of pain announced someone's shot finding flesh.

Then the cube had closed sufficiently, and its red beam lanced out. It struck the iron barrel of the cannon. Amaranthe expected shards to blow off, but the intense heat melted the metal on the spot.

The men stumbled backward, their clothing and features illuminated by the beam. Not soldiers, Amaranthe verified from their unshaven faces and longish hair, though she'd already guessed as much.

Torn between fleeing and needing to avoid being shot, the men tried to crawl away on their stomachs. She hadn't thought anyone over there had had time to reload the cannon, but the cube's beam found black powder somewhere. An explosion rang across the field, hurling smoke and shrapnel into the air.

Amaranthe and Maldynado ducked low behind their barrier, but not before she glimpsed the men abandoning their crawl. They leaped to their feet and sprinted across the field, impressively fast given their lack of snowshoes.

When the rain of shrapnel abated, Maldynado rose to his feet. "Huh."

"Don't overwhelm me with your enthusiastic approval." Amaranthe stood as well, still trying to scoop and shake snow from her trousers.

"No, I don't think I will." Maldynado bent a knee toward her and laced his fingers again. "Come on, let's jump in there before that cube grows bored with disintegrating the cannon and comes to visit us."

Though she, too, wanted to catch up with the others—she hadn't heard a peep from inside and had no idea what was going on—Amaranthe lifted a finger. "Wait, we need to check on the soldiers we stayed behind to help. After all, they helped *us* with that initial warning."

One of those soldiers was already running in her direction.

"The professor," he blurted, glancing around. "Where'd she go? Is she all right? And her daughter?"

"Inside." Amaranthe pointed up. She couldn't answer the second and third question yet. She decided not to feel disgruntled that these men were far more concerned about Starcrest's family than her and Maldynado. The soldiers had traveled across the continent to help Starcrest, after all.

"That thing is..." The man stared up at the hull, doubtlessly having a hard time imagining a door up there, but he had to have seen at least part of their group scramble through it. "Unbelievable."

"Among other things, yes," Amaranthe said. "Where's your comrade?"

Not dead, she hoped. Not another one....

The soldier's chin jerked down. "Shot. In the leg. I need to take him to..." He looked bleakly at where Fort Urgot *should* have been. "Back to the city. To a doctor. He's bleeding a *lot*."

"Take him to the submarine. It's not nearly as far to drag him, and I bet Tikaya's nephew has some first aid gear in there." Amaranthe had bandages in her own pack, but she didn't want to delay—she wanted to find out what was going on inside. For all she knew, Basilard needed first aid right that second. Besides, the soldiers ought to have the same gear as she had.

"Yes, right," the man said, "but what about..." He waved toward the hidden entrance.

"We'll take care of them."

The soldier hesitated, glancing back and forth from his fallen comrade to the ship.

"Krater?" his comrade called. "Hurry up, I'm bleeding all over the slagging field."

That made up his mind. He nodded once. "Understood. I'll tell the others. Good luck, ma'am."

Ma'am? She'd apparently been promoted to an actual person, thanks to their shared battle.

"Here." Maldynado, back on one knee again, shook his hands. Yes, he was as worried about Basilard and the others as she.

Amaranthe stepped into his hands, and he boosted her up. She scrambled through the membrane and found herself in a dark tunnel. Dark? Odd, the ship had always been illuminated when she'd been inside, every tunnel, ramp, and chamber brightened to daylight intensity.

A scrape and grunt sounded behind her. Amaranthe turned to see if Maldynado needed help, but he'd jumped high enough to catch the ledge on his own. The snowy field lay visible behind him, as if this were a window instead of some hidden door.

"Do you have the lantern?" Amaranthe asked. The others weren't visible anywhere. She thought about calling out, but decided to wait. Just because those would-be relic raiders with the cannon hadn't found a way in didn't mean other enemies weren't about in the tunnels.

"Yes, one moment."

After a few clanks and thumps, a match flared to light, illuminating Maldynado's face. The grim expression didn't match the foppish nest-of-snakes hat he'd managed to keep on his head through everything.

He lit a lantern and held it aloft.

A long black tunnel stretched out ahead of them, an intersection visible at the edge of the light. There wasn't a sign of anyone else.

CHAPTER 7

TWO HOURS BEFORE DAWN, SICARIUS GLIDED THROUGH
Flintcrest's new camp, following paths freshly
tramped into the snow, his feet soundless on the
hard crust. None of the perimeter guards spotted him, none
of the sleeping soldiers heard him, and nobody saw the heavy
bloodstained bag hanging from his shoulder. He wound through
the trees and tents, searching for the Nurian area. Flintcrest had
moved his men in the night, marching south, choosing a wide
route around the lake, up the eastern side of Stumps, and into the
Emperor's Preserve. Though the wilds were dense, they didn't
span that many acres, and the army wouldn't remain hidden for
long. Flintcrest must intend to strike soon. What target? The
Imperial Barracks?

Sicarius found the Nurian tent, not by the lack of activity
around it this time, but by voices coming from within. Elsewhere,
only snores emanated from the tents, the soldiers sleeping hard
after their night's work. From dozens of meters away, he heard
the Nurians, speaking in their own tongue, their voices raised
in argument.

Though he suspected Kor Nas would know his precise
location, Sicarius slowed his approach to listen.

"The assassin is acceptable," a young man said. "Nobody
back home objects to that method of dealing with enemies, and
using one of their own people to deliver the killing blows, it's
a better choice than the soul construct, but I don't want you to
send him after Enemy Chief Fox."

Who? Sicarius stopped outside the tent flap. He knew the

Nurians gave animal nicknames to their honored chiefs and some of their enemies as well, but he had only worked in Nuria once and wasn't familiar with many of them.

"Your attitude... puzzles me, *He shu*," Kor Nas said. Ah, he was speaking to the diplomat. "To lay his head at your father's feet, would that not be a great prize? Resulting in great honor and prestige for your family? For twenty years, he made the Turgonians untouchable at sea, and he destroyed more of our ships—our crews—than one can count."

An uncharacteristic bout of anxiety wormed into Sicarius's belly. Starcrest.

"If he dies in the fighting here, so be it," the diplomat said, "but I do not wish to be the cause."

Kor Nas did not speak for a long moment, and Sicarius expected to be called inside, anticipating that the practitioner had paused because his senses had alerted him to Sicarius's presence. But when Kor Nas spoke again, it was to continue the conversation.

"I do not understand why you feel that way, *He shu*, but if you do not wish to lay Enemy Chief Fox's head at the Great Chief's feet, allow *me* the honor. As soon as his hiding place is discovered, I will send the assassin, and—"

"No."

Another long pause. "Your stubbornness in this matter mystifies me. He *is* an enemy of Nuria. To have a chance at him and not take it is tantamount to treason." Kor Nas lowered his voice to a harsh whisper. "Your father would not be pleased if he learned that you could have arranged his death and turned your back on the opportunity."

"I do not appreciate the implication that you would go to my father and speak ill of me, Kor Nas." The young man managed an impressive amount of cold menace in his voice. Was he a practitioner as well? One capable of standing toe-to-toe with Kor Nas? It seemed unlikely in one half of Kor Nas's age. If he was one of the Great Chief's sons, perhaps he believed himself untouchable because of his father's influence. An unwise

assumption, perhaps, if he chose to let Starcrest live. Indeed, the Nurians *would* likely see that as treason, even if twenty years had passed since the war. Sicarius understood Kor Nas's logic, but he found himself hoping the younger man had a way to stand up to him effectively.

"Do not force me to do so then, *He shu*."

"Do you think my father will care? We're not here to settle old grudges. We're here because our people are hungry, and our resources are limited. Our soil is depleted after thousands of years of farming, there's scarcely any coal or ore left in the mountains, and few of the great forests remain standing. My father wants a deal with the Turgonians, some of the resources they have so many of, and that is *all* that he cares about."

"He'll be more likely to get that deal if all of Flintcrest's enemies are thwarted. Starcrest can only be here to cause trouble."

"We don't know why he's here. Maybe he heard about the nascent fighting and came to collect whatever family he has left in the area."

"Don't be naive. *Let* me send the assassin."

"What honor is there in killing a gray-haired old man, Kor Nas? It's been over twenty years since he bothered us. He probably walks with a cane, has three teeth left in his mouth, and can't remember half of the crimes he committed against our people."

"He is *my* age, *He shu*." Sicarius had never heard the practitioner so dry. "I know at thirty it seems that anyone over sixty must be doddering and infirm, but I assure you this isn't so."

The diplomat had the grace to clear his throat, but he didn't give up his argument. "Yes, but you're a practitioner, not a warrior. You will retain your power as long as your mind remains sharp. Enemy Chief Fox was a marine."

Kor Nas grunted. "He did not receive that moniker because of his sword arm, boy. I *know* you know that. He will be dangerous as long as *his* mind remains sharp. Are you not worried about *why* he is here? It may be true that your father didn't care about

him so long as he was on that island, but now that he is back in the empire... I'm warning you, to leave him alive be would be treason."

"If his mind *is* still sharp, maybe he'll have no trouble defeating your assassin, leaving you out here without a pet to watch your back while you work your craft."

"Oh, I'm confident in the abilities of my assassin." Kor Nas raised his voice—he needn't have bothered. "Enter, my pet."

Had Sicarius been capable of ignoring the derogatory summons, he would have. Even as his feet led him through the flap and into the tent, he longed to sling the heavy bag at the practitioner's head, yank out his dagger, and drive the blade into his heart. All his arms would do, however, was lower his burden. He untied the cord binding the stained canvas shut and dumped the contents.

Seven heads rolled onto the carpet between the two Nurians.

The diplomat, fully clothed, shaved, and dressed with his flute and pipe ornamentation despite the early hour, didn't stumble backward or flinch at the grisly trophies, but he did stare down at them for a long moment, his mouth set in a hard line. When his gaze lifted to Sicarius's face for a wary few seconds, Sicarius read the fear in his eyes, though he tried to mask his features.

You don't have to fear me, Sicarius wanted to say, for I'll not raise a hand against an ally, acknowledged or not, of Admiral Starcrest's. But he couldn't.

"As you can see, Prince Zirabo," Kor Nas said, "he is effective."

The name, used for the first time, didn't surprise Sicarius. He'd guessed from the conversation that this was one of the Great Chief's sons, the youngest if he recalled correctly. With several older brothers, Zirabo wouldn't likely be put in a position to rule Nuria, but he should have some sway. Not enough to daunt Kor Nas, it seemed. Kor Nas must be high up in the power structure over there as well. The Nurians had sent their best to ensure they received the concessions they wanted.

"Enemy Chief Fox won't have a chance to apply his clever mind," Kor Nas continued, "because he won't see my pet coming until the dagger is plunging into his heart."

"Then you'll forgive me," Prince Zirabo said, striding toward the tent flap, "if I hope the seer doesn't find him."

Kor Nas's smile gave Sicarius little reason to share that hope, not when the man had already located so many of the Forge leaders that had eluded Amaranthe, Books, and Sicarius himself over the last six months. He stared down at the sightless eyes of Worgavic and couldn't help but imagine Starcrest's head in an identical position.

* * *

"Where'd everybody go?" Maldynado whispered.

"I don't know." Amaranthe headed for the dark intersection, holding a lantern aloft. "But if this place was eerie when it was lit, it's even more disturbing now." Her meager flame wasn't much of a beacon against the black, windowless tunnels. It felt as if the oppressive darkness could reach out and snuff the single flame.

"Maybe we should wait here." Maldynado pointed to the translucent membrane, the snowy field and nighttime sky visible beyond it. "We don't have any longbows and whatever it was the professor thought could be used against the cubes."

"Agreed, they might never find us if we wander off, but I want to see if we can see any sign of them from the corner."

Amaranthe stopped at the seven-way intersection. Those ancient people hadn't cared much for standard geometric shapes. Too basic for their tastes? She peered down each passageway until she spotted something on the floor. She almost leaped back. It was one of the cubes. But it wasn't floating. It was...

She dared to shuffle closer for a better look.

Two of the sides had been melted away, the exterior crumpling in on itself, revealing a mess of innards made from the same black as the shell, but with thin boards and fine cables snaking about. An arrow shaft stuck out of the mess, the fletching still attached, though the head had either broken off or perhaps melted as well. A tendril of smoke wafted from the innards.

"That's heartening," Maldynado said.

"It'd be more heartening if our comrades were standing here over the broken husk, beaming with pride as they showed off their victory."

"I don't think Bas knows how to beam. His face is stuck in that saturnine expression of his."

Amaranthe would be saturnine, too, if they couldn't find the others. The tunnel stretched away beyond the cube, and if anything else waited down it, she couldn't tell. She wondered if there was any way to return power to the lights. In crashing the ship, had she broken the entire thing? Given what she'd seen of the technology, it seemed incomprehensible. But, then, it *was* fifty thousand years old. Maybe the furnace had run out of coal.

"There must have been more than one cube," she said. "They'll probably take care of it and circle back."

"I hope there wasn't a *lot* more than one cube," Maldynado said. "The professor didn't have *that* many arrows."

Her quiver had been stuffed, but that didn't mean much. Twenty arrows perhaps. And how many cleaning cubes existed in the vastness of the *Behemoth*? "I wonder why she didn't ask us all to bring some."

"Maybe they were only able to make so much of... whatever was in that jar."

"Something applied to the arrowhead," Amaranthe guessed. "That must be it, or maybe she expected me to be able to guide her right to the control room before we had to face many problems."

"Can you? From here?"

"I might have been able to if we'd gone in a door I'd been through before, but this is a new one."

Amaranthe was contemplating sticking her tongue out at the confusing seven-way intersection when she noticed a scratch on one of the walls. More than a scratch—something had gouged a centimeter-deep hole in the impervious metal. No arrow could have done that. She probed the dent with a finger and found it slightly warm.

"Oh, right," she murmured, remembering the damage in the control rooms.

"Hm?" Maldynado prompted.

"Whatever Retta's assistant did to change the cubes caused them to do more than incinerate people. Their beams started damaging the walls, punching *through* the walls to whatever equipment lay behind them. That's why we crashed."

"That wasn't your fault then," Maldynado said. "I can tell you're blaming yourself for all of this. You shouldn't be."

"Enh." Amaranthe didn't feel like explaining the chain of events that had led to Retta's assistant *making* those changes, a chain she had started as surely as she was breathing now. Instead, she wandered about the intersection, searching for more signs of damage. The number of shots marring the walls confirmed her suspicion that there'd been more than one cube attacking the team. At least two, but maybe more. Tikaya had used her bow to destroy one, but the other must have overwhelmed them and they ran. "I think they went this way," Amaranthe said after a few more moments of study.

Maldynado nodded toward the scarred walls. "Follow the holes, and we find them?"

"I'm assuming the cubes were shooting at our people as they fled."

"You sure you don't want to wait here for them to come back for us? What if they circle back by some other route and we miss them?"

"You'd think they would come back the same direction to stave off that very possibility. We can meet them in the middle."

"Unless they're still fleeing cubes and they *can't* come back in the same direction," Maldynado said. "We could get very lost in there."

"They have exactly one effective weapon between the three of them. I'm not going to stay here and wait when they could need our help."

Maldynado sighed and walked down the corridor at her side. He did not, she was glad, point out that they had exactly *no* effective weapons to help balance the equation. "Just promise me you won't hurl yourself in front of any cannons. At least not when I'm standing close to you."

"I'll try to sublimate any urges to do so."

They continued down the tunnel, watching the walls for scars. In some spots, there was a clump of them. In others, often around bends where their comrades must have gained ground, there weren't any. Amaranthe grew nervous in those blank-walled areas, especially when they crossed an intersection and other tunnels branched off. They had to double back twice to find the trail again.

"I hope random cubes aren't roaming through the corridors, shooting up the walls for their own amusement," Maldynado said.

"Our people wouldn't have run off for no reason," Amaranthe said firmly.

"I'm not so sure. Did you see the way the professor's eyes lit up when she saw this thing? She couldn't wait to get inside. Those other two soldiers are probably at the docks right now, wondering where she is."

Amaranthe stopped walking and lifted a hand. She'd heard something.

A clank sounded in the distance, somewhere ahead of them and... above them? Could that be right?

"Is that—"

"Sh." Amaranthe held a finger to her lips, then jogged down the tunnel. Listening as she went, she tried to keep her footfalls soft and stop the clatter of her gear, though her rucksack thumped annoyingly on her back.

Maldynado ran beside her, stealing glances at her. Hadn't he heard anything? Maybe she'd imagined it.

A blocky shape came into sight in the tunnel ahead. Another destroyed cube. Good. They *were* on the right track. They ran past it without stopping to examine it.

"Look out," someone yelled ahead of them. Mahliki.

"I see it," came Tikaya's response, calm but harried.

A sickly smoke scent, something between burning rubber and

scorched metal, reached Amaranthe's nose. Maldynado picked up speed, outpacing her. Lantern light came into view ahead.

His broad back blocked her line of sight, so she didn't see why he yanked out his rapier, but she trusted he had a good reason. She pulled out her pistol. Neither of their weapons would be effective, but maybe they could distract the cubes.

Maldynado bellowed and took a swing at something in front of him, wielding the blade as if it were an axe instead of a slender rapier. Hugging the wall, Amaranthe went down on one knee and lifted her pistol, expecting a cube to hover in the air ahead of them. She was in time to see his blade clang against something else, something larger but also floating. The blow caused it to bump against the wall and wobble before righting itself. Whatever it was, it didn't retaliate.

Four feet tall and reminiscent of two big snowballs one atop the other, the black object hovered a few inches above the floor. Two thick white beams shot from its body, painting the wall next to it. Maldynado twitched, almost leaping back, but when he saw that the beams weren't aimed at him, he swung again. Again, the contraption hit the side of the tunnel, bounced off, and wobbled, but again righted itself and refocused its beam on the wall, a smoldering patch of wall.

Amaranthe raised a hand to stop him. "I don't think—"

"Not those," came Tikaya's voice from ahead.

Amaranthe and Maldynado were at the end of a tunnel that opened into a strange chamber with a spiky floor plan—she didn't know what else to call it. Long angular alcoves thrust outward in all directions from an open center area, the walls coming together at the shadowy ends of those alcoves like the tips of a triangle with a column of lights at each point. Control stations?

"They're repairing the damage," Tikaya went on. Her head was sticking out from one of those alcoves. "They won't hurt you, but—"

"Look out," her daughter barked again.

"—the cubes will!" Tikaya finished, ducking back into the

alcove before a splash of crimson struck the wall. The sturdy metal didn't explode or even sheer off in great shards, but flakes did rain to the floor as the beam bore in.

"Where's Basilard?" Maldynado called.

"Where's your bow? And that royal gunk?" Amaranthe asked. Now that she'd been told it wouldn't hurt her, she scooted past the large hovering device, ducking to avoid its white beam, though she paused, startled as a putty-like substance floated through the light and affixed itself to the wall.

Not important, she decided and slipped out of the tunnel. From there, she could see the full room, including two cubes floating toward the alcove Tikaya and Mahliki shared. The two of them were out of sight, but if their alcove was like the others she could see down, it dead-ended at one of those columns. Unless those columns housed secret weapons, the women were in trouble. Where *was* Basilard?

She'd no more than thought the question when he sprinted out of an alcove—no, that was a tunnel—on the opposite side of the chamber. Five arrows were clenched in his fist, and he ran toward the women's hiding spot, but he halted, almost skidding on the smooth floor when he spotted the cubes. One stopped advancing toward the alcove and rotated toward him. He only had the arrows and a dagger, nothing that would help him against it.

"Get out of there, Bas," Maldynado barked, jumping out of the tunnel with his rapier.

Basilard hesitated, but didn't backpedal. He glanced toward the women's alcove, then, jaw set with determination, sprinted toward it.

Maldynado charged at the cube targeting Basilard. Amaranthe fired before the men drew too close. Her ball clipped its back corner, but didn't make it so much as twitch.

A red beam speared the air, aiming straight for Basilard's heart. He anticipated it and dove, rolling toward the alcove, arrows held away from his body so he wouldn't impale himself. He came up zigging and zagging, then dove again, this time disappearing from Amaranthe's sight.

Maldynado skidded to a stop a few feet behind the cube.

"Get out of there," Amaranthe shouted. "You can't do anything."

She couldn't either. She dropped her useless pistol and spun about, eyeing the repair device. It had sealed the hole in the wall and was drifting off up the tunnel.

"Oh, no you don't." Amaranthe chased after it and grabbed it around the middle, figuring it couldn't be that heavy—Maldynado had moved it by beating on it with a rapier, after all. She was right, and she was able to pull it back into the chamber.

She came out of the tunnel, lugging the thing behind her, in time to see Maldynado run off down the opposite passage with a cube chasing him. The other one floated at the head of the women's alcove and was firing inside. Amaranthe gulped. It couldn't have hit anyone yet—there would have been screams, surely. But there weren't any arrows coming out either.

Like a sled dog straining into the leads, Amaranthe hauled the repair device after her, hoping the cube wouldn't notice her until she was ready. She didn't know if she could replicate Basilard's acrobatic beam dodging.

She passed a smoldering section of the floor, and her captured device whirred and pulled against her. Yes, it wanted to do its job, and she was stopping it. Intruders were so rude.

Watching the cube every step of the way, she managed to haul the device to within a few feet of the alcove. She shifted her grip, coming around the thing, and started pushing instead of pulling.

"There, you go, a nice chipped corner to work on," she panted and gave it a great shove.

The double snowball jerked and trembled, but the momentum sent it floating in front of the alcove. It crossed into the path of the crimson beam. Amaranthe skittered back, fearing an explosion, but the cube's attack merely bit in slightly, as it did with the walls. The repair device didn't seem to notice. It rotated until its opening faced the damaged corner, and one of the white beams shot out, bathing the black wall in light.

Maybe the machines were talking to each other—as in, stop firing at me, you idiot box—for the crimson beam winked out. Unfortunately, the cube only turned toward the next target—Amaranthe.

She started to spin, intending to sprint back to the tunnel, but a flash of green streaked out of the alcove, just missing the repair device. It whizzed past to lodge in the cube's orifice. An arrow, Amaranthe realized, noting the green fletching even as she kept scrambling back. If the strike didn't work...

The hole flashed red, and a short, angry beam devoured the arrow.

Not good. Amaranthe tried to resume her sprint for the tunnel, but her changes of direction had thrown her off balance, and she tripped over her feet. She landed hard on her hip.

She scrambled back up immediately, risking a glance as she ran. The cube had stopped rotating to follow her. It hung there, motionless and soundless. Halfway back to the tunnel, Amaranthe paused. A slender wisp of smoke wafted from the cube's hole.

"Ah?" she murmured.

Had it worked after all?

More smoke followed, then the cube clunked to the floor, unmoving.

"Thank you, Corporal Lokdon," Tikaya said. She, her daughter, and Basilard had slipped past the repair device, which was still working on the corner, and stood at the front of the alcove. "That gave us the seconds we needed."

Basilard still held four arrows while Mahliki gripped the jar in both hands, the lid having been removed at some point.

"You're welcome," Amaranthe said.

Tikaya touched the top of her head, as if to ensure her scalp was indeed still attached. In her other hand, she held the longbow. Somewhere along the way, she'd lost her quiver and rucksack.

Basilard handed her another arrow and signed, *Maldynado*.

"He went down that tunnel." Even as Amaranthe pointed, footfalls sounded from that direction.

"Need a little help!" Maldynado called, though they couldn't see him yet.

Tikaya dipped the tip of the arrow into the jar and nocked it. Maldynado dove out of the tunnel, tumbling more than rolling as he clawed his way to cover. A red beam cut through the air where his head had been. Missing its target, it streaked out into the chamber.

Amaranthe sidled closer to Tikaya and the others. She wouldn't be above hiding behind that repair device again. The metal tip of Tikaya's arrow was smoking. That gunk would eat through it as surely as it ate through anything else here.

The cube floated out of the tunnel. It angled toward Maldynado, who had found his feet, but didn't look like he knew where to run. In turning in his direction the cube also turned its deadly orifice toward Tikaya.

Without hesitation, she loosed the arrow. The chamber was a good twenty-five meters across, but her aim was true. The arrow clinked into the hole. As with the last cube, it burned away the wooden shaft, but its defiance ended a few heartbeats later.

"Good shot," Amaranthe said, impressed that a scholar from an island of pacifists had such skill.

The cube clunked to the floor.

"Thank you." Tikaya lowered the bow.

Mahliki put a hand on her mother's shoulder. "The answer to the question you asked, oh, about fifteen minutes ago, is, yes, it *could* hurt to stop and try and figure out how to turn on the lights."

"Thank you, dear," Tikaya said. "Why don't you find the lid to that jar? In case we need it again?"

Mahliki disappeared into the alcove.

"Thank you, too, for your help." Tikaya waved at Basilard, Amaranthe, and Maldynado. "What happened to the rest of our burly soldiers?"

Rest of...? Did the professor lump Amaranthe and her team into that category? Amaranthe supposed they hadn't done anything to convince her they were brighter than privates fresh

out of their initial training. "Outside. We ran into trouble with relic raiders. One of the soldiers was injured and the other had to carry him away. I'm not sure where the other pair went."

"So, we're on our own? All right, give me a moment, please. I was close to figuring out how to turn on the lights." Tikaya returned to the alcove and added, "If they're working," under her breath.

Maldynado shambled over to join Amaranthe and Basilard, taking a wide route around the cube on the floor, though it'd been desiccated, eaten from the inside out by the acidic compound.

"I'd like to take this moment," Amaranthe said, "to point out that you two are as crazy as I am at times."

"Me?" Maldynado splayed a hand across his chest.

"Running up to those cubes and hacking at them with a sword isn't any brighter than drawing fire from a cannon."

Basilard's eyebrows rose. *You tried to get a cannon to shoot at you?*

"No," Amaranthe said, "it just happened that way. I thought those men would use their rifles."

Oh. So you tried to get rifles to shoot at you. Eyebrows still elevated, Basilard met Maldynado's eyes and slowly shook his head.

Amaranthe scowled at them.

Over the next few seconds, the light level grew in the room, eliminating the shadows the lanterns had struggled to pierce. If not for the white and red beams flying around during that skirmish, Amaranthe didn't know how they would have seen anything.

Amaranthe peeked into the alcove. Tikaya's rucksack sat on the floor at the end, and she stood before the column, fingers dancing over tiny illuminated symbols while she held a black sphere with her free hand. Amaranthe recognized the object from the desk back at the factory, but she hadn't seen it doing anything. Now, glowing images hovered in the air above it, projected from some tiny hold. It reminded her of the floating interactive pictures in the control room.

"I'm seeing if this station can call up a map as well," Tikaya said. "We're in the… I guess you'd call it the bowels of the ship. This area handles the infrastructure—lighting, life support, routing of water and internal power, sewage."

"Sewage?" Maldynado asked.

"Everybody goes," Tikaya murmured.

"Fortunately, that's a part of the craft that nobody showed me on my various tours," Amaranthe said.

"Oh, no?" Tikaya asked, her back to them as she continued to work. "I would have found it fascinating."

I'm telling you, Amaranthe signed to her men, *there's no way I'm the craziest person in this room.*

Possibly true, Basilard allowed.

"You went on tours?" Mahliki asked Amaranthe. "Does that mean you can find your way to engineering or the control area from here?"

"Sorry, no. This isn't the way I came when I was here before."

"Ah."

Amaranthe didn't think there was condemnation in that soft syllable, but she wished she could take the lead and walk them straight to the control room nonetheless. Right now, she *did* feel like little more than the hired grunts.

"This should be it." Tikaya twisted a final rune and turned around, facing the center of the chamber.

The air shimmered, then a large, three-dimensional image formed two meters above the floor. Retta had created something similar when she'd showed Amaranthe and Books how to reach her assistant's room, though this was much larger with level upon level on display, along with massive open areas. In a steamer, she would have guessed they represented boiler and engine rooms. Who knew with this craft?

"Hm." Tikaya turned back to the column, manipulating a few more symbols.

Amaranthe tried to decide if the way she knew exactly what she was doing was comforting or disturbing. Retta had been obsessed with the ship. She hadn't had any interest in

destroying it or burying it at the bottom of the ocean. What if Tikaya grew equally intrigued and didn't want to let it go? What did Amaranthe truly know about the woman, after all?

"There we go." Tikaya turned again, extending a hand toward the schematic.

A blue line had formed, weaving down one level, up several others, and into the core of the craft. The spiky medium-sized chamber it started in appeared to be their own.

"Who's memorizing the route?" Amaranthe asked, daunted by all the intersections the line passed through.

"I've got it," Tikaya and her daughter said at the same time.

They shared smiles, Tikaya's fond, and Mahliki's more of a wry smirk.

"I don't think I could even find my way back to the door where we came in," Maldynado muttered.

Me either, Basilard signed. *This place is… I wish to complete our work here as quickly as possible.*

From the eager way mother and daughter gathered their gear and led the way out of the chamber, Amaranthe wasn't certain they would agree.

CHAPTER 8

Sicarius did not want to kill Fleet Admiral Starcrest. He wasn't certain whether he cared one way or another about his own life, but, as he lay on the carpet in the dark tent, like a hound at the foot of Kor Nas's cot, he was certain of that one fact. If Starcrest was in the city, it was because Sicarius's letter had brought him. To turn that letter into a trap, as if he'd planned to assassinate the legendary admiral all along, the man he'd dreamed of emulating as a boy, it was unthinkable.

He still remembered the day when Hollowcrest had dropped Fleet Admiral Starcrest's *Mathematical Probabilities Applied to Military Strategies* into his hands. He'd been nine. At that age, he'd already read Starcrest's simpler and more useful, at least for Sicarius's future career, *Applications of the Kinetic Chain Principle in Close Combat,* along with numerous other books on tactics and strategies from other authors—though Hollowcrest hadn't anticipated that Sicarius would need a thorough military education for his work, he hadn't discouraged the interest. Sicarius had also studied the careers of the important Turgonian admirals and generals from the empire's history, so he'd been aware of Starcrest beforehand, but this had been the first thing he'd read that had been written in first person by the admiral himself. *Probabilities* had been too advanced for him to understand at that age—some of the math was still too advanced for him, he admitted dryly, and with a little sadness for an education that Hollowcrest had deemed finished once he was completing missions for the throne—but he'd devoured the real world examples from Starcrest's own victories, and from the rare losses. In that book, a hint of the man's self-effacing personality had shown through, and something about it had drawn Sicarius to want to learn more about him.

Not disapproving of the obsession, Hollowcrest had supplied third-person accounts of his battles and even copies of a few of Starcrest's personal reports and mission summaries. Those had been brief, though, without any of the... personality that had occasionally shown up in *Probabilities*. Looking back as an adult, Sicarius wondered if Starcrest had been trying to excite future officers about the field of mathematics. Either way, he'd been secretly—oh, so secretly—delighted when he'd stumbled across *Captain Starcrest in the West Markiis*. Ten years old at the time, Sicarius had been reporting to an officer-tutor in the intelligence office for linguistics lessons when he'd spotted the book on the man's desk. The lieutenant had cleared his throat and hastily stuffed it into a drawer, but not before Sicarius saw the title. He'd returned in the middle of the night to sit under that desk and devour the story by candlelight. Over the next year, he'd risked much to acquire other titles in the series. Hollowcrest had forbidden Sicarius to read fiction, calling it a waste of time, and he'd been caught twice with the books. It had been his own fault for daring to keep some of the copies he'd acquired, favorites that he'd wanted to read again. The first time, the punishment had been tolerable if unpleasant. The second time... had convinced him not to hunt down any more of the books. But for months afterward, he'd lain in his bunk at night, imagining himself as a young officer on the *Striker* or the *Emperor's Wrath*, performing heroic feats to win Starcrest's regard and eventually working himself up to second-in-command.

Sicarius sighed and rolled onto his side, the lumpy snow beneath the carpet pressing into his ribs. He was surprised at how much he remembered of those days, and how vivid the memories were. To be forced to kill Starcrest now...

Kor Nas couldn't know that he'd been given that assignment twice in his life already and refused to accept it both times.

But now, he wouldn't be able to. He could slag himself for ever sending that letter.

If he could have foreseen these events...

Enough. He needed to do more than lament his fate; he needed to find a way to avoid it.

Yes, how?

Kill Kor Nas, he thought promptly and not for the first time. But he'd already tried. The first night they lay like this, the Nurians snoring on their cots and Sicarius on the carpet, he'd stood, silent as a shadow, and tried to plunge his dagger into the practitioner's chest. He'd managed to lift the blade overhead, but his muscles had locked. The opal embedded in his temple had flashed an angry warning, sending a stab of pain into his brain, and his arms had never started their downward descent. He'd stood there, seconds bleeding past as he mentally wrestled with it, trying to find a way around the artifact's power, but he'd failed. A few minutes later, he'd lain back down, breathing heavily, but not so much as to wake anyone. Kor Nas had slept through it all, not concerned in the least that his "pet" would—*could*—turn on him.

So get someone else to kill him, eh?

Sicarius let the thought hang in the silence for a while, considering it from a few different angles. With Kor Nas's death, the power of the opal should fade, or at least have no direction. The leash might remain until he could figure out a way to remove it, but the handler at the other end would be gone.

But who could kill Kor Nas? Thus far, the practitioner had sent Sicarius out on independent missions—assassinations— while remaining in camp, but if Flintcrest meant to march on the city, he'd want his Nurian wizard along, blowing things up and adding to the enemy's chaos. In such a battle, Kor Nas might be a target, but he would keep Sicarius at his side. That was what Nurian battle wizards did—employ bodyguards to allow them to concentrate on their Science. In such a situation, Sicarius had no doubt he'd be compelled to protect Kor Nas.

So, he needed to pit Kor Nas against someone capable of both

bypassing Sicarius *and* killing a practitioner. Or simply killing them both. The bleak thought didn't repel him as much as it would have once. With little left to live for, this might be more apropos than suicide. If he could take Kor Nas down with him, and in doing so, assure Starcrest would live... Starcrest was the one person, he believed, who might achieve what Amaranthe and Sespian had failed to do: create a better empire.

Yes. Sicarius rolled onto his back again and placed his hands behind his head. This would be an act worth dying for.

But how? Surprisingly, or perhaps not so surprisingly, Amaranthe's face was the first one to pop into his thoughts as someone who could concoct a scheme that would bury a wizard and his bodyguard beneath a mountain of rubble. But she wasn't around any more to do that. And she'd risk herself trying to save him, anyway, instead of accepting that he and his master—in the darkness, with nobody watching, Sicarius allowed his lip to curl at the word—had to be slain. His belly shivered at the idea of Amaranthe approaching him while he was under Kor Nas's influence. Once again, he remembered Darkcrest Isle and his fingers wrapped about her neck.

Stop it, he told himself. She's dead. It's moot.

He needed someone else capable of the job. Starcrest himself was the logical person. But Sicarius had defeated him the one time the admiral had attacked him, and Starcrest was twenty years older now. Slower. While Sicarius was still in his prime. Or close to it anyway.

True, Starcrest had seen him as a boy back then and had underestimated him. He wouldn't make that mistake again. Still, Sicarius would win in a purely physical confrontation between the two of them. But if the admiral had *warning*, time to plan something...

A snort came from the cot above. Sicarius's thoughts hiccuped to a halt. Had Kor Nas woken? Had he been listening to Sicarius's mind spin all along?

The snort, more of a gurgle, came again. Kor Nas rolled over and started snoring.

Sicarius exhaled slowly. No, the practitioner slept on. Here, and here alone, he could think without being monitored. He had to take advantage of that and come up with a plan before dawn.

Go in person? He couldn't. For one thing, he didn't know where Starcrest was. Beyond that, Kor Nas would wake if Sicarius tried to escape. He'd tried to walk away before and had been compelled, after a blast of pain seared his brain, to return. Kor Nas had been waiting for him, a slit-eyed glare on his face.

Maybe Sicarius could send another letter. Encoded like the first. But through whom? Some soldier in the camp? True, some of them might be swayed to Starcrest's side if they knew he existed, but Sicarius had no way to ferret out which ones. He had to assume everyone here, in committing themselves to this march on the throne, belonged to Flintcrest.

Although... there was one person in the camp he could be certain didn't want to see Starcrest killed.

Sicarius felt his heart rate quicken.

Dare he approach the man? Try to get him alone without Kor Nas finding out?

You still have to figure out where Starcrest *is*, he reminded himself. A letter couldn't be delivered without an address. And somehow he had to keep these thoughts locked down deep so Kor Nas wouldn't stumble across them as soon as he woke up. The practitioner might like his new pet, but that wouldn't keep him from killing Sicarius and finding another if the situation warranted it.

* * *

Sicarius scrambled up the granite cliff, his fingers finding purchase in the slender cracks and on the ledges where snow gathered. His pace was fast, but not fast enough. The terrifying howl of the soul construct echoed from the canyon walls, following him as he climbed. The beast followed him, too, hulking and black in the dark night, not affected by the snow gusting sideways down the ravine. It bounded from ledge to ledge, knocking rocks and huge clumps of snow off with each leap, but finding a way to scale the cliff nonetheless.

Sicarius didn't glance back, but he had to sense it gaining. Surely, he did. Amaranthe, watching from some impossible viewpoint floating behind him, tried to scream a warning. It's gaining on you. Do something! But the snow and the wind stole the words.

The top of the cliff came into view, and Sicarius charged the final meters toward it. But his foot slipped, and the handhold beneath his fingers gave way. He dangled from one arm, legs hanging above the thousand-foot drop. A tiny frozen stream wound through the canyon far below, amidst boulders that might as well have been spikes. Sicarius reached for a new handhold. He would have made it, would have finished the climb, but the soul construct caught him then. It leaped, fangs biting, claws slashing, and tore him from the cliff.

Together they fell, spinning into the dark depths below. Before he plummeted to his death, Sicarius's accusing eyes met hers, and he asked, "Why, Amaranthe? Why didn't you come help when I needed you?"

Amaranthe woke with a gasp, her heart trying to jump out of her chest. For a disoriented moment, she stared about, surprised she wasn't on a mountainside with snow streaking through her vision. Instead, she lay on her back, using her lumpy rucksack for a pillow. The black floor of the control room stretched before her. She remembered reaching it, watching Tikaya and her daughter lock the doors from cuboid intrusions, then setting to work. And she remembered feeling useless as the two women had called up the floating images—the control interfaces, Tikaya had called them—and taken turns manipulating them and considering journals full of notes. She'd announced that her team would get some rest, which had unfortunately resulted in Maldynado and Basilard conspiring to ensure *she* slept while one of them stood watch.

Amaranthe sat up, wondering if she should be disappointed

or relieved that her nightmares had evolved into something new. Neither. That one hadn't been any better than the others. Her sweat-soaked shirt stuck to her back, and strands of hair that had fallen from her bun lay pasted against her face and neck.

Thirsty, she unclasped her canteen from her rucksack. She hoped the thirst meant she'd actually slept for a number of hours this time, instead of her usual fistful of minutes. She also hoped the two women had, thanks to their interest in alien sewage and plumbing, found something that qualified as a washout. Last time, her team had been forced to make do with... well, Amaranthe hoped neither of her Kyattese explorers had opened that cabinet thing on the far wall. Though maybe the cubes or repair devices had cleaned in there. They'd scoured the floor of the control room of any memory of the fight. The bodies were all gone, not so much as a drop of blood or strand of hair left behind to prove those people had existed. Some funeral pyre.

Someone touched her shoulder. Basilard.

He sat with his back to the wall, a rifle across his knees while Maldynado, using his silly hat for a pillow—how *did* he keep from losing that thing when he was fleeing killer technological constructs?—snored, his face smooth and relaxed as he slept. No nightmares haunted him.

With concern in his eyes, Basilard signed, *Bad dream?*

They all are these days, Amaranthe signed back, not wanting to disturb the quiet room.

Tikaya and Mahliki still worked, though now they were sitting, heads bent together over an image displayed on that black sphere. Stuck on some problem? Amaranthe didn't wish to disturb them.

Pike? Basilard asked, mimicking an actual pike for his sign.

Not this time. Sicarius in trouble.

Oh, Sicarius, she thought, if you'd figure out a way to show me where you are, I'd come help. True, she had no way of knowing if he needed help, but it'd been four days since anybody had seen him, maybe more.

I have wondered, Basilard signed, *if he's...*

"Still alive?" Amaranthe murmured.

Basilard hesitated, watching her face, afraid he'd upset her maybe. *Injured*, he decided on.

"Me too."

I think it would surprise him, but I'd miss him if he were gone.

"Maybe not surprise so much as perplex." Amaranthe tried to smile, but couldn't. She'd been better at false cheer before. Maybe it'd been required too much of late.

Yes. He was just getting...

Human, Amaranthe thought. "Interesting?" she responded aloud.

Less unpleasant, Basilard signed. Perhaps realizing that wasn't much of an accolade, he added, *It was a noticeable improvement. Not bad for a year's influence.*

"Your influence?"

Yours. By the time you've been married for ten years and have a pile of children, he might be almost approachable.

Amaranthe almost fell over. "Children?" she squeaked. "Him? Us? Er."

Her voice had grown louder, and Mahliki glanced in their direction. Amaranthe blushed and made sure Maldynado was still asleep. He'd rib her endlessly for a discussion like this.

You don't envision it? Basilard asked.

Amaranthe went back to signing, not wanting people she barely knew overhearing the rest of the conversation. *I suppose I've thought about it from time to time as possibly happening in some distant future.* Though she also wondered if the injuries she'd received from the makarovi would preclude her ever having children. *I didn't realize you, any of you thought about it, or that he'd... that we'd be...a good idea.* Books had been disapproving for months, and Maldynado kept trying to send her on picnics with other men.

Not all of the others, perhaps. Basilard glanced at Maldynado. *But you are a good team. Your strengths complement his weaknesses and vice versa. And you are a good influence on him. The world is safer because he's with you.*

Amaranthe didn't feel like she could be a good influence on anyone anymore, but Basilard's approval warmed her heart nonetheless. So few people seemed able to see Sicarius as anything other than a heartless killer, even those with whom he'd spent an entire year in close quarters. It shouldn't surprise her that Basilard would be the one to glimpse behind the facade, at least a little. It took an observant man to find a tasty herb in a urine-beleaguered alley.

After all this is over, will you return to your people? Find your daughter perhaps? Amaranthe hadn't asked his thoughts on the matter in a long time. She should have. She'd been too buried in her own inner world.

Basilard fiddled with the strap of his rucksack and avoided her eyes. *She wouldn't want to see me. After my crimes... it's better for her if I don't try to make contact.*

You're making assumptions, Amaranthe signed. *Don't you think you should at least plan a trip to find out the truth? For all you know, she wonders every day what happened to you.*

Basilard swallowed. *Even if that were true, when she found out what I've done...* He spread his hand toward his face and head to indicate his scars, and those he'd killed to receive them. *She would be shamed. She would not want anything to do with me.*

Do you still want anything to do with her?

He dropped his forehead into his palm, but not before she glimpsed a damp sheen on his eyes.

"Basilard," she said, because he wouldn't see signs if she made them, "don't give up on her without finding out how she feels. Even if she is shamed, because that's what her culture has taught her to feel, you don't have to give up. You know... or *do* you know—" she lowered her voice to a whisper, "—that everything Sicarius has done these last couple of years, even before we met him, has been for Sespian's sake? At first to protect his son, and later because he wanted a relationship with him, even though Sespian has always thought him a monster. And unlike in your case..." Amaranthe stopped herself from saying Sicarius really *was* a monster. She didn't believe that, but she couldn't think of a better way to say Sicarius's crimes had been greater than Basilard's. Given the strict pacifist nature of the Mangdorian religion, he might not agree anyway. "He hasn't given up on Sespian, and, if it matters to you, *I* don't think you should give up on your daughter."

Basilard lowered his hand from his face. He didn't look at Amaranthe, but he signed, more to himself than to her, *I'll consider your words.* He shifted his weight and grimaced. *The idea of Sicarius being a better father than I* would *be difficult to swallow.*

Feeling she'd won a victory, Amaranthe chose not to argue Sicarius's merits in the parenthood department. She fancied he might do just fine though, without meddling from emperors or other superiors.

Basilard leaned back, a newly thoughtful expression on his face. *He did seem to be getting closer to Sespian there at the end. Or I guess I mean Sespian was letting Sicarius get closer to him.*

"How so?" Amaranthe asked.

They went off on a spy mission together for the general. Sespian was the one to suggest it. I gather it was harrowing for him, but he seemed pleased he lived to talk about it. He was visibly disappointed when Sicarius left to hunt the soul construct on his own.

Amaranthe tried to imagine the adventure they must have had that night. She wished she could have seen it, especially after Sespian had said he might understand his father better now that he knew his past, but that he didn't want anything to do with him. Hah, boy. What Sicarius lacked in charm, he made up for in persistence.

Out in the center of the room, the two women stood, returning to one of the images floating above their heads. In addition to the piles of notebooks and the familiar sphere decorating the floor around their packs, a few small black objects Amaranthe hadn't seen before rested amidst their gear. Items brought from

Kyatt? Or were they shopping for goods to take home and study? She frowned at the idea. If not for "goods" collected from those tunnels twenty years ago, the Kyattese Polytechnic wouldn't have started a research division to study the ancient language and technology, and the *Behemoth* wouldn't have turned Fort Urgot into a graveyard.

Amaranthe climbed to her feet and joined the women. "How are things going? Have you figured out how to dump this in that trench yet?"

"I believe so," Tikaya said, not tearing her eyes from the shifting and changing images to meet Amaranthe's gaze. "But this ship is incredible. It can do *so* much. I could spend the rest of my life in this room and not come close to understanding everything available here. Rias should be out here, using it as a command headquarters for his troops. It'd be a lot easier to defend than a molasses factory, and look." Tikaya prodded one of the images.

Amaranthe shifted her weight as a new image popped into existence in front of her. The professor's enthusiasm disturbed her; it was too akin to that which Retta had displayed.

The image wavered and coalesced into a map of Stumps, the lake, and the surrounding area. Not just a map, Amaranthe realized when she spotted trolleys moving along Waterfront Street, a display of the living world around them. Daylight had come, and the city was awake with more troops than ever roaming the streets.

"Fascinating," Mahliki murmured. "You wouldn't think that'd be possible without some sort of..." she groped, searching for an adequate word, "floating observatory in the sky above us somewhere."

"*Mkor Mratht*," Tikaya said.

"Pardon?" Amaranthe asked. Mahliki didn't look enlightened either.

"There's no word for it in either of our languages, but that's what these people called it. I am, of course, taking liberty with the pronunciation."

"Of course," Amaranthe said.

"Floating observatory, yes," Tikaya said, "but in space, orbiting about our planet like a moon. They left them there tens of thousands of years ago. I read about it in the encyclopedia." She waved toward the unassuming sphere. "Until now, I had no way to know whether they were still functioning—after all this time, I certainly wouldn't have guessed that to be the case— but... it's magnificent, isn't it?"

"Ah, yes," Amaranthe said. "About that trench..." She trailed off, taken in despite herself, when Tikaya swiped her fingers through the image, shifting the view. Instead of the waterfront, they were now looking down at the *Behemoth*, an aerial view of it, the snowy field, and the lake to the south of it. Along with a whole crowd of people. "Emperor's eyeteeth, where'd they come from?"

Men and women, mostly in civilian clothing but with a few army uniforms mixed in, circled the base of the *Behemoth*, staring up at it. There were a few children too, though mothers had them pulled in close. Afternoon sun gleamed off the snow—Amaranthe had indeed slept for some hours—but failed to make so much as a glint on the inky black hull of the ship. It swallowed light instead of reflecting it.

"Tourist attraction?" Mahliki mused.

"Indeed," Tikaya said. "When it first appeared, everyone must have been too scared to investigate, at least en masse. But now that it's been sitting here for more than a day, without anything deleterious occurring since the crash..."

"Communal gawking?" Amaranthe shook her head. "They'll run off when we lift this monstrosity from the ground."

"You want to move the ship with all those people watching?" Mahliki asked. "Give them a demonstration of what it can do, and people might get it in their heads to go looking for it."

"If that trench is as deep as your father says, it won't matter. Besides, it already flattened an entire fort and thousands of men. I'm sure the brighter people out there already have an idea as to what it is."

"I believe I've found something that will more completely do what must be done with this ship." Tikaya exchanged a long look with her daughter, a look tinged with reluctance and sorrow.

"Oh?" Amaranthe prompted.

"There is a sequence in here that commands the ship to destroy itself from within."

Amaranthe perked up. That would be an ideal solution. "The way a Turgonian captain would blow up his own ship, rather than letting it be taken by enemies?"

Tikaya frowned at her, or perhaps at Turgonian military practices. "We can only guess as to their motivations, but perhaps so. It's taking much searching to figure out how to initiate the sequence. I gather it was designed to be accessible by a limited few, such as the captain and first mate."

"You wouldn't want some disgruntled private fresh off a reprimand to be able to blow everyone across the stars," Amaranthe said reasonably.

"While I keep researching, Mahliki, why don't you and Amaranthe use the mapping device to figure out where the rest of the troops are currently located? Rias will doubtlessly be pleased to gain that information."

It was a brushoff—the stop-bugging-me-so-I-can-work kind—but in this case Amaranthe didn't mind. She should have thought of intelligence gathering herself when that map had first popped up.

"Yes, Mother." Mahliki, too, sounded a tad disappointed at the brushoff.

Amaranthe tried a sisterhood-of-the-underappreciated smile on her and got a wry twist of the lips in return.

"I'll take notes," Amaranthe volunteered, leaving Mahliki to manipulate the image.

She dug a journal out of her rucksack. Maldynado was still snoring. Basilard was facing the women, but his eyes were unfocused, lost in thought.

"Heroncrest's army was surrounding Fort Urgot two days ago," Amaranthe said. "It'd be good to know where they went.

At the time, they were wearing blue armbands. I haven't seen more than a handful of Flintcrest's men yet, but his army was rumored to be gathered somewhere west of the lake. Yellow armbands, I believe. Marblecrest should have forces in the Imperial Barracks, and his men have the river checkpoint at the bottom of the lake and at least one of the railroads into the city as well. White armbands."

"Understood." Mahliki manipulated the image, and it was as if she and Amaranthe were flying about in one of those dirigibles, looking down upon the city. They cast no shadows, though, and nobody looked up, able to sense their eyes. How the technology worked was so far over Amaranthe's head she would have needed a rope and grapple to get close to having a clue, but she had no trouble taking advantage of what it offered, and she scribbled notes as fast as she could write.

Flintcrest's troops had moved into the Emperor's Preserve. Heroncrest must not have been close enough to the crash to have lost many of his men, for he'd taken over the University campus, using the student housing for barracks. Classes were, no doubt, on hold. The sheer number of troops clogging the streets daunted Amaranthe. There had to be tens of thousands of uniformed men in Stumps. What could she, Sespian, and Starcrest and their five hundred do against them?

"There's a lot of fighting going on in the city, especially here." Mahliki pointed out squads of men in the streets around the Imperial Barracks, blue and white armbands clashing.

"I see it," Amaranthe said. "Someone must have made a move in the night or early this morning. Things were quiet by comparison when we left. I wonder if they've discovered our factory and our people yet."

A worried expression crossed Mahliki's face.

"I'm sure your father wouldn't jump into the middle of trouble," Amaranthe said, though she admitted that Starcrest might indeed become a target once people learned he was in the city. With hundreds of men in the factory, someone might well be a snitch for the other side. Emperor's warts, she couldn't

even be certain the snitching wouldn't start in her own camp, not when those two recruits of hers were new and untried. And Deret... she should have spent some time with him, reassuring him that she was behind him, before haring off with the professor. She hadn't even gone to check on the captive she'd ordered him to take.

"No, he wouldn't jump into the middle," Mahliki said, "but he didn't come here to work on his suntan. I wouldn't be surprised if he's already enacting some plan or another."

Though Tikaya seemed engrossed in her research, her lips flattened at this comment. Yes, she'd be worried about her husband too. Amaranthe wondered how much of an argument there'd been about whether or not to come to the empire and poke their collective nose in this hornet's nest.

"Can you make the perspective closer to those men fighting in front of the Barracks?" Amaranthe asked. It'd be convenient if Ravido, Heroncrest, and Flintcrest all managed to kill each other in some pointless squabble for Arakan Hill, as if having possession of the physical throne truly meant one were emperor of Turgonia. It might be an important symbol, but surely other things mattered more.

Like a bird swooping down from the skies, they descended. It was too far at first, and Amaranthe twitched as the perspective focused on a close-up of one of the old cobblestone streets. The wheel of a steam lorry rolled across the frost-edged stones.

"Oops," Mahliki murmured and twisted her fingers to pull the viewpoint back.

Ah, not a steam lorry, but an armored carriage. One of many rolling up a street toward the Barracks.

"I bet it's a diversion," Maldynado said. He'd woken up at some point and was yawning and watching the show. "Like at Fort Urgot. If you hunt around, I bet you'll find guarded holes where tunnel borers are working. Sespian said that's Heroncrest's big plan."

"If that's true," Amaranthe said, "it'd be useful to know the location of the tunnel entrances. A back door for us later, maybe."

Mahliki manipulated the image, and their aerial viewpoint swept across roofs and up and down streets.

Basilard scratched his jaw. *Would they be attempting to bore tunnels during daylight hours?*

Watching the fighting in the streets—a soldier driving a lorry was shot by a sniper on the rooftop of a building right in front of them—Amaranthe did not answer. Bodies occupied the streets, too, and she couldn't help but wonder what the death count was if one included those killed at Fort Urgot. And how could one *not* include them? They were victims of this internecine political madness as surely as a man shot in the chest.

Back when she'd vowed to throw her support behind Sespian, to hide his secret heritage and to keep him alive, this was exactly what she'd wanted to avoid. She'd failed. In so many areas, she'd failed. Maybe it had been hubris to think that she, one person, had ever had the power to stop this. It was disheartening to realize it might have been better, or at least less bloody, if she'd kept her hands out of the stewpot. Forge would have slid right into power. But what future would that have given the world? One in which a select few controlled the global economy and inexorably drove the majority of the population into a clandestine sort of indebted serfdom.

They couldn't turn around the bloodshed now; they could only find a way to end it as swiftly as possible. She hoped Starcrest truly was working on a plan to do precisely that.

"They could have started the boring last night," Maldynado said. "Gotten the machines underground where nobody would notice them and then thrown something over the hole to block it."

Amaranthe stirred herself from her thoughts and tried to focus on the larger images sweeping past rather than the bodies. "It wouldn't be that easy to hide the evidence of the excavations. They'd have a lot of earth to move out of the way. Mahliki, can you take us northwest of the Barracks? To the Emperor's Preserve? It's a forested area, the only large one left anywhere near the boundaries of the city. It'd be a long dig from there, but that's where I'd start a tunnel. Indeed, there are already tunnels that

lead from there to the Barracks, though it would take someone with inside knowledge to find them." Neither Maldynado nor Basilard had accompanied Sicarius on the mission to research his heritage, so she couldn't get verification, but she added, "They're supposed to be protected by wards now too."

Mahliki blinked. "The Science? In the empire?"

"Forge hasn't been above importing wizards and shamans to work for them. There's at least one in the Barracks, I understand."

The perspective had flown through the streets and over Arakan Hill, where squads of soldiers manned cannons and other mounted artillery weapons, and they were now reaching the Preserve. Fortunately, many of the snow-lined tree branches were bare, or they wouldn't have witnessed much with the bird's eye view. The scrubby evergreens did blot out some of the ground, but not so much that they couldn't see soldiers moving about. More soldiers than Amaranthe had expected.

"Tents?" she asked. "Someone's moved his whole camp into the Preserve."

Maldynado pointed. "Yellow armbands. Flintcrest."

"He's moved a *lot* closer," Amaranthe said. "He must have marched yesterday or all night to get around the lake and over to this side of the city. Someone would have noticed that, but maybe he's planning to make his move soon. While Heroncrest's men are squabbling at the foot of the Barracks."

"Is that a Nurian outfit?" Mahliki murmured and adjusted the image, pushing them closer to a silver-haired man in a vibrant yellow and red robe.

"Stop," Amaranthe blurted. "That gray-haired fellow walking up to him. Is that…?"

Maldynado, more familiar with all the warrior-caste families, nodded. "Yup, that's the satrap governor, Lord General Flintcrest."

The man was pointing at something beneath the trees and seemed to be arguing with the Nurian.

"I wish there was a way to hear them." Amaranthe supposed she should already be tickled with the degree of spy information the *Behemoth* was giving her. For the first time, she found herself understanding the temptation to study the ship rather than destroy it, or at least keep a few of the useful-in-a-non-deadly-way tools.

"I see it," Maldynado said. "Ewww."

Beneath the evergreens, poles had been thrust vertically into the frozen earth, and... Amaranthe's stomach did a queasy flip. Severed heads were mounted atop them. The branches hid the faces of many of them—there had to be at least twenty—but her breath caught when their perspective drew closer, and she could pick out the features of one of the unseeing visages. *Familiar* features.

"Dear ancestors, that's Ms. Worgavic." She swallowed. "It *was* Ms. Worgavic."

"The one who ordered you tortured?" Maldynado asked. "The one who was stroking the senior Lord Mancrest's snake to get control over the *Gazette*? The one who happens to be a Forge founder?"

"Yes." Amaranthe stared at the grisly trophy. Whoever had retrieved the head had brought Worgavic's spectacles and mounted them appropriately on her nose.

"How is Flintcrest finding Forge people?" Maldynado asked.

Good question. It'd taken Amaranthe and Books the better part of the year to collect names, and even then, it hadn't been until she'd been forced into that mind link with Retta that she'd learned who the founders were. "That might be why he brought in the Nurians."

"Are those *all* Forge people?" Maldynado pointed at the decapitated heads.

"I can't see all of the faces," Amaranthe said. "I wouldn't necessarily recognize them all anyway. One wonders what kind of message Flintcrest is trying to send and to whom with the poles. If they were in a public square somewhere, it'd make sense, however gruesome that sense, but is he trying to alarm his own troops with how dangerous and bloodthirsty he is?"

"Would Turgonian troops be alarmed by severed heads mounted on spears?" Mahliki asked mildly, though her face

seemed paler than usual. She'd lowered her hands and was wiping them on her trousers, as if she might clean them from their association with the image. "It was my understanding that your people weren't squeamish about such things." She glanced at her mother, but Tikaya was frowning at some incomprehensible display of symbols.

"Oh, we're not squeamish," Maldynado said, "but like the boss said, the heads on a stick usually go in plain view of the *other* bloke's camp, not your own."

"Maybe that's what Flintcrest was pointing out so vehemently," Amaranthe said. "That his Nurian ally got it backwards. Mahliki can you pull away so we can see them again? Professor Komitopis, is there any chance you recognize the gray-haired man? I'm wondering if he's someone important or powerful in Nuria. Is he a wizard?"

Frowning at the symbols, Tikaya didn't respond. She may not have heard.

"Sometimes you have to poke her to get her attention when she's deep into her research," Mahliki said. "That's what Father does."

"He *pokes* her, eh?" Maldynado smirked. "It's good to know the old admiral hasn't grown too senescent for that sort of thing."

Amaranthe swatted him. Not only was Mahliki too young to be exposed to his lewd commentary, but no one wanted to hear implications that one's parents engaged in sexual exploits regardless.

Mahliki surprised her by saying, "Indeed not. Where the poking happens and with what depends on whether we kids are around, of course." She walked over to Tikaya and tapped her shoulder.

While their backs were to him, Maldynado grinned and signed, *I like her.*

Amaranthe managed not to roll her eyes. Barely. *Allow me to remind you that I've become friends with Yara. If you intend to thrust your rapier into someone else's sheath—*

Maldynado waved a quick, *No, no. Even if I weren't slightly intimidated by the fact that Starcrest,* the *Starcrest is her da, I wouldn't wish to abandon Yara. Or jeopardize the progress I've made with her. I'm* this *close*—he held his thumb and first finger up, a hair's breadth apart—*to getting her to let me use her first name.*

Amaranthe snorted, but smiled. Good. *Only* slightly *intimidated, eh?*

Gray hairs or not, Starcrest had an inch of height on Maldynado and still looked like a formidable warrior. And then there was all that reputation he could swing about.

Yes, Maldynado signed. *I should think he'd have to glower at me for at least three seconds before I wetted myself.*

Distracted by the conversation, Amaranthe hadn't noticed when Tikaya and Mahliki turned in their direction. They exchanged glances, and Mahliki whispered, "Interesting how many of those gestures of theirs are straightforward enough to guess."

"I didn't catch much of the exchange," Tikaya murmured back, "but I do hope we won't be witnessing more of what was in that cabinet over there."

Amaranthe cleared her throat, wishing the two had chosen to speak in their native tongue. Although she might have guessed the meaning of the words anyway. "I was wondering, Professor, if you recognized that Nurian with Lord General Flintcrest there."

"Tikaya," came the correction, then she added, "Which one?"

"Er." The image, Amaranthe reminded herself, was live, so people came and went. The silver-haired fellow and the scowling general were still talking, this time with fewer gestures, but two more people in Nurian garb had joined them. These two were younger, in their thirties perhaps. "The older fellow. I'm guessing he's in charge."

"I'm guessing not." Tikaya drew closer to the image and adjusted her spectacles. "It's been a while since I've seen the boy, but that flute he's wearing, it means he's a diplomat, probably in charge of the Nurian side of the mission. He also happens to be Prince Zirabo, son of the Great Chief."

"*The* Great Chief?" Amaranthe found the Nurian way of organizing political and tribal power confusing, at least insofar as remembering which chiefs were which—they had, she recalled, everything from sub-chiefs to lieutenant-chiefs to big chiefs, and then there were hunt- and war-related ones, such as wolf, fox, and bear chiefs—but the Great Chief, that was their equivalent to an emperor.

"The ruler of Nuria, yes," Tikaya said.

"Are any of the lords trying to get the throne *not* someone's puppet?" Maldynado asked. "I'm not surprised my brother would let someone control him—he's not clever enough to think up a usurpation plot on his own—but Flintcrest too? As a satrap governor, I'd expect him to have a brain of sorts. Those are appointed positions, after all, not inherited."

Sort of, Amaranthe thought. One still had to be warrior caste to be appointed.

"It's possible the Nurians are allying with Flintcrest, not trying to control him," Tikaya said.

"Who's that?" Mahliki asked, drawing Amaranthe's attention back to the hovering image.

Her jaw dropped to her chest. In a clearing near Flintcrest and the Nurians, a blond-haired, black-clad man fought with four shirtless soldiers, each covered with fresh lumps and bruises, and two with blood streaming from their noses as well. Not fought, her stunned mind realized after watching for a few seconds, *sparred*. He was training with the men, taking on four at once for the challenge he required.

Maldynado made a choking sound. "The person who brought those heads in, I'll bet. But *why*? What's he doing with *them*?"

Sicarius spun, sweeping the legs out from beneath an encroaching opponent, and in that moment, that rotation of his head, Amaranthe knew. "Oh." She goggled at the glowing stone stuck to—no, *embedded in*—the flesh of his temple. "Oh, no."

CHAPTER 9

I N THE DARK TENT, SICARIUS LISTENED TO THE SOFT
exhalations of his Nurian roommates for a long time
before rising from his spot at the foot of Kor Nas's cot.
Everyone had drifted off, he was certain of it. And tonight, for
the first time since Sicarius had been in the camp, Prince Zirabo
slept in one of the cots. There'd been one set up during the prior
nights, but it had remained empty. Maybe he had a Turgonian
lover somewhere. It didn't matter. This was Sicarius's chance—
possibly his *only* chance.

He crossed to the Nurian's cot and considered his options
before acting. If he woke Kor Nas, his chance would be gone. He
wouldn't be able to explain what he was doing without thinking
of Starcrest and the letter in his pocket, one he'd written the
night before, before the practitioner woke for the morning. It'd
been hard enough keep his thoughts away from the topic during
the day. Kor Nas had sent him off to collect a few more heads,
and that'd served as a distraction. After that, he'd asked for a
practice session, ostensibly to keep his skills sharp, but in truth,
he'd needed to keep thoughts of his plan away from the surface
of his mind, from where Kor Nas kept plucking thoughts, even
when Sicarius tried to disguise them.

With few other options, he gently shook the prince's shoulder.
In the darkness, Sicarius couldn't see Zirabo's eyes open, but he
sensed it in the sudden rigidness of the body, followed by the
reaching for a dagger at his waist.

Sicarius had hoped curiosity might stay the prince's hand,
and that he might be led outside for a quick meeting, but it

seemed not. Sicarius dropped a hand across his mouth and caught the wrist before the fingers found the weapon. Before the prince could recover, Sicarius hoisted him from the cot and propelled him through the tent flap, barely stirring it despite his captive's attempts to struggle. The prince tried to yell, and some noise escaped through Sicarius's muffling fingers, but by then, they were outside, and there were other sounds to mask their quick walk away from the Nurian tent.

This close to the city, with the potential for an attack high, a full night shift remained awake with numerous soldiers patrolling the camp, the inside as well as the perimeter. Sicarius hunted about for a quiet place to take his prisoner, one where they could talk openly, but that wasn't far from the Nurian tent. From experimentation, he knew he had the freedom to walk off far enough to piss without the stone implant chiming an alarm in Kor Nas's head, but not much farther.

A lorry rested in the shadows behind the chow hall. Lanterns burned inside the tent, and a few voices and the thunks of tiles being played drifted from within, but the back of the lorry lay dark and empty. Sicarius forced his prisoner in that direction. When they reached the cargo bed, and had to climb up to enter it, the Nurian tried to tear free. He was smaller and lighter than Sicarius, without a lot of muscle on his frame, truly a diplomat and not a warrior, and it didn't take much to squash the outburst. In a few more seconds, Sicarius had him inside, pressed against a tall pile of bags of rice. There were benches along the walls, and two men might sit, facing each other to converse, but he had to convince the Nurian to talk to him first.

"I wish to speak with you, that is all," Sicarius whispered. "It's about Admiral Starcrest."

The prince didn't relax, but he did stop struggling.

"You did not seem to want him dead." Sicarius loosened his grip on the man's mouth, ready to clamp down again if anything except a quiet response came out.

He didn't get a response at all. Not surprising. The Nurian would not see him as anything other than an enemy, one that couldn't be trusted. That Kor Nas had... domesticated him would not change anything. Judging by the exchanges Sicarius had witnessed, the prince didn't consider the practitioner a close ally anyway. He'd have to keep talking, convince the man they had a common interest. Too bad none of Amaranthe's charisma had fallen into his boots the time she'd tried them on.

"I do not wish him dead either," Sicarius murmured.

The prince snorted. "Of course not. He's one of your people."

"I've killed many of my people in the last two days."

"Because Kor Nas forced you to through his artifact."

"I've killed many Turgonians in the last few years too," Sicarius said. "There are few who have ever mattered to me one way or another. Most of those who do—who *did*—are gone now."

The prince, still pressed into the rice bags, heavy iron pots hanging on racks all about his head, said nothing. Sicarius searched for something else that might draw him into a conversation. He didn't know how much time he had. As soon as Kor Nas woke up and found him gone...

"Except Starcrest?" the prince asked.

"Yes. I've only met him twice, but he was a brilliant commander in the eyes of our people. In my eyes as well," Sicarius said, suspecting he'd have to be more open with this man than he was wont to be with others if he wanted to earn his trust in such a short time. "I read all of his books as a boy and those written about him."

"Strange then that you chose to become an assassin." Coldness had crept into the prince's voice. "Enemy Chief Fox was honorable. You are Sicarius, are you not? You were Emperor Raumesys's personal assassin. You came to Nuria over twenty years ago and killed my uncle. He was my father's older brother, and he would have been Great Chief. Your emperor did not think my father, who was studying medicine at the time, would be accepted as a leader; he thought there'd be war."

Now it was Sicarius who didn't respond right away. He hadn't known he'd ever been identified by the Nurians as the

perpetrator of that assassination. Gaining the prince's trust in this matter would be harder now. Dissembling or flattery would not do; he could only be blunt and hope the Nurian respected such traits.

"As you have been sent to take advantage of our succession issues, so I was sent two decades ago." It'd been one of his early missions—he'd been only sixteen at the time—one that had involved months of travel, and it'd been the one that had finally convinced Raumesys of his capabilities and usefulness. "We do as our masters bid us to do. I was raised to be an assassin for the throne. For the first thirty years of my life, it was all I knew. Did you ever have a choice to do anything except serve your father?"

The prince shifted his weight. Sicarius took a chance and leaned away from him, letting him turn around. He still blocked the exit, standing so he could keep an eye on the prince and an eye on the camp outside, and also so he could stop his prisoner from escaping if need be. But when the Nurian sat on one of the benches, Sicarius allowed it.

"What do you want, assassin?" the prince asked. "Why risk punishment—" he waved toward Sicarius's temple, "—by dragging me from my cot?"

"Kor Nas will send me to kill Starcrest as soon as his location is determined. You know this. You were there, arguing against this act. I heard you."

"Did you." It wasn't a question. The prince rested his elbows on his knees and considered his hands. There wasn't any light nearby to judge the expression on his face.

"If I'm sent after him and cannot control my actions—" Now Sicarius was the one to wave at the artifact, "—I will kill him. He is a brilliant man and a capable fighter, but he is not my equal with a weapon."

"No," the prince whispered, still studying his hands, "I saw you practicing today."

"I would try to warn him, but I cannot leave this camp. If he were warned, I believe he could figure out a way to avoid me." Sicarius did not voice his true thoughts. He didn't know why this man wanted to protect Starcrest, but he highly doubted those feelings would transfer to betraying his people. Even if he had no fondness for Kor Nas, he must have been trained to be loyal to Nuria and to his family, much as Sicarius had once been trained to be loyal to Hollowcrest and the emperor.

The prince snorted. "I believe he could figure a way to defeat you."

Sicarius said nothing. In truth, he was pleased to see that Starcrest had admirers, even amongst his enemies, but he did not want to lead this man to suspect the depths of his plans. "He means something to you," Sicarius said by way of diversion, and also because he was curious how it could be. He judged the prince to be in his early thirties, too young to have battled against Starcrest in the Western Sea Conflict. Had he been to the Kyatt Islands at some point in his life?

"We've met," the prince said, "when I was a foolish boy. He saved my life. I had the opportunity to repay the debt not long after, but... I would still not raise a hand against him, unless given no choice."

Good. This might work out yet, if Sicarius could keep Kor Nas from discovering his thoughts. What sort of punishment might the prince receive for helping protect Starcrest? Would he be immune from his father's wrath? Or might Kor Nas retaliate by arranging some... earlier punishment? Sicarius imagined himself forced to kill the prince and the wily practitioner proclaiming that it'd been accident, that his "pet" hadn't been monitored and had found a way around the device. Indeed, the opal hadn't tried to stop him or even sent a warning stab of pain into his mind when he'd dragged Zirabo from his cot.

"Do you know where he is?" The Nurian sat up, considering him. "No, you mustn't, else Kor Nas would have dragged the information out of your head. Telepathy wasn't his primary mode of study, but he's competent enough at it. In the morning, he'll know of this meeting."

"No, I can keep it a secret. I had training from one of your wizard hunters as a boy."

Training that hadn't done much good against Kor Nas yet.

"Hm," was all Zirabo said, though he managed to convey a lot of doubt in that one syllable. "What do you want of me? If you don't have any better an idea of where he is than I, then I could no more warn him than you could."

"Your comrade is a seer."

"Yes... but, if you were trained in our ways, you should know this: a seer must have an item that belongs to the person they seek. It's like a hound following a trail after sniffing a scrap of clothing that carries the owner's scent."

"I know," Sicarius said. "I thought it might be possible..." He unsheathed his black dagger and held the weapon up to the back of the wagon, so the prince might see its dark outline against the white snow of the forest. "Starcrest gave this knife to me twenty years ago."

"That's a long time. I doubt there'd be any residue. Did he have it for many years before that?"

"No, he only handled it for a short time." Sicarius had feared nothing would come of the idea, but he'd had to try.

"May I see it?" the prince asked. "That's one of those... it's from that strange ancient technology, isn't it?"

"Yes."

"Ji Hoc may be able to See using the technology itself. Aside from that rather ill-placed... thing that landed on the north end of the lake, it's quite rare, isn't it? Would Starcrest have any of it? I understand he and his wife have studied it and were on the original mission that first discovered it."

The depth of the prince's knowledge wasn't surprising—surely, spies would have uncovered any number of truths, given twenty years—but it certainly would have flummoxed Raumesys, were he still alive. "At one point, he had a knife similar to this. I do not know if he carries it with him." As an assassin, Sicarius had had no end of uses for the blade over the years, but, for all he knew, Starcrest used it for a letter opener in his office back on Kyatt.

"May I borrow this to let him use?" the prince asked.

"Is he loyal to you? Or to Kor Nas?"

"He *better* be loyal to me."

That did not answer Sicarius's question. He stared at the prince, hoping for a more compelling affirmative.

But the Nurian only spread his palm and said, "I'll tell him to give me the information on Starcrest's whereabouts first."

A risk. Sicarius had no other choice but to take it. He placed the dagger in the prince's hand, and he also withdrew a folded note. "My warning for Starcrest."

"May I read it?" The question was asked casually, but the prince probably didn't trust Sicarius entirely yet. Why would he? Sicarius might be here on Kor Nas's behalf in some attempt to entrap him, or to distract Starcrest from the real attack.

"Yes. But it's encrypted with an old military cipher."

"I... see. Will *he* be able to read it? In time?"

Time, yes, there was that. How long until Kor Nas learned what was going on around him? Even if Sicarius could successfully hide his thoughts, could the prince? Or the seer? On the Kyatt Islands, there were legislative and social rules against telepaths delving into the minds of others, but he'd heard the Nurians were less restrained. Those who commanded the mental sciences ruled over there, and they were rarely questioned.

"He may remember the key," Sicarius said. "If not, his wife will. They presumably decrypted my last message, since they are here."

The prince accepted the folded note. "Then we better hope Starcrest is in a bunker somewhere with his wife, not out planning mayhem to trouble the troops."

* * *

Amaranthe shook her hand, trying to alleviate a writing cramp. Her notebook was jammed with hastily sketched maps, troop numbers and movements, incoming weather fronts, and everything else they'd been able to discover that she deemed worthwhile. She hoped Starcrest would have a good use for the information. In the short time they'd watched, the fighting

around the Barracks had escalated, and she'd witnessed skirmishes around the river and railroad checkpoints too. Of course, Amaranthe's mind kept drifting to Flintcrest's camp and the image of Sicarius sparring while that cursed stone glowed cheerfully in his head. She wanted to stalk straight to the Preserve and rescue him, but destroying this ship had to be the priority. Besides, she didn't know *how* she could rescue him. After they returned to the factory, she would gather the others for a planning session.

When Amaranthe lifted her head to massage a crick in her neck, she found Tikaya gazing at her. It was one of the few times the professor hadn't been riveted by the control room's myriad options.

"Are we ready?" Amaranthe asked.

"I believe I've discovered how to engage the self-immolation method."

"And?" Amaranthe didn't know if she cared for that word choice, but perhaps it would be best, leaving nothing behind to be studied by unscrupulous sorts.

"Two problems. It must be activated from here." Tikaya pointed at the floor of the control room. "And I haven't been able to determine how damaging it will be to the surrounding area."

"How much more damaging could it be than squashing an entire army fort?" Maldynado asked. He and Basilard had grown bored of standing an assiduous watch, given the lack of trouble encroaching through the locked doors, and a travel-sized Tiles game sprawled across the floor between them.

"I don't know," Tikaya said. "If there's intense heat or shrapnel or, goodness, I can only imagine how they might accomplish this feat—I gather it was usually done in outer space, not while landed on a planet—it may be destructive for miles around."

"Miles... as in the city?" Amaranthe asked.

"Possibly. At the least, those gaping civilians and would-be relic raiders wandering about the outside of the craft would be in danger. For us..."

"I can't imagine they'd require someone to die with the craft," Amaranthe said. "See if there's some sort of delay. There are lifeboats, or there should be. Unless all of them were fired when we crashed. Maybe you can check on that too. As for the rest..." She closed the journal and sat down. "I don't want to risk the city. Can we lift off and *then* immolate?"

"Let me check on those things." Tikaya returned to the images.

Amaranthe had been thinking of the professor as being in charge, as someone who saw her as nothing more than a bodyguard along to shoot things. That she'd asked for Amaranthe's opinion, and even seemed to be following her... yes, they'd been orders, surprised Amaranthe. Maybe Tikaya figured it wasn't *her* city and they weren't *her* people, so it'd be appropriate to ask for a native's advice. Or maybe she wanted to pass the blame to Amaranthe.

"Just what I need," she muttered. "More deaths on my shoulders."

Nobody was around to hear her. Mahliki, the closest person, was still manipulating the viewing image, trying to find those tunnel-boring machines or evidence of a fresh underground passage. She frowned deeply and murmured something of her own.

"What is it?" Amaranthe shook out her hand again, in case she needed to put her pen to use once more.

"I... don't know. Come look."

Amaranthe gazed up at the image. Their "bird" was providing a view from near the Emperor's Preserve again, but it was focused toward the horizon instead of downward. The eastern mountains, their white craggy peaks thrusting skyward, were... burning? She wasn't sure. Smoke smothered one of the peaks directly east of the city. It seemed to be drifting up from the front slope of the mountain.

She lifted a hand, intending to ask Mahliki to take them closer, but a brilliant explosion burst from the hillside, yellow and orange flames leaping into the air so high they would have been visible from the city by the naked eye. It might have been

audible too, even across the miles and miles of intervening farmlands. Before, there'd been a smoky haze above the area, but now huge black plumes rose, darkening the sky.

"Whose demented ancestor caused that?" Maldynado asked. "And why?"

"What's out there?" Tikaya asked.

"A pass," Maldynado said. "There's a road up into the mountains. We were there last spring. It..." He trailed off, chewing thoughtfully on the side of his mouth.

"More than a pass," Amaranthe said, guessing her thoughts matched his. "There's a hidden dam and a lake up there that supplies all the clean, fresh water to the city. Although... can you get closer with that thing?" She waved toward their floating map. "That explosion came from lower on the mountainside, I think."

"There are a lot of old mines up there," Maldynado said.

"Which would be pointless to blow up," Amaranthe said. "The city's water supply though... If they blew up the dam, they'd flood Stumps, and nobody wins there, but..." She snapped her fingers. "I bet it's the aqueduct. There are reservoirs in the city, but with a million people, we'll start to run out of water within three or four days."

"I don't understand," Mahliki said. "There's a lake right there."

"A lake we pump our sewage into," Amaranthe said. "It gets pretty diluted I think—people swim out there after all—but I've heard that if you drink much of it, you and your family can expect to enjoy some lovely bouts of cholera."

"You don't have any filtration systems in place?" Tikaya asked.

"Filtration?"

"I've read of sand filtration systems being used by some civilizations, and my people have experimented with chemicals that kill pathogens." Tikaya lifted a shoulder.

"We never needed to develop anything like that," Amaranthe said. "I'm not even sure we have the technology to do so. If it's not metallurgy or engineering..." She shrugged—those were what the empire was known for.

"But your city's vulnerable if it only has one water source," Mahliki said.

"That's why the aqueduct is *underground*," Amaranthe said. "So it's not easy for enemies to reach. And the existing maps aren't even accurate. They're deliberately misleading about where the water comes from and where the underground lines run. I can't imagine who would know to strike out there." She pointed at the billowing smoke. "My team only knows about all this because of the incident last year. Researching the snarl of lies and altered blueprints confused the spit out of us."

Basilard waved a hand to get everyone's attention, then made a single sign, the finger sweep across his throat. *Sicarius*?

Amaranthe's stomach sank into her boots. If he belonged to that Nurian practitioner, and that practitioner was working for Flintcrest... "Why?" she asked. "What would one of the candidates gain from harming the city? They should want to inherit a glorious capital city, not writhing chaos."

"There's another explosion." Mahliki nodded, not toward the mountains this time, but toward the southwest corner of the city, near the lake and the railway. "Multiple explosions."

It didn't take long for Amaranthe to figure out what the smoking cylindrical husks left behind represented. "The granaries."

"Someone's striking at your city's food supply too?" Mahliki asked.

"There's not much stored within the city itself," Amaranthe said, "not when compared to the number of people here who need to eat. Most food comes in via the rail system from the surrounding countryside and other satrapies as well, but the granaries are symbolic. This is going to cause panic."

"This may be our opportunity to destroy this craft without many people noticing." Tikaya walked over and drew a finger through the map, returning its focus to the *Behemoth*.

The crowd that had been staring at the craft, trying to figure

it out, had dissipated. Some people were gaping toward the eastern mountains, but more were leaving the field, racing back to their homes to check on their families. And to check their food and water stores, or at least that's what they'd be doing when they figured out what had happened.

"I'll take us off the ground and set the destruction mechanism," Tikaya said. "If it blows up in the air, high above the lake, it might put on a good show, but it shouldn't damage anything down here. Though I suppose there could be sizable chunks of shrapnel. I'll move us out over the farmlands farther, where the population is less dense. I think I can give us ten minutes, maybe more, to run to the nearest of those lifeboats, where we can escape and make our way back to the factory."

"Wait." Amaranthe gripped her arm. "This might not be the best time to blow up the *Behemoth*. If Flintcrest wasn't responsible for those explosions, if none of the candidates were, this could represent some new enemy to the city. Someone who's swooped in to take advantage of the chaos."

"But, who?" Maldynado asked. "The Nurians are already here with Flintcrest. Who else would attack? The Kendorians? How would they know about the secret aqueducts? The Mangdorians and the Kyattese prefer peace to war—they've never struck at us in force before. The desert city states haven't shown any ability to come together to make a cogent attack on the empire in the last hundred years, so it seems unlikely they would now."

"I don't know," Amaranthe said, "but we may need this craft to fight... whoever it ends up being."

Tikaya arched her eyebrows. "The technology must be destroyed; I thought you agreed with that."

"I did. I do. But maybe it should wait until after the city is safe. If we have some new enemy to deal with, some army we hadn't anticipated..." Amaranthe imagined a massive invasion force poised on the nearest ridge, looking down upon the city. Was it possible that in all the chaos created by the succession squabbling, armies could have slipped past the border forts?

"Here in the heart of your empire?" Tikaya asked. "I deem

that unlikely. Besides, those explosions weren't acts of armies. They were guerrilla tactics. The kind you'd expect from a small group of desperate men. I have a feeling we should finish here as quickly as possible and go talk to Rias and our group of desperate men."

Amaranthe stared at the professor. "You think... You don't think Admiral Starcrest would have orchestrated this, do you?"

"It's possible things are not as they seem. We've been away from your headquarters for nearly twenty-four hours. Let's not make up fanciful new enemies until we've checked in. Either way, this craft cannot be kept in reserve. We must win this war with our own wits and resources, if it is to be won at all."

Amaranthe hung her head. Had she been the one doubting the professor's willingness to do the right thing when it came to disposing of the powerful technology? And then she'd been so quick to think of the ship as a potential means of defending the city. She wondered if Forge's intentions had started out innocently.

"You're right. Yes, do it." Amaranthe met the eyes of her teammates. They'd all gathered their weapons and gear. "We're ready."

CHAPTER 10

AMARANTHE JOGGED DOWN THE CORRIDOR WITH TIKAYA at her side, she with her rifle and the professor with her bow. Maldynado, Basilard, and Mahliki followed on their heels. Tikaya had supposedly manipulated the cubes so they wouldn't appear to trouble them on their run to the lifeboat, but Amaranthe kept her finger on the trigger. The *Behemoth* was already airborne, hovering over farmlands on the other side of the lake. Tikaya had arranged for an hour delay before the craft "self-immolated." That should be plenty of time, but Amaranthe didn't want to risk being anywhere nearby when it happened. If they could escape in the next five minutes, that would be excellent.

"Left," Tikaya said, her breath winded from the jog, but she was keeping up admirably, especially with all the gear bouncing about on her back. "Two more turns and we'll be there."

Amaranthe surged ahead a couple of paces to round the corner first, in case danger awaited. She stuttered to a halt. It wasn't danger in the form of cubes, as she'd been ready for, but two men dragging a bulging burlap bag down the corridor. Daggers hung from their belts, but neither person was otherwise armed.

A stream of succinct and vitriolic Kyattese words streamed out of Tikaya's mouth. A heartbeat later, Amaranthe twigged to the reason for them. The idiots with the cannon might not have found a way in, but others had. If these two people were on board, hunting for treasures, ancestral spirits knew how many others had found their way into the labyrinthine passages.

One of the men released his bag and dropped into a fighting

crouch, his hand darting for his knife. "This is our claim. We found it, right and honest." He eyed Amaranthe's rifle though, and didn't draw the blade. When Maldynado and the others jogged around the corner, he stepped back.

"We're a mile in the air above the lake," Tikaya said, "and the ship will blow up soon. You'd better come with us, or you'll blow up with it." She cursed again in Kyattese and said something to her daughter.

"You lie," the second man said, not releasing his "claim" bag. "We would have felt it if this place moved. You just want our stuff."

"No," Amaranthe said, lowering her rifle and walking toward them, hand open. "It's true. I'll show you. I have a device in my pocket that's worth more than anything you have in there." She glanced at Maldynado, meeting his eyes and giving a quick nod. The men were watching her hand. She lifted it toward a jacket pocket, thrusting out her breasts for good measure as well—they'd been enough to intrigue those young soldiers on the train, after all—though she suspected the prospect of more treasure was what riveted them.

Flowing around her like water, Maldynado and Basilard jumped the two men while they were watching her. Heads were hammered into the floor, and within seconds the team had two whimpering and grumbling prisoners, their arms drawn behind their backs in painful grips that made them easy to control.

"Good work. Let's go." Amaranthe jogged into the lead again.

"Wait," Tikaya said. "There could be more people in here. I didn't think to check before activating the immolation program. I should have, I *should* have. I didn't think—I was distracted by the explosions, and— Blighted banyan sprites, there could be hundreds of people in here."

The anguish in her voice made a lump well in Amaranthe's throat. Treasure hunters or not, anyone exploring inside the *Behemoth* didn't deserve to die for greed. Emperor's warts, people might have wandered in out of sheer curiosity.

"I know," Amaranthe said. "I didn't think of it either and

should have. Can we check from the lifeboat? We'll get these two in there, and my men and I will go back out to find any others."

If they had time. Blast it, how many people would be left aboard? The *Behemoth* was a... a... behemoth. It could take hours to round everyone up. Hours they didn't have. And those cursed cubes... just because Tikaya had cleared them from *this* route didn't mean they weren't elsewhere in the ship.

The argument got Tikaya and the others moving again, though the professor must have been having similar thoughts. She murmured something under her breath, again speaking in Kyattese. It sounded more hopeful than the earlier cursing. Maybe Amaranthe's words had given her an idea.

"What about our things?" one of the prisoners gasped, as Maldynado and Basilard pushed them around a final corner.

"Can we go back for them?" his partner asked. "We lost Tedak to one of those black boxes. It melted him to *nothing*. It's not worth him dying without—"

Maldynado jostled him. "You'll all die if you don't stitch your lips together and do what these ladies say."

They'd come to a dead end. Amaranthe shifted from foot to foot while Tikaya teased symbols from the wall, big ones such as they'd seen often next to doors, but then a smaller set below, one she took the time to read. Amaranthe wished she had a pocket watch. How much of their hour had already raced past?

"Is this the right spot?" Amaranthe asked. "The lifeboat?"

"Yes." Tikaya removed her gear, opened her rucksack, and pulled out the black sphere. "But if I understand this correctly, the pod is very simple, meant to land escaping personnel safely and nothing more."

"I know that. We've already been in one."

"These interface controls are our last chance for communicating with the ship's systems." Tikaya lifted the sphere, held it before the smaller grouping of symbols, and manipulated a handful of them. A conical white beam came out of the wall, enveloping the sphere.

Amaranthe jumped back, though her brain caught up with her

reactions a second later. It was similar to the white beams from the repair devices, not to the scorching crimson rays emitted from the cleaning cubes. After a moment, Tikaya let go of the sphere. Instead of dropping, it floated within the beam.

"Bloody balls," one of their prisoners whispered. "We hadn't been able to get our gizmos to do anything. We were just picking the, uh, pretty ones."

Tikaya ignored them. An image formed in the air above the sphere, not dissimilar to the larger ones in the control room. A moment later, Amaranthe found herself staring at a familiar map of the *Behemoth's* interior, one with colored dots on different levels.

"Those are the people still onboard?" Her stomach sank. Six different groups. If the ship weren't so spread out, getting to them all might be feasible, but how long would it take to run from level to level?

"Uh," Maldynado said. "How many people can we fit into our lifeboat?"

Amaranthe grimaced at the new concern. "They're not big inside."

"We'll make it work," Tikaya said firmly, her eyes meeting Amaranthe's, as if to remind her of the promise she'd made. "We needn't stay in it for long."

"Agreed." Amaranthe pointed at the sphere. "Is there any way to take this map with us? I can't..." If she had to memorize the complex routes... she'd never be able to do it, not that many. And what if the people moved positions in the time she was trying to get to them?

"Yes, that's what I'd planned to do." Tikaya removed the sphere from the white beam. The map projected above it remained in place. She handed it to Amaranthe.

"Any chance you can add a clock to it?" Amaranthe asked. "To let us know how much longer we have?"

"Not in a language you'd understand. I'll see if it's possible to delay the countdown though."

"Good."

Basilard prodded Maldynado and pointed to one of his pockets.

"Oh, right." Maldynado fished inside of his jacket. "Will this do?" He held up a gaudy gold pocket watch crusted with emeralds and sapphires.

"To pay the team's wages for a year? Yes." Amaranthe grabbed it from him. "How much time do we have currently, Tikaya? Assuming you're not able to change the countdown."

"About fifty minutes."

Amaranthe would have preferred precision to "about," but she noted the time on the watch and only said, "Understood." If they were dealing with translating the minutes across languages, precision wasn't going to happen anyway. She pointed at Tikaya and Mahliki. "You two stay here, watch the prisoners, and figure things out, please."

The two treasure hunters eyed their proposed guards with speculation, and Amaranthe hesitated. Maybe it'd be better to leave Basilard or Maldynado and take Mahliki to hunt for the people. But Starcrest's family *had* to get out of here. Amaranthe had been sent to help them, and she wasn't going to fail. She... she'd get out too. Sicarius needed her. These thoughts were only for... just in case. Besides, she needed her men to handle the people they found, in case they put up resistance. Most of the dots were in pairs, but there were two groupings of multiple people.

She pointed at Mahliki and held the prisoners' eyes. "You two have heard of Fleet Admiral Starcrest?"

They nodded.

"This is his daughter. He's trained her from birth to defend herself and smash men who annoy her into applesauce. If you give her any trouble, she'll tear off your balls and shove them down your gullets." Not her classiest threat, but it had the desired effect. The men grew pale.

Mahliki simply smirked, and Amaranthe wondered if there might be some truth to her statement.

"Let's go," Amaranthe held up the sphere and nodded toward Maldynado and Basilard. They'd already wasted enough time.

"Wait." Tikaya pointed to Amaranthe's rifle, then picked up her bow and the jar of acid. "Trade. You may need it."

"Good point. Thanks."

Amaranthe took the bow while Basilard grabbed the jar.

"Want me to carry anything?" Maldynado asked.

"Your watch." She thrust it into his hand. "Those twenty pounds of jewels would slow me down."

"It's not *that* heavy," Maldynado said, and they ran down the corridor. "Though Sicarius did once make me tread water while holding it above my head during a swimming practice."

"I'm surprised it didn't sink you irrevocably."

It was hard to read Basilard's signs when they were racing down the corridor at their four-minute-obstacle-course speed, but Amaranthe *did* catch, *Sicarius had to pull him up.* After a glance at the hat, he added, *By the tentacles.*

"It's a real shame the ladies don't know what a comedian you are, Bas," Maldynado growled as they ran around a corner and up a ramp.

After that, they focused on covering ground and didn't speak. Amaranthe checked the map frequently, holding the sphere like spun glass as they raced about. If she dropped it and the map disappeared, she didn't like her odds of finding her way back, especially after they zigged and zagged through a series of those seven-way intersections.

They almost crashed into the first pair of relic raiders, a man and woman with stuffed rucksacks, eyes wide as they sprinted down the corridor.

Amaranthe stopped them, raising her hands rather than the bow. Fearing some of the cubes were chasing them, she didn't start with pleasantries. "What're you—"

"How do we get out of here?" the woman shouted. "The door we came in is—it looks like we're a thousand feet in the air!"

Ah. "That's because we are. Five thousand feet, I believe. Come with us. We're going to collect the others, then all of us can get off via the lifeboat."

"A flying lifeboat?"

"Something like that." Amaranthe waved to her men, implying they should encourage compliance physically if needed, but the couple was too terrified to object. They were lost and didn't know how to get off the ship. They'd follow anyone who had a plan.

Her team collected two more groups of people and a single meandering man before circling back toward Tikaya and the others. Amaranthe had expected more trouble, but everyone had encountered cubes—or something else that had scared them—and was eager to escape. Most of their packs were empty—they hadn't had time to find anything useful with which to abscond—but Amaranthe and Tikaya would have to figure out a way to divest the first group of their loot. They could worry about that later.

"We're doing well," Amaranthe whispered to Maldynado as they ran down the ramp that would lead them to the lifeboat floor again.

He tilted his watch in her direction, his face bleak. Amaranthe grimaced at the numbers. Though they'd collected people without any brawls to slow them down, the sheer miles of tunnels in the *Behemoth* were working against them.

"Let's hope Tikaya found a way to give us more ti—curse it all, stop, everyone stop!"

A black cube had floated into an intersection ahead of them. Amaranthe already had the bow in hand, but it took a second for Basilard to remove the lid jar and for her to dip in an arrow. The cube rotated toward them, its dark orifice flaring to life like a burning red eye.

Sweat dribbled down the back of her neck as she made herself take the time to ensure the arrowhead was fully coated. Shouts and bumps sounded behind her as people scrambled back. Amaranthe nocked the arrow and dropped to one knee. She forced herself to take a steadying breath before firing. This had to be perfect.

She loosed the arrow only to cringe when it bounced off the rim of the cube's hole instead of going in. A crimson beam shot out, incinerating it in the air.

Blast, Tikaya had made it look easy. Amaranthe grabbed another arrow, all too aware that they only had four more, and dipped it again. Basilard had set the jar on the floor and he was crouching, ready to sprint at the cube and distract it if he could. She didn't want him to risk himself, but with the arrow disintegrated, the beam sought a new target. Her. It tilted downward, toward her spot.

Amaranthe skittered backward, even as Basilard ran toward it. He ducked before the beam could catch him in the chest and dove under the cube. It rotated, trying to track him. Though safe from the attack, Amaranthe could no longer see the hole.

"Bring it back, Basilard," she called.

He'd disappeared around a corner, and she hated to distract him, but if she couldn't see the hole, she couldn't aim at it. Already, smoke wafted from her acid-dipped arrowhead.

"Wait, just wait," Maldynado said, somewhere behind her. Good, he was keeping track of the people, not letting them run off where they'd get lost again.

Basilard ran into view, skidding back around the corner, and ducking under the cube once more. As before, it tracked him.

Amaranthe lined up her shot, squinting through the wisps of smoke arising from her arrowhead. As soon as the orifice came into view and the angle was right...

She fired.

This time her aim proved flawless. Though she'd seen Tikaya's acid-tipped arrows drop the other cubes, Amaranthe held her breath, afraid it wouldn't work for her. Basilard crouched, ready to run again if need be. After a small eternity during which she would have glanced at the pocket watch again if Maldynado had been near, the broken cube dropped to the floor.

"It's safe," she hollered at the people huddled behind her. "Come, hurry!"

Maldynado had maneuvered to the rear of the pack to prevent escapees, and he pushed at people's backs now, urging them to comply.

A minute later, Amaranthe and Basilard burst around a familiar corner. A door now stood open in the dead end, and Mahliki and the prisoners waited inside the lifeboat. Its interior was even smaller than Amaranthe remembered. With all these people, they would be crammed in there like trout piled in the bottom of a fishing boat's hold. It couldn't be helped.

Tikaya waited outside by the controls, and the single grim shake of her head told Amaranthe everything. She hadn't been able to delay the countdown. Amaranthe wanted to demand details, to ask why someone would build something that devastating without incorporating a way to cut it off, but she didn't dare waste the time.

"Everyone inside," she hollered. "That's our way out." Amaranthe lowered her voice as people streamed past. "Tikaya, we have three more groups."

"I don't think there'll be time," Tikaya said, her eyes haunted. She surely took as much responsibility for this debacle as Amaranthe.

Not your fault, Amaranthe wanted to say, but what came out was, "I have to try. Maldynado, stay here in case anyone gets rowdy." Something that might very well happen if the people realized they were sitting inside a giant bomb with a timer ticking down.

"Got it." Maldynado tossed her his watch.

Amaranthe caught it and stuffed it into her pocket. "Bas, come on."

Sweat bathed his bald scarred head, but he didn't hesitate to race off down the corridor again with her. Amaranthe couldn't guess what she looked like, but she didn't care. She had to retrieve those people. She didn't know why it mattered so much—her ancestors knew, countless others had fallen in the last few weeks—but maybe she hoped it would offer some sort of absolution. She couldn't help those the *Behemoth* had obliterated with its landing, but these few… these she could help.

Basilard was watching the map and their progress toward the next dot. *I don't think we can make it*, he signed, though he kept running by her side.

"We will," Amaranthe panted. The grueling pace was wearing on her, too, but she charged up the next ramp, heading up three levels instead of one this time. They'd go for the farthest out party first. "I'm not... going to... die now."

I'm glad to hear you say that, Basilard signed. *I wondered. You've been reckless of late.*

Had she been? More so than usual? Maybe since the crash.

"That was... before I knew... Sicarius had... gotten himself... in trouble again. He obviously... needs my help."

Basilard smiled tightly. *Obviously.*

Thighs burning, she raced down a new corridor, and they swung into a chamber, similar to the alcove-filled one where they'd fought their first battle. Four men were gathered around one of those columns, trying to—no, they were managing to—disassemble it.

These people were better armed than the others, and one spun at their approach, a crossbow in hand. Basilard was carrying the jar of acid, but he had a pistol, too, and he fired before Amaranthe could decide if she wanted to use a precious arrow. The ball grazed the man's hand, and he dropped the crossbow with a cry of pain. His bolt flew free when the weapon hit the floor, clanking into the ceiling above Amaranthe's head.

"The ship's going to blow up in less than fifteen minutes," she blurted. "If you don't want to blow up with it, you have to come with us. We have a lifeboat."

"Don't believe her, Krageth. They just want our finds." The innards they'd dug out of the column were stuffed into a bag at their feet.

Three more crossbows came to bear.

They hadn't seen a door and didn't know they'd left the ground, nor had the cubes scared them into submission. Amaranthe shook her head. She'd spend too many precious minutes trying to convince them of their danger.

"They're your lives. If you decide you want to escape, go back that way, down the ramp three levels, then to the right. Lifeboat's waiting!"

Watching the crossbows as she went, she and Basilard ran out a door on the opposite side. A quarrel skipped off the corner wall as they ducked into the corridor.

Amaranthe swiped at her eyes, frustrated and angry at the situation.

You warned them, Basilard signed.

"Best we can do."

Time?

Balancing the sphere displaying the map and her bow, she dug out the watch and handed it to him.

Seven minutes, he signed.

Fortunately the next group, a trio of lost and scared women, joined them without more than three words exchanged. They probably would have followed anyone, promises of escape not withstanding.

We should circle back, Basilard signed.

They'd had to slow their pace so the newcomers could keep up. Even tired, Amaranthe and Basilard were faster than most people, at least over a distance, and this cursed ship was all about distances.

"Three more people to collect," Amaranthe said resolutely.

Four minutes. We still have to run back. She said this was an estimate.

"I know, Bas. I know."

He grimaced. *I know you do. I just have to… Sicarius needs your help, remember.*

She blinked sweat out of her eyes. Maybe they were tears. Both probably.

Muscles trembling, she led the way up the final ramp and into a new corridor. Voices came from ahead.

"…brilliant. This is the finest place *ever*."

"…make it our new fort."

It wasn't the extended run that made Amaranthe want to throw up. Children. They'd almost blown up children. She glanced at the watch clenched in Basilard's hands. They still might.

With the rest of their flock straggling behind, Amaranthe and Basilard raced into the room.

"Your fort is about to explode," she shouted, her words coming out in a jumble. She was panting and could barely speak. How could she explain the need for urgency?

The children, a brother and a sister no more than ten years old, whirled toward them, their eyes wide. They stumbled backward. They were going to run away.

"No," Amaranthe managed, flinging up a hand.

Basilard surged into the lead. He solved the problem of convincing them to join by dropping the jar and grabbing one of the children in each arm. Without stopping, he slung them up, one over each shoulder. He spun around, mouthing, "Go, go!" though no words came from his throat.

Amaranthe grabbed the jar and tore after Basilard, waving for everyone else to do the same.

"We just came... from that... direction," one of their followers panted.

Amaranthe had no idea what her face looked like, but when she glowered at the dissident, he raced after Basilard as if makarovi were on his heels.

They hammered down the corridors, ragged breaths echoing from the walls. Amaranthe was tempted to veer toward the chamber again, to take another try at convincing those men to leave, but Basilard was in the lead now, and he chose another route, a shorter one, back to the ramp. She didn't ask about the time. There wasn't any to spare. She knew that.

By the time they reached the lifeboat floor, the people in her group were stumbling, and Amaranthe was half pulling a straggling woman. She almost slammed into the backs of the people ahead of her when they halted.

"Go in," she panted, recognizing the corridor.

"We can't," someone yelled, "it's a dead end."

Amaranthe pushed through. Had they made a wrong turn? She lifted the map. Sweat streamed down her face, and she wiped her eyes so she could see. This *was* the spot.

Dear ancestors, what if the others hadn't waited? What if they'd left? Panting, unable to find the air she needed,

Amaranthe wondered if she was going to hyperventilate. No, you'll be immolated first, she thought.

Then the door slid up.

"Hurry, get in," Tikaya cried.

Amaranthe was pushed to the floor as the stampede of bodies surged around her. By now everybody sensed how short their time was.

A hand grabbed hers, pulling her to her feet. Maldynado. He hoisted her over his shoulder and leaped for the door. It whispered shut right behind them, almost slicing off her feet.

There should have been a great surge of acceleration as the lifeboat took off, but Amaranthe barely noticed it. Maldynado shifted his grip on her, as if he meant to put her down, but he couldn't find a place to do so. Every inch of floor space was covered, people crammed in even more tightly than she'd imagined.

"We're clear," Tikaya announced from the front of the tiny craft.

"Clear enough?" Mahliki murmured. "There might be a big shock wave."

"We'll find out. Any second. No, it should have already happened. Did we... not enter the commands correctly?"

If Amaranthe hadn't been so weary, she might have laughed. Had they spent the last hour racing around for no reason?

Then a brilliant flash lit up the interior of the lifeboat. Still hanging over Maldynado's shoulder, Amaranthe wasn't facing the front and could only assume a viewing window up there allowed the flood of light to enter. A boom sounded right after, though it wasn't as loud as she'd expected.

"That's... quite a show," Mahliki breathed.

Mutters and whimpers came from the throats of the rest of the crowd.

Maldynado finally elbowed enough space to set Amaranthe down. If not for the press of bodies holding her upright, her trembling legs would have collapsed. She twisted around, trying to see over people's heads, but had to accept that she wouldn't have a view of this final devastation. She did have a view of

a familiar man's stubbled jaw. It was the person Basilard had shot, the one with the crossbow.

He stared at her. "You weren't lying."

"No," she said, ridiculously pleased that he'd found his way out. For all she knew, he was a thief or a murderer, but she hoped the rest of his team had escaped too.

"I'm going to forgive you for shooting me," he said.

Amaranthe decided not to point out that it'd been Basilard who'd shot him. It didn't matter, and it would have taken too much effort. "Thanks," she mumbled and leaned back against Maldynado.

"I'm taking us down to the lake," Tikaya announced.

Good.

Maldynado supported Amaranthe with a comradely hand, though that didn't keep him from saying, "I hope one of you heroic types remembered to bring back my watch."

"Will some lady be affronted if she finds out you lost her gift?" Amaranthe whispered, closing her eyes. They'd have to figure out how to get rid of the lifeboat, this one and the one they'd left in the mountains. Though small and simple, they were pieces of the same technology as the *Behemoth*.

Later. That mission that could wait until everyone was safe.

"My mother, actually," Maldynado said.

"She gave it to you? Before you were disowned?" Amaranthe had been under the impression there wasn't much familial adoration between the two of them.

"No, I stole it when she kicked me out of the family. I hear she's still looking for it. I want to wear it to her funeral pyre someday."

"You Marblecrests are an odd lot," Amaranthe said.

"Oh, no argument there. I wonder if the professor would land this thing on the roof of the Imperial Barracks so we could scare my brother's troops a little."

"Let's just worry about getting back together with the others." And finding out whether Starcrest did indeed have anything to do with those explosions, or if they had some new enemy to face.

CHAPTER 11

AS DUSK GATHERED IN THE EMPEROR'S PRESERVE, Sicarius strode into Flintcrest's camp, another sack of heads slung over his shoulder. Most of the soldiers were off on assignment, and he walked the paths unchallenged. He wished he could veer down one of the side trails, letting his feet take him away from the Nurian tent instead of toward it.

Drying blood saturated his clothing and stained the skin of his hands—one of the remaining Forge founders had a Kendorian bodyguard who had sensed Sicarius's approach. The ensuing battle had been more challenging—and messy—than the others. All through it, in the back of his mind, he'd felt Kor Nas's presence, watching and enjoying the show. It was Sicarius's method to make his kills quick and efficient, but Kor Nas liked having the deaths drawn out, a vice that had been growing with each assassination. Maybe Sicarius was his first human "pet," or maybe he'd never operated in a foreign land without anyone around to enforce the rules and mores of his own culture. Power without the potential for repercussion, an insidious temptation.

On the way back to camp, Sicarius had chanced across a newspaper page caught in the wind, flapping and skidding across a frost-slick street. The headline had made him halt for a long moment.

As Intra-Army Fighting Grows Fiercer, Vicious Assassin Slays Innocent Civilians

His name was in the first sentence, followed by a list of "prominent and upstanding members of society" found dead in their abodes, their heads missing, their bodies mutilated.

Worgavic topped the list, along with several other Forge people, though the business coalition itself was never mentioned, simply the names of the "respectable and worthwhile" organizations the dead had run, the charities they'd contributed to, and the scholarship programs they'd financed.

Not surprisingly, the article was out of the *Gazette* and had been penned by the senior Lord Mancrest. The newspaper must have repaired enough of the building and machinery to return to printing its lies. Lies? Sicarius admitted the article was somewhat accurate, if biased and incomplete—it hadn't mentioned Flintcrest or his Nurian allies. How Mancrest had known *he* was the assassin responsible, Sicarius didn't know; he hadn't been seen at any of the kill sites. Perhaps the *Gazette* owner had guessed based on his reputation.

Sicarius would have stopped reading after the first paragraph, letting the newspaper continue scraping and skidding down the street, but a name lower on the page snagged his attention: Sespian.

He'd picked up the newspaper and slipped into an alley, putting his back to a wall to finish reading. It stated that new evidence had been brought forward, proving that the "dastardly and vile" Sicarius, who'd once worked in the Imperial Barracks for Emperor Raumesys, had raped Princess Marathi and that Sespian had been an illegitimate heir all along.

Sicarius had stared a long time at that passage. With Sespian dead, none of it mattered, though he would have preferred it if his son's reputation hadn't been tarnished so. With most of the Forge founders dead, this article was nothing but bitterness and spite. He couldn't help but sigh to himself though, and think of the way Sespian had been concerned about Sicarius's reputation, about improving it so he might one day work for the throne, in whatever incarnation it continued to exist. Now...

Sicarius crumpled the page and dropped it in the alley. It didn't matter, he repeated to himself. Sespian was gone, and he no longer cared who stumbled into power.

Unless, came a whisper from the back of his mind, Starcrest could find the support of the people and somehow...

He shook his head, reminded that his thoughts might be monitored.

Now, as Sicarius jogged to the Nurian tent, he clamped down on those thoughts and all others, turning his mind into a blank, unthinking place.

Before he could sweep the flap aside and enter, sounds inside told him someone was coming out. Head bent, Prince Zirabo slipped outside. He saw Sicarius, gave one quick nod, then strode past.

What did that mean? That he'd located Starcrest? Or arranged for the note to be delivered? Or did it mean that Kor Nas had snaked into his mind and learned everything of their exchange? The prince's face had been grave; that nod might have been a warning.

Again pushing the thoughts out of his mind, Sicarius stepped into the tent, the flap catching on the bulky bag. He came face-to-face with Kor Nas, who stood in the center of the carpet, wearing a fur travel cloak as well as his colorful robes. His long silver hair was tied back in a tight Nurian topknot, a style favored by men about to go into battle. A braided rope belt at his waist supported numerous pouches, some of them giving off auras to those sensitive enough to detect them.

"Starcrest has been located," Kor Nas said, his eyes shut to slits. "But this news is not unexpected to you."

Sicarius said nothing, and he tried to keep his mind from saying anything as well.

"Interestingly, I understand I have you to thank for providing the suggestion that allowed my seer to locate him." Kor Nas held out Sicarius's black dagger. "Less than an hour ago, he gave me the news."

Though Sicarius accepted the blade, and he longed to know when the seer had first learned the news and if he'd informed Prince Zirabo first, he kept his mind a blank.

"Drop those off in Flintcrest's tent." Kor Nas pointed to the bag. "Then join me on the south perimeter. We are leaving immediately."

"Later would be better," Sicarius said. "This early in the evening, Starcrest will still be awake, as will the men he brought with him. I doubt he came into the capital without troops at his back."

"We are leaving immediately," Kor Nas repeated. "Lest he have time to prepare for your visit."

The cold, hard look the practitioner gave before stalking outside said much. He knew that Sicarius had arranged a warning. Had he learned of it in time to stop it? Sicarius guessed not, otherwise there'd be no reason for haste now. He hoped the note had been delivered in time for Starcrest to receive it and read it. Had encoding it been wise? Sicarius had assumed it would be passed through the hands of lesser soldiers before finding Starcrest's desk, and he hadn't wanted others to understand it, but what if it took the wife to decode the message and she wasn't there when it arrived?

If that was the case, he could only hope that Starcrest had expected attacks from assassins all along and was prepared. Sicarius, under the influence of that stone, needn't be his craftiest, but physically, he could be no less than utterly competent. And it was without arrogance that he acknowledged his competence far surpassed most people's best days.

Compelled by the thing in his head, Sicarius delivered the heads, and strode off to join Kor Nas. As he inhaled the crisp freshness of the snow and the creosote taint of numerous camp stoves, he accepted that he was either walking to his death or to Starcrest's death. One of them would no longer live in the morning. Odd to think that all this effort was to ensure *he* was the one who wouldn't see another sunrise. So be it.

* * *

When her weary group slumped into the factory, the first thing Amaranthe noticed was that there were a lot fewer soldiers than there had been when she left. Her first concern was that the factory had been attacked or discovered, forcing men to flee, but all the rucksacks and bedrolls remained. Maybe the men

were simply off working on some assignment? Revolutionaries couldn't be expected to keep normal hours, after all.

Night had fallen again in the time it had taken her group to land the lifeboat, send the rescued relic hunters off on their own way—without any purloined gear—then reunite with Tikaya's nephew and get a ride back to the city. Tikaya and Mahliki had figured out a way to sink the lifeboat to the bottom of the lake. It wasn't the deepest trench in the ocean, but it would have to do for the time being. Basilard had stayed behind to make sure none of the would-be treasure hunters followed the team back to the factory—at least two people had eyed Tikaya's sphere as she returned it to her pack.

The lights burned in the offices on the catwalk. Amaranthe headed straight for the stairs. She already knew she wouldn't find Sicarius waiting for her in the factory—she certainly hoped not, or she'd have to watch her scalp—but she wanted to check in with the others. Not only did she need to know what Starcrest was up to, but she needed to start planning a rescue mission, to figure out how she could sneak Sicarius away from that wizard. Or, more likely, she thought with a determined set to her jaw, figure out how to kill that wizard so his trinket wouldn't control anyone any more.

"Does she always walk this fast?" Tikaya asked from a few steps behind Amaranthe.

"No," Maldynado said, "sometimes she paces about slowly and thoughtfully, such as when she's mulling over some new scheme."

"What does more rapid leg movement mean?"

"She's already thought of a scheme and is about to put it into action," Maldynado said.

"Given what I've witnessed in the last twenty-four hours, I'm guessing we should be concerned?"

"Oh, very much so."

Not bothering to comment, Amaranthe took the stairs three at a time and... halted at the top with her leg in the air. Four shirtless men were jogging toward her. Not toward *her*, she amended as she took in the sweat-drenched hair and gleaming torsos, but toward the stairs, as part of a training circuit. Her breath formed clouds in the air in front of her, so it must have taken them time to warm up enough to sweat in the cold factory.

"Hm." Amaranthe had imagined finding Admiral Starcrest hunched over a desk in the office, head bowed in some meeting with his men, not doing laps with Ridgecrest, Sespian, and Books.

"What's going on?" Maldynado asked, stopping on the landing next to her.

"Strategy planning session?" Amaranthe guessed.

"Yes," Tikaya said. She and Mahliki had stopped a couple of steps below, but were tall enough to see the men rounding the far corner and jogging onto their stretch of the catwalk. "I've learned Turgonians are vigorously active when they're pondering, not at all like our Third Century Kyattese sculptures of people sitting with their chins on their fists, gazing out at the waves, poised in eternal contemplation."

"Who's *that*?" Mahliki asked.

Guessing it was neither her father nor the sixty-something General Ridgecrest who had caught her eye, nor—sorry, Books—her fit but graying scholar, Amaranthe said, "Sespian."

He wasn't as muscular as Sicarius, but the last few weeks of adventure, along with a natural filling out as he reached the end of his teenage years, had added pounds, none of it fat. Though he might describe himself as bookish—or, bookly, as Maldynado called him—he had his father's natural athleticism and jogged along with the older men at an easy lope, speaking and gesturing, not at all winded. Though Amaranthe's tastes had come to favor a certain man with a harder, more chiseled face—and body to match—she had no doubt Sespian would attract any number of young ladies, should he take the time to place himself in their midst.

"The Sespian who was emperor up until recently?" Mahliki asked.

"Yes, that's him." Amaranthe decided not to say, and he will be again, for she had no idea how the tile bag would truly

shake out. Whatever Books was saying to Starcrest, it was accompanied by enthusiastic gestures.

Starcrest might have been listening earlier, but he lifted a hand toward Books as soon as his gaze encompassed those on the landing. His wife and daughter specifically, Amaranthe guessed, and stepped to the side when he surged ahead, long legs swallowing the remaining meters of catwalk. A wise decision, for she might have been flattened otherwise.

Starcrest enveloped Tikaya in a long fierce hug, then extended the embrace to his daughter as well. "That was quite an explosion," he said, striving for casual commentary, though his hoarse voice betrayed his feelings. Amaranthe belatedly realized how the destruction of the *Behemoth* must have appeared to those watching from the ground. From what little she'd seen, packed into the back of that lifeboat, it had been fiery, orange, and enormous in the late afternoon sky. Starcrest must have wondered if his wife had escaped the explosion. "I can only assume the trench-immersion plan was abandoned in favor of a more... complete method?"

"Mother found the immolation button," Mahliki said dryly.

Books gripped Amaranthe's arm and pulled her up onto the landing with him and Sespian. He gave her a hug, too, then stood her out at arm's length to eye her from head to toe. "We're relieved you survived and seem to be intact."

Sespian lifted an arm, as if he might offer a hug too, but he settled for gripping her shoulder.

"I'm intact *too*." Maldynado propped a fist on his hip.

"Yes, we're relieved to see you well too," Books said.

Maldynado squinted suspiciously, expecting some sarcastic addition perhaps, but Books only patted him on the back.

"Everyone in Stumps stopped fighting to stare at the sky," Sespian said. "It dwarfed the manmade explosions in the mountains and in the city."

"Yes, I was wondering if anyone here knew anything about those..."

Starcrest hadn't finished with his reunion—he'd switched to

putting a hand on his daughter's shoulder and asking her a couple of quiet questions—so Amaranthe looked to Ridgecrest instead. The one-eyed general was leaning against the railing, his arms folded across his chest, the accompanying frown making it an aggressive posture. He grunted at Amaranthe's comment, but didn't offer anything more conclusive.

"Come," Starcrest said, pulling Tikaya and Mahliki onto the landing and pointing toward an office door. "We have much to discuss."

As the group filed into the office, Books walked beside Amaranthe and whispered, "I've been telling him *all* about my treatise."

"Has he been listening?" she asked.

"In between reports from his men, yes."

One of those men thundered up the stairs behind the group, pushing Amaranthe and the others aside to reach Starcrest. "My lord!" The young man's heels clacked together and he thumped his fist to his chest.

Starcrest's hand twitched, as if he meant to return the salute, but he stopped himself, opening his palm instead. "Yes?"

Though he'd found a pair of black army fatigues that fit him, he was neither in the military any more *nor* a Turgonian subject. Nobody should have been saluting or "my lord"ing him, but none of the soldiers Amaranthe had crossed while in his presence acted as if these missing credentials mattered.

"Captain Greencrest reports that the—" for the first time he glanced at all the additional people in the room, "—the *items* have been secured in their new location."

"Thank you, Private. Let Colonel Stonecrest know."

"Yes, my lord." The private spun on his heel and rushed out.

"Items?" Ridgecrest rumbled. "He talking about the rice?"

"I assume so," Starcrest said.

Amaranthe perked. "We saw the granaries blow up. The professor suggested that might be... is that our doing? And if so, *why?*" She didn't manage to keep all of the anguish out of her voice, though she told herself to be patient and wait for an explanation.

"You saw it?" Starcrest tilted his head curiously. "From the ship?"

"We've seen a lot," Tikaya said, "and collected a great deal of data on troop positioning, movements, and... allies. Rather I should say, Corporal Lokdon did. I was searching for that—" she glanced at her daughter, "—immolation button."

Mahliki had been stealing glances at Sespian, but marshaled her attention to the conversation at her mother's look. Amaranthe shrugged off her rucksack and dug out the journal full of notes she'd made. She handed it to Starcrest.

He accepted it and waved to the chairs. "Sit. Let me get you caught up."

That "you" was more for his wife, Amaranthe sensed, but his wave did include her and Maldynado. They dragged chairs around the tables, and she ended up between Sespian and Books. Good, if Starcrest didn't answer her questions, she could interrogate them for details. If the jog was an indicator, they'd insinuated themselves into the inner circle.

"We are responsible for the explosions at the aqueducts, the granaries, the freighter docks, and two of the main railroads," Starcrest said. "It will appear to the public that food stores and water supplies have been devastated. We *did* destroy the main lines by which more food can be brought into Stumps, though the railways were attacked in such a way that repairs should not be extensive for a competent team of combat engineers. The Blue Bluff Bridge was in abysmal condition anyway and wouldn't have passed an inspection *I* led."

Amaranthe couldn't believe that in the middle of admitting to being responsible for all of this destruction, he sounded genuinely affronted at the condition of the bridge, a bridge he'd ordered blown up. Or blew up in person. What exactly had he been doing in the night and day her team had been gone?

"*Appear?*" Maldynado asked, his usual baritone on the squeaky side.

"The food in the granaries was moved overnight, before the explosions, and it is safe," Starcrest said. "The aqueducts were not, in fact, damaged, insofar as their capabilities to deliver water. We blew up the *auxiliary* line, which is widely believed to be the main and only line, and have only temporarily dammed the flow."

"How do you know that wasn't the main line?" Amaranthe remembered her thought that Sicarius, having been part of the team that had researched the underground water passages for their mission the year before, had told Flintcrest. But if Flintcrest and Sicarius had had nothing to do with all this... "That's secret information, I understand. Or..." She faced Sespian. "Did you know about it?"

"You'd be amazed at how little I *do* know—" Sespian rubbed his head, perhaps remembering his months of being drugged, "—insofar as imperial secrets go. Raumesys didn't share as much with me as you'd think. I wonder now if he somehow knew, all along, that I wasn't... Well, no, that's unlikely, or he would have killed me."

Amaranthe patted his arm, though she returned her attention to Starcrest.

"My fourth-year engineering professor at the military academy designed the current aqueduct system," he said. "I was one of his student assistants at the time and was much honored to be chosen to help. In the beginning, I assumed I'd be running calculations for him and double-checking his work. Instead, I learned quite a bit about... excavation that semester. I did, however, manage to have myself removed from the laborious assignment, inadvertently I assure you, by presuming to make a few field improvements to the Model 4L Steam Shovel. To this day, I maintain that my improvements made it more efficient. And powerful. Had the operator simply allowed me to instruct him in the changes to a few key controls... Well, it's not my fault he refused to take advice from a seventeen-year-old boy. He—"

Tikaya touched his arm. "In most circumstances, I wouldn't interrupt your enthused rambles, love, but these folks are waiting for an explanation as to why *you*, a presumably loyal imperial man despite your years in exile, are blowing up important parts of the city's infrastructure. I, too, am curious."

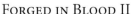

Rias cleared his throat, the faintest tinge of red brightening his cheeks. "Yes, forgive me." He leaned forward, propping his elbows on the table. "We do not have the forces to combat anyone in a straightforward confrontation, so we must use guerrilla methods. Every one of our opponents must protect the city, otherwise they'll win a poor prize should they come out on top. Each knowing that the other wants an intact capital to take over, I'm guessing they will suspect some outside invasion force is responsible for the destruction."

Amaranthe nodded. Hadn't she herself thought along those lines?

"Unless they're self-absorbed idiots, they'll recognize the need to stop these attacks. They'll either band together, to deal with this unknown enemy, or they'll attempt to solve the problems on their own. They cannot, however, afford to ignore the threat. The citizens... Thus far, most of the citizens have been hiding indoors, letting the various armies fight amongst themselves, but they'll no longer be willing to be bystanders once the food and water threat is revealed. Thus our enemies will have problems to deal with on two fronts. Our guerrilla attacks, at which we are not lingering around to address opposition, will force them to place troops at strategic points. Also, the citizens will demand a resolution sooner rather than later, giving our opponents people at their backs with whom to deal."

Sespian and Books were nodding, so they must have already heard all of this and come to accept the plan. Tikaya's frown was more dubious, but she didn't protest aloud. She might be the kind to wait until she was in private with her husband to accuse him of megalomaniacal lunacy.

No, not megalomaniacal, Amaranthe admitted. Just... shifty. If she was honest with herself, it sounded like a plan *she* would come up with. All right, it was a bit grander in scale than most of her plans, but still.

"What will we be doing while all this is going on?" she asked. "Or are all of our—*your*—troops busy with the guerrilla attacks?"

"Our troops," Starcrest said, extending a hand toward Sespian and Ridgecrest. "Many of them are busy planning further mayhem, albeit doing as little genuine damage as possible, to keep our opponents running around with blankets, trying to swat out the fires. But assassins have been striking at the Company of Lords as well as Forge operatives. I've dispatched a team to check on—"

A knocked sounded at the door.

"Come," Starcrest called.

Four natty soldiers in pressed uniforms marched into the room, their rifles gripped in front of them in perfect parade configuration. A bald man with heavy jowls, walked between them, a rumpled dressing gown sweeping about his ankles. His fur-lined boots were the only piece of clothing appropriate to the cold night. Alarming, since he couldn't have been less than eighty years old.

Amaranthe didn't recognize him, but from the way Sespian stirred in his chair, she thought she should.

"Books?" she whispered out of the side of her mouth.

"Lord Delvar Markcrest," Books replied, "one of the senior members in the Company of Lords."

"Lord Markcrest," Starcrest said. "I'm glad you could make it to—"

"*Make* it? As if I had a choice. I'll not vote for you, I don't care which one you are."

"I'm not... any of them, my lord," Starcrest said. "I learned that you and your brethren were being targeted—"

"Targeted? Seven of my colleagues are already dead," Markcrest growled. "That I know about."

"That is why we're offering refuge for those who remain. I wish you to take the first train north. I've sent word to my brother in the countryside, and he'll board you at Ravenwood Estate until the smoke clears down here." Starcrest nodded toward the soldiers. "Continue your mission, please."

"Yes, my lord." They thumped their fists to their chests and marched out.

"Ravenwood Estate?" Markcrest's forehead wrinkled, as if he were trying to dredge something from his memory. He peered more closely at Starcrest. "You aren't... are you... General Kreg Starcrest's boy?"

Starcrest blinked. It must have been a long time since someone referred to him as his father's son. "Yes, sir."

They stared at each other for a long moment, and nobody spoke. It was doubtlessly only in Amaranthe's mind that Starcrest stood taller, trying to look worthy in the older man's eyes.

"I've only recently returned from... exile," Starcrest said. "We're attempting to find a resolution to this mess that's been created. We want to work *with* the Company of Lords, not against it."

"I should hope so," Markcrest snapped, though much of his anger had faded.

"Joth," Starcrest asked Ridgecrest, "can you take him down to the cafeteria? See to his needs? Lord Markcrest, I'll come down and talk to you shortly."

Ridgecrest bowed his head and ushered their guest out.

As soon as the door shut, Amaranthe blurted, "You're kidnapping people." Everyone stared at her. "My lord," she added.

"You don't approve?" Starcrest tilted his head, his lips twitching in... was that bemusement? "This morning, at her bequest, I met the prisoner *you* instructed to be kidnapped."

"Er, yes," Amaranthe said. "I mean, no. I don't disapprove, given the desperate nature of these times, and, ah..." Erg, why was everyone still staring at her? "It's just that you're Fleet Admiral Starcrest. I wasn't expecting you to be—" she cut off before uttering "just like me" or, worse, "as crazy as I am." After all, she hadn't achieved *quite* what he had with her unorthodox problem-solving style, and he wasn't some scummy outlaw in the eyes of most of the population. Some unfairness in that, she decided. He *was* exiled—wasn't that every bit as bad as being an outlaw?—yet nobody cared.

Tikaya leaned against her husband's arm. "She expected you to play fair, love."

"Oh," Starcrest said, drawing out the syllable. "Well, I wouldn't have lived past thirty if I made a habit of doing that. How would one win a battle against superior man- and firepower if one stuck to common and acceptable wartime practices?"

"Uh." Amaranthe winced at her lack of eloquence. "I understand. But I'd thought, you being a Turgonian hero..." She stopped herself before she devolved into whining. She would not, for the sake of herself and her ancestors, stand there and sulk about how everyone considered him a hero for apparently using the same tactics that made her an outlaw. "Your tactics aren't what I expected, my lord, but I'm sure they'll get results. In fact, you seem to have your thumb on the pulse of... everything." Had they truly only been gone for twenty-four hours? He'd been *busy*. "If you don't mind, I'd like to take a few of my men and go..." She met Books's and Sespian's eyes. "Flintcrest has Sicarius. No, Flintcrest's Nurian *wizard* has Sicarius. With some kind of magical control device." She tapped her temple. "He's being forced to work for him. There are... a bunch of pikes in Flintcrest's camp with severed heads mounted on them."

Books swore under his breath. Sespian looked out the window. Starcrest... had grown hard to read again.

"Guess that explains who's assassinating the Company of Lords," Sespian murmured.

"I wouldn't be sure," Amaranthe said. "Those heads suggest Flintcrest is dismantling Forge right now. Either way, we—*I*— have to get Sicarius back. There must be a way to kill that wizard or find some other way to free him." With so many people in the room, Amaranthe didn't go into how much she owed Sicarius or how she wouldn't be able to sleep as long as she knew he was out there, being forced to carry out some sadistic bastard's whims again. Curse everything, she'd tried so hard to get him away from that, to create a less violent world for him to live in, one in which... She swallowed and made the simple argument that would ensure their help. "I'm sure none of us wants to see him in our enemies' hands. We all know what he can do."

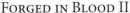

Starcrest and Tikaya exchanged looks.

Yes, they were a part of that "all."

"Maldynado," Amaranthe said, turning, but he had slipped out at some point. To find Yara? "Never mind, I'll get Akstyr. I'll need his advice. And I welcome any other advice."

"Do you intend to walk into Flintcrest's camp?" Starcrest observed her through hooded eyes, no doubt thinking this a bad plan.

"Of course not. Although..." If she allowed herself to be captured, or even pretended to be switching sides, might she not find herself in a meeting with Flintcrest and his Nurian advisers? If she could see Sicarius, talk to him for a few minutes... What, girl? If this was anything like their time together on Darkcrest Isle—she shuddered at the memory—she'd be powerless to get through to him. "No."

"Good," Starcrest said. "In case you might change your mind, I'll point out that my presence in the city isn't widely known yet—with luck, none of those vying for the throne have learned about it—and we have an advantage as long as that remains so. Though I don't know Flintcrest, Marblecrest, or Heroncrest well, it's possible they've read my work."

Possible? Amaranthe snorted. Try likely.

"They may know enough of me to suspect that I'm behind the explosions. It'll be better for our plans if they believe they have to defend against an outside threat to the empire."

"Yes, I understand," Amaranthe said. "I have to figure out a way to get to Sicarius, to his *keeper* though. I'll ask Akstyr if there's any way we can sever the link, but I'm guessing the wizard is the only one who can free Sicarius. Either voluntarily or not." She let the statement hang in the air, figuring they'd know what she meant.

"A likely assessment," Tikaya said. "Only those with a great deal of training can resist mental intrusions from strong telepaths or devices crafted by telepath Makers."

Amaranthe winced, remembering how easily Retta had gotten through her own defenses with that tool. Tikaya was grimacing as well. Sharing a memory of a similar experience?

"Does anyone have ideas on how I can reach the wizard without having to go through Sicarius?" Amaranthe asked. "I'm assuming he's being used as bodyguard as well as assassin. Not unlike a soul construct." Maybe that was what had happened. Sicarius had gotten rid of the wizard's soul construct, then been turned into the replacement.

"Let me think about it and look over the data you brought." Starcrest lifted the journal; he hadn't had time to more than glance at the first page yet. "I'd appreciate it if you didn't go on a mission to save him without letting me know first."

"I won't, my lord." She *would* gather her people to discuss this. She thought about asking Starcrest if he truly meant to think about it or if he was too busy juggling all those others balls. It would seem rude though, or demanding. She ought to be able to come up with something anyway. Sicarius was her prob— no, just hers. "Sespian, Books, do you want to help, or...?"

Maybe she shouldn't have asked. They were helping Starcrest, and they'd probably find that nobler work than worrying about Sicarius.

"I'll help," Sespian said, surprising her. He pushed away from the chair to join her at the door.

Books's lips flattened, but he pushed away from the table too.

"You can stay," Amaranthe told him. "I'll let you know if we need your help."

He continued to stand. "You may need my input during the planning stages, to keep from coming up with something... imprudent."

Amaranthe managed a smile. "When have you ever kept me from imprudence before?"

"I keep hoping there'll be a first time."

Hand on the door, Amaranthe meant to walk out, but a knock on the other side surprised her. She stepped away to let in a nervous private with an arrow clenched in his hands. A piece of paper was tied around the shaft.

"Sir, ma'am," the private murmured, not looking up as he ducked his head toward people. "Uhm, my lord, Starcrest? I'm

sorry to bother you, but I couldn't find my LT, and I thought this might be important."

"What is it, Private?" Starcrest held out his hand.

"I don't know, my lord, but it has your name on it."

"An arrow with your name on it?" Tikaya asked. "That's distressing."

Starcrest grunted and accepted the shaft. The private hadn't dared unravel the note, but STARCREST was indeed written across the visible side, the name in block letters. Starcrest held it up to his wife, his brows lifting slightly. Tikaya considered it through slitted eyes, then shook her head.

"Nothing Made about it, no taint."

Amaranthe hadn't realized Tikaya had personal experience with the Science, but supposed it wasn't uncommon on the Kyatt Islands, hence why Akstyr wanted to move there.

"Where'd you get this, Private?" Starcrest asked as he unfastened the note.

"The side of the building, my lord. Someone fired it toward us from several rooftops away. We, my corporal, I mean, sent men off to try and catch the archer, but I don't think they did. I figured I'd rush this inside right away in case it's important."

"You did well. Thank you, Private."

The soldier took this as a dismissal and scurried out the door.

Starcrest unrolled the note and handed it to his wife. "It's encrypted."

Amaranthe sucked in a breath. "Like the letter from Sicarius?"

"Maybe," Starcrest said. "There's a line of Nurian at the bottom though."

"What's it say?" Though they hadn't invited her to, Amaranthe inched around to their side of the table. She remembered the block letters used to address the first letter to Starcrest, and these looked the same. But why would Sicarius have added Nurian? Unless the wizard had. What if he'd caught Sicarius trying to pen a note? Or—a queasy surge flooded her stomach— what if they'd been working together to write it? It could be a trap. "Would your awareness of the Science allow you to sense if it'd been poisoned?" she found herself asking.

Tikaya gave her a sharp look. "No."

Starcrest grew grimmer, but all he said was, "We've already touched it. What's it say?"

"It's the same code as was used on the letter he wrote to you," Tikaya said.

No longer inching, Amaranthe came to stand at her shoulder. The message was gibberish to her eye. She bounced on her toes, waiting for a translation. Why was Sicarius sending letters to Starcrest instead of *her*?

"He explains that a Nurian practitioner named Kor Nas has captured him," Tikaya said.

Starcrest's gaze shifted upward thoughtfully. "I've heard the name. He's one of their more powerful battle mages and Makers."

"A telepath?" Tikaya waved the letter.

"Meaning does he know that was written?" Starcrest asked. "Probably. We'd better hurry."

"He says he was injured when trapping the soul construct and searching for Corporal Lokdon after the *Behemoth* crashed. He saw where the ship landed and knows who and how many died."

Amaranthe cringed. He'd think Sespian was dead. And Maldynado and Basilard as well. *She* had.

"And he saw Lokdon's body," Tikaya said.

"Pardon?" Amaranthe asked.

Tikaya's finger ran across the line of gibberish, rechecking the translation. "That's what it says. Kor Nas embedded some device in his head to control him, and he's been working as the man's assassin. He can't disobey. Kor Nas has learned—" Tikaya swallowed and gripped her husband's arm. "He's learned you're in the city. He doesn't know where yet, but he intends to send Sicarius to kill you, a tactical move for Flintcrest's army, but more importantly it'd be an honor for this Kor Nas to dump your head at his Great Chief's feet."

Starcrest ran a hand over his hair. "It seems the years and the gray haven't diminished my head's value."

"Sicarius writes to expect him soon." Tikaya jerked her hand downward, the paper crinkling in her fingers. "I knew you couldn't trust—Akahe spit on that blond monster."

"It's not his fault," Amaranthe said. "He's warning you, so you can do something. Sir, my lord," she said, fumbling the honorifics but not caring, "you have to know he idolized you growing up. His life was hard and he had no freedoms, but I know he read your work and wished..."

Starcrest lifted a hand. "I understand. And he's done me a service in warning me, though he may have given away my position as well. If Kor Nas has been in his thoughts, or in the thoughts of the one who arranged to have this delivered, he'll know about this factory. He could come tonight. I wonder who it was that helped him deliver this, and why. Maybe it's a trap. Or even a trap within a trap."

"What's the line in Nurian say?" Amaranthe asked.

"I have noticed that Kor Nas grows intensely inwardly focused when his pet makes his kills. He enjoys the show."

His pet? "Sicarius knows Nurian, but that's nothing he would have written," Amaranthe said.

"No, it must have been an addition from the messenger. It'd be helpful to be able to trust it, but—"

"Wait." Tikaya's grip tightened on his arm. "We saw Prince Zirabo. He's there in Flintcrest's camp."

"Ah? That explains much."

"Not to me," Amaranthe said.

"That's one of the Nurian Great Chief's younger children, isn't it?" Books asked from the doorway.

"Yes, it is." Sespian scratched his head.

Good, Amaranthe wasn't the only one perplexed by receiving assistance from the son of the enemy ruler.

"We saved each other's lives once," Starcrest said. "Long ago. I'm certain he wouldn't betray his father or his people on my behalf, but this small favor?" Starcrest took the letter from his wife's hand and smoothed it onto the table. "This makes sense. I don't think it's a trap."

"Trap or not, love, that assassin is coming to kill you."

CHAPTER 12

F ROM A ROOFTOP A BLOCK AWAY, SICARIUS STARED AT the familiar outline of the molasses factory, its high brick walls and flat roof, the pair of massive cylindrical holding tanks occupying a third of the lot. Had he known *this* was Starcrest's hideout, he could have sent a note days ago. How had he found it? If Sespian, Maldynado, and Basilard had died at Fort Urgot, and Amaranthe, Books, and Akstyr had been killed in the fighting within the *Behemoth*, that didn't leave any of the original team members who might have acted as a guide. Yara? Had she somehow chanced upon Starcrest? Sicarius reminded himself that he'd only seen Amaranthe's body. Perhaps Books and Akstyr had escaped the crash and met up with Starcrest when the admiral was coming to investigate it. Yes, that made sense. Countless people, some curious and some opportunistic, would have visited that site, however gory it'd been. And Starcrest would have been troubled by, if not outright horrified at, the reappearance of that alien technology.

"We may be too late," Kor Nas said from a meter away. They stood, their backs to the smokestacks of their own building, a refinery still filled with busy employees, as they studied the molasses factory. "It's empty."

"You can sense this?" Sicarius lowered a spyglass. Though there wasn't any smoke coming from the factory's stacks, that might be intentional. When Amaranthe had been leading, the team hadn't laid fires in any of the furnaces for warmth and had used only personal lanterns for lighting. They had set a guard though, and Sicarius would have expected Starcrest

to do the same. He didn't spot anyone standing on the roof. Copious footprints trampled the snow on the sidewalks around the factory, and drifts had been cleared from the doors, but that might have happened at any point in the last few days.

"I do. There is no one inside." Ice frosted the practitioner's voice. "Starcrest and his men must have received your warning and moved on."

Before Sicarius could decide if he wanted to respond to the statement, a blast of pain dropped him to his knees. It was as if a cannonball had struck the side of his head, blowing half of it away. Unprepared, it took him a moment to erect his mental barriers, to push aside the pain and bring his rational mind back to bear before his attack-or-flee instincts could take over. Teeth gritted, he staggered back to his feet. The pain hadn't lessened, but he dealt with it. He forced his breathing to return to normal, his heartbeat to slow, and he faced his attacker.

Though he had one hand stretched out toward Sicarius, Kor Nas was barely paying attention to him. His gaze remained on the factory.

He's distracted, Sicarius thought. Attack now!

He bunched his muscles to spring, but Kor Nas dropped his arm, and the pain vanished so quickly it startled Sicarius.

"Wait," Kor Nas said, "there's one person in there."

"Starcrest?" Sicarius was still of a mind to spring, to attack, but when Kor Nas turned his gaze toward him, he felt the subtle presence of the opal again, soothing his muscles, not allowing him to prepare an attack, not at his good master.

Sicarius wanted to let his lips peel back in a snarl of rage— even that seemed too unsuitable a reaction to that much pain— but he found his mask again. Interesting, a detached part of his mind decided, that when the stone had been inflicting pain upon him, some of that control it had over his physical body had faded. Could he use that somehow?

"I cannot tell," Kor Nas finally said. "Seeing was not my field of study. Is it possible he's already laid a trap?"

Yes, Sicarius thought. "We'll find out."

Kor Nas considered him for a long moment. "You go find out."

"You're staying here?" Sicarius waved at the paraphernalia on the practitioner's belt. "Didn't you come for a fight?"

"I came to see Starcrest killed and his head removed. As a practitioner who has survived three wars, I've learned to use tools to handle such things whenever possible." He extended a hand toward Sicarius.

"I cannot act as your bodyguard if we are separated," Sicarius said and tried to keep himself from thinking the follow-up, and you cannot fall into Starcrest's trap if you're not there with me when he springs it.

"A risk I'm prepared to take." The slight smile that curved Kor Nas's lips said all too much, that he knew Sicarius's thoughts.

Sicarius gazed again toward the dark factory. He'd hoped his scheme might result in the practitioner's death as well as his own, thus insuring Starcrest's safety, at least from the Nurians who so dearly wanted him dead, but his own death would have to be reward enough. A release from a captor who enjoyed living vicariously through his assassinations. He'd worked among those types of men for too long. He didn't know when he'd gone from feeling apathy toward the duties they demanded of him to developing a distaste, but sometime in his last year, walking at Amaranthe's side, it had happened. He wished they'd both lived long enough for him to tell her that.

"Go," Kor Nas said. "He's already had enough time to prepare. Don't give him more."

"I understand," Sicarius said, not of his own accord, and his legs carried him to the side of the building. He climbed over the edge and descended into the darkening night.

* * *

Amaranthe walked through the dark factory, her lantern the only light. With the hundreds of soldiers about, the place had felt crowded and cramped. Now only their gear remained, most of it stacked out of the way near the walls, and she alone occupied

the cavernous building. It was impressive how quickly an army could decamp if given the order. She didn't know where Starcrest had moved them, but it didn't matter. The only thing she had to worry about that night was delaying Sicarius so the rest of the team could search the surrounding area and deal with the wizard. Some of Ridgecrest's stealthiest scouts had been sent to Flintcrest's camp in case Kor Nas remained there, observing the planned assassination from afar. If he came in at Sicarius's side, the task was to try and part them somehow, long enough to strike at the Nurian's back. Either way, it was her job to distract Sicarius.

When they'd been discussing the note, Starcrest had originally placed himself in this role, but Amaranthe had pointed out that he, as the target, would be swiftly dispatched, perhaps without ever seeing the dagger coming. But she—seeing her *alive*—ought to muddle Sicarius's clarity of purpose. Oh, it was possible the wizard would simply order him to kill her as soon as he spotted her, but she thought he'd fight it and that she'd have more time. Time in which she could... what? She hadn't figured that out yet. And she didn't know how much longer she had to plan.

She walked along the catwalks, pausing here and there to lean over a railing with her lantern and consider a vat or piece of machinery or some series of pipes snaking from the creation area to the holding tanks outside. Though she hoped Sicarius would fall to his knees and fight off any order to kill her, she couldn't bet on it. Not after Darkcrest Isle. When she'd reluctantly spoken of that event to the others, Tikaya had pointed out that a living practitioner in the prime of his powers would be even harder to resist. So she needed to lay a trap for Sicarius, one that would delay him or separate him from the wizard.

Near the back of the factory, a row of grating traversed the cement floor, running from the vats to a larger square of grating in the corner.

"Must drain into the sewer system," she murmured, "or maybe straight into the lake." Amaranthe didn't know much

about how molasses was made, but figured there'd be a food-grade equivalent of slag, useless liquid or pulp that wasn't employed in the final product.

She jogged down to the floor to investigate the drains further.

A soft bang sounded somewhere above her.

Amaranthe jumped into the shadows beneath the stairs, putting her back to a wall. Ears straining, she listened for footsteps or a repeat of the noise.

Anxiety dampened her palms and quickened her heart. For all her calculating analysis of what Sicarius might and might not do, she couldn't manage to push aside the knowledge that the most deadly assassin she'd ever heard of was now working for the other side, and he was coming to this building with the intent to kill. Kor Nas had no reason to spare her, and somehow she doubted that the Nurian would think kindly toward her because she meant something to Sicarius. Or *had* meant something when Sicarius had been... himself. What would he be like now, under the influence of the wizard's magic? Would he possess his memories? His feelings?

"He must," she whispered, for he'd thought to warn Starcrest.

Or had he? Though Starcrest thought that Nurian prince might be on his side, how could he be certain? This could all be a trap, the other side trying to trap Starcrest even as her team tried to trap the wizard.

The bang sounded again, and she flinched.

"Stop it," she told herself. "It's the wind batting against some shutter or loose tile on the roof." Hadn't Basilard mentioned something about a warm front blowing in?

Besides, if she could rely on nothing else, she could be certain Sicarius wouldn't make any noise when he entered.

Her thoughts so fortified, Amaranthe jogged to the drain system. She reached the three-foot-wide line and pried up one of the grates, revealing a shallow channel that stunk of... She crinkled her nose. She didn't know what to call it. Could sugar turn into mold? If so, it'd probably smell like that, though this had a richer, earthier scent. Many things had probably been funneled down there over the years.

Amaranthe lowered the grate. She might trap a cat in the shallow channel, but not a man. She followed it to the larger square in the corner, one about six feet by six feet wide. Much deeper than the channel, its bottom wasn't visible to her light. She fished out a tenth ranmya coin and dropped it. The copper fell about ten feet before clanging, then bouncing a few times, the echoes suggesting it'd slipped into a drain. Amaranthe winced at the chain of noises, alarmingly loud in the silent factory.

When she was peeking around to make sure nobody had heard and was rushing out of the darkness, her gaze caught on one of the tall upper windows. A spider web of cracks stretched out from a large hole in the bottom pane. A hole large enough to crawl through? She wasn't sure. She also wasn't sure if it'd been there all along—the abandoned factory wasn't in the best state of repair—or if it might be a new hole, such as the sort a person who romped about on rooftops and entered through windows might make. Was it her imagination that she could feel the draft whistling through the gap, its icy fingers teasing her flesh?

Yes, she decided, and stop imagining. There was a trap to be laid.

Amaranthe found the latch for the grate. She had to drop into a crouch and lift with her whole body to raise the wrought iron lattice. Expecting a noisy groan of rusty hinges, she said a silent thank you to whatever janitor had kept them well greased when they opened with a soft whisper.

Too bad the grate lifted up instead of falling downward. She'd had a vague notion of tricking Sicarius into falling into it, but it'd be a rather obvious trap if the huge grate were leaning against the wall behind it, waiting to be dropped shut. Besides, how would she have gotten him to fall in? Throw a carpet over it and stand on the other side? That only worked in the old fables and to animals with the brightness of inebriated sloths.

A cold draft whispered across the back of her neck, sending a shiver down her spine. She lifted her head, eyeing that window again. Maybe the hole *was* new. Or maybe her senses were

telling her something. That she wasn't alone in the building any more.

She stood, ready to abandon her feeble trap idea for something else when a new idea popped into her mind. If delaying him was her main goal, and the way to do that was to keep him busy...

Amaranthe prodded her fingers into the fastening mechanism for the grate. There was a hole where one could fasten a padlock.

"Great, just need a padlock," she whispered and nibbled on the edge of her nail, thinking.

She'd seen one somewhere around the building, hadn't she? On a storage shed outside, yes, but that one was locked. She had a feeling she didn't have time to pick locks.

Oh, there was an open one in her office, hanging on the big metal locker that had housed that horrible frilly dress she'd borrowed. As if something like that needed to be secured. The lock had been left open though. Even as the sequence of thoughts ran through her head, her feet were moving. She raced toward the stairs, running on her toes, trying to keep her steps soft in case her senses were correct and she wasn't alone.

Taking the steps three at a time, she reached the office, rushed inside, and grabbed the padlock. It was still open. She had no idea where the key was, but that didn't matter. She wasn't the one who was going to have to unlock it.

She lunged back through the doorway and spun toward the steps, but halted and, acting on instincts, cut out her lantern.

Blackness swallowed the factory.

She struggled to still her breathing so that its noise wouldn't keep her from hearing what was happening around her—and also so that its noise didn't lead someone straight to her. The light had already betrayed her, but she set the lantern down and backed away. He'd expect her to go down the stairs. She tiptoed in the other direction, into the maze of catwalks overlooking the factory floor.

Again, she wasn't certain her imagination wasn't playing tricks on her, but she thought she'd caught a shadow moving down there, near the wall with all the rucksacks and bedrolls. It had been out of the corner of her eye, and when she'd turned her head to look full-on, it was gone. That was more of a warning than most people got when dealing with Sicarius though, and she'd be a fool to ignore it.

Thankful for the railing, she groped her way along the catwalk, choosing a route that would take her toward that grate. Wind gusted through the broken window, and the night sky and the dark silhouette of the building next door were visible through it. She didn't think the wan illumination would be enough to make her outline visible to someone on the floor below, but she couldn't be certain.

Once she reached the last section of railing, the closest she could get to the grate via the catwalks, she paused to listen. She doubted she could drop down without making a noise. If he didn't know where she was already, he would soon. Did he know yet that it was she and not Starcrest? Did it matter? Did he have that soulless black knife out, ready to cut the first throat he came across?

Amaranthe climbed over the railing and crouched on the other side, her toes balanced on the edge of the catwalk, her arm hooked around the lower bar. Eyes straining, she tried to see into the inky darkness below. She should have put out that lantern far earlier so her vision would have had more time to adjust.

If he *was* down there, he'd have no trouble jumping up and grabbing her if she didn't let go. With that encouraging thought, she lowered herself until only her fingers gripped the edge of the catwalk, then dropped the six or eight feet left to the floor.

She landed on hard cement. Without hesitating, she ran the last few meters to the drain hole, skirted the square blob on the floor—the hole was darker than the surrounding cement so she could make out *that* at least, and patted in the air by the wall. She frowned when her fingers didn't brush against anything. The grate *should* have been leaning against the wall where she'd left it.

An ominous sinking sensation came over her. Swallowing, she crouched and patted the top of the hole. Cold wrought iron met her probing fingers.

She hadn't shut it, and it hadn't fallen shut—there was no way the window drafts were enough to cause that, nor could it have happened without her hearing a resounding clang. If she'd wanted proof that her mind wasn't tricking her and that she wasn't alone... she had it.

Amaranthe eased the hatch open again, high enough that she would be able to slip through the gap. She clenched the padlock between her teeth, the metallic taste against her tongue reminding her unpleasantly of blood.

The plan was to secure herself inside the pit, forcing Sicarius to pick the lock from an awkward angle—she even imagined herself being audacious and knocking the picks out of his hand from beneath the safety of the grate—or find another way past the iron bars. If she was lucky, he might not have his lock picking set with him.

Poised to slip over the edge, she paused. What if he'd somehow guessed her intent and waited down there right now? Her death would be swift if she flung herself into his grip.

No, how could he have guessed such a suicidal plan? Who would lock themselves into a tiny space with an assassin stalking about? Anyone else would flee the building. Except she couldn't do that. She had to keep him busy.

Hoping her logic proved sound, she slipped over the edge, letting the grate fall most of the way shut. Her feet didn't come anywhere close to touching the bottom, so she hung there by her fingers, the weight of the iron on top of them. She shifted her grip until she hung from a bar and the grate was completely shut.

Letting go with one hand, Amaranthe pulled the padlock out of her mouth. With all of her weight dangling from those fingers, her shoulder cried out for her to hurry. She reached up, trying to hook the shackle into the latch hole, but it was a hard target to find from her awkward position. She tried to find purchase on the wall with her feet, but her boots slipped. There were no footholds. Whatever sludge came down this drain, it'd long since dried up, and the grimy residue was slick and frozen. Her fingers, still wrapped around the grating, slipped a few millimeters. A few more millimeters, and she'd drop, just like her coin.

The light level changed above, and her already rapid heartbeat jumped into triple-time. It wasn't bright enough to suggest a lantern, but some faint variation had occurred up there, beyond the grate.

Struggling for the calm precision she needed, Amaranthe stretched up again. Her fingers gave way in the same second that the shank threaded the hole.

An involuntary gasp escaped her lips as her top arm dropped, leaving all the weight hanging from her other hand, from the precarious grip she had on the lock. Fearing that noise had betrayed her position, she gave up on caution. Shoulders burning, she gritted her teeth and flung her free arm up, catching the grate. From there, she was able to find the leverage to push the shank into the lock. A soft click sounded as it caught.

Overhead, a boot came to rest an inch from her fingers.

She'd known he was up there, but it startled her nonetheless, and she let go, as if he might stab down with his dagger should she move too slowly. Her other hand slipped off the lock at the same time. She skidded down the wall and, unable to judge the distance in the inky blackness, hit hard on her heels. Pain lanced up both ankles, but she'd barely registered it before they were sliding out from beneath her. Her butt struck next, followed by her back and shoulders. Not only was the ground icy and slick, but it sloped downward. She skidded several feet before coming to a stop on her backside with her knees scrunched up to her chin.

High above, a second boot had joined the first. He must not fear that she had a weapon with which to shoot him. Or did he know it was she and that she wouldn't hurt him, no matter what the wizard commanded him to do?

Of *course* he knows it's you, she snarled to herself, he can identify you from thirty paces by the shampoo you use.

The boots shifted. For some reason, she could see well enough to know he had gone from standing to crouching. The light was so faint as to be barely distinguishable, but it was more than the pitch darkness that had surrounded the factory earlier. Or was it that she'd simply gone into a deeper level of darkness and it seemed light up there in comparison?

That sounded logical, and she might have believed it, but his face came into view with the crouch. He wore a black knit cap, but a faint glow seeped through the fabric at his temple.

Oh. Right. The stone.

"You are alive," Sicarius said.

His tone was flat and emotionless—that lack of any sort of feeling shouldn't have surprised her, but it dug into her heart like a dagger nonetheless. He knelt at the edge, most of his body out of sight, but his hands slipped through the grate to check the latch.

Amaranthe needed to get him talking, to slow him down from... whatever it was he intended to do to her. "Yes, I'm alive. I'd like to think you have an interest in keeping me that way."

He didn't reply. Not promising.

"I've been wondering where you've been for *days*." She didn't have to feign the anguish in her voice. "The last I heard you'd gone after that soul construct. Maldynado said—"

His hands froze. "Who?"

"Maldynado," Amaranthe said. "Tall fellow. Broad shoulders, handsome face. Ridiculous hat. His current one has tentacles sticking out in all directions. You couldn't miss it, even at a distance." She regretted her flippancy immediately. Of course, he must have thought Maldynado had been killed along with everyone else in Fort Urgot. She had, too, until he, Basilard, and Sespian had showed up at the factory. Oh, she realized with the certainty of a gut punch, Sicarius would have thought Sespian dead too.

Dear ancestors. She dropped her face into her hand. Had he thought *everyone* was dead? That he was the lone survivor? That might explain how he'd stumbled into this wizard's clutches. He might have been grieving or stunned or running around heedless of his safety, in some crazed vengeful state.

"Sespian is alive," she said, then wondered if she should have. Did the wizard hear everything he heard, know everything he knew?

Sicarius's hands hadn't started moving again. That was good, anyway. As long as he was here, he wasn't serving as bodyguard for the Nurian. She felt certain he had come alone to the factory—surely someone less stealthy and less comfortable with moving around in the dark would have insisted on a light or made some noise.

"Where is Admiral Starcrest?" Sicarius asked. There'd been a long gap between her statement and his next words, and she imagined some conversation going on between him and the wizard. Or perhaps some battle of wills. Maybe Sicarius had given in before because he'd had nothing to live for, but might he fight harder now that he knew his son was alive?

"I have no idea," Amaranthe said.

"You will tell me." Sicarius's voice was icier than the frozen sludge pressing against her back.

She swallowed, thinking of Pike and imagining... She squinted her eyes shut. No, she didn't want to imagine something like that. Not with Sicarius holding the knife. He was her best friend, curse it, and... more. The idea of being tortured by the man she loved, it was too horrible to dwell upon.

She didn't have the exact information he wanted anyway. They'd decided it would be best that she not know, in case the team couldn't get to the wizard in time.

Time. Sicarius's fingers were probing the latch again, feeling around the lock. He knelt back. Pulling out his picks, she wagered.

Amaranthe patted around, looking for a stone or something she could throw. She had a knife, but she didn't want to hurt him. That was why she hadn't brought a pistol. But she needed a way to keep him from thwarting that lock. Once he opened that grate, he'd jump down, and his fingers would be around her neck faster than she could duck or dodge, and there'd be nothing she could do about it. On Darkcrest Isle, there'd at least

been a hope of escaping, but where could she go from here?

Wherever the sewage goes, she admitted. An unappealing thought, but if there were a large enough pipe or duct...

Sicarius's hands came into view again. It was too dark to see any tools in his fingers, but she could hear the soft scrapes of metal on metal. Applying those tools through a grate wouldn't be easy, but she had no delusion of that simple padlock defeating him for long.

Amaranthe shifted about, patting beneath her, trying to find the hole through which sludge could escape. Given the sticky gooey nature of the residue, it couldn't be a small easily clogged drain... right?

She chanced across an egg-sized stone, or chunk of some hardened residue perhaps, on a ledge beneath her. While she wouldn't fling knives at Sicarius, a rock that might cause him to drop one of those tools? Absolutely. Knowing she wouldn't find many projectiles down there, she shifted around and lined up the throw carefully. Sicarius would hear her, she had no doubt, but doubted even his eyes could pierce the darkness at the bottom of her pit.

Trying not to make noise and give away her intent, Amaranthe hurled the chunk. Her aim proved accurate, and it should have smashed against the lock or his fingers, but he anticipated it somehow and caught the rock without dropping any of his tools.

"I prefer dealing with soul constructs to you," Amaranthe muttered. "At least those things are dumb enough to hurl themselves out windows. I'm fairly certain they're not well trained in lock-picking techniques either." Though the one she'd dealt with might have been strong enough to tear the grate off the hinges.

Sicarius set the stone on the floor beside him—how unsporting of him not to toss it back down so she could try again—and returned to work. Since her commentary wasn't distracting him, she went back to groping around for that drain.

Ah, there. The ledge covered a vertical hole about a foot in diameter, maybe a foot and a half, but narrow enough that her guts clenched at the idea of squirming into it. There weren't any bars blocking the opening—no excuses not to shift her body around and attempt to crawl inside. Except that she might get stuck. Her breasts and hips weren't huge by feminine standards, but she gauged that they'd get in the way for this task, or that there'd at least be a lot of uncomfortable squishing. And what if the drain narrowed before it reached the lake or sewer or wherever the sludge dumped? What if there were bars or a grate at the other end? If she were stuck, there'd be no way to turn around. Would she even be able to back out the way she'd come?

A soft click came from above. Curse his nimble-fingered ancestors, he'd already thwarted the lock.

Amaranthe had to contort herself into something approaching a U to lever her body under the ledge and into the hole, but, motivated by the knowledge that Sicarius's master wanted her tortured for information, she found the agility to do so. Hands leading, she scrabbled at walls bathed in variegated lumps of mold and less identifiable grime. If not for the winter temperatures outside, the clumps might have torn off when she gripped them, but they were frozen to the sides, hanging on with the tenacity of warts, and she used them for handholds to pull her body fully into the hole.

To say it was a tight fit would have been a supreme understatement. The lumpy walls scraped at her hips, and she couldn't bring her knees up to use her lower body to propel herself along. Her movement relied fully on her arms, and her shoulders bumped against the walls too, limiting her upper body's effectiveness. She couldn't lift her head without cracking it on the top, nor could she glance over her shoulder to check behind her. The air was close and stale, the scent of some animal's scat lingering around her.

The faintest of squeaks sounded—the oiled hinges of the grate opening. Amaranthe pulled herself along faster.

Something brushed the sole of her boot. She yanked her leg away from the touch, banging her knee on the wall. She pulled herself along with her hands, scooting as quickly as she could.

Sicarius. Unless there were rats down there, that had been he, reaching his hand in after her.

"Like there's room for rats," she muttered.

As she clawed her way deeper into the drain—she couldn't see any light ahead, no promise that an end awaited her—she wondered if Sicarius would be able to follow her. His extra six inches of height would make it harder for him to lever himself around the ledge and into the hole, and his shoulders were broader than hers, but his hips were narrower, and hips were the main thing giving her trouble.

She kept pulling herself along, though she tried to listen over the sound of her own breaths and of her clothing scraping and tearing against the frozen sludge lining the walls.

If he *did* succeed in slipping inside, and if he caught up with her, would he be able to kill her from back there? Crawl up as close as he could and drive his dagger into her femoral artery, so that she'd bleed to death? He wouldn't get his information about Starcrest then. No, he'd probably have the strength to drag her out of the drain backwards, with her fingernails snapping off as she tried to retain a hold on the walls.

Your imagination is worse than reality, she told herself. He might not even be back there. What if he'd decided, upon realizing he couldn't squeeze in, to wait for her on the other side? She'd see the exit ahead and lunge for freedom, only to tumble into his grip.

Stop that, she snarled at herself and her all too frisky imagination.

It *would,* however, be useful to know if he'd managed to enter the drain or not.

Amaranthe licked her lips and called, "You know... when I imagined us getting horizontal together, this isn't at all how I thought it'd go."

She didn't slow down to wait for a response, but she did listen intently, ears straining to hear any sign that he was behind her.

A startled squeak came from the other direction, followed by something scampering away. So. Room for rats down there after all.

"I," Sicarius said, but that's all he managed. Even that syllable broke off with a grunt of exertion.

Amaranthe renewed her efforts, pulling herself along as fast as she could. He might be fighting the wizard, but he wasn't winning, not if he was that close behind her.

The blackness ahead seemed to lessen in intensity, fading to a dark, dark gray. The exit? Or some storm drain in a nearby street? Either would work, so long as she could escape through it.

A hint of a breeze brushed her cheeks, carrying the fresh scent of snow, of the outside. Her situation might be improving.

Her fingers smashed into fresh rat droppings.

Right. She'd better wait to see what lay ahead before wasting her energy on optimism. If she ran into a dead-end...

The sound of breathing reached her ears. It was strained, like Sicarius was trying to fight the wizard, but *trying* wouldn't help her. He was close on her heels.

The tunnel curved slightly, and Amaranthe's hips caught in the bend. The dark gray turned to a less dark gray circle ahead. An exit. There were bars across it, but only two and widely spaced, relatively speaking. She might be able to squirm her way between them. She grunted. *If* she could escape the cursed bend. Extra sludge had accumulated on the walls in that spot.

"Should have grabbed some lubricant before thrusting myself into a tight space," she muttered, scraping and clawing, trying to find a larger handhold, something to offer her a good grip. There. She caught some nodule on the ceiling and twisted, using it to pull. The fresh angle let her shimmy free. The escape sent a surge of exhilaration through her, and she brazenly called, "*That*, on the other hand, might have been appropriate for our first horizontal meeting."

She didn't know if he'd heard her first mumbled comment, but somehow hoped he had and that he might find the notion amusing. She didn't know the secret to breaking that hold, but figured displaying her personality, however quirky and inappropriate it might be at times, would remind him of his fondness for her and give him ammunition to continue to fight against the wizard. In lieu of that, she'd be fine with him getting stuck in the bend.

Amaranthe squirmed the rest of the way to the exit and to the two vertical bars, both coated with so many layers of frozen grime that they were twice their original size. She pressed her head into the gap between the two—that would be the sticking point. If she couldn't get her head through, she wasn't going anywhere. If she could, she figured she could twist and gyrate enough to wriggle the rest of her body out.

Out into what, she wondered, even as she scraped the skin off her temples in her first attempt. It was almost as dark outside as inside. If not for the fresh smell of ice and snow beneath her nose, she might not have believed she'd come to an end of the drain. She rotated and ended up on her back before she found an angle that allowed her to slip her head through the bars.

Dear ancestors, I'm vulnerable, she thought, staring up at something dark, her head hanging out of the drain hole, her neck exposed and her body sticking out on the other side. If Sicarius came up on her...

She thrust her arm through and clawed around the outside even as she crooked her knees, trying to push off the bottom of the drain. She flayed off more skin, but she managed to get her other arm through and from there her shoulders.

Oh, those are boards up there, the part of her mind that wasn't busy panicking realized. The underside of a dock. She'd made it to the lake.

She wasn't sure yet where she would run when she had the opportunity, but the notion that she'd be able to do so gave her the strength to haul more of her body between the bars, though it was a painful experience.

"Wonder if... Akstyr's healing book... covered how to graft... new nipples onto a woman," she panted.

When her hips made it through, there was nothing left to hold her back. She skidded down the slope and landed on the frozen lake, her momentum enough to send her skidding several feet. She hardly cared. She was free.

Of the drain, she reminded herself, not Sicarius. Where to next? If his head was any bigger than hers, he wouldn't make it through that grate, but she couldn't swear that it was. They'd never taken out measuring tape and compared. No doubt that was one of those things people waited to do until *after* they'd engaged in physical intimacies.

She rose to her knees, the first part of a plan cementing itself in her head. Race back to the factory, close the grate, and push a bunch of heavy stuff on top of it so he couldn't escape that way. Yes, and then she could run into the city and check in on Starcrest's team—what had they been doing all this time, anyway? Inviting that wizard to a teahouse to share a plate of Emperor's Buns?

"Amaranthe?" came Sicarius's voice from the depths of drain. From around where that bend had been, she guessed.

She'd found her feet and was poised to scramble up the bank and enact her plan, but she waited. "Yes?"

"I'm stuck."

She'd expect him to make that statement in his usual monotone, but a hint of plaintiveness accompanied it.

"Sorry about that, but that *was* the point." She wondered if he'd believe she'd planned for it to happen like that, not that her plan had simply been to desperately survive the next moment, and the next, in the hopes of chance favoring her.

"Did something happen to the practitioner?" Sicarius asked.

"Uh? Why do you ask?"

Maybe Starcrest *had* done his job. Had Sicarius been freed from his captor?

"I don't sense him any more," Sicarius said. "It's possible he was distracted and forgot about me."

Amaranthe crept back up the slope. Though she wanted to believe him, she approached from the side of the hole, so he wouldn't see her from inside. Even he would have a hard time firing a throwing knife from the bowels of a drain that tight, but she wouldn't believe it impossible for him.

"Where are you stuck?" she asked. "That bend?"

"Yes."

"What do you want me to do? I love you, but there's no way I'm scraping the rest of the skin off my head to try to get back through these bars."

"No, I understand. Perhaps some of that lubricant you mentioned..." He chuckled.

A sick feeling washed over Amaranthe. He... *chuckled*? When had he ever...?

It wasn't him. The wizard was trying to fool her. Either the Nurian didn't know Sicarius well enough to know he never laughed, or Sicarius had somehow tricked his captor into believing he shared such activities with Amaranthe.

But what if... what if it *is* him, she countered to herself, and he's so relieved to be free that he let the laugh escape? When they were alone together, he *had* occasionally let more emotion show...

"Yes, of course," Amaranthe said, realizing that long seconds had passed. "I'm sure I can find something. Stay there."

"Naturally," Sicarius said dryly.

Too much emotion, he was showing too much emotion. She was sure of it.

Amaranthe scrambled out from under the dock and ran up the slope and onto Waterfront Street. She sprinted up the hill toward the factory. Funny how quickly she reached the back door, considering the eternity that had passed while she'd been pulling herself through that drain. But if Sicarius was tricking her, her "quickly" might not be quick enough.

She slowed down enough to close the door softly behind her and stepped lightly as she ran through the factory, trying to think of things—and remember where they were in the dark— she could pile onto the grate.

If Sicarius *was* free of the wizard, good. The worst that would happen was that he'd spend a few hours trapped down there while she hunted down Starcrest and verified the Nurian's death. If he wasn't...

She had to work fast. He might not be stuck in that bend at

all, he might be crawling back to the start, even now.

Remembering a pile of machine parts along one of the back walls, Amaranthe veered in that direction. She ran as quickly as she could without allowing her boots to clomp on the cement floor, but Sicarius had the hearing of a hound. She could only hope that backtracking through the tight tunnel would delay him.

In the dark, she almost tripped over the machine parts. She *did* hammer her shin into something unyielding. Another bruise to add to the night's collection. She'd admire it later.

Groping about, Amaranthe found a pole attached to a cylindrical wheel, some sort of grinding device. It didn't matter what it was. So long as she could carry it. She dragged it off the pile, wincing when something else clanked off and rolled across the floor, striking one of the vats with a resounding gong. It wouldn't take a hound to hear that.

Fortunately, the pit wasn't far. She pulled her prize over and patted about, expecting the grate to be open. It wasn't. Sicarius had let it fall shut behind him. Believing she wouldn't have the strength to climb up the wall and open it from below? She shuddered at the idea of that wizard smirking somewhere while she tried.

Amaranthe maneuvered the wheel onto the grate, then ran back for more gear to pile on top. Even Sicarius would have a hard time pushing that grate open from below, but she wouldn't feel safe until she had hundreds of pounds of gear stacked atop it. Starcrest and the others could laugh at the overkill when they came in the morning to help pull him out. So long as the wizard was dead, and Sicarius's mind was free, they could all laugh. She didn't care.

Some rusty pipe sections followed the grinding wheel, then a couple of cement blocks after that. She was in the process of dragging over something that felt like an industrial-sized funnel when a new thought occurred to her. She halted a few inches from the edge of the grate, the certainty of her mistake slamming into her like a wrecking ball.

If Sicarius freed himself from that bend and reached the bars

blocking the drain exit, it wouldn't matter how big his head was. He had that cursed black knife. How many times had she seen the thing cut through substances no normal blade could? Not more than a few weeks ago, he'd hurled it at the floor in the cab of a train, a textured *steel* floor, and it had bit in and stuck. If he reached those bars, he'd cut through them. Or if he came back this way, he could cut through the grate. Sure it might not be like slicing through butter, but she'd be shocked if that knife couldn't do it.

"Emperor's eyeteeth," she muttered.

What if he'd already escaped and was running back to the factory at that very moment? Or—she eyed the broken window and the back door—what if he was already inside again?

Something latched around Amaranthe's ankle.

She shrieked. And was yanked off her feet.

She landed on the cement so hard, the blow slamming into her back, that it stunned her. For a second, she couldn't breathe and couldn't think. Then she was being pulled toward the grate.

Amaranthe flailed with her hands, trying to find something to grab onto. Most of her body was still on the cement, but he'd reached through and grabbed her ankle and—curse him, he had her other leg now too. There wasn't anything to grab onto, and the smooth floor didn't help. Even from his awkward position—he had to be hanging from the grate, hanging from *her*—his power dwarfed hers; she couldn't find any leverage to fight him off.

She twisted and scrabbled at her belt for her knife. She might not have thrown it at him earlier, but, blast it, she *would* stab him through the hand.

The instant she stopped fighting his pull, though, he gained ground, spinning her sideways so that her body rolled onto the grate. She'd no more than unsheathed the knife when his fingers snaked through an opening, tearing it from her grip. It'd been too fast; she hadn't noticed him let go of one of her legs before his hand had been upon her. A clatter sounded below, her blade striking the stone at the bottom of the pit. She didn't have another one.

She froze—he'd pulled her onto her belly, her face mashed into one of the openings—and tried to think of something to say. A quip, a plea, anything to buy time. She found herself staring into his eyes.

He was gripping her with both hands, one on the back of her thigh and one on her opposite shoulder, all of his body weight hanging from those points. He'd lost the wool cap somewhere, and that stone at his temple glowed, a sickly opal with a myriad of colors in it. The light was enough to illuminate his face. And hers, too, she imagined. What terror did he see there? Or did her calculation show in her eyes? Little good it was doing her.

"Where is Starcrest?" he asked, his voice calm and emotionless, no hint of the earlier exertion in it. Was he not fighting the wizard now? Obviously it'd been the Nurian when he'd been trying to trick her at the bend. Where was Sicarius? Still in there? Or utterly defeated? Squashed down into some tiny corner of his own mind, unable to effect any power over his body at all?

"Why don't you let go," she whispered, "and we'll discuss it?"

Amaranthe tried to get her arms beneath her, to brace her palms against the iron bars so she could push away. It'd be futile, though, as long as he held on.

Think, she ordered herself. Do something. What? Spit on him, anything. But such tactics would be useless against him. Talking. As inane as her words sounded in her ears, she had to try, to hope she'd break through somehow and lend him the strength to pull away from the wizard, even if it was only long enough for him to let go. That was all she needed.

He dug into her thigh and shoulder deeper and swung his legs. She ground her teeth to keep from gasping in pain, both from the steel-fingered grip and from the way it mashed her harder into the bars. His legs came up, his boots finding bars to brace against so they lay horizontally, body to body, except for the grate between them. The weight pulling against her lessened, but when she tried to push away, she couldn't gain so much as an inch. She couldn't knee or elbow him—she'd hit the bars.

What was he going to do next? Grab his knife. If he tried he'd have to let go with one hand. That'd be the best chance she had to pull away. She'd save the desperate spit-in-his-face maneuver for that moment.

"It's not that I wouldn't enjoy having you this close under other circumstances," Amaranthe said, searching his eyes, trying to find some sign of the man she knew in there, "but I'd really appreciate it if you let go right now, dropped down in that hole, and waited until my comrades come back." Preferably with that wizard's head on a stake. "Starcrest too. The letter you sent, it brought him. He's helping Sespian. We'll have a resolution before long, I'm certain of it. And the *Behemoth* is gone. Forge is greatly weakened. Er, you know about that part. But with the technology gone, the remaining members will have less to draw on. Victory is close, Sicarius. Don't let this foreigner control you, to make you do... anything you don't want to any more."

His grip on her shoulder tightened. "Where is Star—"

Abruptly, he threw his head back and roared in pain or frustration—or both. She'd never heard such a cry from him, and it startled her, but not so much that she failed to notice his fingers slipping a half an inch.

Now's your chance to pull away, she thought, while he's distracted. Do it!

"Fight it," Amaranthe whispered, not moving. "Just for a moment. That's all it takes."

His arm dropped from her shoulder, and his knife was between their faces so quickly she hadn't registered more than the released grip. She'd missed her chance to pull away. Or... maybe not. The blade was in his hand with the hilt laid bare between them. It was the familiar black dagger.

"Take... it..." he gasped. "Use it... *end* it."

End what? His life? His eyes were pleading with her, and it broke her heart. She couldn't hesitate, couldn't argue—who knew how long he'd hold out?

Amaranthe slipped her hand through the grate, hooking it around a bar to grab the knife. He released it and tilted his head

back again. He was shaking, as if from the effort of holding his bodyweight up in that position, but she knew it had nothing to do with physical exertion.

In a movement as efficient as she could manage, she slashed the knife across flesh. Not, as he seemed to expect, his neck; she cut into the skin around that cursed opal, trying to slice the full circle before he could jerk away. And jerk away he did, his eyes widening with surprise, or maybe that was pain. Agony.

She dropped the knife and grabbed the opal with her bare hand. Digging her fingers into flesh slippery with blood, she struggled to grasp enough of it to pull out.

Sicarius screamed.

The alien sound startled her so that she reared back, yanking her arm back with her. The hands that had gripped her released. Sicarius fell into the black depths below.

Horrified, Amaranthe stared at her open palm. Slick with blood and gore, the opal pulsed three times, revealing slender tendrils on its underside, tendrils that had, she realized sickly, grown through his skull and snaked into his brain.

After the final pulse, the opal went black. Everything went black.

Tremors coursed through Amaranthe's body. Disgusted by the device, she hurled it as hard as she could. It had grown eerily quiet in the factory, and she heard it hit one of those vats and clunk to the floor.

"Sicarius?" she whispered, her voice hoarse. "Sicarius, are you...?"

She couldn't say it. Tears welled in her eyes. If that thing had been so intertwined with him... with his brain, had its destruction destroyed him too?

CHAPTER 13

P AIN. HE'D EXPERIENCED IT COUNTLESS TIMES IN HIS LIFE, and this, he told himself, was no different. He set about erecting the barriers in his mind, walling off the areas that were affected. Later he could meditate and work on healing those areas, but first he had to regain full consciousness and assess the exterior situation. He couldn't remember exactly what, but something important had been going on.

Breathing. He hadn't been doing it, he realized, so he focused on that for a time. The expansion of his lungs, in and out, drawing in rejuvenating air. He gradually grew aware of cold stone beneath his back. The grate, the drain. Amaranthe. The memories returned in a rush, bringing a fresh wave of pain, if a different kind.

She was alive!

And he'd almost killed her. *Again.*

Sicarius had experienced a surge of pure joy when he'd realized she was the one in the factory, that he'd been mistaken and that she'd somehow survived that crash. But he'd rushed to squash the feeling, afraid of how Kor Nas would react. Now shame and anguish filled him, underlaid with frustration for his inability to thwart that cursed Nurian. The memories of the man's thoughts, of what he'd wanted Sicarius to do to Amaranthe, the pleasure he'd derived from learning that "his pet's woman" still lived and could be tormented as punishment for Sicarius's attempts at defiance. Or maybe Kor Nas's fantasies hadn't had anything to do with anything as logical as punishment. He'd simply delighted at—

No, Sicarius told himself. Push it aside, like the physical pain. Kor Nas was gone, or at least Sicarius was free of him.

She'd done that. Yes. He owed her again. He hadn't been certain if the stone could be removed without killing him—or if some fate worse than death might await. Having his throat slit had seemed a superior alternative. She'd made the decision for him though. Good.

A new sensation pierced the cloudy haze of pain and awakening awareness that surrounded him. Moisture. On his face, his cheek and nose. Saltiness touched his lips.

Tears. His?

No...

It took an eternity before he could open his eyes—he needn't have bothered, for only darkness awaited—and he realized that he remained in the pit. And that Amaranthe was down there with him. Her arms were around him, his head cradled to her breast, her fingers twined in his short hair.

"Should let you... cut that... sometime," he whispered, his voice hoarser than a blade rasping across a whetstone.

Amaranthe stiffened, lifting her head. Her forehead had been pressed against his, he realized when an unpleasant coolness replaced the warmth of her flesh.

"You're alive," she blurted.

"Yes."

"But you weren't. You weren't breathing."

"A temporary setback," Sicarius said.

"Did you... did the wizard..." Her grip tightened about him. "Is he gone? Are you... you?"

He remembered her asking those exact words once before on Darkcrest Isle, and a fresh surge of disgust came over him for his inability to do better this time. Focus on her, dolt, he told himself. She'd asked a question.

"I believe so." Sicarius lifted his fingers to his temple and probed about the crater in his flesh. That would take a while to heal. He hoped he hadn't endured brain damage that might afflict him later in life. "My body will suffer another scar though. Allying with you remains deleterious to my health."

Amaranthe let out an explosive laugh, or maybe it was a sob, given the way her chest trembled against his head. "That *has* to be you. No Nurian wizard would be so..."

"Sespian suggested he and I may share hereditary tendencies toward social awkwardness."

Amaranthe snorted and wiped her eyes. "An understatement, though he's not so awkward as his father." She lifted her gaze toward the open grate above. "What are the odds of either of us, being rather battered and broken, climbing out of here and finding a more comfortable place to sit? Perhaps even growing so ambitious as to apply bandages to each other."

Sicarius didn't feel up to standing, much less climbing out of the pit. He'd be content to continue to lie there for some time with Amaranthe cradling his head. Such weaknesses shouldn't be admitted aloud. Besides, he didn't know how long she'd be willing to cuddle with him once she learned about the atrocities he'd committed for Kor Nas. Or how little he'd fought to avoid committing them. If he'd known she was alive... and Sespian too. To learn they'd survived delighted him of course, but it deepened his shame as well.

"I'll construe your silence as a stolid, 'I could if I truly wished to, but I'm suitably comfortable here right now,'" Amaranthe said.

"Indeed," Sicarius murmured.

"There are things I should tell you," Amaranthe said. "I... oh, let's save it for later."

Her fingers traced the side of his face, the side without the raw wound, and he let his head loll back, content to let his mind rest and to appreciate the ministrations. He had a notion that he should return them, in some manner or another, but his mental war with the practitioner had exhausted him in a way physical skirmishes never did. Another time, he thought, then reluctantly added, if she wished it. If she saw the newspaper article, or, worse, the row of heads on pikes that Kor Nas had set up to show Flintcrest how effective his Nurian allies were, Amaranthe might not wish to accept any "ministrations" from him.

He reminded himself that he was appreciating, not thinking, and for a time his mind lay quiet.

"In retrospect," Amaranthe mused, "I should have tied a rope up there and climbed down that way instead of flinging myself into the pit."

"Such premeditation is rarely part of your strategies," Sicarius said. He hadn't meant it as an insult, rather a bit of that teasing she'd encouraged him to do, but her stroking fingers stilled, and he worried he'd hurt her feelings. After all that he'd put her through that night, he would not wish to cause her further upset.

"True, I must admit," Amaranthe said. "I'm not sure when that happened. I used to go by the book and consider consequences before enacting a plan. Maybe my plans just grew so unprecedented and grandiose that I couldn't foresee the consequences, so I stopped trying."

She sounded chagrinned but not hurt, so he attempted teasing again, thinking it might lighten her mood more than a terse affirmation. "You could not foresee the consequences of jumping into a pit without a rope?"

"Not that." She swatted him on the chest. "The *Behemoth* and its... landing spot. This—" she pointed toward the lip of the pit, "—is simply a result of me being too worried you were dead to think of more than hurling that junk aside and jumping down here to check."

"Ah. Your solicitude is appreciated then. Almost as much as a rope would be." Though she wouldn't see the faint smile that touched his lips, he hoped she'd hear it in his voice.

"As if you've ever needed a rope."

"As you pointed out, I was recently in a non-respirating state. I remain grievously weakened."

"A non-respir... you *are* socially awkward. Now I see the real reason you've never talked much."

No doubt it was a reflection of said weakened constitution that his smile lingered. It was too much effort to maintain the mask, and in the darkness alone with Amaranthe, what did it

matter? Sicarius closed his eyes and hoped she'd go back to stroking his face.

"Are you in much pain?" she asked instead, her voice gentler, serious now. "I'm sure I could claw my way up there and find a rope and a first-aid kit."

He hadn't taken a thorough inventory of his body, but found he could move his arm. Nothing corporeal seemed damaged from the fall; it was only his brain that ached. Given their positions, with his upper body in her lap, wrapping that arm around Amaranthe was awkward, but he did it anyway. "Stay."

"Not exactly an answer to my question, but I suppose it wouldn't hurt me to obey *your* orders once in a while."

He might have found another teasing response, but she bent, touching her forehead to his. Some of her hair had come free in the... he couldn't bring himself to think of it as anything other than a harrowing trial. It had been for both of them, though certainly more so for her. The locks of hair brushing his cheeks made him forget the role he'd played in it, at least for a moment as he inhaled the smell of her shampoo. The delicate cherry and almond scent was far more pleasant than the smells of cold sweat and fear that lingered about both of them. He thought of teasing her again, this time about the new blonde coloring of her locks, but her lips brushed his, gentle and sweet, and he forgot all about hair.

I do not deserve kisses, he thought—bless her ancestors, didn't she know he'd been trying to catch her to torture her, to please that sadistic prick ruling his mind? He should have turned away, told her exactly why her compassion was misplaced, but his lips betrayed him. They parted and invited her to explore. For days, he'd thought her dead, that he'd never again stand at her side and feel the warmth of a smile directed at him alone. To have her back only to push her away? He couldn't.

Later, if she decided she couldn't stomach the level of... monster he'd reverted to, he'd understand. For now, he accepted her tender kisses, finding them far more of a balm than anything in a first-aid kit.

Sometime later, a door banged open in the factory above. Voices sounded, too muffled to identify, but there were a number of them.

Amaranthe sighed and her lips left his, though with a palpable reluctance, and she kissed his eyes, careful to avoid the wound at his temple, before drawing away fully. He wanted to capture the back of her head with his other hand and pull her back down. It might be their last kiss—why let it end because of a few people roaming about upstairs?

"I suppose those are the reinforcements," she murmured, "here belatedly to save me from you." She chuckled as she said it, as if the thought—the memories—weren't horrific, but the reminder quenched his passion as surely as a hot iron being thrust into a bucket of water. "Maybe we can get them to supply our rope," she went on, unaware of his thoughts.

Frantic bangs and shouts came from above. They were calling her name, not his. Understandable. He'd been the villain of the night. Who, except Amaranthe, cared if he'd survived?

"Down here," she called when someone came close enough to their corner to hear.

The yellow glow of lights preceded the appearance of two familiar faces, Books and Akstyr.

"Amaranthe!" Books leaned over the open pit, his lantern extended. "Are you all right? Is that... uhm?" He squinted, probably trying to pick out Sicarius's black-clad form in the gloom.

"Yes," Amaranthe said, "and yes. We could use a rope and some bandages."

"Of course, I understand." Books scurried away.

Akstyr remained. He wore a self-satisfied grin as he thrust out a familiar rope belt adorned with several pouches. "Look what I got."

Amaranthe regarded the item without comprehension. "If you've been out shopping with Maldynado, I would have expected something more stylish. Or at least grandiose and flamboyant."

"Nah," Akstyr said, "this belonged to the practitioner who was controlling Sicarius."

"You killed him?" Sicarius asked, not having to modulate his voice to make it come out cold and flat.

If *Akstyr* had killed Kor Nas when Sicarius hadn't been able to so much as give the man a hangnail... He ground his teeth. He hadn't thought he could feel like more of a failure than he already did.

"I did." If Akstyr had lifted his chin any higher, he would have fallen over backward. "And I was the one who found him, on account of the Science he was working. Sort of. At first I couldn't do more than get the general vicinity down. He was able to mask himself somehow. Starcrest had his team and our people searching building by building. But then we heard this yell of pain."

Yes, it didn't surprise Sicarius that Kor Nas, too, had felt a mental backlash to the breaking of that bond.

"He was on the rooftop," Akstyr went on. "Starcrest wanted to storm up there with all of his forces, but I didn't wait for him to finish explaining. I thought the practitioner might sense them coming, even when he was in pain, and that he'd run away. So I crept up there first while they were still deciding things. He sensed me coming, and I thought he'd kill me, but I told him I'd been looking for him all over the city, that I wanted to be his apprentice. That little lie let me get close. I thought maybe I could stick a dagger in his chest. But he was a telepath and rifled through my mind. He flattened me—" Akstyr's face grew sheepish at this, "—and I figured my plan hadn't been so bright after all. But by then Starcrest and Maldynado and Basilard and the others were all climbing up to get him, blocking all the escapes, and he panicked. I got my chance and stuck my dagger in his back. Then the others were swarming all over him, finishing him off before he could hurt anyone else. It was great." Akstyr grinned again and waved his belt. "I haven't gotten a chance to see what all he had yet, but I hope I can learn from it."

Something to his left drew his gaze—Books returning with the requested items.

Sicarius hadn't removed the arm he had wrapped around Amaranthe, and he took this last moment alone with her to rub her back. "You made that happen," he said, trying to let his approval seep into his voice. "If you hadn't cut that thing out of my head, he wouldn't have cried out. They never would have found him."

Though it remained dark at the bottom of the pit, he heard the grin in her voice. "Can we pretend it was some premeditated brilliance then and not utter desperation? Much like me shutting myself down here and crawling out the sewage hole?"

"Yes." Sicarius levered himself into a sitting position and would have kissed her, Akstyr's observing eyes be cursed, but several more figures stepped up to the ledge above them.

"Amaranthe!" Maldynado called.

Basilard raised a triumphant fist.

"Are you all right?" Yara asked. "We were afraid... it took so long, everyone was afraid we were too late."

Sicarius heard and saw them, as well as Books, Deret Mancrest, and a handful of soldiers with ropes and grappling hooks, but it was the silver-haired man in insignia-less black fatigues onto whom his eyes locked. Fleet Admiral Sashka Federias Starcrest. The man he'd asked to come to the empire, and the man he'd come to the factory to kill that night. Aside from the hair color and deeper lines around the mouth and eyes, Starcrest hadn't changed much. He'd gained a few pounds, but he'd been on the edge of gaunt at their last meeting, fresh off that time on Krychek Island. He appeared hale and fit, as befitting a warrior.

"Corporal Lokdon," Starcrest said, his voice quiet but carrying to the bottom of the pit regardless. "I am relieved to see that your plan worked." His gaze shifted, and he nodded once. "Sicarius."

This wasn't how Sicarius had envisioned them meeting again after twenty years. He'd wanted... what? To be able to march with pride at the head of an army he'd built? Perhaps not, but at least to be able to hold his head up and know he hadn't spent the last few days as some wizard's lickspittle.

At a wave from Starcrest, one of the soldiers dropped a rope down. Sicarius touched Amaranthe, indicating that she could go first. After she scrambled out of the pit, he marshaled his strength, crouched low, and leaped up, catching the lip. He pulled himself over the side. Who he meant to impress by ignoring the rope—Amaranthe? Starcrest?—he didn't know, but he hadn't wanted to appear weak. He already knew his appearance, with dried blood streaking his face and gore smashed beneath his fingernails, did not match the tidy one he preferred.

Of course, Amaranthe was equally blood- and gore-covered, but that did not keep her from greeting her comrades with hugs and offering Starcrest a firm handshake. He accepted it and added a comradely, or maybe fatherly, pat of approval to her shoulder.

Sicarius kept his face composed in his stony mask, showing nothing of the chaos and pain that remained in his mind, nor the childish feeling that *he'd* like a pat of approval from the great admiral.

He noticed another man standing back from the gathering, and it took a great deal of effort to maintain the mask he'd so carefully reapplied. Sespian. Amaranthe had said he was alive, and he'd believed her, but it wasn't the same as seeing his son with his own eyes.

Sicarius strode around the others and toward Sespian. For a moment, he had a notion of hugging him, but his approach evoked a look of hesitant wariness. Sespian glanced at his temple, as if he worried Sicarius might still be under someone's control. Or maybe he was more aware than Amaranthe of what Sicarius had done in the last few days.

Instead of extending his arms for a hug, one he realized with lament he'd been far closer to receiving on that water tower, Sicarius stopped a pace away and clasped his hands behind his back. "I am pleased to see that you are alive and undamaged."

"Uhm," Sespian said, and Sicarius sensed his simple statement hadn't been the correct one, or at least not the one Sespian expected. "Thanks."

"I thought you'd died at Fort Urgot."

Sespian winced. "I should have. I was lucky. Thousands of others weren't."

"So I understand." The stiltedness of the conversation pained Sicarius, but he did not know how to smooth it out.

"Heroncrest's army had tunneled under the walls. Maldynado, Basilard, and General Ridgecrest, and I were fighting the troops trying to enter that way."

The tunnel borer, of course. Sicarius hadn't thought to hope that it could have somehow come into play in saving Sespian. He was relieved the soul construct had interrupted their spy mission, for, given enough time, he might have thought to sabotage that equipment.

Sespian's gaze shifted over his shoulder. Sicarius glanced back in time to catch Amaranthe mouthing something and making a gesture toward Sicarius. She caught him looking, shrugged, and returned to a conversation with Books and Deret.

Sespian cleared his throat. "I am... pleased to see that you are alive as well. And only... somewhat damaged."

It wasn't the hug Sicarius would have preferred, and Amaranthe had goaded the statement out, but it was better than stiff coldness.

Sicarius nodded once. "Good."

"You're supposed to say thank you to something like that."

"An artificial social construct that is no more of an acknowledgment of your statement than my 'good.'" It was an automatic response, not a well-thought out one, and, as soon as Sespian shook his head, Sicarius knew he should have simply voiced gratitude. This was why he didn't get hugs...

Sicarius sighed to himself, wondering when he'd ever figure out how to interact with his son.

* * *

After washing and changing clothes, Amaranthe was on her way to join Starcrest and the others in a midnight planning meeting, but Deret Mancrest blocked her path. He stood at the base of the catwalk stairs, his swordstick in one hand and the other on the railing as he spoke with a blonde-haired woman in spectacles. Though Amaranthe had never seen her in person, she knew exactly who this was. The nose, in particular, was quite familiar, though the woman was a little stouter than she had been in her ten-year-old tintype. She was smiling as she spoke to Deret, a pleasant smile with dimples, but it disappeared when she spotted Amaranthe approaching.

The wry smile Deret issued suggested he'd intentionally put himself—and Suan Curlev—into Amaranthe's path. Yes, he knew she'd been avoiding this chat for days. Suan was neither bound nor gagged, though enough soldiers guarded the factory perimeter that one might be deterred from escape attempts. Or perhaps she'd been given her parole in exchange for... what? Some promise from Deret? She was standing closer to him than one would expect from a pair of enemies, or rather, kidnapper and kidnap victim.

"Ms. Curlev," Amaranthe said, and that's as far as she got. How did one say, "I'm sorry I had you kidnapped and, oh, did I mention that I'm responsible for your sister's death? No? Sorry about that too."?

"Corporal Lokdon," Suan said. "Lord Mancrest assures me that your assassin will not be knocking on my door tonight, but I would like to hear these assurances from your mouth. Does being imprisoned by you indeed grant protection?"

Er, what?

"You won't be assassinated while you're here," Amaranthe said, "but Sicarius is his own man, not *my* assassin." After what he'd been through, the last thing she wanted to do was claim ownership of him. That was sure to make him bristle, no matter who tried it.

"Then you can't promise he won't kill me the way he's single-handedly annihilated most of my sisters?" Suan frowned at Deret.

Sisters. She meant the Forge women, not Retta, but the link made Amaranthe wince nonetheless. Did Suan know about Retta

yet? Or did her knowledge only extend to what had been in the latest newspapers?

You'd know, Amaranthe told herself, if you hadn't been avoiding her.

"He will not," came Sicarius's voice from behind her, "kill any of Corporal Lokdon's prisoners."

Though his words were for Suan, he stopped beside Amaranthe, standing shoulder to shoulder with her. She'd missed that this last week, and she drew strength from his presence. Retta's death had been regrettable, but she had to accept it, and accept whatever this woman's reaction would be.

Suan had taken a step back at Sicarius's approach, her fingers tightening on the railing like vise clamps. Despite Sicarius's words, Deret shifted to stand protectively in front of her. Surprise flickered in her eyes, but, after a moment, she shifted her hand from the railing to Deret's arm.

It occurred to Amaranthe that, however last-minute and desperate her order to have the woman kidnapped had been, she had one of the Forge founders in her hideout. Maybe she could use that—and this friendship she'd apparently developed with Deret—to put an end to the bloodshed. The Forge bloodshed, anyway. Amaranthe was happy to leave the ending of the military bloodshed to Starcrest and Sespian.

"Ms. Curlev," Amaranthe said, "Sicarius was under a wizard's control when he killed those people—" his lips flattened; he doubtlessly did not wish to be reminded of the fact, and she resolved to move the conversation away from it quickly, "—but that has ended. You're safe as long as you're here, with us. Should you choose to escape and conspire with what's left of your comrades..."

"Was he also under a wizard's control last month when he killed Ambree, Sia, Tabthra, and so many others?" Suan asked.

The image of Books's notebook, the one he'd used to research Forge members, popped into Amaranthe's mind, along with the neat checkmarks Sicarius had made beside the names of each person he'd assassinated. She didn't know how to

explain that his actions that night had been a retribution for the threat to Sespian—it wasn't as if that fact could legitimize assassinations anyway.

"No," Amaranthe said. "If you're aware of his relationship to Sespian, which most of the world seems to be now, then you'll understand why he took those actions. He doesn't kill... whimsically." She glanced at Sicarius, wondering if that would draw an eyebrow twitch. No, he was wearing his facade of granite, with neither his face nor body hinting at his thoughts. He'd washed and changed into a fresh set of his black clothing, but that didn't make him appear any less dangerous. He either hadn't been offered, or more likely hadn't accepted, a bandage for his temple, and the fresh puckered wound only gave his visage a new degree of deadliness.

"I've lost so many old comrades." The edge in Suan's voice softened. "And... Retta? Do you know... I can only imagine she died in that explosion. But maybe...?" She lifted hopeful eyes.

"She died in the crash," Amaranthe said. "Ms. Worgavic's shaman friend tried to stop some deadly alien devices with fire and Retta was caught by the blast." Leaving out the fact that Retta had only been in the line of fire because of her didn't sit well with Amaranthe, but if Suan could be convinced that her "old comrades" were in the wrong, and she could become some conduit through which a new law-abiding business class could be created, might not the omission be acceptable? For the greater good?

"I see," Suan said. "I feared this plot of theirs would not end well. Though I never thought..." She closed her eyes for a long moment. "I never thought Retta would end up in the middle of the fire. All she ever wanted to do was study in her field."

Amaranthe latched onto the word "theirs," noticing Suan hadn't said "*our* plot." Might she have disapproved all along?

"Do you think Forge will be finished with... their plot now?" Amaranthe asked. "If you're no longer a threat to Sicarius, or those he cares about, he'll have no reason to pursue you."

"From what I understand..." Suan watched Sicarius, not

meeting his eyes, but making sure he didn't come closer to her. "There's not much left of Forge anyway. What *is* left will have little reason to target Sespian now. As you pointed out, his heritage has been made public and will disqualify him from the throne."

"*Possibly* disqualify him," Amaranthe said. "None of the other potential candidates is doing anything to ingratiate himself with the public by marching through the city, imposing martial law, and killing members of the Company of Lords. Dead ancestors know what else they're doing by now. You might be best served by ingratiating yourself with... someone else."

Sicarius gave her a sharp look. She ignored it. Surely turning one's enemies into allies was a military strategy with a long tradition.

"Ingratiating isn't quite the word I'd use," Suan said, "but, yes. I spoke with Lord Starcrest. I understand political changes may be in the air. If they are, it'd be wiser for me to work with the new regime rather than against it. I imagine someone who gets in early could have a substantial say in the way businesses are treated by the government going forward."

Huh. Starcrest must have tried to plant the same seed. "I imagine that might be the case," Amaranthe said.

"Excuse me, please." Suan glanced at Sicarius again, then released Deret's arm and stepped away. "I told Lord Starcrest I'd write up a proposal." She hustled away, and Amaranthe wondered if her sudden urge to do homework had something to do with Sicarius looming nearby.

Deret gazed after her for a moment, then frowned at Amaranthe when she tried to pass him. "Are we still keeping her as a prisoner?"

"I don't think I'm in charge here any more," Amaranthe said. "Why don't you ask Admiral Starcrest?"

Deret looked toward the offices at the top of the stairs. "I wouldn't want to bother him, but..."

"Deret, old boy, hasn't any plucky young private shot you yet?" came Maldynado's voice as he approached from across the factory floor.

Deret's lips flattened. "Not yet."

His lips flattened even further when Maldynado, who was passing Suan, gave her backside a speculative eyeing.

"Given the size of your head," Deret said, "I'd think you'd make a more appealing target."

"I've been out of the city on an important mission. They can't shoot me if they can't find me." Maldynado winked at Amaranthe.

Sicarius headed up the stairs, apparently disinterested in listening to the old friends banter. Remembering her own mission, Amaranthe waved to the men and followed after him.

"So," Maldynado drawled to Deret, "that Forge girl is cute. Have you ever considered crashing your train into her bunker?"

Deret made an exasperated noise, but allowed himself to be drawn in. "Isn't the expression gliding your train into her station?"

"Yes, but that sounds terribly sedate. I suggest something more vigorous."

"I see. Your Yara appreciates that?"

"She's not an inhibited woman."

Their conversation faded from hearing as Amaranthe reached the landing. Sicarius slowed so they could walk side-by-side to the well-lit center office.

"Still think I'm crazy?" she asked.

"Did I say you were? Recently?"

"I sensed the thought in the look you gave me."

Sicarius gripped the knob to open the door for her, but he paused. "I have occasionally dwelled upon your unique interest in attributing feelings, emotions, and thoughts to my impassive stares, stares that other people find unreadable."

"They only find them so because of the menacing under-layer; it discourages analysis."

Sicarius did not respond, though he did give her a long scrutinizing look. It failed to achieve menace status, though she did wonder what he was thinking.

"Are you saying I'm incorrect in my assumptions?"

Amaranthe asked. "That you *weren't* thinking I was crazy?"

"No."

"I thought not." She pointed to the doorknob. "Are you going to open that or stand there caressing it until dawn? I only ask because such effort seems wasted on a door."

He stared at her, neither removing his hand nor responding to the comment... until he said, "I am vastly pleased that you are not dead."

Amaranthe bit down on her lip to restrain the toothy grin that wanted to dance across her face. Vastly. Not even Sespian had earned such a riotously enthusiastic adverb from him. Still, she couldn't help but tease... "I appreciate the sentiment very much, but when you say things like that, you should bounce on your toes or wiggle your hips or let out some physical manifestation of your emotional exuberance. It helps relay the message."

Sicarius looked down at himself. "My... hips?"

"Never mind." She stood on tiptoe and kissed him on the cheek before dropping her hand to his. They opened the door together.

She'd figured everyone inside would have their heads bent over the table, intent on their plots and machinations. But Starcrest spread a hand toward them as soon as they entered.

"Precisely who I wished to see."

He, Ridgecrest, a pair of colonels, Books, Sespian, Tikaya, and Mahliki all sat around the table, with the two women sharing a corner opposite the window. Mahliki was smirking, and Amaranthe would have calculated the angle required for her to have witnessed that conversation and quick kiss—surely the door had blocked her and Sicarius's private moment together?—but Starcrest was pinning her with his serious, legendary-admiral gaze.

"Sir?" she asked. "Or did you mean..." She nodded toward Sicarius. Given how much Starcrest meant to Sicarius, he'd probably appreciate being the one the retired admiral wished "to see."

"Both of you," Starcrest said. "Especially Sicarius."

Though he stood behind Amaranthe, she sensed him straighten to rigid attention. "Sir?" he asked.

She smiled, warmed by the earnestness in the single syllable. Would Starcrest recognize the feeling in it? Few people she'd met read the faint nuances in Sicarius's seeming monotone.

Yes, the "sir" caused genuine warmth to spawn in Starcrest's eyes, she was certain of it. He understood. Even if his wife never would. Tikaya was shifting uncertainly at this first face-to-face meeting with Sicarius since their adventure—misadventure?— twenty years earlier.

"Flintcrest is dealing with our diversions," Starcrest said. "The loss of his wizard hasn't derailed him."

No, Amaranthe thought, if the expression she'd seen on Flintcrest's face when he'd been arguing with the Nurian had been typical, he'd *appreciate* the loss of the wizard.

"Heroncrest has troops in the streets," Starcrest continued, "but we also believe he's scheming up something, an attack with the tunnel-boring machines perhaps. Marblecrest is holed up in the Barracks with his most trusted forces. It seems this brave soul is worried about food and water shortages and, rather than venturing out to do anything to this perceived threat to the city, has decided to hide and wait out the chaos."

"There are several months' worth of food and water in the Barracks," Sespian said. "Enough to supply the entire staff and guard regiment."

"Marblecrest will have more people in there than that," Books said, his fingers laced on the table, "but the stores will still keep them supplied through a short siege."

"What a heroic individual," Tikaya said. "Is he truly related to your comrade who helped us in the ship?"

Amaranthe nodded. "Maldynado's older brother."

"Remarkable."

"Does the older brother wear silly hats too?" Mahliki asked.

"I don't know," Amaranthe said, "but the only time I've seen him, it *was* in a clothing store."

Starcrest lifted a hand and the room fell silent. "Strictly

speaking, controlling the Imperial Barracks doesn't offer a military advantage, but it *is* symbolic, and now that the civilians are in the streets, many taking up arms, it could be important to make a visible move that resonates in the minds of the populace. Also, capturing one of our enemies and convincing him that no, he does not want the position of emperor, would simplify things." He'd been speaking to everyone, but now he focused on Amaranthe and Sicarius. "I understand you've both been in the Barracks and are aware of alternative entrances."

"I'm only aware of *escaping* the Barracks," Amaranthe said.

"We can get in," Sicarius said.

"Won't those wards have been reset?" Books asked.

"We can take Akstyr," Sicarius said. "He can further refine his system for altering the plane on which the wards operate."

"You'll want to take your whole team for this," Starcrest said.

"You want us to do more than sneak in and kidnap him?" Amaranthe asked.

"That's a possibility, but I'd prefer having the Barracks taken over and the doors thrown open for us." He nodded, in particular, at Sespian.

"Didn't you say there are thousands of people in there?" Amaranthe asked.

"Yes, I imagine it'd take some unique scheme to get the best of them. I understand that's your specialty."

Books smirked at Amaranthe. "How's it feel having your own spiel played on you?"

"Odd," she admitted. "I suppose once one had control of Marblecrest, one could control his legions. They might desert on the spot after realizing they'd chosen to side with the wrong candidate. Though it'd be nice to have some kind of distraction to keep people busy while we swoop in and locate the general."

Starcrest nodded, encouraging her, she thought.

"When I escaped from the dungeon, I distracted my guards with jars containing... I'm not certain I ever got the real name, but they called them Fangs. They transmit Hysintunga, a fatal disease. I was already infected, so the bugs didn't matter to me, but they terrified the guards. Of course, I only had to scare four people then, not four thousand."

"Fangs?" Mahliki perked up. "You mean *Mexisahil creatat* order *eractus?*"

"Ugly black bugs, halfway between a lizard and a wasp?" Amaranthe asked.

"That's them."

"Know where we could find any around here?" For a second, Amaranthe had a vision of thousands of soldiers fleeing the Imperial Barracks, their arms flailing about their heads as they strove to ward off attacks. Then she remembered the men she'd shared a cell with, men she'd watched die from the disease. "No, never mind. I wouldn't wish that punishment on anyone, certainly not fellow Turgonians."

"They're native to the equatorial regions anyway," Mihlaki said, "though there are other insects with properties that could be exploited in... interesting manners." She tapped her chin.

"I like interesting," Amaranthe said encouragingly.

"As do I." Starcrest gave his daughter a fond smile.

Mahliki opened her jacket, causing dozens of tiny clinks. Amaranthe couldn't guess when she'd found time to dig under the ice or whatever she'd been doing, but she'd filled a number of those vials. "Not these... We'd need... Hm, I need to think. I'm not as familiar with this area as my own climate, but I have a bunch of books in the submarine. And Lonaeo has been studying entomology longer than I have. He might have some ideas. I'll go talk to him."

"If you're able to come up with a useful solution," Tikaya said, "make sure their team can employ it without needing an entomologist along on the incursion."

"Mother." Mahliki touched her fingers to her chest. "Whatever are you implying? That I'd deliberately come up with a plan that forced me to go off on some interesting new adventure?"

"I'm *implying* you're too young to go on an infiltration of a building full of belligerent marines. Turgonians aren't—" Tikaya glanced around the room, the Turgonian-filled room. "Not all Turgonians are like your father."

Starcrest was leaning back in his chair and watching this exchange, a bland expression on his face.

"It'd be a strange nation if they were," Mahliki said. "Not that I was planning to get myself invited on their mission, but I'm sure *Father* was infiltrating buildings—or probably ships—full of belligerent marines when he was seventeen."

Amaranthe observed with amusement as Professor Komitopis, a woman who reputedly knew dozens of languages, in addition to having all that cryptographic expertise, floundered for an inoffensive way to say, "It's different for girls."

"Actually, I was still at the military academy when I was seventeen." Starcrest smiled at his daughter, but made a shooing motion with his fingers. "Get to work, and let's see what you can come up with."

"From the stories you've told me," Tikaya said, after Mahliki left, "I doubt your academy years were devoid of belligerent marines."

"Belligerent instructors, perhaps. The infiltrations were all sanctioned, a part of my training, with little possibility of loss of life. Unless one did something stupendously stupid. That did happen on occasion."

"How often did it involve you?" Tikaya asked.

"Me? Never. I was a tranquil and studious cadet, much loved by my instructors."

Tikaya folded her arms on the table and raised frank eyebrows.

"I was, admittedly less well loved by my older, larger, stronger schoolmates," Starcrest said. "Still, I maintain that Cadet Badgercrest, that brutish fellow who kept trying to stuff my head in Colonel Pondcrest's humidor—as if a simple volume equation wouldn't have told him that was impossible—burned down the upperclassmen's barracks all by himself. I merely failed to point out the flammable nature of lacquer when he came up with his super-quick-automatic-floor-buffing scheme."

Amaranthe found this aside amusing, though it tickled her more that Sicarius listened with the attentive mien of a bird dog focused on a rustling bush.

"Tell them who modified the automatic floor buffer," Tikaya said.

Starcrest cleared his throat. "I might have tinkered with it. That old model was in need of a performance boost."

Hm, if his daughter took after him at all, Amaranthe supposed she should plan on having something interesting—and possibly volatile—to use on their infiltration. She had better assemble and brief—*warn*—her team.

"How soon do you need the Barracks secured, my lord?" she asked.

"I'd say by dawn, but that's only a couple of hours away. Plan to go tomorrow night. And plan to be careful. Going by the reports I've received, it's getting dicey out there in the city. The gangs are rearing their heads, and the black market is thriving. As soon as we can remove Marblecrest and Flintcrest from the equation, someone on our side will very publicly and very heroically find a way to repair the supposedly broken aqueduct, put engineering teams to work on the bridge—teams that won't be harassed the way Heroncrest's men are sadly being—and find emergency rations from little known imperial reserves." Starcrest was gazing at Sespian as he spoke this last sentence.

"Me?" Sespian blurted. "You want to set me up to be the hero in charge of all of that?"

Amaranthe was almost as surprised. When last she'd spoken to Starcrest, he hadn't been certain he wanted to back Sespian as a candidate for the throne. Tikaya nodded firmly at this exchange though. Had she been whispering in her husband's ear? Something along the lines of, "Straighten this mess out and put an acceptable candidate on the throne so we can go home, dear?"

Books was frowning, but he didn't speak.

"The will to solve struggles with claims of superior blood is a familiar one, for it simplifies the issue and ensures certain agencies remain in power," Starcrest said, "but we've entered an age where more and more Turgonians are literate, and though the education system is designed to create good soldiers and

factory workers, not future rebels and anarchists, I think you'll find that the civilians are ready for a change." Starcrest nodded toward Books, causing his frown to fade into a thoughtful nod. "If not in this generation, then in the next. Regardless, the common man has always been ready to accept a hero as a leader."

"But I wouldn't be a hero," Sespian said, "I'd be a fraud. We *made* this problem. For me to come in and supposedly fix it, it wouldn't be honest."

"Honesty and politics rarely ride in the same wagon," Books said.

"You don't approve of this scheme, do you?" Sespian asked him.

"I... don't know. It's not ideal, but I would not fault you for taking advantage of an opportunity."

Sespian looked to Sicarius, as if to ask his father for advice, but he must have decided against it, for he stared at his hands instead. Amaranthe checked Sicarius's face, wondering what advice he might give to his son. Take the chance, or walk away from it all for a safer life? He'd mentioned something along those lines to her once, that he wished he'd taken Sespian away from Raumesys and from the Imperial Barracks, figuring out a way to have him raised as his own man, one who'd have a choice in the careers he picked. She couldn't read past Sicarius's mask though, not at this moment.

"Sespian," Starcrest said, "I'll not pressure you into a decision, but might I point out that you merely requested the assistance of a military adviser, trusting in him to find a solution to what couldn't be, given their numbers versus our numbers, anything except guileful?"

"I requested?" Sespian touched his chest.

"Your father did, then." Starcrest nodded toward Sicarius. "Fathers have been attempting to do what they believe is right for their children since time immemorial. I posit that there's no blood on your hands here. If there are critics of my methods, I'll take the blame."

"Mmm." Amaranthe touched a finger to her lips and shook her head at Sespian. She thought about signing the rest of her message, but Tikaya didn't have much trouble reading Basilard's code. Might as well make her comment public. "If you want the throne, take the credit for this, or at least for hiring the admiral. I suspect... The food isn't truly gone, nor is the water, and it sounds like the railroad damage is minor. I think this will be seen as a guileful plot, yes, but smartly so. If not next week, when people are feeling duped and affronted, then in the months and years ahead. There's a reason the Nurians call him foxy, eh?"

One of Starcrest's gray eyebrows twitched. "Enemy Chief Fox is the phrase they use." And not, his tone seemed to say, anything so effeminate as "foxy." At his side, Tikaya lifted her gaze ceiling-ward.

"I concur with Amaranthe," Books said. "I don't think the military or the populace will see this as dishonest, not in the long run. Sespian... if you want the throne back—" his lips twisted downward, "—this is your opportunity to have it."

"And what if..." Sespian traced a crack between the desks jammed together to form a table. "What if I want to throw my weight behind Books's manifesto and suggest a restructuring of the empire—of Turgonia—into something fairer for the people and more suitable for a modern world?"

"Constitution," Books said.

"Pardon?"

"Manifestos are what you have before elections, being largely temporary and fleeting. My work is called a constitution. Not temporary."

"Would you run for office?" Amaranthe asked Sespian. "For president, or whatever Books has decided the head chief should be called?"

"President, yes." Books frowned. "A fact you'd know if you'd read my work."

"Sorry, I've been getting shot at and blowing things up. It's kept me busy."

"I fail to see how you couldn't find the time to read a short document in between drawing fire and crashing alien aircrafts," Books said.

"*Short?*"

"I think," Sespian said firmly, drawing their attention back to him, "my age would make me a less than ideal candidate to lead a republic."

Books beamed at him, less, Amaranthe suspected, because of his wise acknowledgment and more because he'd used the correct name for the government entity Books had defined.

"Perhaps I could run for an ancillary role," Sespian said. "Second to someone more experienced, someone whose reputation for fairness around the world could do more to establish peace between Turgonia and its enemies than armadas of warships." He looked to Starcrest, and everyone in the room followed his gaze.

Tikaya didn't flinch exactly, but she dropped a hand—a warning hand?—onto her husband's shoulder. It might have been because she didn't want anything to do with Turgonia, or perhaps she didn't want to see Starcrest burdened with all the responsibility, or maybe she feared for his life, as any state leader was wont to be a target for assassins and zealots. All legitimate reasons for concern.

"I didn't come here to run for office," Starcrest said.

"There is a saying in the desert city-states," Books observed, "that a man who seeks power should be feared. Only he who seeks to avoid power should be granted it."

Starcrest and Tikaya opened their mouths at the same time, said a few words over each other, then acquiesced to the other, but neither started again.

"You'll have to discuss it in private, I'm certain," Sespian said.

"All of this is premature," Sicarius said. "Our enemies remain on their feet with armies at their backs."

"A true point," Starcrest said. "Your team must make plans to secure the Barracks. Meanwhile, Ridgecrest and I will see what we can come up with to capture, or at least further constrain Flintcrest."

"Yes, sir." Sicarius bowed his head and held the door open for Amaranthe.

They walked onto the catwalk together, Amaranthe already thinking about who she wanted to take. Akstyr, for certain, as they'd doubtlessly run into the shaman setting wards in the Barracks. Basilard was always an asset. Maldynado? Could she pry him away from Yara? Amaranthe hadn't seen much of Yara since the other woman had railed at her, flinging accusations. She'd be an asset, too, but would she join the mission?

The door clanked open behind them, and Sespian jogged out. He hesitated, a hand on the railing, when Amaranthe and Sicarius faced him.

"I... I'd like to go with you." He glanced at Sicarius. "Both of you. I think I can... uhm."

Amaranthe nudged Sicarius. "I think he missed working with you. That infiltration I heard about must have made an impression."

"I'm simply looking for my cat," Sespian said. "I don't know if anyone's been taking care of him."

"Ah, yes, I understand," Amaranthe said. "Of course."

Sespian's cheeks colored.

A clank sounded, and Yara strode through the back door and onto the factory floor. She veered for Maldynado and Deret at the base of the stairs. Deret must have finished trading insults with Maldynado, for he headed off at her approach. Well, Amaranthe had wanted to talk to Yara...

"I'll meet you back in one of the other offices for planning," Amaranthe told Sicarius and Sespian, then walked down the stairs to intercept the other woman.

It wasn't hard. As soon as Yara saw her, she said something to Maldynado, waved for him to give them some space, and walked up to Amaranthe.

Amaranthe had only a couple of seconds to decide whether to mention their last conversation, or to pretend it hadn't happened. "How are you doing, Yara?" She was having a hard time exuding bright perkiness lately, but she gave it her best.

"I've been assigned the task of putting together a team to infiltrate and capture the Imperial Barracks. Are you interested in joining?"

A finger raised, Yara had been about to say something herself, but she stopped, her finger still hanging in the air. "You never give up, do you?"

"Rarely. But to what specifically are you referring?"

"Recruiting people to your insane schemes. No matter how horribly the previous ones failed."

"Ah." Amaranthe feared pretending their previous conversation hadn't occurred wouldn't work. "I'll admit that it may be some sort of disease that's difficult to fully eradicate from the system, but I have, in fact, been assigned this mission, and it'd be unwise of me to believe I can handle it by myself. Therefore... recruiting."

"Assigned. You're letting someone give *you* orders? I didn't think you knew how."

"I *was* an enforcer for seven years," Amaranthe said, deciding the conversation was promising. Yara seemed her usual gruff self, not that irate tear-ravaged person who'd hollered at her in the office. "I was very good at biting my tongue and not arguing with my superiors, no matter how shortsighted their orders might have been. Of course that didn't get me far in my career."

"Hm."

That didn't exactly invite further details, but Amaranthe wasn't ready to give up. "I'll be asking Maldynado to come too. It might be fun."

"Or it might be crazy."

"There's no ancient super advanced technology in the Barracks." A true statement, Amaranthe hoped. "I'm certain things can't get *that* crazy."

"Really," Yara said, her tone flatter than a stone paver.

"Starcrest's daughter is thinking up something involving insects, but other than that..."

Yara snorted. "Look, Lokdon..." She glanced around. With Starcrest's troops running all over the city to enact his plans, not many people lingered inside the factory. Yara lowered her voice anyway. "I don't think I was wrong about some of the things I said the other day, but I know you already felt awful, and I shouldn't have…"

"Stomped on me like a makarovi?"

Yara grimaced. "I should have waited before reacting and saying things…"

Things that she regretted? Would she regret them if Maldynado hadn't returned? Even if he had, most of the rest of the fort hadn't.

"They were valid," Amaranthe said. "I don't think anything we accomplish here can justify… no, nothing can ever justify that. It was surely accidental, but that doesn't help those people, their families."

"I know." Yara stared down at a crack in the cement. "But we have to go on anyway, right?"

"Wallowing on a blanket in a corner of an office only satisfies you for so long. Eventually you get bored."

"So… insects you say?"

"Insects or something derived from them, I'd guess. That area of study is the girl's specialty."

"Studying bugs. Huh. The Kyatt Islands must be an interesting place."

"So I hear. It'd be nice to visit them someday." Someday when they didn't have so much work to do. Counting Yara in, Amaranthe headed off to gather the rest of her team.

CHAPTER 14

HIGH ABOVE THE FACTORY FLOOR, SICARIUS SAT CROSS-legged in the rafters, his chin propped on his fist, watching as men came and went below. Actually, he was watching Amaranthe's door. She'd spent the remains of the night putting her team together, all of her usual men plus Yara and Sespian, then retreated "to get some sleep," as she'd said. He should be resting, too, as the night would doubtlessly be a busy one, but he kept wondering if she was in there, plagued by nightmares. Before this... divergence with Kor Nas, he'd promised to teach her how to meditate. It would be negligent of him to rescind his offer now, but if he showed up at her door, would she think he expected more? Did he still? With so much fresh blood on his hands?

He sighed. He appreciated his freedom from the practitioner, and from the others who had caged him before and made his decisions for him, but admitted life was simpler when all one had to do was follow orders.

The back door banged open, and two young people entered amidst snow flurries. Starcrest's daughter walked side-by-side with a relative of the professor's, judging by the fair complexion. Speaking rapidly to each other, they were too involved with their conversation to shut the door—or acknowledge a half-asleep soldier on the floor who complained about the draft. With their arms full of shopping bags, they headed for the stairs. The lettering on the bulging canvas sacks read *Madolich's Insect Farm and Emporium* in large text and in small print underneath: *Lizard food, medicinal ants, venom sacs, and more!*

Sicarius was familiar with the establishment, though he hadn't visited in some time. A wizened woman who worked in the attic sold poison-making supplies. He wondered what sort of concoction the pair might come up with that could be used in a large-scale application.

They climbed the catwalk and the girl used her elbow to thump on a door. Starcrest himself answered, listened to their words, and watched the excited gestures, then pointed them toward the cafeteria. They scampered back down the stairs.

Instead of returning to the office—from his perch, Sicarius glimpsed other men sitting inside, including Sespian—Starcrest stepped to the railing and surveyed the floor. He yawned and rubbed his face. Taking a break? No, there was more to it than that; he was looking for something.

Sicarius sat taller. He didn't have any reason to think Starcrest might want to speak with him, but might it not be so? He hadn't decanted his information on Flintcrest's camp, troop numbers, and last heard plans. Starcrest hadn't asked for the intelligence, but he would doubtlessly find it useful.

Then why haven't you talked to him yet, he asked himself.

Sicarius didn't know where he stood with the admiral, not after coming to the factory with the intent of assassinating him. Twenty years earlier, they had parted... not as friends precisely, but not as enemies. It had taken time for Sicarius to unravel the admiral's last words to him and to understand his reasons for not continuing to serve the emperor. A part of him wanted to tell Starcrest that he understood now, but an unfamiliar feeling of trepidation left him reluctant to speak with the admiral alone. Odd how one could face a boyhood hero as a youth, filled with confidence in one's own abilities, brazen in one's beliefs as to his own superiority, and not be intimidated at all. Now, older, he was less certain of the world and his place in it than he'd ever been.

Starcrest's gaze lifted toward the rafters. Sicarius wasn't hiding—if he were, no one would see him—but simply sitting where he could observe and nobody could approach him

unaware. The admiral's eyes met his. *His* face was hard to read. Interesting turnabout. Starcrest pointed toward the third office door, the one that Books and Akstyr had given up for him, and arched an eyebrow. An invitation?

Starcrest stepped inside, leaving the door open. Sicarius stood, trotted along the beam, and dropped onto the catwalk by the office.

Though bedrolls were spread for two, and Kyattese journals and notes cluttered the desk, only Starcrest waited inside. He stood, hands clasped behind his back in a loose parade rest.

Unconsciously, Sicarius came to a military-style attention, heels together and back straight, as Hollowcrest had once demanded from him when he was delivering reports. He launched into a description of Flintcrest's numbers, last known location, and camp layout, followed by a point-by-point analysis of the general's defensive and offensive capabilities.

"Thank you," Starcrest said at the end, a hint of amusement in his voice. It made Sicarius wonder if he'd already possessed the information, via spies of his own. "It is good that you were able to keep your wits about you during your ordeal."

As always, Sicarius kept his wince internal. "Yes, sir."

"I appreciate your thorough report, but it was actually a personal matter about which I wished to speak with you. A matter of curiosity."

"Yes, sir?" Sicarius wondered why he felt like a youth again, seeking to impress a tutor with his rigid attentiveness. Oh, he recognized the psychological reasons, but he'd thought he would be past seeing Starcrest as more than a man. He'd thought he might... what? Ask him out to the drinking house to become inebriated and swap stories of adventures they'd had? An unlikely scenario given that Sicarius didn't drink and few Turgonian warriors would be delighted by tales of assassination.

"Nearly twenty years ago, I sent sealed letters to old colleagues and relatives over here," Starcrest said. "They included instructions not to be opened until a certain date which came and went some years ago. Emperor Raumesys was alive

at the time. I had assumed there'd be, if not retaliation, at least some action taken when the contents were revealed to him. I believe you were still working for him then. Do you know anything about this matter?"

"Yes, sir," Sicarius said. "It was revealed that the Kyatt Islands were originally claimed by Turgonian colonists, and that when the first Kyattese explorers landed, they sought the chain for themselves. They used a plague to weaken our ancestors, then kill them, so they couldn't report back to the mainland." *Our* ancestors, he'd said without thinking, forgetting that Hollowcrest's records proclaimed him half Kyattese. But he'd been raised here. He'd never think of himself as anything other than Turgonian.

"I see. You know quite a lot about it then."

"I was there when the emperor and Hollowcrest read the letter."

Starcrest cocked his head. "What was their response?"

"Hollowcrest seemed indifferent, though he rarely grew impassioned about anything, at least not visibly."

"Yes, the few times I met him, he struck me as... passionless, yes."

Sicarius sensed that was a more civil word than Starcrest had first thought to use. "The emperor was livid. He wished to attack the Kyattese and reclaim the islands. Our ships were on alert in the Gulf at the time, due to all of the pirate raids, and Hollowcrest talked Raumesys into delaying hostilities. The emperor reluctantly agreed, but did wish to send an assassin to kill you."

No hint of surprise made its way to Starcrest's face. He nodded as if he'd expected nothing else. "You being the assassin who was in the room, I'll assume he wished to give you the job."

"Yes, sir. I refused it. That was when I looked up your postal address and tried to mail a warning. Your questions now lead me to believe it never arrived. I am not surprised."

"Yes, either the emperor's spies or the Kyattese government may have intercepted it. The Kyattese were particularly twitchy

then—though presidents have come and gone, their government remained aware of the threat. I must thank you then for—" Starcrest looked at himself, then Sicarius, and gestured to chairs. "There is no reason to stand in military stances while we speak. Please, relax." He sat in one of the chairs.

Sicarius hesitated. Relaxing wasn't something he did while discussing important matters with people, nor had he ever found sitting in chairs particularly calming. People could sneak up on someone sitting in a chair with its back to a door, and one could not easily spring into action from the seated position. As a boy, one of his tutors had always squatted when he grew weary of standing, and Sicarius had adopted the habit.

"They're not as comfortable as a hammock on a Kyattese lanai, I'll admit," Starcrest said, "but they aren't booby trapped. You needn't look at them so suspiciously."

"Yes, sir." Sicarius shifted one of the chairs around so his back wouldn't be toward the door and perched on the edge of the seat.

"As I was saying, I thank you for refusing to assassinate me. Twice now." Starcrest gave him a dry half smile. "Or is it three times?"

"Three."

"Last night, a few years ago, and... in the tunnels? Did you have orders to kill me if I didn't accept the emperor's offer?"

"Yes, sir. But you used your superior strategic mind to outmaneuver an inexperienced young assassin."

"That's what you told the emperor?" Starcrest asked.

"I thought I might receive less punishment that way. 'I let him escape' sounded unpromising."

"Ah, and did you? Receive less punishment?"

"It is impossible to judge since I have no way of knowing what the punishment may have been had I voiced the more succinct phrase."

"Of course." Starcrest leaned back in the chair. "Sicarius, I regret that your associations with me have always resulted in pain for you."

Sicarius almost whispered, "Me too," but only gave another, "Yes, sir." Those punishments were long past and inconsequential at this point.

"Is there anything I can do for you now? I would offer you the use of a guest bungalow on Tikaya's land on Kyatt, but if you can't relax in a chair, I can't see you swimming in the surf and lounging on a beach. Though I do recommend the practice. After years of constant fighting, the tranquility is a relief. At least for a time. Until your mind grows restless and dreams up a new challenge. Note, I do not recommend taking up surfing as said new challenge. Well, perhaps in your case, it would not be disastrous. You're an agile sort."

Surfing? For... relaxation purposes? How odd. "I would find it difficult to lie on a beach, visible from afar, vulnerable to anyone who walks past on a bluff above."

"Perhaps a deserted island would be more amenable to you than one full of people who might wish a Turgonian assassin... a bad day."

"Yes, sir. Amaranthe has suggested seeking such a place."

"Good. You two should go somewhere after this is over. Time out of the empire would do you both good, I suspect."

"I... don't think she'll wish to go off with me now." Sicarius didn't know why he'd admitted that. He hoped his voice hadn't sounded as plaintive as it had in his head. He should have simply repeated another, "Yes, sir."

"Oh?"

Was it too late to voice that, "Yes, sir?" Sicarius suspected so. "During the short time I was Kor Nas's slave, I killed and tortured many people for him. I did these things once for the emperor too, but found them less palatable this time. Of late, I have been less inclined to..." Sicarius was used to being able to say what he meant in a succinct manner. Why couldn't he find the words to explain this? "This last year, working with Corporal Lokdon..." he'd already used her first name—why try to put distance between them now? "I resented the lack of a challenge in capturing and torturing the Forge women. They were not worthy opponents." There's more to it than that, Sicarius forced himself to acknowledge. "Amaranthe would not have used such tactics on them. She would not have needed them. Through working with her, I have not needed them. I have grown... accustomed to not needing them."

"So, she's made you a less cruel man, and you appreciate her for that."

That was succinct enough, Sicarius supposed, though he'd always seen himself as pragmatic, rather than cruel. "Yes."

"But you fear she'll see this relapse as an unforgivable failing."

"I did not fight Kor Nas as hard as I could have," Sicarius said. "While he was sleeping, I could have killed myself to prevent him from using me so."

"I doubt she would have wanted to see that."

Sicarius said nothing.

Starcrest leaned forward, his elbows on his knees. "When I was a junior officer, I had a captain who took an interest in developing my career, as good captains are wont to do. I performed my duties diligently, but he saw that I preferred my books or the machine-filled solitude of the engine room to working with other men. I was teased a bit in school, you see, for being younger than the others, and smaller, and rather bookish. I had faith in my ability to become an officer, but I'd always figured I'd be an engineering officer, someday to command a small crew below decks, a crew that I assumed would be made up of bookish sorts not dissimilar to myself. Captain Orndivit had other ideas. He forced me to spend time above decks, ordering around grizzled enlisted men twice my age and commanding the cannon crew when we went into battle. It was because I was up there that my ideas were heard, and I even took command once when the captain and first mate were injured and all manner of chaos descended upon us."

"*Ensign Starcrest and the Blockade Runners' Revenge,*" Sicarius said.

Starcrest blinked. "Pardon?"

"It's a book." Sicarius wasn't one to blush, but he did

feel a tad mortified at bringing up a fictional account of the story the admiral was trying to tell. He shouldn't have spoken. Some delight at recognizing the favorite childhood tale had bestirred him.

"Ah, yes," Starcrest said. "I'd forgotten about those. They don't turn up much in Kyatt."

"It details your adventures with Captain Orndivit. It doesn't mention you being bookish and teased."

"No, I'd imagine that some authors think military admirals are born knowing how to command men and outmaneuver enemies." Starcrest pressed a finger to the desk. "My point is that Orndivit was the sort of man who made you uncomfortable by demanding the application of skills and traits you didn't believe you possessed. It tended to make one a better man."

"Yes," Sicarius said. Starcrest understood. Amaranthe had been that person for him. Not just for him. Maldynado, Books, Akstyr, and Basilard were all different men—*better* men—than they had been a year earlier.

"Now, I don't know Corporal Lokdon well enough to know which types of men she likes to go off to deserted islands with, but it's my understanding that she's taking personal responsibility—*blame*—for the crash of the ancient ship and the subsequent deaths of those trapped in Fort Urgot."

"Typical," Sicarius said.

"Command tends to be glorified, especially here in the empire, but it's been my experience that the downsides often outweigh the upsides. In fact, the so-called upsides are typically greater responsibility, more pressure, and more work. Recognition from your superiors can be heartening, but it can never fully make the downsides go away. Those who are injured or killed as a result of your decisions, their spirits haunt you for the rest of your days, even when they belong to nameless people whom you've never met. Sometimes those are the worst. People whose deaths were incidental, part of the power plays of puppet masters they never knew and never cared to know."

Sicarius thought the admiral should be having this discussion

with *Amaranthe* rather than with him. More sensitive than he, she needed it more. He'd learned to harden himself long ago, and though he might have regrets now and then, few spirits haunted him. Perhaps, he mused, because he'd so rarely been in command. Always a puppet, never the master.

Starcrest seemed to be waiting for a comment.

"It is curious that people choose to seek out command positions," Sicarius said.

That drew a sad chuckle. "Indeed, it is. Some people are driven to it though, by seeing unfairness or injustice in the world and believing that such calamities could be lessened if they took on the responsibility of leadership."

"That is Amaranthe, yes."

"I hope that in the end she will find that the prize—if there is one to be achieved in this situation—was worth the cost," Starcrest said. "In the meantime, I suggest to you that she is probably not going to feel she's in a position to judge *you* for anything you did under this wizard's control. From what little I've seen of her, I doubt she would have anyway. Decisions you make under your own control, that might be a different matter."

Yes, she'd always been disappointed in him—even when she hadn't said it, he'd sensed it—for killing as a solution, even those who'd declared themselves their enemies. "I shall consider your words, sir."

Starcrest nodded, and Sicarius believed himself dismissed. He headed for the door.

Starcrest spoke again. "Sicarius?"

"Sir?"

"Perhaps you already know this, having read the book, but Captain Orndivit was killed at the Battle of Savage Harbor."

Sicarius nodded. "He fell in action along with his first mate, and you had to take command of the ship. Even though you weren't the senior officer remaining, your force of will and what became known as the Wricht's Channel Tactic caused the others to listen to your wisdom."

"Force of will and wisdom, eh? That author certainly put

a grandiloquent slant on me and those events. Regardless, my point is that Orndivit died before I had a chance to thank him for the encouragement that he gave me. Being eighteen and still having some of the surly stubbornness of youth, I was occasionally... if not disrespectful, then sullen about the lengths he forced me to—I often felt he was picking on me, over the other ensigns. It didn't occur to me that he might have seen something in me that was worth drawing out. Anyway, it is one of my longest standing regrets—dear ancestors, it's been over forty years now—that it was only after he was gone that I fully learned to appreciate the man."

"I understand, sir."

Hand on the doorknob, Sicarius didn't move for a moment, wondering if he should let Starcrest know he appreciated him and his counsel, but he sensed that Starcrest would wave in dismissal of the idea. The admiral meant his story to apply to Amaranthe, not himself.

Still... "I appreciate your advice."

The half smile returned, and Starcrest inclined his head once.

Sicarius stepped out of the office and approached the one two doors down. He knocked lightly, but didn't receive a response. The door wasn't locked so he eased it open.

There weren't any lanterns burning, but some daylight crept in from the factory's tall outside windows. Four sharpened pencils, all the same length, all in a tidy row, lay next to a sheet of paper with notes written in Amaranthe's neat hand. Plans for the Barracks endeavor? It was too dim to read the page. He was more interested in checking on her, anyway. She occupied the blankets on the floor behind the desk, scrunched in a ball again, her back to the wall, though she wasn't thrashing about this time. Her chest rose and fell with soft, regular breaths. Perhaps she'd been too exhausted for the nightmares to take hold.

Though Starcrest had inspired him to talk to her—to offer to teach her the meditation he'd promised before—Sicarius would not wake her up to do so. She desperately needed sleep. He thought of returning to his perch in the rafters to find rest of his own.

Or, you could lie down with her, he mused.

Would she mind, if he presumed to do so? He *had* promised to stand guard the last time they'd been alone together in this room, and she'd been amenable to the notion.

Careful not to touch her, lest it waken her, Sicarius lay down beside her and closed his eyes.

He drifted in and out of his meditative rest. Many hours passed before Amaranthe stirred. Her eyes remained closed, but she yawned and stretched out a hand. Her fingers bumped against his leg. Her face scrunched up, and she patted about, trying to identify the unexpected object.

"Musharup?" she mumbled, then blinked bleary eyes.

"I suspect I would need to consult Professor Komitopis for a translation before finding a suitable response for that," Sicarius said.

"Oh. Hello." She pushed the dyed hair out of her face, rubbed her eyes, found them crusty, and grimaced. "I see I'm looking my best for you. I wasn't drooling, was I?"

"No."

"Good." Amaranthe pushed herself to a sitting position, the blanket falling about her lap. She looked him up and down, perhaps noting that he hadn't removed his boots or knives. "Are you here to... stand guard?"

Sicarius knew what she meant, but pretended to misunderstand. "I have been doing that for several hours now."

"*Hours*, eh? By yourself?"

He contemplated whether to respond. With her, there might be hours. By himself? Such needs could be taken care of more quickly. The topic seemed too crude to voice to her in blunt terms, and he was not practiced in coming up with humorous innuendoes.

When he didn't answer, she blushed and waved away the joke, a sheepish expression on her face. He should have risked the faux pas and replied with an answer.

"Do you know what time it is? Or how much time we have before... er, what *do* you have in mind anyway?"

What did he have in mind? To see if she slept better when he was there, holding her in his arms. To see if she might sleep even *better* after a couple hours of vigorous horizontal exercise. All he said was, "Teaching you meditation."

Her shoulders drooped. "Oh. It's not that I don't need that—and I appreciate your willingness to teach me—but I thought... I had something else in mind."

"I did as well when I entered your room hours ago, but you were sleeping. Hard. You may have been drooling."

Eyes chagrinned, she lifted a hand to her mouth. "I was? That's not—you shouldn't just... No, wait. I want you here. No matter how pathetic I look. It's not as if you haven't..." She squinted at him. "Are you... smirking?"

"No." Sicarius flattened his lips into their usual deadpan expression.

"You were. I saw it. You're teasing me, aren't you? Was I really drooling?"

"No," he said, more softly this time, and lifted a hand to brush a stray lock of hair out of her eyes. "I did not wish to wake you. We will be up all night."

She swallowed and leaned her head into his hand. He cupped her cheek.

"How long do we have until it's time to go?" she asked.

"A half hour."

"That's long enough to do... things."

"Some of the others are milling downstairs, making preparations. Someone will doubtlessly come to ask you a question before it's time to go."

Amaranthe opened her mouth to voice some protest.

"I do not know if I could keep from throwing a knife at Sergeant Yara a second time," he said bluntly.

She stared at him, her open mouth forming the word, "second," though no noise came out. It didn't take her long to remember what he was referring to, and her lips curved into a smile.

"Besides," he said, letting his eyelids droop halfway. "I want those hours."

"Oh," she whispered.

"Days, perhaps."

"Days?"

Still cupping the side of her face, he brushed her cheek with his thumb. "Days. I'll bring water. Rations."

"Not those awful bars," she blurted.

"Hm." Sicarius lowered his hand.

Amaranthe caught it and held it in her lap. "All right, you can bring them, but I insist on a couple of pastries as well." She stared into his eyes, serious as she made this proposition.

She'd started stroking the back of his hand, her fingers tracing the tendons, and it distracted him. What had they been discussing? Appropriate food for sustaining physical exertion, yes. He ought to tell her that sugary treats weren't suitable for activities requiring stamina, but a memory flashed through his mind, that smudge of frosting on her nose and his interest in... cleaning it off.

"A compromise would be acceptable," he found himself saying.

"Good." Her gaze lowered to his lips.

Was she contemplating a kiss? Her strokes to the back of his hand were already stirring sensations in his body, along with thoughts he'd been quelling while she slept. If she kissed him, he might forget his resolve to postpone their amorous acts until they had more time. Much *could* be done in a half hour. But a frenzied rush? Surely she'd want more. *He* wanted more for her, and for himself.

Amaranthe dropped her gaze to her lap. "Ah, meditation, was it?"

"Yes," he said. Did his voice sound raspy? Odd. They hadn't even kissed. He put more effort into finding his emotionless tone when he launched into an introduction of the history of meditation.

"You're sure you don't need hours for this too?" Amaranthe asked after a few minutes.

"It can be taught in stages."

"I see. Carry on then, carry on."

She kept stroking his hand while he spoke, eventually turning it over and running her fingers along his callouses. He prevailed against urges that called for him to drag her into his arms and show her exactly what he'd been thinking of while she slept. As he spoke, he did, however, indulge himself in the planning of what they'd do when they did find their hours.

All too soon, a knock came at the door. Amaranthe released his hand. It was time to go.

CHAPTER 15

SICARIUS GLIDED THROUGH THE STREETS, SCOUTING AHEAD for Amaranthe and the others, avoiding the pockets of fighting. Night had come a couple of hours earlier, so most of the skirmishes had broken off, but a few continued. The gangs were about, too, looting, or trying to. Many shopkeepers remained in their stores, fighting off would-be intruders with crossbows and swords. Sicarius stuck to residential areas, picking a winding route toward the Emperor's Preserve and the secret entrances to the Imperial Barracks.

They reached the park's boundaries without incident, and Basilard came up to scout the woods with him. He took point, ahead and to the right of the party, while Sicarius took the left. Footprints and lorry tracks crisscrossed the slushy snow blanketing the ground between the trees. The warming front from the south had come in, and icy clumps melted from bare branches, spattering on their heads and shoulders. Shots fired from time to time in the city, but the Preserve remained quiet.

That quietness ended abruptly when the team was halfway to the underground tunnel Sicarius sought. A woman's shriek arose from the west. He paused, turning his head to catch the remains of the cry, pinpointing the direction. He couldn't see the city from there, but given their position in the woods, he was certain it had originated on Mokath Ridge. He would have thought that area, where the wealthy lived, would be neglected by the soldiers, as there was little up there worth acquiring in terms of military maneuvering, though perhaps the gangs had taken their looting to those lavishly adorned homes. The only

reason he'd paused was the sheer terror and pain the shriek had carried. Would someone cry out so at a bunch of teenaged Akstyr-like thugs? If one's life were in danger, he supposed so. Whatever it was, it was unlikely it had anything to do with their mission.

A shadow trotted in from the northeast. Basilard. He carried a lantern, though he had it shuttered. He set it on the ground and released a sliver of light in such a manner as it wouldn't shine into their eyes—he only needed enough illumination for his hand signs to be seen.

I caught the scent of blood, he signed and pointed toward the northeast.

Human blood?

I believe so.

There may have been fighting out here earlier in the day. Flintcrest's camp is nearby. Though Flintcrest's camp should have been more to their east by now.

There was something else... something familiar.

Yes?

When he wasn't signing, Basilard was plucking at the seam of his trousers and glancing over his shoulder. *I'm uncertain. I would like your opinion. They shouldn't be down here.*

They?

But Basilard had already picked up the lantern. He jogged in the direction from which he had come.

Sicarius thought of returning to the team to warn Amaranthe—and let her know they were going to investigate something suspicious—but the others were a half a mile back yet. Traveling with the aid of lanterns, they were picking their way more cautiously across the forest floor, and Maldynado and Books carried a heavy burden, a four-foot-tall canister Starcrest had devised to hold his daughter's concoction. Amaranthe had more details as to what it was and where they'd use it. First they had to reach the Imperial Barracks. Sicarius wondered if they should be wasting time, following the scents of blood, instead of heading directly to the passage. Nonetheless, he

trailed Basilard, pausing only once, when he crossed the trail the others would come up. He broke a couple of sticks to form an arrow on the snow, indicating their northeasterly direction.

As he loped after Basilard, he tested the air again, as he'd been doing throughout the evening. He detected the scents of the forest, of coal smoke, of military rations, and... He sniffed again. Yes, the smell of blood tainted the air.

Freshly spilled blood, a lot of it.

The air held another odor as well, one that was earthy and musky. And familiar. One he hadn't smelled since last spring, since they'd been in that dam up in the mountains. Makarovi? Down here? Basilard was right. They were a hundred miles from that dam and hundreds of miles from what remained of makarovi territory. It was possible that one of the ones he, Amaranthe, and Maldynado had hurled downstream had found its way to shore and migrated in this direction, finding food to sustain it as it went, but such beasts did not tread lightly upon the earth. Someone would have reported the deaths, and the story should have made its way into the newspaper.

His nose, however, did not make mistakes, not like this.

His first urge was to find Amaranthe, remembering that makarovi chose female targets when possible, preferring the taste of their reproductive organs. His fear for her rose in his chest, so intense that he almost spun about and ran to her. But that would leave Basilard to possibly face one alone. Amaranthe had several men around her, enough to slow an attack should it come, and Sicarius would hear the sounds of melee. He could run back in time. She was competent enough to deal with a fight as well—if nothing else, she couldn't do worse than his example with the soul construct: fleeing up a tree.

Hoping he wouldn't regret the decision, Sicarius increased his speed until he caught up with Basilard.

"Slow down," he whispered. "We should approach with caution."

Basilard started to unshutter the lantern, but Sicarius stopped him, guessing at his question.

"Yes, I smell it too."

Moving more slowly now, they circled a copse of evergreens so they could approach from downwind. In this part of the park, boulders mingled with the trees, and some of the outcroppings towered above a man's head. Though hunters and the creep of civilization had long ago driven large game out of the valley, it was the sort of area where an animal might make its den.

He and Basilard picked a careful route, listening and smelling as they went. To Sicarius, the faintness of the makarovi odor implied the creature wasn't still about—their pungent, earth scent was overpowering in close proximity—but makarovi could move quickly on land, and just because it wasn't in the area didn't mean it couldn't choose any moment to return.

Sicarius spotted the body first, a dark form crumpled against the trunk of a tree. The paleness of the snow made the blood spatters stand out. Clawed plantigrade footprints surrounded the area. Basilard stopped and pointed at the body. He raised the lantern questioningly.

Sicarius nodded. "Take a look. I'll stand watch."

As Basilard peeled back the shade on his lantern for a close look at the corpse, Sicarius listened for the approach of the others—or for anything else that might be about. Plops sounded as melting snow continued to fall from the branches, but little else disturbed the night. Above the skeletal trees, clouds blotted out the stars and moon. A dark shape in a hollow between two boulders caught his roaming gaze.

Sicarius headed toward it. The number of clawed footprints in the snow increased. With several meters between Sicarius and the lantern, he couldn't be certain of the indentions, but he thought them varied in size. More than one makarovi?

He knelt, spreading his fingers wide to measure one of the prints. Not surprisingly, it dwarfed the width of his hand. He touched another one. It was bigger. He checked a third. Smaller than the first.

Sicarius struggled for his usual calm detachment, but another urge flowed through his veins, an urgent desire to race back and

warn Amaranthe. He made himself stay, probing the edges of the prints, trying to decide how fresh they were from the amount of erosion—the warmer weather was melting snow at a regular rate, but those edges were sharp. Recent. Two hours? An hour?

He rose to check on the dark hollow. More than a hollow, he discovered as he drew closer. A tunnel, freshly scraped from the earth, one large enough for three men to stride through, shoulder to shoulder. Large enough, too, for a makarovi to traverse.

Sicarius sniffed the air. It did smell of the makarovi, but not so pungently as one would expect from a den. The walls were even and tidy, too, more like something dug with machinery than claws. He peered behind him, half-expecting Heroncrest's tunnel-boring machine to be sitting under the trees somewhere, beside piles of moved earth. When he didn't spot anything in the trees behind him, he skirted the edge of the boulder formation. He'd only taken a couple of steps before he rounded a bend and found his moved earth. Great piles of dirt had been dumped behind the boulders. Snow blanketed some of them, but other piles had been recently dumped, the dark earth standing bare to the night.

The location behind the boulders would hide the evidence of extraction from the trail Amaranthe and the others were on. The hint of a large, dark form, too bulky and square to be a pile of earth—or belong to a lurking makarovi—hunkered beside one of the piles of fresh earth.

Sicarius jogged toward it. Another dark shape in the snow to the side made him hesitate. Another body. The light would help with investigating those, so he'd leave it for Basilard.

A few more steps, and he was close enough to make out more details. It was a vehicle. It lacked the conical front of the tunnel-boring machine, possessing instead the stub nose of a lorry with a large cargo bed ideal for moving earth. Two more battered bodies awaited in the snow, their arms akimbo. One's neck had broken upon landing. It was as if he'd been torn from the cab of the vehicle and hurled at a huge velocity. Sicarius checked the lorry's furnace. Heat radiated from the metal, and

red embers burned inside. The gauge had fallen below ready, so some time had passed, but the vehicle had been in operation earlier that evening.

Lights came into view, lanterns bobbing and weaving with the steps of men. Basilard stood and waved.

Relieved nothing untoward had happened to the group, Sicarius jogged in that direction.

"Are we there yet?" came Maldynado's moan from the trees. "This canister is *heavy*. Does anybody else think we should have been given an armored attack vehicle for carrying our equipment and for infiltrating a highly secured imperial building?"

"Are you whining again?" Yara asked.

When Sicarius joined the group, his silent appearance cut off whatever response Maldynado might have made. Good.

"It would be unwise to linger in the area," he said without preamble. "Makarovi have been about, no more than two hours ago."

One hour, Basilard signed, joining them. *That soldier's body is fresh.*

"Bodies? Makarovi?" Amaranthe spoke with admirable calm, but Sicarius didn't miss her darting glances toward the trees and the boulders. After nearly dying to makarovi claws last spring, she had more reason than any of them to fear the creatures. And he had more reason than ever to keep her from coming up with schemes to thwart them.

"The tunnel-boring team is dead," Sicarius said. "Four men. At least."

Basilard glanced at him. *Tunnel boring?*

"Their earth hauler is behind those rocks."

"So... the makarovi came out of the mountains and rushed into the tunnel, mauling everyone on the way?" Amaranthe asked. "That could work to our advantage, if we can avoid them. I wouldn't wish that pain—and death—on anyone, but if fate has delivered it... we *were* looking for a good distraction."

"The type of distraction where my older brother gets skewered by claws and turned into a makarovi appetizer?"

Maldynado dropped his end of the canister, causing Books, who had been walking backward, carrying the opposite side to jerk in surprise and lose his grip. He glowered at Maldynado.

"Eww," Akstyr said. "I hate those things. Aren't they the ones that eat women's... lady parts?"

"Yes," Amaranthe said.

Yara, who'd been trailing the party with Sespian, grimaced. "I hate those things too."

"If they've found a way into the Barracks," Sespian said, "and the building and courtyard gates are locked down, whoever's in there will be trapped."

"They didn't go inside the tunnel," Sicarius said.

Silence fell as the team considered his words. He took advantage, listening to the night forest around them. More plops of snow fell, but he didn't hear anything else, no further screams, nor the moist snuffles of those creatures advancing through the trees.

"They killed the tunnel team and moved on?" Amaranthe asked.

"No," Sicarius said. "They came *out* of the tunnel and moved on."

Basilard shook his head. *That doesn't make sense. You must have read the tracks incorrectly.*

"I did not," Sicarius said.

Amaranthe patted Basilard on the arm. "Now, now, you know you insult him when you say things like that."

She kept her teasing tone light, though Sicarius sensed that her jocularity was not sincere. As she so often did, she was trying to remain strong, insouciant even, so the others would not worry. Indeed, Yara had turned to face the shadowy trees to the rear, the rifle in her hands clenched tightly, her shoulders tense. Working as an enforcer sergeant, she too had been up near that dam, and she too had seen what the makarovi could do.

Perhaps the creatures traveled into it, used it as a den, and came back out again, Basilard signed.

"Makarovi came out," Sicarius said. "They did not enter."

I do not wish to belittle your tracking skills, Basilard signed,

but... He faced the others. *Sicarius did not see the tracks by the light of a lantern.*

"He's right," Sespian said. "It must be a mistake. Having makarovi come from inside the Barracks doesn't make any sense. We don't grow them in the garden."

Sicarius said nothing, though having his skills doubted by his son stung slightly. Sespian was right to question, he told himself. It *didn't* make sense.

"Here's an idea," Maldynado said. "Why don't we take the lights over there and all have a looksie?"

"Would you be comfortable dying if those were your last words?" Yara asked.

"I can't imagine any circumstance where I'd be comfortable dying, unless it were in bed, after being heart-stoppingly overworked by a lush, beautiful, and terribly athletic woman."

"More likely you'd be killed in bed, by a dagger from the woman's husband," Yara said.

Maldynado removed his hat and crushed it to his chest, a forlorn expression on his face. "I meant *you*, my lady."

Yara blinked. "Oh."

"Let's take a look at these makarovi prints," Amaranthe said before the conversation could veer farther off track.

"This way." Pointedly not taking one of the lanterns, Sicarius led the way to the tunnel mouth.

"Nice... body," Akstyr said. "At least it's not a girl. It's only deheaded, not de...organed."

"Decapitated," Books corrected.

"Whatever."

"Is there a better word for de-organed?" Amaranthe asked bleakly, her voice devoid of the humor that might have accompanied her words under other circumstances.

"Not that references the specific organs those creatures target," Books said.

"Pity," Yara muttered, still eyeing the forest warily. "I'd hate for there not to be a word for how we'll be killed."

"I'm sure Books can make one up for you," Maldynado said.

Sicarius waited while Basilard investigated the tracks with the help of his lantern. Amaranthe stepped into the tunnel, holding her own light aloft. The flame did little to push back the darkness, illuminating only a few feet into the earthen passage. It was enough, however, to see the round walls and regular cuts made by a boring machine.

"Do you think they made it through to the Barracks?" she asked.

"It's over a mile from here to there," Sicarius said, "via a linear route. This is farther out than the secret entrance to which I intended to lead the group."

"The one labeled sewer access point?" Amaranthe asked. "I've visited that one before."

"Yes." Reminded of their first couple of meetings, Sicarius remembered how callously he'd sent her to see Hollowcrest and how unmoved he'd been when he found her dying on that park bench. It chilled him now to think of how close he'd come to losing her before he understood her worth to him. "It's approximately one fourth of a mile away."

"With a shaman booby trap at the end."

"Ward," Akstyr said.

"We don't know *what* will be there," Books said. "After you fiddled with the last one, that shaman may have tinkered around and improved the security."

"That's... actually a good point," Akstyr said.

"I make them occasionally."

Basilard stood, a displeased wrinkle creasing his forehead. Sicarius waited for him to pronounce the correctness of his findings.

"Basilard?" Sespian asked. He'd been watching the investigation, puzzled, no doubt, as to how makarovi might have originated inside the Barracks.

It does appear that they came out this way. There are no tracks leading inside the tunnel. Basilard tugged off his cap to scratch his scarred pate. *There could be an intersecting tunnel ahead somewhere, allowing entrance from another outside point.*

Sicarius did not disagree with this supposition.

"Shall we check?" Amaranthe pointed into the tunnel. "If the boring team *did* breach the Barracks grounds before this happened—" she tilted her head toward the corpse in view, "—it may be an unguarded way in. I'd prefer not to alert the shaman of our entrance, and if I'm understanding the wards correctly, that could happen even if we find a way to bypass the alarm."

"It could," Akstyr admitted.

"What if *this* entrance is guarded by makarovi?" Yara asked. "That's worse than a shaman."

"First Marblecrest's troops and now makarovi." Sespian sighed. "My poor cat hasn't got a chance."

Amaranthe looked around at everyone, holding Sicarius's gaze a little longer. He nodded. Neither option was amazingly better than the other, and they needed to get on with their mission. The only unfortunate bit would be if this involved walking a mile to a dead end and having to backtrack, but it was worth the risk if it offered them a chance to learn more of the makarovi—such as if these beasts wore shamanic control collars like the ones in the dam had. If one of the contenders for the throne controlled such creatures, Starcrest would want that information. Sicarius had picked up five distinctly different prints from five different creatures before he'd stopped counting. As powerful as the makarovi were, even a force that small could have an impact in a wartime situation.

"We'll try it." Amaranthe took a step to lead the way into the tunnel.

Sicarius cut her off, gliding into the point position. Under many circumstances, he'd accept her going first, but *not* when dealing with monsters that preferred the taste of human women. She didn't object to his usurpation of the lead spot, and he trotted ahead, wanting to feel and smell the tunnel with senses that were superior to sight in such poor lighting. If makarovi raced down the passage toward him, he'd be the first to know it.

* * *

Amaranthe judged they'd walked about a half mile when she caught up to Sicarius. He'd stopped in the middle of the passage, his back rigid, his eyes forward, as if he were a statue. The rest of the team had been walking behind her, their lights bobbing on the dirt-and-rock walls, and they too halted.

"What is it?" she whispered, though she knew there was no point. He'd tell her when he'd fully processed whatever he'd heard or smelled.

"Nothing new," Sicarius said without turning around, "but the scent is growing alarmingly strong."

Basilard stepped up to Amaranthe's shoulder. *I concur. We may run into their den before we reach the end of the tunnel. Perhaps discovering it is what caused the excavation to stop.*

Amaranthe detected the musky scent now, too, and memories shivered through her, excruciating memories. We beat them last time, she reminded herself. Of course the layout of the dam had given them time to enact a plan. Meeting them head on in the tunnel would not offer that same time.

"I will continue," Sicarius said. "Wait here."

"Sicarius, wait—" she started, but he was already jogging away. *Running* away.

Amaranthe was tempted to run after him. To lose him now, when they were so close to... having a full-on, grownup *real* people's relationship... She sighed.

"I'm sure he'll be fine," Sespian said, stepping up to her other side. "I've seen him run. He's quite the sprinter. He should have been an athlete in the Imperial Games instead of an assassin."

We already have a competition-winning athlete in the group, Basilard signed.

"Yes, we do." Amaranthe patted him on the shoulder, though she didn't take her gaze from the tunnel ahead. "Let's keep going. We'll walk while he runs. He'll still see whatever there is to see first."

"As if there were... another option... than walking," Maldynado grunted. "Anyone else want to take a turn at carrying this thing?"

"Sorry," Amaranthe said, "but I couldn't lift it when I tried. Alas, I'm not as brawny as you and Books."

Books looked mollified at being called "brawny," though his face had an unhealthy turnip-like hue. Amaranthe was glad when Sespian said, "I'll take a turn."

Maldynado smiled brightly, though it faded when Sespian replaced Books instead of himself. "Hmmph," he announced loudly.

"What are we going to do with this big can anyway?" Maldynado added a few steps later.

"It's full of... I don't remember what exactly Mahliki called it," Amaranthe said, "but it's a liquid compound she derived from the venom sacs of... I forget that too. Some kind of spider. I remember that she was relieved that the city's main bug farmer had the correct specimens in suitable numbers, due to most bugs dying or hibernating in the winter." Amaranthe was lucky to remember that much of the explanation she'd received, as the young woman had spoken rapidly, sometimes slipping into Kyattese and sometimes into technical bug-babble that Amaranthe had followed even less than the foreign language. "The venom sacs contain a poison that paralyzes insects, so the spider can easily snack on them."

"I hope the plan isn't for us to go around shooting my brother's men full of poison and then eating them, because I had some of Basilard's chicken dumplings before we left, and I'm not in the mood to snack."

Amaranthe met Yara's eyes. "Did you want to smack him, or should I?"

"That's most likely my duty," Yara said, "though I wouldn't want him to drop that barrel, especially now that I know it's full of paralyzing poison."

"Actually, that's not quite it," Amaranthe said. "Mahliki and her cousin performed some fancy alchemy to turn it into an anesthesia of sorts. We're to pour it onto the coals in the basement furnace that warms the air that flows into the ducts of the building. It'll waft out of the vents as a colorless gas, supposedly without much of an odor either. We'll wait a few minutes, and when we come up, most of the resistance should be groggy or outright unconscious. Those on the inside of the building anyway. We'll still have to deal with the guards in the courtyard and on the walls."

"She made an anesthesia from spiders innards?" Akstyr asked. "How old *is* she?"

"Seventeen, I believe," Amaranthe said.

"That makes me feel less... special about my ability to use the Science to pull down people's trousers."

Amaranthe couldn't remember ever hearing Akstyr sound impressed by anyone, not out loud anyway. He usually rolled his eyes or curled his lips at the admirable feats Sicarius and his teammates could accomplish. Perhaps it was Mahliki's age. Or the fact that she was beautiful. Amaranthe decided not to mention that she'd caught Mahliki glancing Sespian's way a few times during the team meeting. "Don't belittle your skills," she said. "They've saved our lives a few times now."

"Wait," Maldynado said. "Akstyr's running around, forcing people to model their undergarments? When did he learn this new talent?"

"Don't ask," Books said, "or he may try it on you."

"I'd rather we head to the dance halls together, so he can demonstrate that skill on the pretty—ouch."

"Thank you, Yara," Amaranthe said without looking back.

"You're welcome."

Basilard jogged in front of Amaranthe and dropped to one knee, examining the dirt. The ursine makarovi prints weren't as perfectly defined as they had been in the snow, but one could make out partial tracks in the soft earth, not to mention the finger-thick punctures that marked the spots their long claws had set down.

"Same number of them as we saw at the entrance?" Amaranthe asked, though logic suggested the answer had to be yes. They hadn't passed any side tunnels or exits.

Basilard nodded. *The smell is getting stronger.*

Amaranthe hoped she wasn't directing the team into the heart of a makarovi den. Maybe they should have chanced dealing with shamanic alarms and booby traps instead. She peered into the darkness ahead. Sicarius hadn't returned.

"I thought that was Maldynado and Books smelling that bad," Akstyr said, "on account of working so hard to tote that big can."

"Ha ha," Maldynado said, "your sharp quip has skewered me like a venison kebob for a grill."

"How come he didn't include Sespian in his witty lambast?" Books pointed to the rear, where Sespian trudged along, now carrying the back half of the canister.

"He doesn't seem to sweat much," Akstyr said. "Even when he's not doing bookly things."

Sespian shook his head.

Basilard stood, pointing ahead. A moment later, Sicarius jogged out of the darkness. Yes, jogged, Amaranthe noted; he wasn't sprinting as if a herd of… makarovi were after him. Good.

"Come," he said, turning as soon as they saw him.

"No, no," Amaranthe said. "No need to tell us what you saw. We're not the curious sorts."

He'd already disappeared into the tunnel depths.

Amaranthe grumbled, but strode after him anyway. The others followed, this time without the banter. Sicarius hadn't appeared any grimmer than usual, but there'd been an urgency about his terse command and quick retreat.

A breeze drifted down the tunnel, bringing with it the scent of earth and snow, though the makarovi musk nearly smothered those more delicate odors. Amaranthe noticed her hand pressed against her belly, against the scars she'd forever have, a tangible memory of her last encounter. We're not heading into a den, she told herself. If she smelled snow, there was another exit to the tunnel.

Soon sounds as well as smells came from ahead. A din that Amaranthe couldn't place: bangs and clangs and shouts. They ought to be close to the Barracks; could they be hearing sounds

of an attack? Starcrest wouldn't have sent men to charge the gates, would he? As a diversion? No, he didn't have many men, and certainly none to spare for something foolhardy. Maybe Flintcrest or Heroncrest were attacking. Except that her team had already stumbled across Heroncrest's men. He'd been the general with the tunnel-boring machinery. His original plan of attack had to be on hold now.

Metal glinted ahead, not in the center of the passage, but off to the side in a hollow. Thus far, the tunnel had been straight without so much as a wall niche for holding the canteens and lunch boxes of the workers.

Sicarius stepped out of the hollow at the same moment as Amaranthe drew close enough to identify the metal object. The conical head of the tunnel borer stuck a few inches into the tunnel, with the rest of the vehicle backed into the nook.

When she took a step toward it, thinking to peek inside the cab, Sicarius lifted a restraining hand.

"There is nothing to see except mauled corpses. They were trying to turn around, to escape. Presumably the machine's forward speed is greater than its reverse speed. Either way, it wouldn't have mattered. Makarovi can cover ground quickly."

"I see."

"There are two exits ahead. One where the borer came up in the root cellar, and another in the courtyard where the ceiling caved in—or was pulled in—" Sicarius made an upward grasping motion with his hand, and Amaranthe imagined makarovi claws tearing into the earth. "That's where the tracks diverge."

"Root cellar?" Sespian asked. "Was the food destroyed? That's where most of the stores to feed the compound are kept. If Marblecrest was depending on those rations for his men..."

"I'm more concerned about what he means about tracks diverging," Amaranthe said. "Are we dealing with more than five makarovi?"

"At least twelve," Sicarius said. "More than half of them went up into the courtyard instead of down the tunnel."

"*Twelve?*" Maldynado groaned. "And us without a dam to hurl them off?"

"Maybe we can lead them to the lake," Books said. "The ice will be weakened with the warmer weather, and their corpulent frames ought to break through a couple of inches regardless."

"Lead them with *what* bait?" Yara frowned.

Sicarius gave Amaranthe a quelling expression. She hadn't planned to volunteer for that job again anyway.

Sespian raised a finger. "Just to be clear, you're saying they originated in the root cellar? How would that be possible?"

"An empty portion was sectioned off and turned into a cage, a cage secured with thick steel bars. The tunnel borer came up underneath it."

"That must have surprised the piss out of the operator," Maldynado said.

"Heroncrest's people must have thought the root cellar would be the ideal place to bring up the borer." Sespian touched the cone, its metal blades scraped and pitted after so much use. "It's underground, of course, and out in the courtyard, not attached to the main building. Unless a few servants were out collecting supplies for breakfast, who would hear the rumbling of the machinery underfoot?"

"Yes, good plan from Heroncrest," Yara said, "but is anybody else wondering how a bunch of makarovi got into the root cellar to start with and *why* they were brought here?"

"Maybe..." Amaranthe withdrew a kerchief and wiped earth off the borer's grimy blades. "Maybe Ravido wasn't planning on being a figurehead for Forge after all."

"You think my *brother* caught twelve makarovi?" Maldynado blinked. "He shot one of our cousins when he was out on a stag hunt with Father. After that, he was encouraged to abandon the hobby."

"With the money your family has, I imagine he could have hired someone to do the capturing for him," Amaranthe said. "Maybe he learned about our shaman friend from the mountains. Maybe he even excavated that cave we collapsed and found some of those collars..."

"You believe Ravido Marblecrest brought the makarovi here

and imprisoned them to be unleashed on the Forge people?" Books asked. "Once they'd secured his place on the throne?"

Basilard nodded in grim agreement. He must have been imagining the scenario too.

"Forge is comprised mostly of women." Amaranthe's hand strayed toward her scars again before she caught herself. She returned to cleaning the blades. "Makarovi like women."

"*Like*," Yara choked. "That's not the way I'd put it."

Gunshots erupted in the distance, drowning out the muffled shouts and general din drifting down the tunnel from the courtyard ahead.

"That's a despicable plan," Sespian said and frowned at Maldynado. "Your brother is a monster."

Maldynado touched his hand to his chest. "Do you hear me disagreeing? I wouldn't be surprised if Father had a hand in this as well. Anything to assure the family's place in imperial history."

Sicarius caught Amaranthe's hand before she could stand on tiptoes to clean the top part of the drill head. She didn't plan to fall into it, but supposed she *was* leaning precariously close to the sharp blades. There was no point in cleaning the machine; she just hated to leave those crusty edges alone. She gave him a sheepish shrug.

"Let someone else deal with eradicating the makarovi," Sicarius said. "There are soldiers all over the place, and the creatures can be killed by attrition—enough bullets to the head will stop one of them."

"What about twelve?" Sespian murmured.

"Now would be the time to enact our original plan," Sicarius said.

"Put people to sleep while they're defending themselves from man-slaying monsters?" Books balked.

"I climbed out of the hole in the courtyard long enough to assess the situation," Sicarius said. "The Barracks doors have been barricaded, the shutters on the first floor closed and barred. Many people are inside, and more are on the ramparts, trying to kill the makarovi and keep them from climbing up or escaping into the city. I do not believe any made it into the building."

"You don't *believe*?" Sespian asked. "What if you're wrong? How many did you *see* in the courtyard?"

"Two, but I didn't explore. I had to warn you." Sicarius met Amaranthe's eyes. "Currently, there are no barriers between us and the makarovi running around the courtyard. It is only their distraction that has kept them up there, but it's unlikely there are women on the walls amongst the defenders."

"No, but there'll be women inside," Amaranthe said. "Maids and kitchen helpers if no one else."

"Yes, one of the makarovi was clawing at the front doors, trying to get inside."

"Dear ancestors." Yara started pacing.

Amaranthe would have lifted a fingernail to her lips for thoughtful nibbling, but Sicarius hadn't released her hand. Given that it was the first time she remembered him holding it with others around, she wasn't about to yank it away. Alas, it probably represented a concern that she might race off and, at the urging of some foolhardy scheme, put herself into a makarovi's path, rather than a sudden interest in public displays of familiarity. She squeezed his hand, letting him know she'd had enough of risking herself stupidly, thank you very much. And after the debacle with the *Behemoth*, she wasn't in a hurry to risk anyone else either, not without agreement from the rest of her team.

"Any chance our anesthesia will put makarovi to sleep as well as people?" Amaranthe glanced from Sicarius to Books, guessing they'd be the most likely to know, though she was starting to wish Starcrest had sent his daughter along after all. Mahliki had been more than willing to come.

"Unknown," Sicarius said.

"Entomology is outside my area of expertise," Books admitted, "though it's possible. Mammals share some of the same aversions to venoms—a rattlesnake bite will kill a dog as surely as a man. It would, however, take a much larger dose to affect such a substantial creature. If it affected it at all."

"I think... we need to get inside the building before we

decide," Amaranthe said. "Let the guards on the walls handle the ones outside. They have far greater firepower than we do, and—"

A scrape, then a pattering of earth sounded in the tunnel ahead of them.

As one, everyone stared in that direction. Something knocking dirt loose? Something jumped down into the tunnel? Amaranthe swallowed. A makarovi? More than one?

She pulled her hand from Sicarius's grasp and signed, *How far are we from the courtyard entrance?*

Not far.

Any chance, Books signed, *that was nothing more than loose earth falling free? Because of all the activity above us?*

A heavy thud sounded, followed by more dirt pattering to the ground.

No.

CHAPTER 16

"**G**ET YARA AND AMARANTHE INTO THE CAB," Sicarius barked, stepping into the center of the tunnel. He crouched, his black dagger out and ready.

Before Amaranthe could decide if she wanted to object, no less than three sets of hands grabbed her. She was hoisted into the air like a sack of rice, ported into the tight aisle between machine and earthen wall, and stuffed into the cab. She landed on her rump between the back of the steering chair and the furnace. A dead man's half-severed arm hung over the back of the chair. Amaranthe gulped.

"Let go of—ouch—you oaf!" Yara was deposited next to her.

"Stay," Maldynado said, his eyes serious, all the lazy humor gone from his tone.

Assuming the order was for Yara, Amaranthe shifted to her feet. Maldynado pointed a finger at her chest, his hard gaze promising punishment if *either* of them went anywhere. Basilard, Sespian, Books, and Akstyr had already left the side of the cab to join Sicarius in the center of the tunnel.

The familiar musky scent of the makarovi rolled toward them, hanging so thickly in the air now that it stung Amaranthe's eyes. Someone fired, and two more shots followed, the bangs thunderous in the confined passage.

"We can't sit in here and do nothing." Yara scrambled to her feet. She glanced at the door, then at the body in the chair, and decided against jumping out. Yes, she knew what these beasts could do and who their preferred targets were.

"I don't disagree." Amaranthe turned around, considering the furnace and coal box. Plenty of fuel remained. If the boiler were cold, it'd take a long time start up, but if Heroncrest's men had been using the vehicle recently...

More shots fired out front.

"Look out," came Sespian's voice.

"Into the hollow," Sicarius said. "It'll have a harder time—"

He leaped out of sight, his black knife raised overhead.

"We have to do something," Yara repeated. "They can be killed, yes, but not without a ton of firepower. More than they have."

Amaranthe opened the furnace door. The flames had died down, but the embers glowed red and heat bathed her face. "Help me shovel coal."

A makarovi shriek pierced her eardrums, ricocheting down her spine. It made her want to cringe and crawl under the dead man's chair. Or maybe crawl into the furnace and shut the door. If not for the burning embers, she might have been tempted.

"I hope that means Maldynado shot its balls off," Yara growled. There wasn't a second shovel, but she hurled coal in with her hands.

Amaranthe had to stop her lest they smother the fire with their vigor. She grabbed a bellows and blew fresh oxygen onto the embers. Flames burst to life.

"Take over." Amaranthe thrust the bellows at Yara and turned to the controls. One of them would have to figure out how to work the machine.

Forward and reverse were easy enough—the lever was labeled—but how did one operate the drill? And where were the gauges to signal the boiler's readiness? And—she grimaced—why did that man's horribly mauled body have to be *right* there in the middle of the workspace?

Sicarius would have pushed it out of the cab, but she couldn't bring herself to be so callous. She tried not to look as she studied the controls.

"Look out, Amaranthe!" came Books's bellow from outside.

She lifted her head at the same time as a hulking figure leaped around the razored cone and toward her, a mass of shaggy black fur and fangs. It landed on top of the drill head, inches from the windshield. Claws like knives gleamed as it lifted a paw.

Amaranthe ducked behind the seat. "Down, Yara," she almost had time to shout. In the middle of her words that paw smashed through the glass.

Claws slashed, tearing through the air, groping for Amaranthe. She was aware of bullets firing, but more aware that they weren't effective. The paw tore off the head of the dead man and the back of the chair as well. Both items flew out the door, slamming into the wall of the hollow.

Yara cursed and yanked out her pistol. Amaranthe, flat on her back now, trying to avoid that swiping claw, did the same, though she feared the weapons would be useless. She fired anyway, trying to hit the beast in the eye. The top of the cab blocked the target, though, and her round disappeared into the fur of its shoulder. If it hurt the creature at all, she couldn't tell.

Then it grunted, moist saliva flying from its mouth, as its head was thrown forward. It cracked against the roof of the cab, and hot droplets of spittle flew through the broken window, spattering Amaranthe and Yara.

A black knife snaked around the creature's neck, and she realized the reason for its grunt. Sicarius had climbed onto his back. His blade plunged into fur, seeking a vital vein.

Amaranthe thought that might be the end, but the makarovi reared up, gyrating in the air, and did a clumsy but effective somersault. It landed beside the drill head and charged back into the tunnel, batting aside rifles shooting in its direction. The wild move had flung Sicarius free, but he dropped feet-first to the earth and raced back into the fray.

"Even these fancy new Forge cartridges don't do a cursed thing," Yara snarled, checking the rounds, as if they'd betrayed her somehow.

"No, we need a *bigger* weapon." Amaranthe found the control she'd been looking for and shouted, "Watch out for the drill," over the chaos.

"Don't skewer our own people."

"No, it'll have to be just right..." But Amaranthe couldn't see much of what was in front of her with the massive cone in the way. This vehicle must typically employ ground guides to drill. She leaned out of the cab. "Trap it in the tunnel, right in front of us!"

Only gunshots answered her.

"Yara, would you risk...?" Amaranthe jerked her chin toward the space between the machine and the wall.

"Oh, sure, I'd love to. Never mind that there's a dead man's head right down there." Her voice had grown squeaky and loud, but she clamped down on her terror and gave a quick enforcer's salute before jumping to the ground.

"Get it," Sespian cried. "Yes, the eye, the eye!"

Amaranthe couldn't tell if they were working to follow her order or not. Maybe they hadn't heard her over the screeches of the beast and their own gunshots. She was about to lean out of the cab and see for herself, but Yara shouted at her.

"Now, Amaranthe, now!"

Trusting her, Amaranthe shoved the accelerator to maximum. The vehicle lurched forward with a surge of power. She gritted her teeth, tenser than a bowstring. If one of the men got in the way...

With an even greater lurch, the borer slammed to a halt. For a second, she could hear the sheering of flesh and the grinding of bone as the drill spun, but a high-pitched squeal drowned it out.

"Hold," Sicarius shouted. "I'll finish it."

The gunshots Amaranthe had been aware of halted. Unwilling to remain blind, she jumped out of the cab on the opposite side from Yara so she could see. She wished she hadn't. The drill was still going—worried more about ramming the creature, she'd forgotten about it—and blood and fur spattered the walls and continued to fly through the air. Sicarius, his dagger sunken hilt-deep in that rubbery sheath of flesh, finally found the jugular. More blood spurted, and Amaranthe shrank back from the macabre sight.

"Uh, I think you can turn it off now," Akstyr said.

Glad for the excuse to climb back into the cab, where she couldn't see the pulverized beast, Amaranthe cut off the drill and backed the vehicle into the hollow again.

"Yup," Akstyr said a moment later. "It's dead. Real dead."

Someone vomited.

Amaranthe supposed she couldn't escape the tunnel without walking past that mess again. She wondered how long she could delay the unpleasantness. No, she needed to check and see if anyone was wounded.

Before she summoned the fortitude to walk back into the carnage, Sicarius hopped up beside her.

"You'll note," Amaranthe said, "that I did obey your order to stay in the cabin." Actually, Maldynado had barked that blunt, "Stay," but she was certain Sicarius would have agreed with it.

"So you did." He gripped her arm gently. "Good work."

"Thank you."

He was contemplating her with... admiration? Satisfaction? As usual, he was hard to read, but enough warmth seeped through the expression to please her.

"Just so you know," Amaranthe said, "I'd be happy to kiss you at a moment like this, but you have makarovi guts in your hair and a tuft of fur stuck to your jaw."

"This is a problem for you?"

"I prefer my lovers to be clean and gore-free. It puts one in the proper mood to express physical endearments."

"I shall remember your preferences." Sicarius lifted a finger and scraped ichor off her jaw. Right, she must look as bad as he. And he didn't care. He sounded... disappointed.

You almost died, girl, she thought, *again*. And the night was young. They could both end up dead. So why was she making jokes? Idiot.

"I changed my mind." Amaranthe placed a hand on either of his shoulders, rose on tiptoes, and pressed her mouth to his. She had a sense that an I'm-glad-we-didn't-die-and-there's-still-work-to-do kiss shouldn't be overly passionate or involved, but she found herself breathless when someone spoke in the tunnel, and they drew apart. Sicarius's hand, she noted, had found its way to her back, and she fancied she felt the warmth of his flesh even through her jacket.

"One down, eleven to go," Maldynado was saying.

It didn't sound like anyone had noticed their leaders smooching in the cabin. A good thing, most likely.

Sicarius drew back, though he let his hand linger on the small of her back. Yes, she preferred that faintly pleased expression on his face to the disappointed one, even if, she was certain, nobody else could tell the difference.

He hopped out of the vehicle and offered her a hand, as if they were disembarking from a steam carriage or trolley and heading in for a night of fine dining. Amused, she accepted the help down.

Up front, Akstyr was kneeling by the creature's head. He lifted a tuft of fur, revealing a silver chain around its neck.

Amaranthe groaned. "Sometimes I hate it when I'm right; I'm guessing those are similar to the ones the makarovi at the dam were wearing?"

"Not similar, the same," Akstyr said. "If not the same pieces, they were made by the same Maker."

"These aren't the *same* makarovi, are they?" Books asked. "Could someone have found them wandering around the mountains at some point this last year and recaptured them?"

"I know a way to tell," Maldynado said. "Lift up his leg and see if he has a big old scar in his nether regions. That's how we hooked them and slung them off the dam."

Books eyed the mangled, fur-coated groin area, considered his hands, then clasped them behind his back. "No, thank you."

"It's not important," Amaranthe said. "They're here. We have to deal with them."

"Anyone else think we should take the monster-grinder with us?" Maldynado tapped the gore-slick drill bit.

Amaranthe grimaced. So much for the earlier cleaning of the blades. It'd take a lot more than her kerchief to duplicate the feat now. At least her team had survived the fight without any serious injuries. Blood streamed from a gash on Basilard's arm and a cut on Books's jaw, but both men were still standing, swords and rifles at the ready.

"It would take time to drill a new tunnel at an angle sufficiently slight enough for the borer to climb into the courtyard," Sicarius said.

A boom sounded somewhere above them—a cannon.

"I don't know if those people up there have time," Amaranthe said. Not to mention that another makarovi might catch her scent and hop into the tunnel. It might be *more* than one next time.

"This way," Sicarius said, taking the lead again.

"Leave the canister," Amaranthe told the men. "We'll come back for it once we see how things are going up there."

They didn't need to walk far before the blackness ahead faded, and the caved-in hole in the ceiling came into view. Enough lamps burned in the courtyard that some of the light seeped below.

Sicarius made everyone wait while he hopped up, catching tufts of grass near the ragged edge, and checked the courtyard. When he dropped down, he waved them forward.

"Only one makarovi is in sight now, and it's up on the parapet. Continue to the root cellar." He waited for the others to pass, clearly intending to guard their backs.

A lantern in hand, Amaranthe hustled forward. The stench of the makarovi grew thicker, and she chose not to breathe through her nose. "If anyone invited me to a dinner at the Imperial Barracks right now, I'd have to pass, if the potatoes came from this cellar anyway."

"Agreed," Books said, his voice altered, as if he, too, was trying not to breathe through his nose. "What a dreadful place to house a cage."

You wouldn't think so from their strong smell, but with the proper seasoning, Makarovi steaks are quite edible, Basilard signed. *Or so they say. The rarity of the beasts means I've never partaken personally, only heard from old warriors.*

"They're not nearly as rare as I'd like for them to be," Amaranthe said.

"Agreed," Books repeated. He'd given up on his earlier method of avoiding the scent and had pinched his nostrils shut.

There wasn't a source of illumination in the root cellar, and Amaranthe almost missed where the tunnel ended and it began until her light played across steel bars. Her first thought was that they wouldn't be able to get out this way, having entered into the cage itself, but she realized she could turn sideways and slip through the widely spaced bars. They might hold a makarovi in, but most people could squeeze through.

Maldynado cleared his throat. "Anyone have a key?"

He'd slipped an arm and his head through, but the chest proved a sticking point.

Footsteps thundered past overhead, the echo changing as they passed from earth to the wooden cellar door back to earth again. A shout of terror followed after them.

"Look for the key," Amaranthe told the others, already moving toward the door, hoping a hook might hold a ring. Though she didn't know yet how she might help those in the courtyard, their obvious distress filled her with urgency.

"We could simply pull him through," Books gripped Maldynado's arm. "If he can suck in that belly."

"My *belly* isn't the problem. It's my well-developed pectoral area."

"Oh, please," Yara said.

"At least he didn't say it was his third leg that was too big to pass through." Akstyr snickered.

Just when Amaranthe thought the boy was growing up...

"Ouch—oomph!" A thud followed this unmanly cry.

Amaranthe abandoned her key search. Books and Basilard had succeeded in pulling Maldynado through.

Sicarius jogged out of the tunnel and slid through the bars with much less trouble.

"No belly on him," Books said.

"It *wasn't* my belly," Maldynado growled.

"The doors and the shutters remain secured," Sicarius said. "There aren't many men fighting from the walls. A few snipers are on the roof, but it looks like everyone else has retreated inside, leaving the others to deal with the makarovi."

"I thought Marblecrest had *troops* in there with him," Sespian said. "What are those cowards doing? Why're they sacrificing *my* men? I mean men who used to be mine, curse him."

"If Ravido is the one who brought the makarovi," Amaranthe said, "he may not want them killed. He may still believe they'll do their job, if they can escape the Barracks."

"Some of them have already done so." Sicarius waved toward the tunnel, indicting the prints they'd first seen. "I saw one more dead in the courtyard, and one living, but no others were in sight, nor were there sounds of a fight coming from the other side of the building."

"I'm going to flatten Ravido if I see him." Maldynado clenched a fist. "Even if the collars lead those monsters to Forge people, they're going to kill tons of other people on their way through the city. And women will get... gar, those things are horrible."

"There aren't even that many Forge people left, are there?" Books avoided looking at Sicarius.

"No," Sicarius said.

"What a mess." Amaranthe pushed a chunk of loose hair behind her ear and frowned—it was crunchy with dried gore. "In all possible ways."

"I want Marblecrest out of the Barracks more than ever." Sespian regarded first Amaranthe, then Sicarius, as if he wondered if he could make it an order and anyone would listen to him.

Amaranthe had never planned to give up, not when Starcrest had explicitly given her this mission, but she was glad to see the others nodding their heads in agreement with Sespian. Sicarius, too, gave a single nod when she glanced his way, though that surprised her least of all. He wouldn't give up on a Starcrest-assigned mission either.

"I concur," Books said. "Maldynado, why don't we go back and fetch that canister? I imagine some stealthy assassin can find a route into the basement furnace room from here."

"You'll have to lift that barrel up through the hole in the roof back there," Amaranthe said. "We haven't found keys for this gate."

"We'll have to go through the courtyard to reach the door anyway," Sicarius said. "There are shadows. And the soldiers are busy."

"Maldynado." Books slipped back through the bars, heading for the tunnel.

"Perhaps Sespian would like to go with you. He's a slighter fellow with less substantially developed pectoral muscles."

"Yes," Books called back, "no belly either."

Sespian lifted a hand in acknowledgment, then jogged after Books.

Maldynado propped his fists on his hips. "Yara, you've seen me naked. Do I have a belly?"

"Not at all," Yara said. Before Maldynado could appear too mollified, she added, "I assumed it was your fat head that got stuck between the bars."

Books was the one to smile.

Sicarius and Basilard, too professional to be drawn into the debate, had scouted the root cellar and, apparently finding nothing more insidious on this side of the bars than potatoes with eyes, headed up the stairs for the door in the ceiling. Crouching, Sicarius lifted it a few inches.

After a moment's observation, he said, "It's relatively quiet now. The makarovi who came up in the courtyard have either escaped or been killed. We'll still want to use caution, as we have to cross two dozen meters to reach the basement and dungeon entrance."

Amaranthe didn't want to think about the dungeon entrance. Her time spent there had been only slightly less unpleasant than her days with Pike on the *Behemoth*. Maybe there was some justice in using insects again, or an insect-derived product, on her return visit.

"We're ready," came Sespian's soft call from the tunnel.

Sicarius led the way into the courtyard.

Blood spattered the churned snow beneath their feet. Not for the first time, Amaranthe wondered how Maldynado could be related to Ravido. What a monster, to think up such a plan. Though she'd been guessing as to his intentions so far; they didn't have proof that he was behind the makarovi.

Sicarius pointed most of the team toward the basement entrance around the back of the building, while he and Basilard jogged to the gaping hole a few meters away. Amaranthe went with them, keeping an eye on the walls and the courtyard as they bent to pull up the heavy canister from below. Shadows, Sicarius had said, but the courtyard was too well lit for her tastes. The guards would have to be wounded and unconscious not to notice a knot of strange men pulling up a—

"You there," someone called from the auto-cannon station on the nearest wall—the gun was pointed *into* the courtyard instead of away. "What are you men doing?"

Basilard and Sicarius had already lifted the canister out of the hole. Books jumped, caught the lip, and pulled himself up at the same time as he knocked a small avalanche of dirt and snow inside. Ignoring the guard for the moment, Amaranthe grabbed his arm and helped him over the side.

Though he was having trouble—more earth crumbled away as he rolled toward her—Books was the one to respond to the soldier. "We got the makarovi poison the captain asked for."

Amaranthe snorted. She didn't know if that would work, but it wasn't any worse than anything she would have come up with.

Sespian scrambled out of the hole with less trouble. He and Sicarius lugged the canister toward the basement door.

"Poison?" the guard responded. "What poison? And *which* captain?"

"Intelligence," Books called back. Not a bad try. Most of the regular soldiers kept a wary eye on the supposedly sly officers who worked in that department.

"If you've got poison," someone else from the wall called, "bring it up here. We need it."

"Gotta report in first," Books called. He and Amaranthe were jogging after Sespian and Sicarius. A few more meters and they'd round the corner of the building and be out of sight, at least to those on that particular wall.

"How come you're not in uniform?" the first man called.

The second jogged over and nudged him.

"Hurry," Amaranthe urged, though the men couldn't go any faster while carrying that heavy load.

The auto cannon shifted, away from melee in one corner of the courtyard and toward her team.

"Get close to the building," Sespian said. "They won't risk shooting a hole in the first floor."

When makarovi were involved, Amaranthe wasn't so certain.

"Wait, that's a woman!" Someone pointed at her. "Girl, you need to get out of there. As soon as those ugly bears catch a sniff of you—"

Amaranthe ducked around the corner. The canister gripped between them, Sicarius and Sespian were already jogging down the icy steps leading to the basement, as if they'd been carrying heavy loads together all of their lives. The metal barrel, almost too large for the walled in stairwell, scraped and clunked against the cement foundation. Fortunately the rest of the team held the door open at the bottom. It'd either been unlocked, or they'd found a way through that lock.

"You next," Books said, a hand on Amaranthe's back, guiding her toward the stairs.

Behind them, footfalls approached, crunching on the snow. Amaranthe hurried, expecting troops with guns.

But one of the makarovi leaped around the corner behind them. It roared, the bellow powerful enough to send the stench of its breath rolling over them. Books's heel slipped off the top step. He would have gone down, but Amaranthe caught his arm.

"Don't worry about me," he yelled. "Go, go!"

The makarovi bounded toward them. Amaranthe pulled Books down the stairs. Halfway down, they both slipped on ice. Gravity threw them together, and they thumped and rolled to the bottom.

At the top of the stairwell, the makarovi reared onto its hind legs, its forelegs rising into the air, dark claws promising death.

A thunderous boom split the air in the same moment that someone grabbed Amaranthe's shirt and yanked her through the basement doorway. Before she lost sight of the stairs, she saw the makarovi get clipped in the shoulder by a cannon ball. The creature spun into the air above the stairwell, a mass of black fur and legs flailing. Then Amaranthe was inside, the door slammed shut, and she didn't see the rest. Though she did *hear* thumps on the stairs.

She tried to sit up, but she and Books were entangled, with someone standing over them.

A heavy bar thudded into place to secure the door. Sicarius, legs spread, was the one standing above them, and he gazed down, one eyebrow twitching ever so slightly.

"So," Amaranthe said, "they're *not* all gone from the courtyard."

"I may have been mistaken," Sicarius said, stepping aside.

"I've longed to hear those words for months." Books groaned and rolled to a sitting position. "Though it was always in response to my claims that you chose obstacle courses entirely too long and difficult for our team's collective abilities. Especially mine."

Sicarius did not answer, though he bent to offer Amaranthe a hand up.

"Thank you," she said.

"No, I'm fine." Books lifted his own hand. "I can get up on my own."

Several feet farther inside, Maldynado nudged Yara. "I'm not the only one who whines."

"No, it's a common trait amongst—"

Something slammed into the door, and Amaranthe didn't hear the rest. She considered the thick metal hinges and the solid oak boards. "Makarovi aren't as strong as soul constructs, right? It shouldn't be able to break in here, should it?"

"Unlikely," Sicarius said, "but we should act swiftly regardless."

Another thump rattled the door.

"Oh, I agree, in every possible way."

Akstyr and Basilard were in the lead, and Amaranthe and the others followed them through a short hall and down more steps. Before they reached the whitewashed walls of the dungeon, they stopped on a small landing and turned into a less inimical space: the basement. It smelled of wood and coal, scents she decided were pleasant when compared to the musk of the makarovi.

They found the furnace room—not much of a challenge since Sicarius, Akstyr, Books, and Sespian had been there before, albeit entering via a different route—and set the canister on the ground.

Maldynado, who'd been among the last to carry it, rubbed his back. "Let's tell Admiral Starcrest that his next poison delivery mechanism should be lighter weight. Pocket-sized would be ideal."

"I'll let you be the one to tell him that." Amaranthe fished in her pockets for the instructions the admiral had given her on setting up the barrel. There were hasty notes about temperature requirements and dispersion rates, too, the latter penned by his daughter. "I'm sure he's even more impressed with complaining than Yara is."

"Maybe, but I'm not trying to ensure his good opinion so that he'll keep sleeping with me."

"Sicarius..." Amaranthe drew him aside as Yara made some retort about her good opinion having yet to be earned. "We need someone to make sure the vents and flues are adjusted so that our special smoke doesn't flow out into the night." She glanced at Books, and he nodded. "Also, we absolutely cannot put people to sleep up there if there's a chance there's a makarovi inside the building. If there's a duct you can squirm through, would you mind taking care of this business?"

"Squirm," he said in one of his flat tones.

"You'd prefer a different word?"

"I do not squirm."

"Even in bed?"

"No."

"Fine, is there a duct you can thrust yourself through in a manly manner? Thrust is an acceptable word, I hope." She bit off an inquiry about whether he performed *that* verb in bed, deciding it was a tad crass.

That eyebrow was in danger of twitching again, but another bang sounded back at the exit door, and he must have decided the time for play was over. Sicarius jogged beneath a massive duct leading from the furnace and into the wall and unscrewed what she guessed was the vent to a maintenance shaft. He glanced at her before, yes, *thrusting* himself through the opening. If any squirming went on, he waited until he was out of sight to do it.

"Let's see that paper, Amaranthe." Books had tipped the canister upright beside the furnace and unfolded something similar to, but more complicated than, a hose and spigot. "We should have this ready as soon as he returns."

Basilard was standing watch next to the exit leading to the stairs, and he closed the door firmly. *I don't believe that basement door will hold.*

"What happened to our allies with the cannon?" Maldynado asked.

"It's hard to shoot a cannon around a corner and down a stairwell," Sespian said.

"Just when you think technology is helping civilization progress in a useful way."

Amaranthe handed the sheet of paper to Books, happy to let him puzzle over the details, and joined Basilard at the door. She touched the wood. Though these boards were oak, too, they weren't so stout as the ones upstairs.

It won't have much trouble breaching this door, Basilard signed, echoing her thoughts, *if it makes it through the one above.*

One that wasn't as substantial as the thick gold-gilded entrance doors to the main floor—Amaranthe remembered their stoutness from her first trip. They'd been opened by steam technology rather than by a butler with a burly arm. Though there'd be women inside the Barracks, the makarovi might find those in the basement a more attainable prize.

"Let me know if anything changes," Amaranthe said.

Basilard, his ear already pressed to the door, nodded once. If nothing else, they could escape into the ducts the way Sicarius had gone. The makarovi would be too big to follow them. They'd have to leave their canister behind though.

"Ah, there's a foldout handle too," Books said. "What a clever little contraption. I'd love to take it apart and see how the inside works."

"Perhaps after we've dispensed the anesthesia," Amaranthe murmured.

"When did he have time to build this?" Sespian asked. "Has anybody seen Admiral Starcrest *sleep* since he got here?"

"Aw, he's been retired for twenty years," Maldynado said. "I'm sure he had plenty of time to rest then."

Amaranthe thought of the submarine she'd seen and the hints Tikaya and their daughter had offered as to some of their adventures. "I'm not sure retired is *quite* what he's been."

A crack and a crash came from outside. Basilard met Amaranthe's eyes.

"Akstyr, I don't suppose you have any Science tricks for distracting makarovi?" she asked.

"I don't know. I guess I can't pull down its underwear."

Books frowned at him. "Surely, your creativity can fathom other applications of similar skills."

"You want me to pull its fur down?" Akstyr asked.

"Never mind."

"Is that contraption working yet?" Amaranthe pointed at the canister, now with tubing in a coil at its base.

"Yes, but you want to wait for Sicarius's return, right?"

"I want to—"

Loud snuffles crept through the door. A few meters away, claws clacked on a cement floor.

Amaranthe clamped her mouth shut, and everyone else stopped talking, as if sound were what had led the creature to the basement.

She grabbed the end of the hose, unraveling it as she returned to the door. She slipped the tip into the crack beneath the boards. The clacking claws halted, and the loud, moist sniffs filled the hallway outside the door.

The door is not much of a barrier for the passage of air, Books signed. *The gas may affect* us *too.*

We can escape into the ducts if we start to feel groggy. Amaranthe pointed at the handle on the canister.

I hope it's that simple. With obvious reluctance, Books turned the handle.

With the hose placed, Amaranthe backed away from the door.

She caught Maldynado signing, *What if the gas seeps through and knocks us out without hurting that beast at all?*

Books shrugged bleakly.

A smash rattled the door. It might have been a paw or a shoulder. It hardly mattered. Under that first exploratory blow, the hinges groaned.

Sespian, Books, Yara, and Maldynado drew their weapons, but they also eased closer to the maintenance shaft into which Sicarius had disappeared. Basilard waited beside Amaranthe, a pistol in one hand, a dagger in the other.

When another blow battered the door, she took Books's place at the canister and turned the handle up farther. A soft gurgle came from the hose. Right, she reminded herself, it was a liquid, not a gas. Not yet. It needed to be heated first.

"Akstyr," she whispered.

He had moved close to the shaft, too, though he had his eyes closed, his forehead furrowed in concentration. She started to wave for someone to bump him, but he opened his eyes of his own volition. He shook his head at her.

"That collar isn't just controlling it; it's protecting it."

Uh oh. Would it protect the creature from their concoction too? Or only Science-based attacks? There was no time to ask and debate about it.

"There should be a bunch of liquid on the floor out there," Amaranthe said, her words punctuated by another blow. One of the old boards cracked under the force. "I need you to heat it up. I *know* you can do heat."

"Oh, yes." Akstyr brightened. "Even if I can't attack the makarovi directly, I can make that hallway hotter than the sun's armpit." He rubbed his hands.

"Just make sure the liquid is heated," Amaranthe said.

He waved and closed his eyes again.

Another blow hammered the door. This time a hinge popped, and the top half tilted inward a couple of inches.

"Now would be a good time," Maldynado said. "Yara, get in the duct."

"I'm not turning coward and fleeing," Yara growled, though her tone lost some of its fierceness when long claws slipped over the top of the door.

The beast was probing, but in a second, it'd attack in full force.

"Akstyr," Amaranthe urged. At the same time, she waved the others toward the vent. "Yara, go. We can come back later, when it wanders off." *If* it wandered off. The beasts had cursed singular minds where female prey was concerned. She turned off the handle on the canister. If the liquid hadn't worked by now, it probably wouldn't.

Yara hesitated, but Maldynado hoisted her from her feet and shoved her into the shaft. Grim-faced, he stalked toward Amaranthe.

"You're next."

"Wait," Akstyr blurted. "It's burning. That gunk is all over its feet. I think—"

The deafening roar of startled distress almost had the power to blow the door down on its own. The claws flexed on the boards. A snap sounded, the final hinge breaking free.

Amaranthe ran to join the others at the vent, though she knew there'd be no time for everyone to climb in, not before the creature rushed inside.

Flames danced in the hallway, surrounding the makarovi. It reared and roared, smashing its head and shoulders against the ceiling, but didn't come in. The heat poured through the doorway, competing with the furnace. Amaranthe couldn't tell if the creature was being burned, but it was surely alarmed.

"Inside you go." Maldynado snatched her around the waist and thrust her through the vent opening with the same maneuver he'd used on Yara. "Books, you next."

Shots fired. Amaranthe didn't want to hide—she wanted to see if the gas worked—but someone was pushing against her—or being *jammed* against her—and she had to crawl deeper into the shaft. She found the first bend—and Yara's feet. Yara seemed as reluctant as she, and wasn't moving quickly.

"More coming," Amaranthe said.

On her knees and elbows, her head brushing the low ceiling, she sped along as quickly as she could. Behind them, more shots fired, and she tried not to feel like a coward for fleeing while her men were fighting.

"Books?" she asked over her shoulder. "Who's still out there? With the door down, there won't be any barrier. If they fall unconscious and the makarovi doesn't..."

"I'm aware of that problem," he bit out from a ways back. He'd stopped before the bend.

Amaranthe stopped too. She sniffed the air, trying to detect... whatever it was the gas would smell like. Mahliki hadn't mentioned that.

The gunshots had stopped. Nobody had cried out or screamed. She hoped that meant something. Something good. Because if the men were unconscious, they might not wake as the makarovi claws tore into their chests.

Bile rose in her throat as the image of the mauled driver of the boring machine jumped into her mind.

"Books..." She didn't know what she wanted to ask. "We should go back and check."

"I don't know how long it takes for the gas to dissipate. We might fall asleep in the ducts and drown in our own drool."

"We're a grim lot tonight, aren't we? Who's behind you? Did anyone else make it in?"

"I thought... I thought Sespian did, but... No, nobody's behind me."

In the utter darkness ahead, Yara cursed. Amaranthe wiped

sweat from her brow. There might be snow on the ground outside, but it was hot and stuffy in the vent.

"Let's go back," Amaranthe said. "We have to know what's happening. What happened."

"I don't hear a thing," Yara said.

"Neither do I." Amaranthe backed up. Without any room to turn around, she had to squirm—yes, there was no way anyone could navigate this tight shaft without squirming—her way around the bend again, feet first this time.

She caught up with Books before he escaped the shaft. "Sorry," she said after sticking her boot in his hair for the third time.

"Never thought you were the type to kick a man when he was in a horizontal..." Books sniffed a few times. "Do you smell... I'm trying to decide if I feel groggy."

"I see the light from the furnace, just past you. You're almost there."

"I'm not sure if that should encourage me to continue on or not," Books said.

"It depends on whether you want my boots in your face again. I'm going through to check one way or another."

"Pushy woman." Books sniffed again.

Amaranthe could smell the odor, too, though the stink of the makarovi was stronger. The gas reminded her, of all the unlikely things, of lilacs. Maybe Mahliki had given it a fake scent to override something less pleasant, something that might make people flee to escape it.

"If you're that worried about it, stop inhaling," she said. "Pull your shirt up and hold your breath."

Amaranthe couldn't decipher the grumbles that followed, but she did hear the deep inhalation, then scuffles as he moved again. She continued scooting back. The light brightened. Books had crawled out.

She hurried to join him, lest he was even now passing out and being eaten at the same time. She was in such a hurry that she fell out in an ungainly tumble. When she tried to roll to her

feet and spin toward the door, she tripped over a body on the floor. Her heart jumped into her throat. Dear ancestors, if they were all dead...

But the makarovi hadn't moved past the threshold. Akstyr's flames had burned out, and the furry mass lay across the threshold, its bulk taking up two-thirds of the doorway. Not two feet from it, Basilard was sprawled on his side, his dagger stretched out toward the creature. Akstyr, Sespian, and Maldynado all lay flat on the floor around the maintenance shaft, their weapons also in their hands.

With relief, Amaranthe noted the rises and falls of their chests. Everyone was breathing. Unfortunately—she ventured closer to check—the makarovi was too.

She hadn't taken a breath since she entered the room. She had no idea whether it was safe or not. Either way, they had better kill the makarovi before it woke up. Since Basilard's dagger had a long, sharp serrated blade, she chose it instead of her own. It took a few seconds to pry it out of his hand. She approached the beast grimly, not certain she'd be strong enough to kill it even in this state.

Let me, Books signed and waved for the knife. He'd pulled his shirt over his nose and mouth. *You hold the fur away, so I can...* He shrugged.

What a fun use for teamwork. Grimly, she obeyed, parting the thick fur and baring the black skin beneath it. Sawing a board wouldn't have been any easier, but at least the anesthesia kept it asleep. Amaranthe watched tensely, expecting it to rise at any moment, to rise and *leap* at her, claws slashing.

As the moments passed and the blade sawed deeper, blood started to flow, then spurt.

"I think I got the jugular," Books panted, "finally." He blinked a few times and looked at Amaranthe in alarm. "Do you feel—I'm groggy. Tired. Sleepy."

"I know, me too. Cut a little further, will you? Just to make sure." She yawned, fighting off the effects of the lingering odor. Lilacs. Definitely lilacs.

"It's dead," came a new voice.

In her woozy state, it took a moment for Amaranthe to identify it and locate the source. Sicarius stood by the shaft entrance, gazing at her.

"Yes, good." Amaranthe stood up. She had to brace herself on the wall. "We decided to test the concoction. Starcrest and his daughter do good work."

"I see."

"Anyone mind if I take a nap?" Books hadn't bothered with standing; he'd simply flopped against the wall, his head lolling back.

"There are no makarovi in the building," Sicarius said. "And I found Ravido's location."

"Good." Amaranthe staggered toward him, having a notion that the air would be clearer farther from the hallway. She tripped on someone's outstretched arm. Sicarius was thoughtful enough to catch her. She smiled up at him, fighting off another yawn.

"I heard a conversation that gave me information that one person in this party will deem important." Sicarius studied Sespian's inert form at his feet.

"What's that?" Amaranthe asked.

"His cat is alive. And irritating Ravido."

CHAPTER 17

THE STENCH OF THE DEAD MAKAROVI MADE IT DIFFICULT to smell anything else, but Sicarius stood beside the doorway, his back to the wall, his senses attuned to the hallway on the other side of the body. The scents of snow, blood, and black powder drifted down from the broken basement door, but the sounds of battle had faded. Nobody had entered via the basement stairs either. The soldiers on the wall and in the courtyard were probably relieved the makarovi had disappeared beneath the building and had no interest in following it. Sicarius remained alert regardless and kept an eye on the open vent as well while Books and Basilard moved the large metal canister closer to the furnace so he could redeploy the hose. Akstyr had lost a game of private-sergeant-captain and was shoveling coal into the firebox to increase the hot air available to flow through the system.

"Judging by how long it took everyone to wake up," Amaranthe said, "we'll have about fifteen minutes between the time the gas disperses and the time the people up there return to their senses. In theory, we could run back down here and send out another dose, but that might be difficult to coordinate, especially if one team runs into trouble. I'm also not sure what the effects of being dosed over and over might be."

"I can tell you I have a blazing headache." Maldynado pressed a palm to his skull.

Sicarius waited for Yara to accuse him of whining, but she was standing next to him, almost leaning against his shoulder, and gave him a concerned look. The battle must have been

more harrowing than anyone had let on. Sicarius was relieved Amaranthe and the others had found a way to handle the makarovi without him; he'd been three stories above the furnace room and had rushed back as soon as he heard the roars of the beast, but traveling through the duct systems was tediously slow. He'd cracked his elbows and his head more than once in his haste to return to help. He resolved not to let Amaranthe send him away from her again, not while makarovi remained alive.

"Though I'm terribly grateful that you three came back to kill our new furry doorstop," Maldynado added.

"Yup," Akstyr said, "it would have chewed donkey testicles if the makarovi had woken up first."

"That, and I'd hate to have been nominated as the one to finish it off." Maldynado grinned. "Books did a decent butchering job there, didn't he? All we need now are some steaks so Basilard can prove to us that makarovi actually *does* make a decent meal."

"I'd rather eat one of Sicarius's greasy bars," Akstyr said.

Books had opened the furnace door and snaked the hose as close to the flames as he dared. "I'm prepared."

"Go ahead and start." Amaranthe stepped away from the furnace. "It'll take a while to wind through all those ducts and affect people."

"What's the plan for dealing with those people once they're out?" Sespian asked. "If we're only going to have fifteen minutes, and there are thousands of men…"

Amaranthe nodded. "A difficulty. I propose that we split into three teams. Maldynado, Yara, and Akstyr on one team, and Sespian and Basilard on another. Books will remain here, ensuring that nobody disturbs the dispensary device while we're up there." The last thing they wanted was for somebody to figure out what was going on and turn it on while her team was roaming the halls. "You'll race through the floors as quickly as possible, picking out high-ranking officers and carting them down to the dungeon and locking them in cells. Don't bother with the staff. Sespian, before you and Basilard drag anyone out, I want you to run up to your rooms and find a dress uniform. Put it on with

all the imperial accoutrements you have time to grab. When people start waking up and see you here while Ravido and their superiors are missing, I'm hoping they'll be eager to switch sides, or at least won't want to pick a fight."

"You're going for Ravido?" Sespian asked.

"Sicarius and I will fetch him for questioning. I want to know if we've guessed right about these makarovi or not. It's possible the Forge people *aren't* their target. I've been wondering why half of the pack stayed on the premises while half ran off into the Emperor's Preserve."

"Into the city," Sicarius said. "I heard screams from Mokath Ridge, and the tracks we saw headed in that direction too."

"Were those the well-mannered makarovi who did as their collars commanded, or were those the rogues?"

"Unknown," Sicarius said, though he suspected her question had been rhetorical.

"We'll focus on securing the building first," Amaranthe said. "Anyone have questions? Disagreements?"

"What about the practitioner?" Akstyr lowered his shovel and swiped sweat from his brow. "The one who set the wards might also be the one who altered the collars so the makarovi have a new target."

"I'm hoping she took the night off," Amaranthe said. "But if anyone sees her, grab her. We'll have to set a guard on her. Even then, I don't know—Akstyr how does one imprison a practitioner and keep him or her from using mental powers to escape?"

"There are some Made devices that can subdue prisoners." Akstyr glanced at the wound at Sicarius's temple. "Otherwise, you have to keep them as distracted as possible."

"The Nurians use a form of water torture," Sicarius said. "Lay the practitioner on his back and pour water over his face, so that he has to concentrate on not choking, thus not letting him focus his thoughts on anything else."

"How... lovely," Amaranthe said.

"Killing her would also be an option, for whoever finds her while she's asleep." *If* she was asleep, Sicarius thought. If the practitioner figured out what was happening to her comrades before she succumbed herself, she might be able to fashion a way to protect herself from the tainted air.

"Uh." Amaranthe glanced at the dead makarovi, but seemed disinclined to order the same fate for a human being. "If anyone sees her, bring her back here. We'll handle her the best we can. She might be worth questioning, especially if Ravido slips away somehow."

Sicarius had spotted Ravido alone in Raumesys's old office, drinking brandy as he stared glumly out the window—he had no intention of letting the general slip anywhere. He expected the man, too cowardly to run out and fight the makarovi or help anyone, to still be in the room when he and Amaranthe returned. He didn't argue with her order though.

"The gas is flowing," Books announced.

"Are the ducts the only way for us to get from the basement to the main floors without going outside?" Amaranthe asked Sicarius.

"No. There's a coal elevator and servants' access ladders in the room next to this one."

Sicarius climbed over the slain makarovi and into the hallway. Amaranthe and the others followed him as he entered a large storage room with chutes in the ceiling. Full coal bins lined the walls. He led them to a ladder at the back of the room and up to a trapdoor where he stopped to listen. A few thumps reverberated through the floor. They didn't sound like footsteps. More like people falling to the ground.

At the base of the ladder, Amaranthe lifted her eyebrows.

"The servants quarters and lounge are up here," Sicarius said. "It's a busy area."

"Is it *still* a busy area?"

He held up a finger. He caught a bleary, "Wha's going on?" then another thump.

Several seconds passed without a sound. Sicarius lifted the trapdoor a few inches and eyed a tile floor covered with shabby area rugs and unconscious people.

"We should wait a couple more minutes," Sicarius said, "for the gas to reach the top floor, then Books can turn off the flow."

Basilard was standing nearest to the door. He nodded and left to deliver the message, then returned a few minutes later. *It should be safe.*

Sicarius checked the room above again, then climbed out, inhaling to see if he could detect the odor of the gas, or anything else that would suggest danger. The kitchens weren't far off, and the odors of hams and cloves were the most noticeable, though he caught the lingering scent of lilac too. One wouldn't think of a poison or anything nefarious if one caught a whiff, though he did sense a hint of something alien underneath it, a chemical scent that must come from the venom used to create the compound.

He would have liked to remain by the trapdoor until he was certain the scent had faded and wouldn't affect him, but they didn't have much time. Amaranthe had already climbed up the ladder beneath him and waited, a question on her face.

"No one is awake," Sicarius said.

Amaranthe waved to the others. "Let's go." She spoke in a whisper, though he doubted it mattered. These people wouldn't be roused by noise, not until the gas wore off.

The men ascended the ladder, and the teams departed without a word. With Amaranthe behind him, Sicarius jogged down the narrow servants' corridors and to ladders and utility lifts that led to higher levels. They climbed to the third floor, at which point they had to head into the main hallway. Fewer bodies lay crumpled on the polished floor tiles than he expected, but when he glanced through the open door to the library, he spotted dozens of people on the carpet near the windows. That made sense. People had been gathered to watch the chaos outside and ensure the makarovi weren't finding entrance.

"I'd forgotten how big this place is," Amaranthe whispered. "I'm afraid our men won't be able to pull out more than a few handfuls of people."

"Ravido is the most important one."

Sicarius turned down a side corridor that led toward the suites for the imperial family and closest advisers. He stopped before the rooms Raumesys had once claimed. The door was locked. When Sicarius had observed the general, he'd done so from the vent in the wall.

"I suppose knocking won't be effective." Amaranthe reached for her belt. "Do you want to pick the lock or shall I?"

Sicarius touched the double doors. They opened inwardly and though made of solid wood weren't as thick as the building's exterior doors. Nor as sturdy. He turned, drew in his leg, and unleashed a sidekick. Wood cracked, and a door flew inward, banging against the wall.

Dagger in hand, Sicarius lunged inside. He didn't expect opposition, but he scanned the room anyway, listening and smelling, as well as eyeing the shadowy niches.

"I see," Amaranthe said from the hallway, "*you're* volunteering to pick the lock. Excellent."

A fire burned in a hearth taller than Sicarius, though a bin of coal also waited next to a stove in the corner. There weren't any lamps lit in the outer seating room, but light came from the office on the other side. Deep phlegmy snores also drifted from the room.

"Is that Ravido?" Amaranthe whispered.

"He was alone when I saw him."

"Goodness, I better warn Yara."

"About what?"

"That Maldynado could sound like that one day," Amaranthe said.

A particularly noisy snore reverberated from the walls in the office, punctuating her statement.

Sicarius strode for the office door, but hesitated, an offensive odor reaching his nose. Another door opened to the left. Though it was dark inside, he could make out the frame of a massive bed and a clothing wardrobe. A distinct smell came from that direction. Urine. Cat urine.

"Something wrong?" Amaranthe whispered.

He almost said no, but decided she'd be amused. "We may have a secret ally in Sespian's cat."

Her nose crinkled as she caught the first hint of the odor. "Ah, I see. Er, I smell."

Sicarius trotted into the office, his dagger still at the ready. Ravido lay crumpled by the window, his dress green uniform rumpled, his cap askew, brandy dripping from a flask that had fallen from his hand. Sicarius surveyed the room before approaching him, but didn't see anyone hiding amongst the bookshelves and display cases holding models of old-fashioned artillery weapons.

Amaranthe moved around the desk to stand at Ravido's head. "We have a few questions for you, Lord General Marblecrest." She lifted her eyes. "You're carrying him, right?"

"You have not been practicing your over-the-shoulder one-man carry?" Sicarius sheathed his knife and strode to her side.

"On men who weigh two hundred and fifty pounds? Oh, all the time, but I thought you might want to show off your ability to lift heavy objects. Thus to display your rippling muscles to fuel my imagination and ensure I'm in the mood for when we have those *hours* together."

"Shouldn't I be shirtless for that?" Sicarius grabbed Ravido's hand and hefted the big man over his shoulder in a smooth motion.

"It's up to you. I'm willing to make allowances for winter."

The office door slammed shut.

"Uhm," Amaranthe said. "I don't suppose that was a draft."

"There are no windows open." Sicarius strode around the desk and, balancing Ravido over his shoulder with one hand, reached for the knob with the other. With his fingers an inch from it, he halted. His sixth sense flared, a warning bell clanging in his mind. He lowered his hand and stepped back. "Our shaman is awake."

Amaranthe groaned. "I so wanted there to be a draft."

Sicarius tipped Ravido to the floor. "Tie him up. I'll go through the ducts and try to locate her. If she saw us come in here, she should be nearby."

"I hear you didn't win your last battle with her," Amaranthe said casually, though concern laced the statement.

"She didn't win either." Sicarius found a vent beside the bookcases and unscrewed it. "Try to be distracting in here, so she's focused on you."

"I'll do my best."

On his hands and knees, Sicarius was about to squirm—no, he corrected the thought, shimmy—into the duct, when he caught a thoughtful, "Hm," from Amaranthe.

He paused, wondering if he should admonish her not to blow anything up. Sage advice usually, but in this case, that might be the sort of distraction he'd need. He decided to allow her to use her discretion.

* * *

Amaranthe decided Ravido looked good in purple velvet bonds. He was a handsome man, after all, so a few plush accessories, sliced from the curtains and applied to his ankles, wrists, and mouth, could only accentuate his features.

That work done, she returned to the door, listening for the shaman's approach. Akstyr had mentioned it was a woman. Was she waiting in the outer room for them to try and come out? Amaranthe raised a hand to the knob, wondering what trap might have been placed upon it—Sicarius hadn't tried to open it.

Before she could decide if she wanted to wrap her fingers around it, heat radiating from the brass convinced her to leave it alone. The office door opened inward, so Sicarius's sidekick maneuver wouldn't do much good. Barging out wouldn't be a good idea if a shaman was waiting out there anyway. Amaranthe thought of the female practitioner from the *Behemoth* and the way she'd torched poor Retta. Was this the same woman? Someone living in the Barracks, but working for Forge? It seemed likely—how many female Kendorian shamans could be traipsing about Stumps anyway?—though Amaranthe didn't know how the deduction helped her.

"Distraction," she muttered. "I'm supposed to be making

a distraction." The silence outside might mean the shaman was already aware that Sicarius had left to seek her out. That wouldn't do. "You're going to focus on me and this room."

Amaranthe grabbed the iron poker from the side of the coal stove and rattled it around in a copper waste bin, then knocked over the bin. There—that ought to sound intriguing to someone listening outside, almost like a fight might be taking place inside.

She paced around the office, eyeing everything on the shelves. She picked up a few of the models, imagining herself lining up the tiny artillery weapons on the desk and rigging them to fire all at once when someone barged through the door. Alas, while a few had moving parts, none included niches for the insertion of black powder. Nor was there a handy keg of the stuff sitting on a shelf.

Using the lamp on the desk, she could start a fire easily enough, but that didn't sound like a winning idea when she was stuck in the room. She nosed into a few cabinets and pulled out a bottle of liquid. Though she'd dismissed the fire idea, she wondered if it were flammable or otherwise useful. Furniture polish, the label read.

"Lovely. Maybe the shaman would like the smudges buffed out of her coffee table."

Amaranthe started to return the bottle to the cabinet, but paused. Maybe she was trying to come up with something too clever. Simple could work, especially if Sicarius was putting himself into place behind the shaman somewhere and only needed a brief distraction.

She gave the door another once over, her gaze lingering on the area rug sprawled in front of it. She nodded to herself. "Yes, let's give it a try."

She rolled up the rug and leaned it in the corner. The old hardwood floor, dating back to when the Barracks had held open bays of bunks for soldiers rather than suites for the emperor and staff, held more scars and scratches than Basilard, but they'd been filled in, the boards smoothed and polished to a gleam

that nearly matched the marble tiles in the hallway. Amaranthe poured the polish out of the bottle and smeared it around in front of the entry.

"All you're lacking is a bucket of water to prop on top of the door..." Not that she could open the door even if she had a bucket.

Now if she could convince the shaman to race into the room... That might be the hardest part, given that several minutes had passed and she hadn't shown any inclination to do so yet. What was she waiting for? For her soldier allies to wake up and lend their assistance? If she knew she faced Sicarius, that might be exactly it.

Maybe if she thought her prisoner was escaping...

Amaranthe picked up the waste bin, strolled past Ravido, who had yet to stir, and chucked it at the window. She'd jumped through a similar window a year earlier and knew it was breakable. The waste bin didn't shatter the panes as thoroughly as her own crazy leap had, but she finished smashing out the window with the iron poker. She thought about hollering something like, "The makarovi are all gone—let's get Marblecrest out this way," but knew Akstyr could tell how many people were in a room. Surely this shaman could too. Had she figured out that Sicarius wasn't in there?

The courtyard *was* clear of makarovi, so far as she could tell. She thought about hoisting Ravido up to the sill and shoving him out, but it was a three-story fall, and he could break his neck. He might deserve that fate, but she'd have a hard time getting all that dead weight through the window.

Footfalls in the other room made the decision for her—*rapid* footfalls.

Poker still in hand, Amaranthe darted around the desk to take up position beside the door. The last thing she had time to think was that her plan was infantile and would never work. Then the door burst open and a gout of flames streamed into the office, engulfing the desk. Even off to the side, Amaranthe felt the heat searing her cheeks.

The shaman ran in behind her attack, her fingers outstretched. Her heel hit the slick patch on the floor, and both legs flew into the air. The flames disappeared.

Amaranthe swung the poker at the side of the woman's head while she was still in midair. The heavy iron slammed into her skull harder than Amaranthe would have intended, had the flames—and the memories of what those flames could do—not been pumping fear through her veins.

The shaman landed on her back and didn't move.

Holding the poker like a club, Amaranthe crept closer and nudged her fallen foe with a boot. The shaman didn't twitch. Her eyes were open, staring at the ceiling.

Amaranthe stared at the poker, hardly believing she could have killed someone with the blunt weapon.

A shadow crossed the threshold. Amaranthe spun, raising the poker.

Sicarius stood in the doorway, his expression as bland as ever. "Neither your sword nor pistol were sufficient?"

If her cheeks hadn't already been burned by the searing air, she might have blushed. "I didn't plan on killing her."

Sicarius rolled the shaman over and withdrew one of his throwing knives from her back. "*She* planned on killing you."

Amaranthe touched her tender cheeks. "Yes, I think that may be so."

A groan came from the window. Afraid their new prisoner might have taken some of that inferno, Amaranthe rushed around the desk. Either the furniture had shielded him, or the shaman had known he was by the window and hadn't let her attack carry that far, Ravido was unwounded. The effects of the gas were simply wearing off.

Sicarius checked his bonds, then hoisted the general to his shoulder. "Others will be waking."

Amaranthe nodded. Time to find Sespian and see how the rest of the team had fared. He needed to start parading himself around the Barracks soon if they were to have a chance at subduing or subverting the rest of the people.

CHAPTER 18

I T WAS STRANGE WALKING AT SESPIAN'S BACK AS HE marched around the Imperial Barracks in full dress uniform. Sicarius had pictured himself in this role numerous times in the past, in particular on the day when he'd grown tired of letting Raumesys torment his son and had arranged the poisoning that would simulate a heart attack. He'd set things up for Emperor Sespian to rule as he believed right, to march about with his faithful assassin guarding his back. Too bad Sespian had fired him on his first day free of Raumesys's shackles. Or... perhaps not. Odd how the years had changed Sicarius's perspective of that fantasy. Not only would he find it difficult to take orders from his own son, but he'd come to realize that he'd never truly wanted the throne for Sespian. That much responsibility was nothing kind to be chained with, especially not for the young. Leadership should be given to one who'd proven himself over and over and whom the people already respected.

Sespian stopped before an unadorned door in the back of the building and adjusted his collar. "I wish your team had collected these people when they were unconscious."

"This office was locked," Sicarius said. "Also, they weren't familiar with the Barracks layout and didn't know its significance."

"The officers inside won't be easy to lure back."

Sespian looked at Sicarius, expecting... what? Encouragement? Support?

"It is within your capabilities to regain their loyalties," Sicarius said.

"And if I don't?" Sespian eyed Sicarius's daggers.

They hadn't worked together privately or spoken one-on-one since Sicarius's return to the factory. He didn't think Sespian had been avoiding him, but perhaps he'd been reminded of his father's ability to kill—and his willingness to do so.

"The decision is yours," Sicarius said. "This is your milieu."

They'd already confronted a handful of young soldiers, men who'd gasped—then squirmed in discomfort—when Sespian had appeared before them. He'd given them a chance to return to his side that night, that moment, or to resign from the service forever. He hadn't threatened them, but the men had seen Sicarius hovering behind him and had nodded vigorously in agreement. Sespian had ordered them to form up in the courtyard with most of the rest of the team—Books, Akstyr, and Yara—and prepare to protect the city from makarovi. The young men had drawn themselves up straight and ushered an enthusiastic, "Yes, sir." They must not have appreciated their commander's orders to hole up in the Barracks, their tails tucked between their legs.

Amaranthe and Maldynado were questioning that commander right now. Sicarius trusted she would learn as much from Ravido using her own methods as he might using his.

Sespian pulled a key ring off his belt, selected a key, and tried the lock. It didn't turn. "They've replaced it." He lowered the ring. "Maybe we should leave this office and try again later."

"Those who've been plotting against you will have time to escape then. Better to confront them now."

Sespian's grimace suggested he might be happier if they *did* escape.

"You said it yourself, Forge controls, or controlled, many of the intelligence officers in the department. It would be unwise to let them run free where they might reunite with their remaining employers and cause other trouble. You must either win them back or—" Sicarius stopped himself from using the word kill, "—imprison them."

"I'll let you open the door then." Sespian stepped aside.

Sicarius didn't try kicking it open; he remembered the office

well and knew the door was reinforced. "Watch my back." He pulled out his lock picks and knelt.

"You've never given me that command before."

"I've given you few commands. Previously you were my emperor."

"Hm." Sespian pulled out a pistol, ostensibly watching the hallway, but asked, "At my fath—Raumesys's funeral pyre, when I was officially acknowledged as his successor with Hollowcrest as my regent, were you... Well, you were there. Would you actually have served me? Obeyed my orders?"

"That was always my plan." The lock had numerous pins, and it took concentration to wrestle them into submission, but Sicarius forced himself to go into more detail—Sespian had never asked about that time. "I thought you might employ me differently than Raumesys and Hollowcrest had, and that you might eventually consider me as an adviser, not simply a tool. I did not think you would fire me before Raumesys's body had finished burning."

Sespian cleared his throat. "I didn't think I could trust you."

He didn't add, *I was afraid of you*, but Sicarius knew and understood.

"Would you have told me the truth?" Sespian asked. "If I hadn't pushed you away?"

"Eventually. Preferably after you'd decided..." Sicarius wrangled the final pin into place and turned the lock. He replaced his tools.

"Decided what?" Sespian asked. "That you weren't a, uhm."

"Monster?"

Sespian nodded.

"I didn't know if that would be possible, but I thought you might come to accept me as *your* monster."

Sespian didn't have a response for that, so Sicarius pressed an ear to the door. It was thick wood, but he thought he heard a faint drip of water. That was odd. He'd expected voices. It might be the middle of the night, but these rooms were supposed to be manned around the clock, if only to protect the centuries of

secret files contained within the cabinets and vault. Even the makarovi shouldn't have driven everyone from their posts.

Still kneeling on the floor, he touched a hand to the smooth marble, seeking the vibrations of footsteps. All he felt was the cool stone.

He stood to one side, waved Sespian to the other, and pushed open the door. Nobody fired a gun, or shouted, nor did a single sound come within, save for the drip of water. A lamp burned somewhere, so the space hadn't been abandoned for long.

Sicarius blocked Sespian from stepping inside first, taking the spot for himself.

A large room full of tables and desks waited inside, with doors opening to interior offices. Cabinets and shelves filled the windowless walls. The headquarters for the Imperial Intelligence Network hadn't changed much since he'd last visited, save for the contraption sitting on the same table as the lamp.

"What's that?" Sespian whispered.

A cylinder wrapped with wires lay on its side, strapped to a block of ice. The corners of the block had worn smooth as water dripped off and trickled over the edge of the table. A puddle lay on the floor. Some sort of stiff string stuck out of the cylindrical device, hovering an inch above the flame. Not a string, Sicarius realized. A fuse.

"Blasting sticks." He strode toward the table.

"They booby-trapped the office?"

Sicarius's first instinct was to yank the lamp away, so the fuse wouldn't descend into the flame, but the ice was melting slowly, so he took the time to walk around the table and examine the bomb, lest it hold extra surprises.

"Why?" Sespian asked. "To blow up the records? Some angry bit of sabotage?"

"More than the records." Sicarius counted twenty blasting sticks in the bundle. *Old* blasting sticks with crystals of nitroglycerin edging the sides. He'd have to move them carefully. "There's enough power sitting on the table to take out the back half of the building."

Sespian's head jerked up. "The dungeons too? And the basement? Amaranthe's almost directly under us, down two stories."

"The blast itself might not, but the building could implode in the aftermath of supports being blown out."

Sespian stared at him. "In other words, Amaranthe and all the people we just put in the dungeon would be crushed." He reached for the lantern. "Get it out of there."

Sicarius caught his hand. "Wait."

His first walk around the table hadn't revealed anything more untoward than the bomb itself, but with only the single lantern in the windowless room, the lighting was poor. He inhaled, smelling the sweet scent of the glycerin and a hint of black powder as well. "Interesting."

He crouched low. A second device—more like a soft pouch— was pasted to the bottom of the table, right under the lamp. Though he couldn't tell exactly what it would do, he spotted the firing mechanism from a flintlock rifle, a string wrapped around the trigger. The other end of the string disappeared through a tiny hole in the table. Ah, lift or move the lamp, and the string would be pulled taut, firing the trigger and causing a spark that ignited the powder. That would, in turn, ignite the fuse on the blasting sticks as surely as the flame from the lamp would.

"See if there's another lantern you can light," Sicarius said.

Sespian had squatted down on the other side of the table. His face grew pale. "All right."

A minute later, he returned with another lamp. With it shedding illumination under the table, Sicarius stuck a finger into the firing mechanism to keep the trigger stationary and sliced through the string. He laid the pouch on the table and did another study of the area, searching for hidden trip wires. When he was convinced he'd caught everything, he cut off the flame in the lantern on the table. Sespian stepped back, a hand raised, as if that would provide any protection if the blasting sticks exploded.

They remained inert.

"How fortunate that we thought to check here," Sespian breathed. "All those people below..."

"There may be other bombs." Sicarius removed the wire-wrapped cylinder of blasting sticks from the ice.

"In here?" Sespian frowned at the office doors.

"They could be anywhere. If the rogue intelligence officers wanted to strike a last blow against you, they might have set multiple traps."

"How... encouraging. If their Forge people can't have the throne, no one can." Sespian frowned again. "That'd be a likely place for a bomb. The throne room. Even if it's decorative these days and only used for ceremonies." He licked his lips. "How long do you think it would have taken that ice to melt down?" And for the bomb to go off, he left unspoken.

"A half hour perhaps." Sicarius picked up the blasting sticks. "Come, we'll gather the others and search the Barracks."

Sespian followed him out of the office, but said, "Evacuating the Barracks would be a better plan, don't you think? It's not worth risking lives for a building, however historically significant."

"How will you keep people imprisoned then? You have few men you can rely on to guard them."

"I'll think of something. But we can have them search for twenty minutes and then evacuate the building if we still need to."

Sicarius headed for the nearest set of stairs. He would have broken into a jog, but the nitroglycerin crystals that had seeped out to the sides of the old blasting sticks meant they were even less stable than usual. Intelligence must have done a rushed search of the armory and found them in a back corner.

Sespian glanced at the bundle. "Is there a reason you're cradling that like a baby and bringing it with us?"

"To show the others what to look for. You should run ahead and warn the rest of the team. We'll want as many men as possible searching the building."

"Just don't trip and blow yourself up. That'd be an ignoble way to end after all the scrapes you've survived."

"Your concern is noted," Sicarius said.

"What concern?" Sespian smiled briefly. "I don't want the building to collapse on top of me while I'm down in the dungeon warning everyone else."

* * *

"Good evening, Lord Marblecrest," Amaranthe said. "My name is Amaranthe Lokdon, and I work for Sespian Savarsin. You're familiar with my associate." She inclined her head toward Maldynado.

He stood next to the furnace, one hand on his hip and the other leaning against the top of the canister. A scowl she'd rarely seen stamped his face, and none of his usual warmth softened his brown eyes. His older brother had the same eyes, and they were even harder as he glared back and forth from Amaranthe to Maldynado. Kneeling, his wrists and ankles still bound by strips of curtain, Ravido wasn't in a position to do anything more threatening.

"As you can see from our new threshold decoration—pardon the stench, by the way—we ran into a few makarovi on our way to visit you." Amaranthe clasped her hands behind her back and smiled invitingly at him, though it wasn't a sincere smile. If he had anything to do with those makarovi, she wanted to unleash Maldynado to pummel him. Sicarius would have been preferable, though he'd do more than pummel. "You wouldn't happen to know how they got here, would you? And how they came to be adorned with those fetching silver collars?"

"Does this confused *girl* truly think I'll answer her inane questions?" Ravido asked Maldynado.

"Do you think I'll answer yours?" Maldynado asked. "Treasonous idiot."

Ravido blinked a few times. Amaranthe had the feeling Maldynado hadn't insulted his older siblings, at least not to their faces, many times.

"Whose idea were the makarovi?" Maldynado demanded. "Yours? Or Father's? I didn't think you'd be cruel enough

to unleash such beasts on the city, but nothing Father does surprises me."

"They weren't supposed to be unleashed on the city," Ravido snapped. "Just those meddling women."

"The women who were going to be kind enough to put you on the throne?"

"Kind! Those bitches wanted to use me as a figurehead. Father wanted to let them, so long as the Marblecrests were on the throne. I wasn't going to be made a play thing for a committee of sniveling *females*." His shoulders flexed, the muscles straining against his uniform jacket, but the velvet bonds proved sturdy.

"So the makarovi *were* your idea?" Maldynado stepped forward, the hand at his side curling into a fist.

His pistol and his rapier hung at his belt, and it was the sway of the weapons that caught Ravido's eyes. He shrank back after glancing up at the lividness in Maldynado's face.

Amaranthe didn't say a word. She had planned to lead the questioning, but Ravido was revealing more to Maldynado than to her. She'd never seen Maldynado this angry either—in fact, she couldn't remember seeing him angry at *all*. Frustrated occasionally, but nothing like this. Judging by Ravido's concerned face, he hadn't seen Maldynado angry before either, not since he was old enough and strong enough to be a threat.

"Padji found the collars in the other shaman's collection, and learned the details from Forge about how they were used before. The rest of the family—" Ravido dared a small sneer, "—those who matter, went hunting for the creatures with her."

"Is Padji the same shaman that put the wards in the Imperial Barracks and who's been seen wandering around with Ms. Worgavic?" Amaranthe asked.

Ravido might be intimidated by his younger brother—she wondered how badly he might have treated Maldynado in decades past—but this did not extend to her. The sneer she received was much larger.

Amaranthe shrugged. "I ask because there's a dead female

shaman on the floor in Raumesys's old office. I thought you might mean her."

"Dead? You killed her?" Ravido tried to surge to his feet and might have made it, even with the bound ankles, but Maldynado shoved him in the back, and he pitched face-first to the ground.

Maldynado followed him down, leaning his weight onto his brother, jamming an elbow between his shoulder blades. Ravido couldn't lift his face from the cement. "This position remind you of anything, old boy? Like the way Dak and Histan used to smash me into the ground, and the way you used to encourage them, saying I needed to toughen up? You were in your twenties then, you sadistic bastard. You shouldn't have egged on boys to torment other boys. There's no way I was going to let *you* become emperor."

"How were you going to stop me?" Ravido managed, one side of his mouth mashed into the floor. "Screw ugly old women for the money to hire mercenaries?"

"You mean like your wife? Do you know how many times she tried to jump into bed with me? It's a pity she—"

Amaranthe cleared her throat. The argument—could it be called arguing when one of the arguers was pinned to the floor?—had devolved, and they weren't getting any new information. Worse, reminding Ravido that his wife was dead at their hands wouldn't convince him to help them.

"Who are the makarovi going after, Ravido?" Amaranthe asked. "Who are they *supposed* to go after?"

He didn't answer at first, but Maldynado leaned harder into him. "Sespian is upstairs collecting your army right now. It's over, old boy. You might as well answer her questions. Maybe she'll let you live if you cooperate. You know that the assassin Sicarius is her man, right? And that he's here too. He'll be down any moment..."

"I don't care, you little brat," Ravido said. "You're not going to kill me. Disowned or not, you're still family, and you already owe Mother. If you rob her of another of her children, her spirit will stalk you for all eternity."

Maldynado had bristled at the "little brat" comment, but he paled at the promise of a vengeful mother. Ravido must have known he'd scored a point, for he locked his lips together.

Amaranthe lifted a finger. "I don't care if your mother is mad at me. *I* can kill you."

Ravido snorted.

Why did men never believe her when she suggested such things? Must be those wholesome eyes Sespian and Sicarius had mentioned. Well, he was a Marblecrest, and if he was anything like Maldynado, there were other threats that might sway him...

She strolled over to the canister and set a hand on it. "You've experienced one of the gases we have loaded in here, Ravido. How did you like it?"

"One?" Maldynado mouthed, but he didn't say the word aloud, and he was still leaning on his brother, so Ravido couldn't see his face.

"A sneaky and cowardly way of fighting," Ravido said.

"Braver, I'd suggest, than hiding in a building while unleashing monsters on the city."

"I didn't unleash them, that idiot Heroncrest did. Burrowed right up into their cage. I hope they ate him first."

"He wasn't driving the tunnel borer," Amaranthe said. "A young soldier was. He's dead now, his chest ripped out and his head torn off. We saw him firsthand."

Ravido's jaw moved back and forth in agitation, but he kept his lips shut.

Amaranthe patted the side of the canister. "There are two other gases loaded inside. One causes great pain to a person, eating away at his nose, trachea, and lungs when he inhales it, eventually killing him." She wasn't surprised when Ravido's expression only grew mulish. "The other... I had our scientist load it on a whim, knowing I'd be dealing with a lot men over here. Its effects are felt in the, ah, lower regions." His lower regions were smashed into the cement, much like his face, but she let her gaze wander in that direction so he wouldn't misunderstand her.

"What do you mean?"

By now, Maldynado was grinning. "She means she can melt off your balls and turn your pizzle into a dandelion wilted under the first frost of autumn."

"Thank you, Maldynado," Amaranthe said, "that was almost poetic, aside from the mention of anatomical parts."

"It's hard to find poetical words for man bits. Though Lady Dourcrest has a few. Storehouses for the nectars of love, the sword of his desire, his purple-headed warrior..."

Amaranthe made a cutting-off motion with her hand, though Maldynado issued a few more examples before noticing her and desisting. She feared this devolution from the original threat would have let Ravido relax, but he didn't seem to be hearing the list. His gaze was focused on the canister.

"I'll make the switch." Amaranthe moved around to the back and opened a panel. "Maldynado, check his bonds, then leave the room. I, of course, am immune to the gas, but I'm sure you'd be most distraught if you could never experience physical pleasures with a woman again."

"Extremely so." Maldynado tightened the velvet bonds and stood.

"Ravido, are you sure you don't want to talk?" Amaranthe pretended to make an adjustment inside, though all she did was clink her knife against the interior wall—she couldn't begin to guess what the various innards did and wasn't going to unfasten anything in case they needed the gas again. "I'm not certain how long it takes for the gas to start melting off external organs, but—"

"What do you want to know, you vile woman?" Ravido's snarl wasn't as fierce as it had been before, and desperation tinged his voice.

"The makarovi target. Who are those collars telling them to attack?"

Ravido sighed. "The rest of the core Forge people."

"Is that... why some of the creatures stayed here?" Amaranthe asked. "Are there Forge people staying in the Barracks?"

"One of the founders is hiding in here, yes. She wanted protection from that mad assassin slaying all her colleagues." Ravido glowered up at them. "That's your assassin, isn't it? The one you were threatening me with?"

"He was working for Flintcrest then."

"A real loyal bloke, eh?"

"Didn't he get all of the founders, already?" Maldynado asked. "There were only five or six to start with, weren't there? And the papers said he killed a pile of Forge people."

"I haven't kept track," Ravido said. "I just know I wasn't going to sit on the throne and have a bunch of nattering nags whispering in my ear for the rest of my life."

Amaranthe stood up slowly, a new realization filling her. "Uh oh."

"What is it, boss?" Maldynado asked.

"I know where at least one founder is in the city."

"Enh? Who?"

"Suan Curlev, the woman Deret kidnapped."

Maldynado stared. "The woman who's sitting in the fac— our hideout with... all the rest of our allies?"

Amaranthe cursed. If a pack of makarovi turned up at the molasses factory in the middle of the night... Those doors weren't that strong, and most of Starcrest's people were out working, the same as her team. Deret, Suan, Starcrest, Tikaya, and their daughter were the only ones there. Maybe a few soldiers, but... Her stomach twisted at the thought of Tikaya and Mahliki being mauled, their insides torn out and eaten. At this time of night, Starcrest and the others were sure to be sleeping. They wouldn't be prepared for such an onslaught; they couldn't have guessed about the makarovi. Nobody could have.

"We have to get back there," Amaranthe rasped.

CHAPTER 19

S ICARIUS REACHED THE BASEMENT DOOR AS AMARANTHE and Sespian were jogging out, with Maldynado trailing behind, forcing Ravido Marblecrest to walk ahead of him. The general's wrists were still bound, though his legs had been untied for the forced march. Maldynado had a pistol jammed into his back.

"Looks like we have another problem," Sespian told Sicarius.

Amaranthe's gaze grew bleak as it fell to the bundle of blasting sticks. "We'll have to split up. Somebody has to warn Starcrest and his family about the makarovi, if it isn't already too late, but somebody's going to have to lead the search and evacuation of the Barracks. Without—" she lowered her voice as Maldynado and Ravido strode past, "—letting the possibly nettlesome prisoners out."

Sicarius kept his mouth shut on the logical approach to dealing with "nettlesome" prisoners. "Why would the makarovi be a threat to Starcrest?" he asked instead.

Another shade of bleakness darkened Amaranthe's face. "Suan. Ravido and his shaman friend decided they weren't going to put up with Forge. The collars are instructing them to go after the heads of the organization."

"I'll stay here." Sespian smoothed a hand down the front of his dress uniform. "I'm the logical choice and the most likely to be obeyed by the average soldier. I'd appreciate it if you leave me a couple of burly fighters though, in case it's necessary to deal with miscreants."

Amaranthe looked to Sicarius, a question in her eyes.

"You are not going makarovi hunting without me," he stated.

Yara and Basilard jogged up to them, both frowning at the blasting sticks.

"That's what we're looking for?" Yara asked Sespian.

"Yes, they might be attached to a cube of ice and a lantern. Check for booby traps around the bomb—this one would have killed us all if Sicarius hadn't been more thorough an investigator than I."

Basilard and Yara nodded, then ran inside.

During the exchange, Sicarius hadn't stopped staring Amaranthe in the eyes, as if he could will her to choose the safe route for once. "You should be among those who stay here."

"Except there have been makarovi around here too," she said.

"If you must go, I will go with you," Sicarius said, though the idea of leaving Sespian here, especially with Ravido still alive, distressed him.

"I'll be fine." Sespian must have sensed Sicarius's concern. "Amaranthe, leave me Basilard and Maldynado, please. Maybe Yara too. You don't want more women than necessary down there, do you?"

Amaranthe sighed. "No. All right, take those three. Sicarius, do you want to see if there's an idling lorry or carriage anywhere that we can confiscate? Even better if it's armored, filled with guns, and features anti-makarovi heavy artillery weapons mounted on the roof."

"I do not believe such a conveyance will be idling anywhere," Sicarius said.

"Do the best you can. I don't want to jog the five miles to the waterfront, not when there's fighting in the streets." She waved for him to go. "I'll round up Books and Akstyr."

Sicarius paused before he rounded a corner on his way to the vehicle garage, giving a last long look toward Sespian. He hoped he wouldn't regret leaving his son here. But the makarovi were more dangerous than men, and he had to trust that Sespian could take care of himself. Indeed, he was already hustling off, giving orders and directing troops. *He* didn't send a long look in Sicarius's direction.

Because he was taking care of business and not worrying needlessly. Sicarius jogged off.

Though the skirmishes had subsided, he stuck to the shadows as he trotted around the back corner of the building toward the garden sheds and vehicle house near the side wall. A woman's body, crumpled and eviscerated in the snow, made him pause. It was an older, well-dressed woman, her hair still neat in its bun despite the claw marks slashed across her face. Her velvet slippers were inappropriate for the slush-filled courtyard, and she had come outside without a jacket or weapons with which to defend herself.

Sicarius glanced up, and understanding dawned. Of course. A second-story window yawned open. If the makarovi had been hunting Forge founders, and one had been in the Barracks, someone must have decided to rid the building of the bait luring the beasts to attack. That explained the quietness that had come over the courtyard, though sounds of fighting rang out in the city below Arakan Hill.

Soldiers remained at their stations on the parapets, but the makarovi that had lingered at the Barracks must have been killed. Or—he paused near a stairway, noting a mauled body lying athwart several steps—with their mission complete here, the beasts had gone over the walls and escaped into the city.

Sicarius regretted hurling his knife into the shaman's back. Had they taken her prisoner, she might have been coerced into deactivating those collars. But seeing her charge into the room where Amaranthe was trapped, the woman's hands raised to attack... He'd thrown that knife without thought. He should have trusted that Amaranthe had a plan and could take care of herself.

It cannot be changed now, he thought, slipping into the back door of the vehicle house. However tough they were, makarovi were not soul constructs; enough bullets—and cannonballs—would bring them down.

A couple of lamps burned in the front of the carriage house, and the soft hisses and groans of steam machinery greeted him.

Two armored lorries idled before the wooden double doors in the front wall, and a pair of firemen were shoveling coal in the cab of a third vehicle still in its parking stall.

Convenient. He could take one before the two men had time to react.

He climbed to the top of a small lorry in front of him and jumped from the top of one vehicle to the next to avoid walking down the wide center aisle where he might be spotted. A few seconds before he reached the end of the row, the front doors swung inward. A row of armed soldiers trotted inside, rifles in hands, swords at their belts. The squad split into groups, jogging for the cabins of the waiting vehicles. They didn't look like men trying to escape, but they also didn't look like men obeying the orders Sespian would be giving to search the Barracks for bombs. Maybe they'd come down from the battlements and didn't yet know Sespian was around.

Sicarius hopped down from the parked vehicle, landing in front of a soldier who'd been angling for one of the cabs. The man blurted a surprised curse and swung his rifle around.

Sicarius could have flattened him, if he'd been willing to kill, but instead he hefted the bundle of blasting sticks. Until that moment, he hadn't been certain why he'd still been carrying the bomb, other than a notion that it ought not be left lying around where someone could stumble across it, but the soldier's eyes widened when he saw it.

"Shooting me wouldn't be wise at the moment," Sicarius said. "This bomb might go off. The blasting sticks are old and unstable. Why are you men not among those searching the Barracks for more booby traps?"

Several other soldiers had come around the front of the lorry, forming a semicircle. Sicarius listened for sounds of people coming up behind him. No one had yet, but there were three other men on the other side of the vehicle, and the two firemen readying the third.

"Booby traps?" a private blurted. "We have to go after the makarovi. They've escaped into the city."

A sergeant jammed an elbow into his ribs. "That's that assassin, Sicarius. Don't talk to him." The sergeant fingered the trigger of his rifle, though he also eyed the blasting sticks and didn't raise the weapon.

"My team is prepared to deal with the makarovi," Sicarius said, "and I am taking this vehicle so that we can do so. You people should report to Sespian."

"Sespian!" The private glanced to the sergeant. The rest of the men did too.

"Sespian is dead," the sergeant said.

"Sespian has returned to reclaim the throne." Without drawing attention to his hand, Sicarius loosened the wires around the bundle of blasting sticks. "Ravido Marblecrest is his prisoner. If you don't want to be punished or discharged for serving a false master, you should report to him now. He's at the back of the building. Get his orders." And get out of my way, so I can get this lorry for Amaranthe, he thought. He was wasting his time; these men wouldn't believe him. But the alternative was to take action that would harm—or kill—them.

"Shoot him, sergeant," another private whispered. "You've seen the papers, seen what he's been doing. And we all know how many of our brothers he's killed in the past. It's worth dying here if he'll die too."

Sicarius thought about saying he'd been working for Sespian in killing the Forge people, but that might cause backlash for his son. The sergeant's eyes hardened, his chin firming with resolve, and the time to talk was over anyway.

Sicarius pulled out one of the blasting sticks he'd loosened from the bundle and lobbed it toward the sergeant. He sprinted for the rear of the lorry.

"Look out!"

"Catch it—don't let it—"

Their focus on the stick kept them from shooting at him. Sicarius ran to the far side of the second lorry, intending to leap in and drive it away before the soldiers could coordinate an attack... so long as the blasting stick didn't explode, blowing up the vehicles and bringing the roof down.

A hint of movement came from his left, from down the center aisle. With the blasting stick bundle still tucked under one arm, he hurled a throwing knife. He *could* have taken the fireman in the throat—the man had stepped around a vehicle with a pistol in hand—but the blade bit into the flesh of his hand instead. The pistol dropped to the floor, and its owner leaped back behind the lorry, cursing.

"Got it," one of the privates yelled.

The remaining three soldiers were standing near the cab of the vehicle Sicarius intended to take. One was glancing around the front, toward his clamoring comrades, but the other two were facing the rear, right where Sicarius came out.

He sprinted at them without hesitating, watching the fingers on their rifles. When the weapons came up, aimed at his chest, Sicarius zigged to the side. Figuring one might anticipate an attempt to dodge, he leaped in the less obvious direction: toward the vehicle.

The rifles fired, but the shots didn't come close. Sicarius ran up the side of the cargo bed three steps, jumping before his momentum broke, and launched himself at the pair. He twisted in the air and kicked out with both legs. The soldier on the right caught a booted heel in the face and flew backward. The man on the left reacted more quickly, and almost evaded the kick, but, in midair, Sicarius hooked his leg and clobbered him in the side of the head.

By then, the third was spinning toward the fight, but Sicarius landed too close for him to fire. Instead of reverting to hand-to-hand, the soldier tried to leap back so he had room to use his rifle. Sicarius caught the barrel and yanked, pulling his foe off balance. Knowing he had no time for finesse, he grabbed the back of the man's neck and slammed his face into the front of the lorry.

The other two men were trying to rise. On his way into the cab, Sicarius stomped on one's hand and kicked the other's knee out from under him. He lunged inside, gripping the controls without bothering to sit. He did take a second to gently rest the

remaining blasting sticks on the passenger seat, then he thrust the vehicle into forward. Startled shouts came from the front— the men he'd diverted with the blasting stick racing over to join the fight. Too late.

Sicarius barreled past them, ducking low in anticipation of shooting. It came, but not until he'd rolled past their positions. A bullet entered the cab from the side and erupted through the windshield.

Others ricocheted off the side of the lorry, but that first shot was the only one to come close. Still, the men chased after him. As soon as Sicarius cleared the vehicle house, he turned a hard right, the wheels throwing up slush, pelting the fastest soldiers. Not much of an attack, but their curses elicited a modicum of satisfaction within him.

"Throw the blasting stick," someone yelled.

"It's a dud."

"No, you have to light it. Here."

Sicarius pressed the lorry to greater speed. His diversion might backfire on him if they ending up using the stick to blow *him* up.

As soon as the vehicle reached the end of the Barracks, he turned a hard left to bring it parallel with the back of the building. More slush sprayed, this time striking men who were standing in an orderly queue guarding other men. The prisoners, Sicarius realized. Sespian must have ordered them brought up from the dungeon for the evacuation.

He spotted Sespian's tidy black uniform with its gold piping, and Maldynado and Basilard at his side. Amaranthe was coming up the basement stairs, Akstyr and Books trailing.

A harsh squeal rent the air as Sicarius threw on the brakes. Dozens of surprised faces turned in his direction. Fortunately, Amaranthe, Books, and Akstyr hustled toward him without hesitation, each carrying a rifle or pistol, swords, and bulging ammo pouches.

"Get in," Sicarius barked, leaning out to check on his pursuers.

The fastest of the soldiers rounded the corner of the building.

The rearmost man gripped the blasting stick in one hand and a lantern in the other, both raised, as if he meant to light the fuse at any second.

"Halt," Sespian called, stepping forward and lifting a palm. Perhaps more influentially, Maldynado and Basilard raised rifles at the oncoming men. Two soldiers, men he must have already recruited, stepped in front of Sespian, also with firearms at the ready.

"Put down your weapons," one of them, a man with lieutenant's rank pins, called.

"But, sir," one of the lorry's pursuers protested. "That's Sicarius. The assassin."

While this exchange was going on, Amaranthe, Books, and Akstyr piled into the cab behind Sicarius.

"We're ready," Amaranthe urged.

Sicarius waited, though, wanting to make certain his son had everything under control. With the prisoners nearby and men who'd been working for Ravido not fifteen minutes before now supposedly on his side, the situation could quickly devolve into chaos.

"Where's Ravido?" Sicarius asked. "Being kept with the general prisoners?"

"No," Books said. "Someone—" he gave Amaranthe a long look, "—decided he should be involved in the search for more incendiary devices."

Akstyr snickered, as if unaware of the tension outside. "Yara is bossing him around the way she does Maldynado. He'll probably end up stepping on a mine just to get away from her nagging."

"I am aware of that," Sespian said, responding to the man with the blasting stick. "The others are outlaws. I'm giving them a chance to redeem themselves by defeating the makarovi."

"But we were going to chase after the makarovi. Sir. Sire. Uhm." The confused soldiers looked at each other. The one holding the blasting stick and lantern lowered the items.

"There is a situation here that requires attention. Fill them in, Lieutenant." Sespian didn't take his eyes from the men, but

he did wave at the lorry. *Get out of here*, that gesture said. *Do your mission. I'm fine.*

Yes, Sicarius decided, it seemed he could. Pleased that his son had brought the situation under control, he nudged the lorry forward. With so many people now gathered behind the Barracks, he steered through the courtyard at a less frenetic pace, but as soon as they passed through the gates—someone had instructed the soldiers to open them—he pushed the vehicle to a greater speed. In the city, fires burned up and down the hills sloping down toward the lake; there was more trouble about than the makarovi could account for.

* * *

Amaranthe gripped the back of the seat beside Sicarius and stared out at the dark, slushy streets. They'd already started passing mauled bodies. Not many—the collars had sent the makarovi on a mission, after all, and they were taking the most direct path toward it—but enough. Shouts came from the rooftops of buildings, and lights burned behind shuttered windows and locked doors. The entire city seemed to be awake.

Aside from the bodies, the streets were empty, at least around the base of Arakan Hill. Torches moved in the distance, down by the waterfront. Her chest tightened, and a slight tremble shook her belly, one that had nothing to do with the vibrations of the lorry. She hadn't wanted to be right about Suan and the makarovi, but Ravido had confirmed it. How much time had passed since those first creatures had left the tunnel? Hours, she feared. Even if they'd paused to... hunt along the way, they were sure to have reached the factory by now. Amaranthe had barely gotten to know Tikaya and Mahliki, but she nonetheless dreaded the thought of losing them.

"Since nobody else is asking," Akstyr said from his spot behind Sicarius, "why are there blasting sticks in the other seat?"

Sicarius, his face intent as he concentrated on the slippery roads—and perhaps he was watching those torches, too, thinking similar thoughts as Amaranthe—did not reply.

"I assumed that Sicarius, aware of Amaranthe's tendency for

causing explosions, thought to facilitate her ability to induce them by giving those as... a gift," Books said. "Blasting sticks get more reliable and, ah, speedier results than setting up catastrophic boiler failures in steam vehicles."

Books was standing in the middle, gripping the ceiling to keep from flying out when they turned corners. Nobody had dared pick up those sticks and slide into the seat next to Sicarius.

"Aw," Amaranthe said, "did you bring these along for me, Sicarius? That *is* quite thoughtful." She almost added a comment about appreciating them as much as her pastry from Curi's, but didn't know if he'd want her letting others know he'd done something so domestic as bringing her sweets. Besides, the shock might cause Books to lose his grip on that ceiling bar and fall out of lorry.

Sicarius's cool sidelong glance convinced her that the thought had been correct. He wasn't in the mood to be playful. Understandable, since they'd left Sespian with a mess and were heading into another one.

"Look at that fire." Akstyr thrust a finger toward a two-story brick building on a corner ahead. Flames leapt from the broken front windows, shards of glass gleaming orange on the cleared sidewalk below. The door had been busted in as well.

"That's Curi's," Amaranthe blurted, reflexively stepping toward the exit, an image of leaping out and running for buckets of water flashing through her mind. But... Curi was allied with Forge, or had been. No matter how tasty her pastries were, maybe she deserved this end. Besides, with the way those flames were jumping, taming the chaos would take the Imperial Fire Brigade, not a couple of people with buckets.

"Looting," Books said with disgust. "Hoodlums."

As the lorry neared the intersection, two youths in oversized clothing slouched out of the shop, carrying bulging bags of stolen goods. One held a display platter full of sweets tucked under one arm. Again, Amaranthe was tempted to order Sicarius to stop, so they could jump out and deal with the thieves. Even if Curi deserved a bad turn for her alliance to Forge, criminals

shouldn't get away with pillaging and vandalism. The team couldn't delay though, not when they were already hours behind those monsters.

Akstyr shrank away from the side of the cab. The pastries stuffed into the youths' mouths didn't hinder their ability to make crude gestures. Amaranthe couldn't tell if they were aimed at the lorry in general or at Akstyr. The backs of those hands were branded, though she couldn't tell with which marks.

Sicarius turned the corner, and the gang members disappeared from view. More buildings burned on either side of the wide street ahead, though there were fewer people out than she would have expected. Looting could grow widespread quickly. Where were the enforcers? Chasing makarovi?

The canal and a bridge came into view. Not much farther to the waterfront. Ah, there were the enforcers—a steam wagon rolled over the bridge at the same time as Sicarius crossed from the other side. Both vehicles scooted to the far sides, allowing room for the other to pass.

An enforcer leaned out of the back of the wagon with a megaphone. "Makarovi are loose in the city. Return to your homes. Do not take up arms. We will handle it." It sounded like a litany he had repeated many times that night.

"How do they propose to handle it while they're driving in the other direction?" Books asked.

"I'm sure there are numerous vehicles patrolling and looking for them. Or maybe enough are already at the factory to handle things."

As they drove closer to the waterfront, they passed army vehicles as well with men on the roofs manning search lights, probing the alleys on either side of the streets.

"This way," Amaranthe wanted to yell, "we know where they are."

In truth, she didn't know that. The makarovi might have already dealt with Suan and moved on to harassing the city at large.

Sicarius took them down the final long hill that led to

Waterfront Street. More bodies littered the route, some on the sides, some out in the middle. More than once, he had to steer the lorry around one to avoid crushing it.

A block up from the waterfront, Sicarius turned onto the street that held the factory, but he had to brake immediately. A barricade had been erected from sidewalk to sidewalk, and two parked enforcer wagons further blocked access.

At first, Amaranthe thought that help must have arrived in time and maybe the law had been able to thwart the makarovi, but the silence of the street instilled a sense of eeriness. Wind gusted through, and clothing flapped somewhere. Amaranthe leaned out of the cab to see around the wagon—and wished she hadn't. Two enforcers lay on their backs in slush turned red with their blood. One's uniform jacket had been torn half off of him, and it flapped forlornly, as if it could fly away and escape the fate its owner had suffered.

Amaranthe listened for the roars of the makarovi, figuring that if they remained in the area it would imply they still sought their prey, but that flapping jacket was all she heard.

"We'll try Waterfront Street," Sicarius said. "If that's blocked, we'll proceed on foot."

Amaranthe nodded. It was only three blocks to the factory—they would walk from here—but she remembered the effectiveness of that tunnel borer and was reluctant to leave the lorry behind. Even if it didn't possess a giant drill bit, it might be able to pin beasts against the walls so the men could attack them.

Waterfront Street had been similarly blocked. If barricades alone had spanned the route, Amaranthe would have urged Sicarius to drive through them, but she doubted he'd be able to roll over the enforcer wagons once again parked inside the barrier.

"Should we try circling all the way around?" Amaranthe asked.

"We can come back for the lorry if we need it." Sicarius parked the vehicle.

Something in his word choice made Amaranthe think they wouldn't, that they were already too late.

Sicarius rose from the seat and grabbed the shovel in the rear. "I'll stoke the firebox so it's ready."

Amaranthe, Books, and Akstyr climbed out. There weren't any boats out on the lake tonight. The ice that had been forming earlier in the week had receded, though it still edged the shoreline and cupped the pilings of docks. She listened again, hoping to hear the sounds of the makarovi, or at least of living beings, but it was as if the city's entire population of one million had disappeared. Except for the looters. Fires continued to burn on the inland hills.

Amaranthe and the others did quick checks of their gear—weapons, yes, ammunition, yes, but would there be an opportunity to use them? She cringed at the idea of finding Starcrest and his family slaughtered in their blankets.

Sicarius hopped down from the cab, and the team squeezed past the barrier and strode up the street. He was carrying the blasting sticks under one arm.

When he noticed her eyeing them, he said, "You forgot your gift."

"Ah, silly me. It's kind of you to tote it along for me."

"Yes," he said.

"Those sticks look... volatile. I suppose it'd be impolite of me to ask you to walk on the other side of the street while you carry my gift."

"Yes."

Books lifted a finger. "What if *I* make the request?"

The look Sicarius gave him lacked amusement.

As they strode through the next two blocks, they passed more enforcer bodies. Even at night, nobody had to stop for a close look to see how they'd died; the gouges left by the long makarovi claws were distinct.

They rounded a corner, and Sicarius pointed. At the intersection next to the factory, a massive furry heap lay in the street. Two more human bodies had fallen in the vicinity, but at least one makarovi had been killed. Amaranthe tried to guess how many remained. Six? Seven?

A shot rang out to the southeast—a block up and a block inland. That ought to be the factory.

"Someone's still alive." She surged forward, but Sicarius caught her by the elbow, his grip implacable.

She expected an order to stay behind, lest her scent drive all of the makarovi toward her, but he merely pointed to the rooftop of the nearest warehouse. "The shot was fired from an elevated position. We may find greater safety in a similar approach."

That warehouse took up the whole block and, standing on opposing corners from the factory, would let them have a view of most of the area. "Let's do it," Amaranthe said.

Sicarius led the way, choosing a sturdy drainpipe. He shimmied up, using his boots and one hand to grip it, since he still held the blasting sticks in the other. Amaranthe couldn't imagine a scenario where they'd lob explosives at the factory—especially if they believed people were still alive in there—but so long as he continued to carry her gift instead of asking the chore of her, she didn't care. One-handed drainpipe climbing wasn't in her repertoire of skills yet.

"Never have I wished more for his safety," Books said, watching Sicarius climb, or perhaps watching the cylinder of sticks under his arm.

"Yes," Amaranthe said. "I wouldn't care to have him drop those, given our positions directly under him."

She waited until Sicarius reached the roof, then hustled up after him. Books and Akstyr followed, though Akstyr whispered, "Blasted drainpipes. I looked this factory over when I was standing watch on the roof over there, and I distinctly remember a fire escape around the corner."

"If makarovi can climb fire escapes, that'll be the first thing I target with my gift." Amaranthe reached the top and scrambled onto the roof. It was a flat one with low walls around the top. A small water tower perched in the center next to a couple of chimneys. A lone door allowed access to the interior.

Not surprisingly, Sicarius was checking the shadows for danger rather than rushing to the corner for a look at the factory. Amaranthe took that job for herself.

Almost sprinting, she bounded across the rooftop, reaching the corner in a few seconds. This building was taller than the factory, so she had to look down to spot the... what *was* that?

She'd stood a guard watch or two on that roof, too, so she knew what was and what wasn't up there. Aside from the smokestacks there wasn't a lot. Usually. Now some towering rectangular assembly of bars—or were those pipes?—had arisen. Lanterns dotted the rooftop, so she could see the stocky silver-haired man kneeling at one of the corners with a wrench. She didn't know what he was doing, but seeing him filled her with relief.

"Admiral Starcrest is alive," she called back to her team. Sicarius, Akstyr, and Books were all approaching. "And there's..." The shadows were thicker away from the contraption, but she made out the figure kneeling at the edge of the roof with the rifle. "Deret." A shot was fired from the far side of the factory roof, the flash of black powder briefly illuminating two more figures over there. Soldiers, she guessed from the fatigue uniforms. A few more knelt around the perimeter of the building, all with rifles and ammunition.

"His wife and daughter?" Books asked, coming up beside Amaranthe.

She swallowed. Where indeed were the women? The makarovi hadn't caught them, had they?

Glass littered the street below. More than half of the windows had been destroyed, and the door visible from their warehouse lay uselessly across the threshold, torn from the hinges.

"There." Books gripped Amaranthe's shoulder with one hand, the other thrust toward the twin smokestacks.

Three women—Suan, Tikaya, and Mahliki—knelt between the chimneys, assembling something. Parts for Starcrest's... project? It didn't matter. They were alive. And well enough to scheme up—she'd have to ask and find out what that was. Some sort of makarovi trap, she guessed.

"Is that Amaranthe Lokdon over there?" came a call from the edge of the roof. "Or am I hearing voices?" Deret had

lowered his rife and was squinting in her direction. "It must be her, because no other female would be reckless enough to come *toward* a makarovi hive."

"You say you have an infestation of some sort?" Amaranthe called back. "Maybe we can help you come up with a suitable pesticide." If the makarovi were roaming around inside the building, she envisioned lobbing burning blasting sticks through those broken windows. Then she envisioned one landing too close to a support post and the entire structure coming down. It was possible her idea needed refinement.

"That's good," Deret said, "because—"

A rifle cracked behind Starcrest's project. There were two more soldiers in the center of the roof that Amaranthe hadn't seen. One rushed to push a crate back atop the trapdoor that led to the interior.

"—the pests are particularly problematic this time of year," Deret finished, his voice grim.

By now, Starcrest and the others had heard the exchange and noticed their company too. The admiral lifted a hand, but otherwise continued to work. Tikaya responded similarly. Suan wore a someone-get-me-off-this-roof-now-please expression. Did she have any idea that the makarovi were there for her?

Mahliki abandoned her project and raced to the edge of the roof. "My gas. Did it knock them out?"

Akstyr snickered. "Not all women can say things like that, but she's pretty enough that I wouldn't mock her for it."

Amaranthe swatted him on the chest. "It did," she called to Mahliki. "But we ran into trouble. The makarovi came from the Imperial Barracks."

"What? How?" Deret called.

Starcrest lifted his head for more than a second this time.

"It seems Ravido Marblecrest wasn't planning to be Forge's spineless figurehead after all. He schemed this up with a shaman comrade. Those collars control them. They're being sent to kill the remaining Forge founders. And I think they've accomplished their mission, save one."

Suan lifted a hand to her lips. Yes, it's you, Amaranthe thought.

"That explains their uncharacteristic tenacity," Starcrest said.

"You might be able to shoot off their collars," Amaranthe called. "We were able to break one that way last year."

Deret cursed. "I didn't even see any collars with those shaggy necks."

"The fur makes them difficult to see, but they're there. Of course, it's not all that much better when they're free of control."

"Understood," Starcrest said. "We'd have a hard time getting at them anyway, as they're all downstairs right now, tearing up the inside of the building, but I'd rather they stay here in one place than wander into the city and kill people wantonly."

"Trust me," Amaranthe said, "they did plenty of that on their way down here."

Starcrest and Deret both grimaced.

"They're... dead because of me?" Suan asked. "I haven't even... I mean..." She stared down at her hands.

Tikaya gripped her shoulder and said something Amaranthe couldn't hear.

"What are you building, sir?" Books pointed to the pipe rectangle—it had to stand more than fifteen feet high.

"A very large mousetrap," Starcrest said. "With bait, I thought we might lure the makarovi outside to one spot." He waved toward the street below the roof. "And drop it over them. It's very heavy—they shouldn't be able to lift it without a combined effort, and I don't believe they have that much intelligence." He pointed to the smokestacks. "We're making a winch, to lower it down."

"Now they know who would work as bait," Akstyr said.

"I'm just happy it's not me this time," Amaranthe muttered.

Another shot fired from the center of the roof. This time, she saw the trapdoor and the crate atop it jump several inches. After the soldiers stationed there had shoved their obstruction back into place, Starcrest asked them a question. They returned affirmative waves, if shaky ones.

"How many are down there?" Amaranthe asked.

"Six."

Amaranthe wished her people could see the makarovi through the factory's broken windows, thus to pepper them with rifle fire and whatever else they could come up with, but she hadn't glimpsed so much as a shadow moving. The beasts must all be up on the catwalks, jumping for that trapdoor.

"Scoot back." Sicarius touched her arm.

Amaranthe allowed herself to be guided back from the edge. "What is it?"

"There are vehicles driving down the street from the canal, and I spotted a boy observing us from the shadows up there." He pointed up the street their warehouse and the factory shared, the one running perpendicular to the waterfront.

"Observing *us* specifically? Or the intersection in general?" Amaranthe waved to include the factory rooftop.

"Our group," Sicarius said. "He ran back into an alley when he noticed me watching him back."

"Gangs?" Akstyr took a big step away from the edge of the roof.

"He was scruffy, with ill-fitting clothing."

Akstyr had once again dressed in *his* collection of ill-fitting clothing when the team had returned to the capital, and he scowled at this description.

"Why would they come here?" Books asked. "Are they unaware of the makarovi? They're out in the streets; they *must* have seen the ravaged bodies."

"What they *saw*," Amaranthe said, "was a whole lot of chaos and a prime opportunity for looting."

"Two of them also saw us drive by," Sicarius said. "We were not making an effort to disguise ourselves."

Akstyr stomped his foot. "Curse those frosting-sucking brats at the bakery. Don't I have enough to worry about right now?"

"Your bounty is meager in comparison to Sicarius's," Books pointed out. "They may target him instead."

"Thanks, Books," Amaranthe said drily, because she knew Sicarius wouldn't.

"They'll go after me," Akstyr grumbled. "I don't have that deadly reputation. And they'll be mad because of the way I embarrassed some of them at the docks last week."

"We have the high ground," Sicarius said, "and are well armed."

"Let's not worry yet. We'll keep an eye on them—" Amaranthe nodded to Sicarius, silently assigning him the task, "—but let's see what we can do to move this makarovi trap along." She faced the factory again. "Admiral, we may have unpleasant visitors coming. Is there anything we can do to help you?"

"What kind of visitors?" Starcrest asked.

Amaranthe hated shouting everything for the whole neighborhood to hear, but doubted Tikaya would be able to read hand signs from that distance. She was busy with the winch anyway.

"Gangs," Amaranthe said.

"Do they fancy themselves makarovi hunters?"

"Unlikely. They're extremely superstitious when it comes to magic, and they know Akstyr's a wizard. Also, three out of the four people on this roof have bounties on their heads." Amaranthe lowered her voice to add an aside to Sicarius, who had returned from a check of the corners and the door leading into the warehouse below. "By the way, you really should spank Sespian someday for putting that bounty on your head."

Akstyr made a choking sound at this image.

Sicarius grunted. Wistfully? Amaranthe wasn't sure.

"At the least, he could have removed it before he asked us to kidnap him," she said.

"He hasn't removed your bounty either, has he?" Books asked her.

"No. Shortsighted of him. We should have made that a condition of our rescue."

"Perhaps you should be spanking him too." Akstyr grinned. At least the conversation seemed to have brightened his glower a touch.

"I don't think I have that right as a non-parent," Amaranthe said.

"If you and Sicarius were to marry, you'd be his stepmother," Books pointed out.

"Alas, there's probably an age when one can't get away with spanking a young man anymore."

"Well," Books said, "there's an age where being spanked by a woman becomes less disciplinary and more... titillating."

"Really, Books, the shocking things you say at times."

"There are lights moving around over there." Sicarius pointed to the street on the other side of the factory. "I'm going to make another round. Keep an eye on that building up the hill—it's higher than ours and they might have projectile weapons."

"Understood," Amaranthe said.

He hadn't said they were foolish to be bantering, but it was implied, and he was right. Someone was coordinating things to surround them.

"You might want to leave," Starcrest called. Though he was still working on his trap, one of the soldiers had come to his shoulder for an extended talk—probably reporting the same findings as Sicarius. "If they surround your building, you'll be stuck. And you can't do anything to help us from over there."

"We have blasting sticks," Amaranthe called back. "Even a makarovi shouldn't be able to shake off one stuck down its gullet."

"Uh, and who's going to do the sticking?" Akstyr asked.

"Maybe you could use the Science to float them in, light the fuse, and insert them in the appropriate mouths." Amaranthe supposed the notion was wistful.

Starcrest digested her blasting-sticks comment for a moment. "Are you proposing we climb down, run into the factory, and attack them?"

"If we can end this with a short skirmish, we can all get out of here," Amaranthe said. "I don't have any particular love for that building."

Tikaya lifted her head and said something to Starcrest. Her words didn't carry, but her tone was sharp, and Amaranthe could guess the gist: *You're not young enough anymore*

to leap off buildings and lead foolhardy charges against man-eating monsters.

Judging by the way Starcrest's head came up, he took affront to being called "not young enough" or whatever she'd truly said. He met his daughter's concerned eyes, though, and sent a finger waggle toward the women. It might have meant *I concede*, or *I'll consider your argument.*

"I might be able to float the sticks and ignite the fuses." Akstyr had been staring at his feet since she made the comment, and he lifted his head now. "But I need to see where I'm aiming. I couldn't will them to stick themselves into makarovi mouths. If I were in there though, I'd need a real good bodyguard so I could concentrate…"

He wanted Sicarius. Yes, understandable, but…

"Even he can't keep six of them off your back," Amaranthe said. "Though I suppose he could be running around and lobbing blasting sticks too… Books or I could be your bodyguard."

"No." Books pointed a finger at her nose. "You're not putting yourself in their path again."

"Someone has to do it."

"Not you."

"Why? Because they want to eat my organs? They kill everyone they see. What does it matter if they eat part of me after the fact?"

"You know there's more to it than that," Books said. "They go crazy when they lock onto the scent of a female."

Sicarius ran over and joined them.

Amaranthe was about to ask him his thoughts on streaking into that building and hurling blasting sticks, but he spoke first.

"We need to get off this roof."

"What happened to having the high ground?" Amaranthe asked.

"There are far more than I realized." He waved her back toward the edge, though he made a "down" gesture.

She approached in a crouch, sticking only her head over the low wall.

"There." Sicarius pointed down the street paralleling the waterfront.

When she leaned out, she could pick out the barricade and abandoned enforcer vehicles and—she gulped—a mass of people with torches, muskets, crossbows, and swords, some of the weapons far too nice—too expensive—for the grimy hands and patched clothing of their wielders.

"Any chance those are angry citizens, come down to take revenge on the makarovi?" she asked.

"They have gang brands on their hands." Akstyr knelt beside her.

She couldn't see that from this distance, but maybe he had other ways of detecting such things.

"They're coming down the other streets as well," Sicarius said. "There are hundreds of them."

Books gaped. "How did they gather so many so quickly?"

"They must have organized earlier tonight for the looting, and it was luck that they saw us going by," Amaranthe said.

"*Luck?*" Akstyr groaned. "*Bad* luck. Unless you mean it's lucky that the makarovi might smell them and come out and eat them."

"A plan is needed," Sicarius said. "Do we run before they get here or stay and attack?" He pointed to the factory.

"Where would we run if we're surrounded?" Books asked.

Sicarius waved toward the waterfront, perhaps suggesting a swim, but his focus was on the factory. He didn't want to leave Starcrest and the others. Neither did Amaranthe.

"Any chance we can find some rope?" she asked. "And invite Starcrest's party to come visit our rooftop? We'll be stronger together, and maybe we can use the blasting sticks to drop that building on the makarovi heads before they sense that Suan has left."

Sicarius considered the distance between the buildings—since the molasses factory was set back from the corner, with a parking area, loading docks, and tanks between the walls and the street, it wouldn't be a short stretch of tightrope walking. Some fifty meters at least. "I'll look for rope in the warehouse," he said. "Watch for attacks from the streets. You'll have to convince Starcrest to leave his trap."

"He likes to give me the fun jobs," Amaranthe said.

"I wouldn't want to go down in the warehouse," Akstyr grumbled. "I bet the gangs will try to find a way in down there and come up that way."

"You better think of a distraction to keep them away then, eh?" Amaranthe scooted closer to the edge again. "Admiral, we're searching for rope and a way to launch it over there." She lowered her voice to mutter to Books, "Whose idea was it to come up here without a harpoon launcher?"

"Perhaps you should have requested a different gift from your devoted paramour," Books said.

She shot him a dirty look, mostly because Sicarius hadn't *paramoured* anything with her yet.

"You're inviting us to the rooftop populated with the people the gangs are after?" Deret hollered.

"Given that we're planning ways to collapse your rooftop onto the makarovi milling in the factory, we thought you'd find it a more appealing perch."

Starcrest left his project and walked to the wall. The approaching crowds were only a block away and coming down three of the four streets leading to the intersection. Voices drifted in from the direction of the docks too. It'd only be a matter of time before people headed in from the waterfront as well.

"Books," Amaranthe said, "grab a rifle and see if you can convince the gang leaders to take cover. Slow their approach. Akstyr—" She stopped. He was kneeling a few paces back, his eyes closed in concentration. She hoped he had something large and spectacular in mind.

"If we crossed that way," Starcrest called, "we'd be vulnerable to anyone with a bow or firearm. It'd take some time for all of us to make it over there, if everyone is able." He glanced at the women. Tikaya propped a hand on her hip. Suan appeared more concerned than affronted.

"We're going to distract the gangs," Amaranthe called.

Books fired his first shot. It took one of the leaders in the thigh. The young man tumbled to the ground, but the others around him weren't as scared as Amaranthe had hoped. A few of the ones in front, who realized what had happened, darted toward the sides of the street, seeking shelter in the shadow of buildings, but other people simply surged into the lead, some stepping on their own downed comrade.

"Sicarius is up there," came a distant shout. "A million ranmyas for his head. We'll all be rich men!"

A cheer went up. A million ranmyas split hundreds of ways would still be decent booty for those people.

"It'll take more of a distraction than that," Starcrest called, but he'd come up to Deret's side and gave an order, then circled the rooftop to speak with his soldiers. Soon, they were shooting at the ringleaders down there too.

"We're working on it," Amaranthe responded.

Akstyr lifted a hand in the air and clenched a fist. The cries of "Sicarius" and "reward" halted, at least from the street directly in front of their building.

"Oh, that might work. Good, Akstyr, good," Books crooned.

Amaranthe started to ask, "What?" then spotted what was alarming the crowd. Four makarovi had run out from behind the factory's massive tanks. Two charged up the hill and two more ran below Amaranthe, barreling toward the front of the mob. They paused and reared up, thumping their chests like gorillas.

"Don't make them dance this time," Books said.

"Those are... Akstyr's invention?" Amaranthe asked. "Are we sure?" The saliva gleaming on those fangs and the fur rippling on the stout limbs appeared realistic to her.

They must have appeared realistic to the gang leaders, too, for they skittered backward insomuch as they could on a street packed sidewalk to sidewalk with people.

"Amaranthe," came Sicarius's voice from behind her.

He nodded for her to step away from the corner. He'd found a coil of lightweight rope and a crossbow. Er, no, he hadn't "found" the crossbow. Blood spattered the weapon and the back of one of his hands. He'd taken it from someone.

"Are the gangs in the warehouse?" she asked.

"A few scouts. I took care of them, but there'll be more. I put a bar through the handle on the door leading up here, but there's no way to lock it from this side. We'll need to watch it." Sicarius leaned over the edge of the roof, eyeing the rampaging makarovi. "That won't fool them for long."

He knelt to tie the rope to one of the crossbow quarrels.

"Best we can do." Amaranthe had the blasting sticks in mind for a further distraction, if they needed them, though she'd prefer to save them for the makarovi—the real ones.

"Incoming," Sicarius yelled, then fired the crossbow.

The quarrel arced high into the dark night sky. Normally it might have traveled a hundred meters or more, but the weight of the rope shortened its trajectory. It was enough. The bolt skipped down onto the roof and skidded toward Starcrest's cage, wrapping around one of the pipes.

"Good choice," Amaranthe said. "That thing looks heavy enough to hold the weight of a tightrope-walking makarovi."

As Starcrest and Deret knelt to secure the rope, another blow to their trapdoor sent the crate skidding off the top. A gap appeared, and a long makarovi arm lashed out. The nearest soldier fired, but he was standing too close, and the claws hooked his ankle. He crashed to his back, the weapon flying free.

The second man had been leaping for the crate to shove it back over the trapdoor, but he forgot it, lunging to help his comrade. That makarovi paw pulled its victim closer. The soldier twisted onto his belly, clawing at the roof, trying to find a handhold.

Helpless from her spot, Amaranthe cringed, not wanting to see the man hauled through the trapdoor to certain death. His comrade caught his arm and threw his weight back, pulling in the opposite direction. The soldier hollered, his body stretching as claws ripped into his leg.

Starcrest and the others on the roof were charging toward the scene, but they wouldn't be fast enough. The trapdoor was flung all the way open. A makarovi head rose, filling the entire space. Maybe its shoulders and torso would be too big for it to

get out. The creature was still pulling its captive—pulling both men now. The standing soldier's feet were slipping. In a second, he'd be on his backside too.

Though the soldiers were younger, Starcrest, with his long legs, was the one to reach the trapdoor first. He kicked the makarovi in the face and jammed downward with a dagger, sinking the blade into that rubbery flesh. The weapon didn't pierce far—Amaranthe could tell even at that distance—but it surprised the creature enough that its grip loosened. The entrapped soldier was able to yank his leg free, and his comrade nearly tumbled over in his haste to pull him back from the trapdoor.

The rest of the soldiers came within range and fired at the black furred head. It ducked out of sight.

Starcrest thrust his hand toward the crate, saying, "Get something heavier to block that door," then knelt to speak with the injured man, his words too soft to carry.

"He still moves fast for a gray-haired fellow," Amaranthe said.

"Secure the rope," Sicarius yelled. He'd tied his own end to a sturdy vent pipe and sounded slightly annoyed that everyone over there had turned toward the trapdoor instead of finishing his task. "Mancrest, you do it."

Deret had limped a few paces toward the fight, but stopped when he saw the others had control of the situation. He waved an affirmative and soon had the rope tied off. Suan had run over to him. Was she volunteering to go first? Amaranthe couldn't blame her for wanting to get off that cursed roof, but wasn't sure she'd have the strength to climb fifty meters hanging from a rope.

"She needs to go last," Sicarius told them. "The makarovi will sense it when she leaves the building."

Footsteps pounded on the roof behind Amaranthe. "We have a problem," Books announced.

"A new one?" She eyed the illusory makarovi in the streets. They'd stopped at the end of the building, a dozen meters from the crowd. The gangs had scooted back at the monsters'

appearance, but they hadn't fled. Men were firing. Trust Turgonian men not to flee in the face of a battle, even grubby street thugs. It was only the darkness of the night that had kept them from noticing that their musket balls and crossbow quarrels were going *through* the makarovi instead of embedding in flesh.

"Not that." Books pointed toward a corner of their building, one facing the waterfront. "Some of them have ropes and grapples and they're trying to get up here, to get us. I shot one, but with the makarovi down there, they have a lot of incentive to want to get off the ground. More than simply money."

"See them across," Sicarius told Amaranthe. "I'll take care of the climbers." He took her rifle as well as his own and ran for the corner.

Two of Starcrest's soldiers were starting across the rope. Amaranthe worried that it would give under their combined weight, but between the gangs and the makarovi, she doubted they had time for a safer, more leisurely crossing. As soon as the thugs below figured out they were facing illusions, their attention would return to the roofs. The gangs might attack the people on the rope, thinking they could also be outlaws with bounties on their heads. Amaranthe thought about announcing that one of the men on that roof was Fleet Admiral Starcrest, but didn't know if his name would raise the same adoration in a mob of illiterate street roughs as it did amongst soldiers and more educated men. Those men down there might shoot him simply for being a Crest and for having been born with comforts and privileges they'd never known.

With Books and Sicarius running along the perimeter, targeting anyone who attempted to climb up, and Akstyr busy maintaining his illusions, Amaranthe felt she should do something more helpful than cheering for the men crossing the rope. She rummaged in one of the rucksacks and found a lantern and matches. If they needed the blasting sticks, they might need them in a hurry.

By the time she'd lit the lantern, the first two soldiers reached her corner. She helped them off the rope.

"Not a much better view over here," one observed.

"It stinks less."

"I don't know. I smell urine. Why do people always piss on roofs? Or is it just that they do it in the alley and the smell wafts up?"

"That's probably it."

Lovely, Starcrest had sent his comedians first. "Could you two help those two?" Amaranthe pointed at Books and Sicarius. "We have gang members trying to—"

"It's fake!" someone shouted in the street below. "All the makarovi are."

"Wizard," another shouted. "That's Akstyr, he's the wizard."

"Kill the wizard, kill the wizard!" Men ran through the makarovi illusions, their chants rising in volume as they grew more sure of themselves.

Amaranthe grabbed one of the blasting sticks. A part of her wanted to let the gangs surge closer, in the hopes that they'd draw the *real* makarovi out of the factory, but it'd be a massacre, especially after Akstyr's illusion. The youths wouldn't know to be afraid of the flesh-and-blood creatures until it was too late.

Out on the rope, Tikaya and Mahliki were making their way across. A nightgown peeped out from Mahliki's jacket, and she wore nothing but socks on her feet. Tikaya wore a dress and boots but no parka or gloves. As Amaranthe had feared, the factory had been caught unsuspecting—and asleep—when the makarovi showed up at the door.

While the women advanced, Starcrest stood on the rim of the roof, his feet planted on either side of the rope, a rifle raised to the hollow of his shoulder. Face set in stone, he was prepared to fire at anyone who threatened his family. Amaranthe didn't think the mob had noticed the rope or the people crawling along its length overhead, and she'd keep it that way if she could.

"Distraction coming," she called to warn the women—the last thing she wanted to do was startle them into losing their grips—then lobbed the first blasting stick.

It sailed toward the center of the street, a few meters ahead

of the crowd. The stick landed on the worn cobblestones and lay there. The flame danced along the fuse, then went out. Amaranthe groaned. And here they'd been worried about the sticks being so volatile. So much for her distraction, and so much for demolishing that building over there. They'd have to—

An explosion roared in the street. Three stories up, the force of it was diminished, but a gust of wind still sent Amaranthe stumbling away from the edge.

She scrambled back, afraid bloody chunks of human beings would litter the street and splatter the walls. When she'd timed her throw, she'd thought the weapon would go off sooner, that it'd be a scare tactic, not a true attack.

The brick building walls weren't awash in blood, but there *were* many injured people near the front. Limping, or clutching arms or torsos, they staggered to the sides, trying to find an escape route past their own men.

"We have more blasting sticks up here," Amaranthe yelled. "Back off or we'll throw them."

"Wait until the women are across to use more," Starcrest ordered.

Amaranthe winced, wishing he hadn't yelled that—there were gang people close enough to notice him, maybe even decipher the words. On the rope, Tikaya and Mahliki had paused and curled in upon themselves, like turtles ducking into their shells. Starcrest's face was grim, as if he was thinking about raising his rifle in *Amaranthe's* direction. She gave a wave of acknowledgment.

Books jogged over to grab more ammunition. "Where are the blasted enforcers?"

Akstyr, still kneeling, wiped his brow. "Does anyone else think it's strange that we're trying to save those idiots when they're here to collect on our bounties?"

Amaranthe shook her head, not having a good answer to either of their questions. "The enforcers are—"

A distant boom came from the depths of the city, and it took Amaranthe a surprised moment before she realized

what it must have been. "Not the city," she whispered. "The Imperial Barracks."

From their rooftop perch, they could see past the miles of intervening buildings and to the top of Arakan Hill, to the great fiery blaze erupting from the center of the walled courtyard at its crown. Flames leaped into the black sky. Amaranthe couldn't see the building or how much of it had been damaged, but one thing was clear: Sespian and the rest of the team hadn't found one of the bombs.

CHAPTER 20

SICARIUS STARED, TRANSFIXED BY THE LEAPING FLAMES. Sespian. He forgot about the gangs mobbing the street, the men banging at the rooftop door, and the youths scaling the side of the building. For a moment, all he could wonder was if he'd made a mistake in leaving the Imperial Barracks.

From across the rooftop, he found Amaranthe's eyes, and saw the same fears reflected in them.

Her mouth moved. She was too far away for him to hear over the din in the street, but he read the words on her lips: "He's fine, I'm sure if it. He knew there might be more bombs. He would have evacuated everyone. And himself."

Yes, he must believe that. But, as she turned away to help Komitopis onto the roof, Sicarius let his gaze be pulled back to those flames.

Only when a ringing clatter arose from the center of the rooftop did he jerk his focus back to the battle. The bar holding the door shut. Someone had knocked it loose. Sicarius lunged in that direction, but a scrape and grunt from behind him alerted him to another danger.

He dropped and spun. A dagger swooshed over his head and clattered on the roof behind him. Two men Akstyr's age had clawed their way over the edge, their eyes wide with anticipation—and greed—when they spotted him. One was recovering from the blade he'd thrown, but the other man held a pistol, his finger on the trigger. Anticipating the shot, Sicarius hurled himself to the side. As he rolled, he yanked out a throwing knife. He twisted and threw, and the blade lodged in his attacker's eye. Sicarius jumped up, sprinting for the edge. Seeing him coming, the second man stumbled back and tried to catch his rope again as he disappeared over the side. He missed it and fell forty feet, landing on the mob below. Sicarius tugged his knife free of the first man's eye before that body, too, tilted backward and dropped to the street.

After a quick scan to see if any more men had made the roof—Starcrest's soldiers were engaged in their own battles on the waterfront side, but they were keeping the gang members from reaching the top—Sicarius ran toward the door. If Amaranthe and the others hadn't heard that bar drop...

More men than he'd expected had already raced out of the stairwell. They sprinted straight toward Amaranthe's corner, clubs, swords, and crossbows raised. She had her back to them, helping Mahliki onto the roof. Books knelt beside one of the rucksacks, stuffing fresh ammunition into his pouches. His back was to the mob too. With the clamor all about the building, they didn't hear the threat.

"Look out," Sicarius yelled, though at the same moment, Akstyr acted. Still kneeling, he'd been facing the door, and now he threw up an arm. A curtain of fire erupted from the roof between the team and their attackers, but not before three of the men ran into it. One screamed, but the others didn't. Had they made it through? Or had they been enveloped in the flames? Sicarius, also behind that curtain, couldn't see his comrades or anything around them.

"Wizard!" someone on his side of the fire shrieked. "There he is. Get him!"

Sicarius pumped his arm once, then two more times, hurling knives. All three blades slammed into the backs of those at the rear of the crowd. His targets went down. Two at the front hurled themselves at the flames, as if they believed them as illusory as the makarovi they'd faced. They screamed, their clothes catching on fire. They dropped to the ground, rolling. Those with crossbows fired, and Sicarius's gut clenched. If one of those stray shots struck Amaranthe...

Someone on the other side of the flames fired a rifle, but nobody went down. His comrades couldn't see through the flames either.

Sicarius leaped into the remains of the cluster of attackers, his black dagger in hand. He slashed two throats before the men knew he was there.

"Akstyr, get out of there—" someone shouted—Books.

Another crossbow quarrel zipped into the flames.

The fiery curtain vanished. Books stood at Akstyr's side, his rifle raised like a club. Akstyr was down on one knee, a hand clenched to his side. Books parried the wild swing of a desperate man whose clothes had been seared by fire. Akstyr stretched out a hand, probably trying to bring back the flames, but his teeth were gritted against whatever injury he'd sustained.

Sicarius meant to sprint the last few meters to fight back-to-back with them, but one of the men who'd been burned by the flames scrambled to his feet. He swung wildly at Sicarius. It might have been an attack or nothing more than pained flailing—he didn't take the time to sort it out. He slammed his dagger into the top of the man's skull. Leaving his blade there, he grabbed a pimple-faced youth who was trying to run around Books to get at Akstyr's back. When the man saw him, he tried to pull away, but he stumbled on one of his fallen comrades. Sicarius didn't bother drawing another knife. He yanked the thug toward him with one hand and slammed the palm of his other into his nose.

Books downed the second of the two people who'd evaded the flames and almost reached Akstyr. He gripped Akstyr's arm. "Are you all right?"

Knowing that door was still open behind them, Sicarius didn't relax. He spun, intending to run back and jam the bar back through the handle. Two more men stood at the top of the stairwell, both with crossbows raised.

A mistake, the analytical part of Sicarius's mind acknowledged, you should have secured the door first. These thoughts came even as he lunged for one of the serrated blades in his boot—he'd spent all of the throwing knives in his arm sheath with the first attack. He never took his focus from the men, but they weren't aiming at him; they didn't even seem to see him. Their eyes, filled with some sort of zealous hatred, remained on Akstyr.

"Look out," Sicarius warned in the same beat as he threw his knife. He reached for a second as soon as it spun from his fingers, but he knew he couldn't hit both men before they fired.

The serrated blade wasn't balanced for throwing, but it slashed across his target's neck, slicing into the jugular before he loosed his shot. The second gang member, however, fired before Sicarius's second knife left his fingers. Hoping the crossbow had missed, Sicarius glanced at his comrades.

Across the pile of fallen bodies from him, Books had lunged in front of Akstyr. Now he crumpled to the roof, his hand clutched to his chest.

"No!" Akstyr shouted.

Sicarius ran for the door. His knife had taken down the man who'd fired, but two more gang thugs were about to lunge out of the stairwell. They saw their death approaching in Sicarius's eyes and stumbled backward. Sicarius yanked the door shut, grabbed the pipe he'd used earlier, and jammed it back through the handle.

"Akstyr?" came Amaranthe's voice, an uncharacteristic quaver to it. "Is he...?"

After another check to make sure no climbers had gained the roof, Sicarius ran toward the group, though he slowed before he reached them. Books lay on his side, facing the door. He wasn't moving.

Akstyr dropped down beside him, forgetting his own wound—blood saturated the side of his baggy brown shirt. Amaranthe rushed over, falling to her knees.

"Why'd he do that?" Akstyr whispered. "Why'd he step in front...?"

Amaranthe shook his shoulder. "Help him. You can heal him."

Books's eyes were locked open. It wasn't his chest that he

was clutching but a crossbow bolt sticking out of it. It was as if he'd meant to pull it out, but he hadn't been able to. It wouldn't have mattered. It'd struck his heart. He was already dead.

"I can't," Akstyr whispered. "It's too late. He's—"

"No, curse your ancestors." Amaranthe grabbed both of Akstyr's shoulders and shook him. "You healed me when I was dying. You can do it. All those books, you—" Her voice cracked, and she shook him again.

Akstyr threw a desperate look at Sicarius.

That stirred him to action. He stepped around Books's body and grasped Amaranthe's arms, trying to pull her away from Akstyr gently, but she wouldn't relinquish her grip.

Sicarius made his own grip firmer. "We'll *all* be dead if we don't concentrate on the rest of the fight."

Komitopis and Mahliki glanced in his and Amaranthe's direction. They'd taken over her position and were helping Deret and another soldier onto the roof.

Sicarius released Amaranthe, trusting she'd gather herself, but he might need to take charge for a moment, at least until Starcrest joined them. He grabbed a couple of blasting sticks. With Books down, any inhibitions he might have had against blowing up gang brats was gone—such inhibitions would have been out of respect for Amaranthe's wishes, not because he thought any of those thugs worth saving.

The remaining soldiers were climbing across the rope while Starcrest, standing beside Suan, waited for the last slot. Nobody was left guarding their trapdoor, a trapdoor the makarovi must still be banging at.

"Come," Sicarius shouted.

Starcrest glanced at his giant unused trap, then squinted behind Sicarius. "What is your rope tied to?"

"Smoke vent."

Starcrest shook his head once and held up two fingers. He must have made a mental calculation and was certain that was all the rope could hold safely. Sicarius didn't know if they had time for safety though. People were spilling into the

intersection below, and more thugs with ropes and grapples were running toward the warehouse walls. Others funneled into the first-floor doors.

As the last two soldiers climbed off, Sicarius waved again for Starcrest to go. He lit a blasting stick and threw it to the north of the intersection where a wave of reinforcements was coming in. He didn't bother aiming where nobody was standing, as Amaranthe had done; he targeted a thick knot of people.

"Look out!" someone cried. They were pressed in too tightly for anyone to run.

Sicarius never would have thought the gangs would work this hard and risk this much for his head, million ranmyas or not. Though the chants that floated up continued to be, "Get the wizard, kill the wizard!" Through his own actions, Akstyr had riled them up into a furor.

Watching the wary slowness with which Suan climbed onto the rope was enough to make one start tearing hair out. Sicarius didn't care if she plummeted, but Starcrest obviously did. He knelt, whispering what could only be encouragements. Since he'd taken the last position, he couldn't cross until she did.

A crack sounded on the far rooftop, and bars clattered. The crate and whatever else the soldiers had shifted onto the trapdoor tipped off.

Makarovi paws appeared, grasping either side of the opening.

"Starcrest, go!" Sicarius barked.

Starcrest scarcely needed the order. He'd swung onto the rope as soon as the crack sounded behind him. Suan inched along ahead of him.

Too slow. If the makarovi was willing to throw itself from the roof to get to them...

Sicarius clenched his fist around a blasting stick. The first creature pulled itself the rest of the way through the trapdoor. A second head appeared behind it.

Sicarius dipped the fuse into the lantern flame. He backed a few steps, lining up a throw. Starcrest's eyes widened. Yes, if Sicarius took out the part of the trap their rope was tied to, it'd be trouble for them. But being knocked from the rope by a makarovi would be trouble too.

"What are you doing?" Komitopis blurted.

Sicarius had to risk it. Better for them to fall a couple of stories than to be shredded to death in midair. He dodged Komitopis's grasp, ran forward, and hurled the burning stick. It flew, toppling end over end through the air. He swore it moved even more slowly than the woman on the rope. The makarovi were lumbering creatures, but at that moment the lead one's gait seemed to have the speed of an avalanche. It couldn't have been more than ten feet from the edge, from leaping after Starcrest and its target, when the blasting stick bounced to the roof at its feet. The fuse was still burning down, and Sicarius believed it'd explode too late. He was about to lunge for a rifle, out of some vain notion of shooting the makarovi in the eye as it leaped from the roof, but the stick blew, right between the beast's legs. He'd been expecting that all night—for one of the sticks to explode on impact—but it surprised him nonetheless.

Smoke swallowed the makarovi, and an undulation ran along the rope stretched between the buildings. Suan squealed. Her legs had been crossed over it, but they slipped free. Starcrest hastened toward her, dropping a hand to steady her. The makarovi was no more, but shrapnel rained down all around Starcrest and Suan—broken metal pipes flying free from the trap Starcrest had been making. The trap had lost the top and part of one side, but the section holding the rope remained stable. Sicarius let out a soft exhalation of relief.

"They're everywhere," came a cry from one of the soldiers defending the warehouse roof. "Why are they so slagging eager to get up here?"

"Wizard, wizard," continued the chant from the street.

"And where are the slagging enforcers?" another of Starcrest's men yelled.

At the Imperial Barracks, Sicarius thought, and grabbed another blasting stick, this one for the mob. The first had kept people away from the intersection, but they were encroaching again.

"Get those people up there," someone in the street shouted. "They're going to help the wizard. And the assassin!"

Sicarius thrust the fuse into the flame. *Nobody* was getting "those people."

Mahliki rushed to the edge, gripping the low wall. "Hurry up, Father!"

Starcrest had righted Suan, and her ankles were locked over the rope again. They'd reached the halfway point. He gave a smile that was probably meant to be encouraging, but bleakness edged it.

"Stay back," Sicarius told Mahliki and lobbed the blasting stick.

A second before it landed, a musket boomed from the street corner. Starcrest's body jerked, his hands flying from the rope.

No. Sicarius grabbed a rifle, not even sure who had shot, but wanting to put a bullet in his eye.

"Rias!" Komitopis screamed.

Suan screamed as well and finally got her hands moving faster. Sicarius was tempted to shoot *her*.

Rias hadn't dropped entirely—he hung from the rope by his ankles. One arm dangled below him, and the other was tucked to his chest. Shoulder shot? Sicarius couldn't tell.

As Rias swayed, his face grew visible for a moment, along with the rictus of pain that contorted his mouth. Definitely shot. He flexed his abdomen and curled up, his good arm reaching for the rope. He almost had it when the blasting stick Sicarius had thrown chose that moment to explode.

Shouts of fear and shrieks of pain erupted from the street. The blast was close enough to set the rope to swaying and buffet Suan and Starcrest again. Starcrest's grasping fingers missed the rope, and he dropped again. One of his boots slipped, but he made a quick adjustment and caught himself.

Komitopis cursed a stream of Kyattese, the words spewing forth so quickly Sicarius could only make out one in three. They weren't flattering. She slammed a palm into his shoulder, the blow harder than he would have expected from her, and shouted,

"Stop throwing those things. Let them cross!"

Sicarius didn't point out that he'd thrown it before Starcrest had been in trouble. Suan had made it to the roof. When Sicarius didn't move to help her, others did. Deret and Amaranthe. She gave him a look he couldn't read.

Out on the line, Starcrest swung himself up again. This time he caught the rope. His head dropped and he stared at his destination upside down. He couldn't get his other arm up to help himself along. Would he be able to complete the crawl with one hand? He twisted his neck, eyeing the street below.

Sicarius read the look. Starcrest was considering how much trouble he'd be in if he dropped.

Sicarius handed his rifle to someone, ordering, "Cover us," to no one in particular. He slipped out onto the rope and skimmed along it until he reached Starcrest.

"I hope you brought the painkillers," Starcrest said.

"Grab me, sir."

"You can't carry me."

"I will," Sicarius said.

"Look out," someone below cried.

"Nah, it's more stupid magic."

With Suan no longer on their rooftop, the makarovi, the *real* makarovi, were running out of the factory.

This was taking too long. Their chance to collapse the building on the monsters was gone, if they'd ever had a chance to start with. This whole night—what chaos and stupidity. Sicarius vowed that if he lived, Ravido Marblecrest wouldn't.

Sicarius grabbed Starcrest, wrestling with limbs and gravity to find a position they could use. Starcrest refused to climb onto Sicarius's back and put all of his weight on him, and ended up grabbing Sicarius's belt with his good hand. Starcrest left his ankles wrapped around the rope, and they managed an awkward upside down crab walk toward the warehouse.

The first scream of pain came from below as the mob learned that *these* makarovi were not illusions. Sicarius wondered if the gangs would stay and fight. With those numbers, they might wear down the remaining beasts by attrition, but there was no money promised for slaying *them*.

"That's the assassin," someone shouted. "Get him—a million ranmyas."

"You shouldn't have come out here," Rias said.

Sicarius picked up his speed—another ten meters and they'd reach the building.

A shot fired, not from below but from the roof. Amaranthe stood on the low wall, smoke wafting from her rifle. She'd taken the idiot yelling about assassins in the center of his chest.

The makarovi tore into the mob, distracting anyone else from the men on the rope. Sicarius reached the roof and shifted about so Mancrest and Akstyr could grab Starcrest first. After the admiral was safe, Sicarius pulled himself over and collapsed on the roof. For a weary moment, he considered not getting up. What was the point? Let the makarovi destroy those people down there. And vice versa.

He looked at the spot where he'd left Books. He hadn't been moved, and seeing his body there, alone on the roof, filled Sicarius with remorse he hadn't expected. There had to be a point, he thought. Or what had his death been for? He looked to Amaranthe, for some reason thinking she might have an answer for him, one that made sense.

She stood, her face more grim and determined than ever, holding a blasting stick in each hand. The last two, Sicarius realized.

"I had an idea while you two were out there," she announced. "I don't know if there's any molasses left in those tanks, but I'm figuring there might be. The business left all their equipment in the building, so maybe some of their product is still here too."

"You think you can blow them up?" Akstyr asked.

"We only have two sticks left," Amaranthe said, "and throwing them at the mob isn't doing much. Maybe we can at least get the makarovi too sticky to attack people." Her mouth twisted. A joke? If so, a bleak one. There wasn't a hint of humor in her eyes.

Komitopis was trying to make Starcrest sit down so she could tend to his shoulder, but he stepped back to the side of the roof and gazed at the sizable tanks. Each one rose three stories high, and Sicarius didn't know if even a blasting stick would rupture the metal walls.

Someone fired below, and Komitopis pulled Starcrest back.

"*Rias*," she hissed. "Stop trying to get yourself killed."

"I'm going to throw it," Amaranthe said, "before the makarovi get too far away for it to matter."

She knelt to thrust the fuses into the flame, but Starcrest dropped down beside her and blocked the lantern with his hand.

"What?" she asked.

"Let me do it." Starcrest opened his palm, asking for one of the blasting sticks.

"She can throw it that far," Sicarius said, not understanding Starcrest's objection, but sensing it might stem from a doubt in Amaranthe's abilities. "And with accuracy."

Starcrest's smile held no joy. "That is not my concern." He met Amaranthe's eyes. "Enough blood stains your sword for this lifetime."

In the second while she was puzzling this out, Starcrest took a blasting stick from her. Her eyes widened with understanding, but he'd already lit it, stood, and hurled it toward the tanks beside the building.

This time, the stick did not explode on impact. Unnoticed by those in the streets below, it skidded to a stop beneath the closest tank. Sicarius watched the fuse burn down, curious as to what the results would be. Nothing if the tanks were empty, though the shrapnel from the explosion might damage those near the intersection. If there was liquid inside, would getting "sticky" truly deter the makarovi?

A heartbeat before the stick blew up, his mind caught up with Starcrest's, the estimates for a volume equation forming in his thoughts.

The tanks dampened the explosion, and Sicarius worried the force hadn't been enough to damage the sturdy walls. But a resounding pop sounded over the fading boom from the blasting stick. Rivets shot in a hundred directions with the velocity—and destructive power—of bullets. Screams burst from the people crowding the intersection, and no less than two dozen fell to the ground, struck by the shrapnel. One of the makarovi was hit, and its roar turned to the squeal of a pig gone to slaughter. Those who died in the initial blast suffered the least.

In a chain reaction, both of the tanks were destroyed, their bellies ruptured. One was empty, but the other... was not. Molasses, brown and thick and almost as fast-flowing as water, gushed into the streets. Sicarius had never seen a tidal wave, but he imagined it must look like this: channeled by the surrounding buildings, the liquid rose ten feet high and bore down on the people in the street. Too fast to outrun, it swept over them, the force knocking them from their feet and pulling them under. Even the heavy makarovi couldn't resist its power, and the beasts roared in terror as they were tugged into the deadly flow.

Like water, the molasses obeyed gravity and found the path of least resistance. It gushed down to the waterfront, then broke like a wave, its height diminishing as it flowed across the docks and into the lake. Sicarius stared down at the intersection and the streets leading up to it, at the swath of brown gunk left behind, and at the disappearance of the crowd. Oh, a few beslimed people lay unmoving in the streets, and a survivor clung to a lone standing lamppost—the others had been flattened and torn away. From the shouts within the warehouse, a few more had survived by being on an upper level when a gush had torn down the doors and broken the windows to sweep through the building. Those who hadn't been swept away were hacking to rid their lungs of fluid and staggering away from the scene. A few cast stares of disbelief up at the warehouse roof, but most simply scurried into the shadows as fast as they could.

"Are they gone?" Amaranthe rasped, a hysteric edge to her voice.

Sicarius knew she meant the makarovi, not the people. She

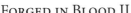

never would have, of her own volition, chosen to kill human beings, not even gang thugs who were trying to kill *her*.

"Guntar," Starcrest called to a soldier on the far side of the roof, someone with a better view of the waterfront. "Makarovi?"

"Looks like they all drowned, sir. Lots of those gang brutes did too. We shouldn't have any trouble getting out of here."

"Understood," Starcrest said. "Thank you."

Amaranthe dropped her face into her hand. To cry? Sicarius couldn't tell, but surely she deserved a release after all this. His own gaze lifted toward Arakan Hill. The flames had died down—or been put out—but the night sky didn't hide the black plumes of smoke pouring from whatever remained of the Imperial Barracks. He wanted to race up there and find Sespian, but he wouldn't leave until he knew Amaranthe would be all right. She was strong, but she'd been through so much, and Sicarius didn't think she'd be able to let Starcrest accept the blame for the deaths her idea had wrought. She'd never failed to feel for those who had died at Sicarius's hand, after all, not when he'd been in her employ.

"That was..." Akstyr was staring down at the carnage in the street. Sicarius expected him to say, "brilliant," or, "the best revenge ever," but he wiped his eyes instead and finished with, "not worth the price." He walked over, sat beside Books's body, and buried his face in his hands.

"If this is how it had to end anyway," Amaranthe whispered, staring at the barren streets, "I wish I'd thought of it sooner."

She lifted her head to find Sicarius's face. Her eyes were like pools with rivulets escaping down her cheeks. Her hand twitched toward him, and his feet swallowed the three steps between them. He pulled her into a hug, wishing he'd thought to do so immediately, but she always tried so hard not to let her emotions or her... human fallibility show in front of the others. This time was different, he realized, and lifted his hand to the back of her head, letting her cry into his shoulder.

* * *

The enforcer wagon crawled up Arakan Hill, and trepidation tightened Sicarius's fingers on the steering controls. Starcrest sat in the seat beside him, with his family, Amaranthe, Akstyr, Mancrest, and the soldiers in the back. Books's body was back there too. Amaranthe and Akstyr had refused to leave it behind, and both had glared at Sicarius when he'd pointed out that nobody would take it.

As the Barracks walls came into view, with the heavy double doors charred and blown half off their hinges, Sicarius wondered how many people they'd be preparing a funeral pyre for. Not Sespian. Sespian had known the danger, known there might be more bombs. If he'd gotten himself killed...

A pair of enforcers standing outside the warped gates frowned at their approach. It was still a few hours until dawn, and Sicarius doubted they could tell who occupied the shadowy interior of the cab, but he watched their eyes—and their hands—nonetheless. A sergeant wearing the reds of the Imperial Fire Brigade jogged up to them, and Sicarius drove through into the courtyard without being stopped. With so many enforcer wagons and army lorries, one more shouldn't seem strange. Besides, Sicarius thought, as the front of the Barracks came into view, what was left to protect?

Black bricks and charred wood lay all about the slushy courtyard, along with pieces of furniture, clothing, and a set of purple velvet draperies that were wrapped around the flagpole. The face of the building had been blown off; the remaining walls and floors, their edges crumbling, stood open to the elements, laid open like a giant diorama. Water dripped from it all, courtesy of the Imperial Fire Brigade's hoses. With the fire quenched, they'd been turned off, but they still snaked across the ground to fire plugs in the corner of the courtyard, and steam still rose from the rubble crowding the base of the building.

Sicarius drove to one side, passing the vehicle house he'd taken a different vehicle from earlier. That vehicle remained on the street where they'd parked it; molasses had reached three feet up the side of it, leaving a sticky mess of the engine.

Though he remained alert for danger from the enforcers they passed, Sicarius searched the rubble for bodies and searched the courtyard for signs of Sespian.

"The back half of the building is relatively undamaged," Starcrest observed.

Sicarius didn't care about the building. Where was Sespian?

"I don't see any bodies," Starcrest added quietly.

A more useful observation. If Sicarius hadn't been busy hunting for his son, he would have realized it too. Sespian—or someone—must have succeeded in evacuating the Barracks.

"Where is everybody?" Sicarius asked. He had rounded the back of the building and come out on the other side. He could almost see back to the courtyard gate, but he hadn't spotted Sespian or anyone else on the team. Enforcers and Fire Brigade personnel roamed everywhere, taking notes, searching the inside of the building, and making inspections to figure out if the rest would collapse, but where was everyone *else*?

"Stop, and I'll ask," Starcrest said.

He climbed out gingerly, his bandaged arm cradled against his abdomen. In a hasty bit of field surgery that Starcrest had insisted upon, Komitopis had removed the musket ball from his shoulder while his daughter had filled the role of nurse. Their practiced professionalism—and the way Komitopis had shaken her head while glaring and *tsk-tsk*ing at her husband—had led Sicarius to believe it wasn't the first musket ball they'd removed from Starcrest's body.

"Root cellar," Starcrest said when he climbed back into the cab. "It was undamaged, aside from the addition of a smelly makarovi den." He raised his eyebrows, silently asking if Sicarius already knew about this and of the cellar's location. When Sicarius nodded, Starcrest added, "It's been claimed as the headquarters suite for now. Most of the troops and staff that were in the Barracks were evacuated to hotels in the area."

Sicarius barely heard the addition. He would have simply run to the root cellar, but there was enough light in the courtyard that people would spot—and recognize him—so it was best to get closer using the vehicle. Besides, Amaranthe and the others would want to rush in to see the rest of the team too.

Four soldiers stood guard around the reinforced root cellar door. Sicarius stopped the vehicle.

"I'll talk to them," Starcrest said.

Not interested in waiting—or being the recipient of rifle fire when the soldiers figured out who he was—Sicarius slipped out of the cab and used the vehicle to cover his approach to the ragged hole in the lawn. He hopped into the tunnel, breathing the makarovi scent anew. It was almost better than the smoke that lingered in the courtyard, the smell of wet, charred wood dominating everything else.

Sicarius heard voices as soon as he landed, and he found himself sprinting up the slope and into the makarovi cage. Numerous lamps burned in the root cellar, and the number of bodies holed up inside made the room warm. Sespian, Yara, Maldynado, Basilard, and a handful of officers were standing around a food crate turned into a table. Their backs were to him. Another man lay bound and gagged in a corner by a box with air holes. Ravido.

Sicarius paused only long enough to make sure nobody with a pistol stood ready to shoot him, then slipped through the bars. "Sespian."

A profound relief filled him when Sespian turned, his hair tousled and his uniform rumpled, but with no injuries marring his flesh. Before his rational mind caught up to his reflexes— his feelings—he'd grabbed Sespian and wrapped him in a hug.

Startled, Sespian leaned back, as if to pull away, but he decided to accept the embrace and offered an awkward back pat. It warmed Sicarius's heart.

The door creaked open. "Fleet Admiral Starcrest and Corporal Lokdon here to see you, sir," a soldier called.

"Thank you," Sespian said. "Send them down."

It wasn't until footsteps sounded on the earthen stairs that Sicarius released Sespian and stepped back. A faint furrow creased Sespian's brow.

"We saw your explosion from the waterfront," Sicarius said, realizing the hug had been out of character and likely puzzled his son. "I did not know if you lived."

"Ah," Sespian said, nodding in understanding.

"What's this?" Maldynado asked. "No hugs for us?" He smirked at Sicarius and opened his arms in an invitation.

Basilard's eyebrows twitched up, and Yara stared at Maldynado as if he'd grown a new eye in the center of his forehead, right under that idiotic tentacle hat that he'd managed to retain throughout the night's action.

Sicarius was almost tempted to take a step toward the man, to see what he'd do, but he must have taken too long to act, for Maldynado shrugged and faced the stairs, his arms still spread. "I know the boss will hug me!"

Amaranthe *was* on the steps, but she was coming down behind Starcrest, and he was the one to receive the enthusiastic smile.

The admiral raised his eyebrows at the proffered embrace. "Given my injury, I'll pass."

"Er, yes," Maldynado said. "Quite right."

Yara pulled him out of the way of the people coming down the stairs. "Are you always going to be a frivolous buffoon?"

"Of course. You wouldn't want a serious old stick, would you?" Maldynado flicked a glance toward Sicarius.

Before the conversation could go further, and before Sicarius could decide if he wanted to rebut with anything more than an icy stare, an ear-splitting yowl made most people in the cellar wince.

Ravido, his ear inches from the box that housed whatever feline beast was emitting the noise, groaned through his gag. He tried to say something too. It sounded like, "Just kill me; it'd be less torture."

"I know, Trog," Sespian said, "and I apologize, but we'll find you some food soon and a place where you can roam."

So that was the cat Sespian had been looking for. Another eardrum-assaulting screech blasted from the box. Sicarius wondered how he could have missed hearing the creature on his first trip into the Barracks.

"Is that your cat?" Amaranthe asked. "I'm glad you found him. Or is it a her?"

Another yowl.

Yara scowled. "Only a male would complain that much."

"I was worried he wouldn't make it," Sespian said, "that nobody would take care of him with me gone, but he's a survivor. More than that. Apparently, he's been harassing the new troops since Ravido presumed to move onto our floor."

Ravido groaned again, cursing vehemently behind his gag. He might have said, "Piss and cat hair *every*where," but it was hard to tell.

"The makarovi?" Sespian asked over the noise of the belligerent cat.

"Dead," Sicarius said.

"All of them?"

"All of them."

"We paid a price though." Amaranthe so rarely gave anyone a glare of hatred that Sicarius almost didn't recognize it as such; it was directed at Ravido.

Sespian sighed. "With such powerful monsters, I'm not surprised."

Amaranthe exchanged hugs with Maldynado and Basilard. "I'm glad you made it out of the building. All of you." She lifted her head to include Yara and Sespian.

"Where's Books?" Maldynado asked. "Up poking through musty old tomes somewhere with Akstyr?"

"Books..." Amaranthe swallowed. "He was our price."

"Our price?" Maldynado removed his hat to scratch his head, either not comprehending—or choosing not to comprehend—her point.

Basilard's shoulders slumped. He knew.

"We were able to retrieve the body," Amaranthe said. "We'll plan the funeral pyre as soon as..." She waved vaguely toward the Barracks. "As soon as enough is resolved that we can do so."

"Oh," Maldynado mouthed, his body as limp as the drooping tendrils of his hat.

Starcrest joined the officers, and their heads bent together over papers scattered on the table. Sicarius found that he cared little as to what was on that table and what they were planning. Sespian and Amaranthe were alive, and in this tight cellar, he could keep an eye out and ensure that they stayed that way. An unexpected sense of contentedness came over him. It was strange, like nothing he'd ever felt before. What an odd time for it to visit him, in the aftermath of all that chaos, at the end of a night with no sleep, and in the face of the death of one of their comrades. Yet there it was, nonetheless.

Because, Sicarius realized, it's finally over, and the two people who mattered most to him had survived. He leaned against the wall where he could observe all and watch the room's entrances.

EPILOGUE

ON THE THIRD EVENING AFTER THE MAKAROVI FIGHT, Amaranthe left her room in Haiden Starcrest's guesthouse. Haiden, the admiral's nephew, tended the family businesses in the capital and kept an estate on Mokath Ridge. His home hadn't been damaged during the fighting and, with order restored to the city, it had proven a safe and quiet place to recuperate. And mourn.

Amaranthe walked toward a granite bench that sat before a fountain in the center of the courtyard. All of the guest rooms opened up on it, though she didn't know who was around. She hadn't answered knocks to her door during the first couple of days. She'd been too busy staring at the wall with her back to the world. Her meals had been delivered by an incurious servant, and nobody else had intruded upon her rest. Rest. Could she call it that? She'd slept a lot, her body finally demanding it whether her mind found respite in it or not. Her nightmares had lingered, and she'd seen Books's death in them over and over, often waking with a lurch to realize she'd been dreaming… then to further realize that, dream or not, he was still dead.

Having grown tired of her self-imposed exile, she sat on the bench, hoping someone might wander out to sit with her, but quietness embraced the house. Along with the benches, exotic potted plants surrounded the courtyard, creating numerous private nooks, but she didn't hear anything beyond the gurgle of a fountain. Outside, the snow and ice had returned, but glass windows covered the ceiling and the southern wall, and the late afternoon sun peeping through the clouds warmed the interior.

In defiance of the exterior climate, flowers bloomed, their scents lush and serene.

Amaranthe didn't hear anyone approach over the flowing water, not that she would have heard *his* approach anyway, and twitched in surprise when the black-clad figure slid onto the bench beside her. He held a pair of scissors and a newspaper.

"Planning to cut out an article highlighting your heroics?" Amaranthe didn't think any of the knocks had belonged to him. If she had, she would have risen, and invited him inside so she could slump against him for comfort. They'd all seemed too… emotional though. She'd feared Maldynado would be out there, wanting to drag her off to a brothel to share drinks, his idea of commiserating. She hadn't had the heart for it. All of the deaths over the last weeks had been difficult, but the loss of a friend struck at one's heart with far greater acuity than the demises of thousands of strangers. Books had been the one to warn her, the year before—it seemed so much longer ago—that the most profound lessons were taught by failure rather than success and that one often had to lose something to realize how much she'd appreciated it.

"No." Sicarius handed her the newspaper.

She didn't yet know what it said or why he was sharing it, but she leaned in and kissed him on the cheek. "I appreciate you," she whispered.

A single blond eyebrow twitched. "Good."

Sicarius was clean-shaven and smelled faintly of soap. He wore fresh black clothing—where did he find those identical, fitted, humorless outfits, anyway?—but for once wasn't wearing his armory of knives. Though she knew he was still deadly without them, he seemed… not exactly naked, but like a man strolling about in his pajamas. A man at rest.

It had taken her a while to summon the strength to care, but she'd eventually bathed and combed the snarls, soot, and dried makarovi guts from her hair. Her clothing wasn't new, but she'd washed and pressed it. She needed to go out and find something appropriate for Books's funeral, but she didn't want

to venture into the city. She was glad Starcrest and Sespian had taken over planning... whatever it was they were planning. The world didn't seem to need her, and for once she was glad to be forgotten.

"Are you going to read it?" Sicarius asked. "Front page."

"Here we are in a pleasant courtyard, being serenaded by a gurgling fountain and enjoying lush fragrances one wouldn't normally find in the winter. I thought you might like to enjoy the moment with me."

"I could read the article to you."

Amaranthe hoped his determination to share it with her meant it was good news. She was ready for good news. This rare display of impatience piqued her humor for the first time in days—after all, he was someone who could perch unmoving in the rafters for six hours, waiting for his prey to walk by.

"Really?" she asked. "You've never offered to read to me. May I lie on my back with my head in your lap and gaze up at you while you do so?"

Sicarius stared at her, his usual unreadable self, and she was about to pick up the paper, when he said, "Describe the gaze."

"What?"

"Your gaze. What kind would it be?"

She had the feeling he was trying to be humorous, and though it didn't sound particularly natural, she went with it. "Oh, an adoring gaze of course. Will that be acceptable?"

"Sufficient for now."

Sufficient? What kind of gaze had he been hoping for? Hm.

Sicarius set down his scissors, took back the newspaper, and lifted his arms. Amaranthe rearranged herself on the bench, her back against the cool stone, and paused, her elbows braced. She hadn't actually expected him to say yes to this scenario. Though there was nothing menacing about his features, at least not to her eyes—others never failed to find his expressionless facade menacing—but she couldn't decide if they were actually inviting. She needed to teach him to smile. Even if it was only when they were alone.

"Sespian and I discussed this failing," Sicarius said.

"What?"

"My inability to be... encouraging. Which facial expression or body posture would be appropriate now?"

Amaranthe blinked. "A smile is *always* appropriate. Surely you've heard the term encouraging smile?"

"I considered it, but thought you might believe I had an agenda."

"Do you... always think this much when you're deciding whether to emote?" She didn't know if "emote" was the right word for those rare eyebrow twitches, but he'd know what she meant.

"Yes."

Ah, she shouldn't be surprised. "And... *do* you have an agenda?" She glanced at the scissors. Why had he brought them? Dare she hope he had a haircut in mind?

"Yes."

Amaranthe waited for him to elaborate. He didn't.

"Well..." She tried her own encouraging smile. "Maybe we have the same agenda."

"An appealing notion." Sicarius hesitated, then patted his leg.

Amaranthe decided not to tell him that'd be more appropriate for inviting a dog into his lap. Her elbows were getting tired anyway. She lay back the rest of the way, shifting about until she found a thigh sufficient for a pillow.

His lips parted, and she thought he'd say something more, but he looked at the newspaper and read instead. "Fleet Admiral Starcrest's reappearance in the empire has brought what could have been an ugly and prolonged civil war to an end." Sicarius's tone was terse and clipped as always, and Amaranthe decided he'd never succeed as an orator or storyteller. She enjoyed having him read to her nonetheless.

"Only two lords remain of the Company of Lords," Sicarius continued, "the ancient organization having been decimated by cowardly assassinations ordered by Ravido Marblecrest.

Rather than electing new members, the survivors opted to dissolve the Company in favor of a new government paradigm being discussed by many, but being spearheaded by Starcrest. Proceedings are being held at the University auditorium and participation is open to those who wish to shape the future of Turgonia. Before the dissolution of the Company, its remaining members voted to place Lord Flintcrest in exile for treason and crimes against the throne, given that former Emperor Sespian Savarsin was still alive at the time of his would-be usurpation. Ravido Marblecrest was put to death for the assassinations of members of the Company of Lords, for setting explosives in the Imperial Barracks, and for his ghastly decision to bring makarovi into the city as part of his scheme. The deaths attributed to those monsters number over one hundred and fifty."

Amaranthe wondered if Ravido had truly had a hand in the bombs, or if those had been the work of disaffected Forge lackeys deciding that if their side couldn't run the Barracks, nobody else would either. If he was dead, it hardly mattered now.

Sicarius had paused, and he watched Amaranthe for a moment before continuing on. "Lord Heroncrest, another plotter against the throne, was also sent into exile, his death being promised should he return to Turgonian shores. In addition to attacking the loyal troops of the ignobly destroyed Fort Urgot, the siege determined that all the soldiers were locked inside the walls when the mystery craft crashed upon the site, destroying the fort and those poor, noble warriors within. The date of their funeral pyre will be announced, along with an awards ceremony to recognize the fallen."

Amaranthe stared at the frost-lined panes of the ceiling windows. "So. Heroncrest gets the blame for that. I never even met Heroncrest. He was probably the most innocuous of those vying for the throne. No mention of how my squabble with the Forge people caused the craft to crash in the first place, eh?"

"No," Sicarius said.

"This last year, I've come to think it terribly unjust to be blamed for crimes one didn't commit. I fear it's also terribly unjust *not* to be blamed for crimes one *did* commit."

"You did not commit a crime; your recklessness merely resulted in deaths."

"*Thank* you, I feel *so* much better now." Amaranthe searched his eyes for judgment, but, despite his knack for the blunt, did not find any. No, not after he'd been that wizard's pawn, killing and doing only he knew what else as a slave. He couldn't be blamed for any of that, but the deaths had been at his hands nonetheless. No, he wouldn't judge her. He might be the only one who understood fully. "Sorry," she said. "I'm sure that'll always be a difficult subject for me to hear about." She wondered if it'd be hypocritical of her to attend the funeral pyre for those fallen men. Maybe so, but it might be worse for her not to.

"In regard to not being blamed for crimes you committed, Admiral Starcrest says it's worse to be rewarded and praised when there are as many allies dead at your feet as enemies."

"Yes, he understands too." Amaranthe studied those panes a little longer, looking at the fading daylight and the deepening frost. "Sicarius, I don't know Sespian's mind on the matter, but... Starcrest is the logical next leader of Turgonia."

Sicarius nodded once. "I had that in mind when I sent that letter."

"You *did*? I thought you mainly wanted his and his wife's help to deal with the ancient technology."

"Yes, but he was also the logical choice for a ruler. As a Crest, his blood is good enough for those who care about such matters, and the reputation he gained when he was on active duty assured the adoration of the general populace. If anything, his reputation has grown in the last twenty years. In addition, he was the only person in the empire who could ensure peace amongst other nations. The tie to Kyatt assures they wouldn't place themselves as enemies, and Nuria would not dare to take up arms against him either. More, he is respected amongst Nurians. Even the Mangdorians, Kendorians, and desert city-states have heard of him."

"You were thinking of *all* that when you wrote that letter? I had... no idea you cared as to who ended up on the throne."

"I did not foresee Sespian winning the position when word of his heritage got out. I thought he would approve of this alternative."

"All along, I thought I was running things," Amaranthe said, "and here it turns out you're the mastermind."

Sicarius touched his chin. "Here."

"Pardon?"

"Your gaze of adoration. It's focused on the window currently."

She grinned and gazed at *him*. "I apologize."

"Accepted." He rattled the paper. "Do you wish me to continue?"

"Yes."

"You may be further disturbed."

Amaranthe's grin faded. Her team hadn't been mentioned yet. Would it be mentioned at all? Would that be so bad? She'd longed for a place in the history books once, but she wasn't sure how history would see her at this point. "Go on," she said.

"Admiral Starcrest, with family in tow, has not commented on whether his return to the empire will be permanent or not. Many pundits are tossing his name about as a logical leader for the new government that's being bandied about." Sicarius lowered the paper to say, "They're relying heavily on Books's constitution. Mancrest, Starcrest, and many top officers, professors, and notable non-warrior-caste citizens are being consulted and amendments are being made, but his work will not be forgotten."

Tears welled in Amaranthe's eyes. "I'm glad to hear that."

Sicarius lifted the paper again. "The missing food stores that were a concern have been restored, and Admiral Starcrest admits he made the aqueducts appear to be damaged as a tactic to force the hands of those illegally vying for the throne. In fact, the water supply was never in danger and full service has been returned to the city. Starcrest, injured in the action, is grateful for the support from the city and trusts no further military actions will be required to ensure peace."

Amaranthe snorted. Sespian had been so worried that

they were treading a questionable line, but in comparison to the makarovi and the bombings, Starcrest's tactics were so insignificant that everyone would doubtlessly forget them. Some historian would praise them for turning the tide in the skirmishes.

"Also," Sicarius continued reading, "Admiral Starcrest wishes to make known the role Amaranthe Lokdon and a team of wrongfully-accused outlaws, including the assassin Sicarius and the deceased professor Marl 'Books' Mugdildor played in saving the city and himself from tragedy. Though they had no hope of reward for themselves, they fought the makarovi toe-to-toe and ultimately came up with the tactic that slew the vile creatures. In addition, they rid the city of much of its criminal element, sending the looting gangs to a similar fate as to the makarovi."

"The assassin Sicarius," Amaranthe said. "It sounds strange without the usual adjectives in front of it. Nefarious. Insidious. Cowardly. Does this mean people will stop trying to shoot you?"

"Doubtful. Starcrest wasn't able to convince the two remaining curmudgeons on the Company of Lords to remove my bounty. He said he'd try again when the new government has taken power. Your bounty has been cleared though."

"Oh, good." She ought to feel more jubilant, she supposed. Hadn't all of this started because she'd wanted to clear her name? She'd always imagined that victory would be more... triumphant. And less bloody. Why, she didn't know; it wasn't as if Turgonia had a history of bloodless victories. "What about Maldynado's bounty? I know that two hundred and fifty ranmyas bothers him terribly." Though the paucity of the amount had always bothered him more than the fact that it was being offered for his head.

"It remains." Sicarius opened to the second page and pointed to the continuation of the front-page story. "I won't read it all to you, but the Marblecrests are all being regarded with suspicion due to Ravido's choices. The family has been tasked with funding the rebuild of the new government headquarters."

"It's not clear that Maldynado was disowned and didn't have anything to do with the rest of his family's scheming?"

"He is trying to make it clear. There is resistance."

"The poor fellow is never going to get his statue," Amaranthe said.

"He's lobbying Starcrest now."

Amaranthe chuckled. "No shame at all."

"Now that I have read for you, I would request a favor." Sicarius touched the scissors beside him on the bench.

"A… haircut?" Dared she hope he'd finally let her tidy that blond nest?

"You have not been answering your door. I believed it might take a long-coveted prize to convince you to rejoin the rest of the world. And me."

"You think I'd consider cutting your hair a prize?"

"You have often expressed the desire to do so."

"Maybe it *would* delight my… fastidious streak." Amaranthe smiled. "You don't have to sacrifice your recalcitrant locks for me though. As for rejoining the world, I was just waiting for the *right* person to knock on my door." That said, she was glad that he'd waited. Two days earlier, she would have wept all over him and left snotty streaks on his pristine black sleeves. Not much of a prize for *him*.

Sicarius lifted the scissors and held them out to her. He still wanted to let her do it? Even after she'd let him off the hook?

"You wish to look tidy for the funeral ceremony?" Amaranthe asked.

"I wish to look tidy for you."

She swallowed. "That's… thoughtful, but I like you fine the way you are. Well, we could work on your smiles, but physically you're very… nice." She blushed, reminded that she was lying in his lap. And that they were alone in the courtyard.

"You do not wish to cut it?" Sicarius asked.

"Oh, I've *dreamed* of cutting it since I met you. I don't want you to think it's some kind of requirement though, that I'm only willing to be seen in public with men with tidy locks."

"I understand. Shall we do it in your room?"

Amaranthe suspected they were talking about more than haircuts, but either way, her answer was, "Yes."

She lifted her head, and he helped her up. He handed her the scissors and gestured for her to lead the way. She opened the door to her room and walked about, lighting lamps. It had grown dim while he'd been reading.

Though comfortable, with a large bed, a desk, and a private tub and lavatory, it was a single room, and she grew aware of the fact that the bed dominated it.

Amaranthe avoided looking at it and pulled out the chair at the desk. "Have a seat."

Sicarius removed his shirt. The lantern light drew attention to his lean, powerful back and torso, the valleys between his muscles delineated by shadow, the bronze contoured flesh taut even when he was relaxed.

"Uhm," Amaranthe said as he folded his shirt and laid it on the desk. "It's not necessary to disrobe for, ah..." He turned to face her, and she found herself staring at his pectoral muscles. "Never mind," she said. "Sit down, please."

He sat on the chair fully, not on the edge, like an animal poised to flee. He'd once remarked that his reason for cutting his own hair was that he wouldn't trust anyone near his neck with a blade. When had that changed?

Amaranthe moved a mirror from the washbasin to the desk. Even if he trusted her, it might make him less uneasy if he could watch what she was doing. She pulled out a comb. Its wide teeth were meant for her thick locks rather than short tufts, but it would do.

Amaranthe positioned herself behind him and tried to comb his hair into order. Though she'd touched it a few times before, for some reason she always expected it to be coarse and prickly, a reflection of his personality. It was clean and soft, though, a pleasure to stroke, even if those strokes didn't cause it to lie down nicely. She used her hand as much as the comb, letting her fingers trail down the side of his neck to brush his collarbone and those lovely shoulder muscles.

She wondered what he used for shampoo. Nothing scented that might give him away to some enemy, but would she catch a whiff of some cleaning agent if she lowered her nose to his scalp? She imagined those soft hairs tickling her skin and had an urge to turn the imagined into reality.

Under the pretext of addressing some knot, she lowered her face as she applied the comb and inhaled subtly. It was *his* scent that filled her nostrils, not that of some shampoo. Warm skin, freshly scrubbed, without the odor of weapons-cleaning oil that usually lingered about him. She didn't mind that smell, indeed associating it with him, but it tickled her that he'd cleaned up so thoroughly for... his haircut. Maybe he'd remembered her words about preferring her lovers to be free of makarovi gore.

"We will not be disturbed," Sicarius said.

Startled, Amaranthe stood up straight. It was silly but she was embarrassed, as if appreciating his scent while pretending to do something else was like being caught sampling flat cakes she hadn't paid for. "What?"

"Sespian and the rest of the team have gone out to drink to Books's memory, and the Starcrests are retrieving their other children from the family homestead."

"So... you're saying we have the guesthouse to ourselves?"

"For many hours."

"Indeed?" Amaranthe squeaked, then cleared her throat. She distinctly remembered their previous discussion revolving around the word.

In the mirror, his dark eyes were intent, full of purpose. Their intensity was alluring, filling her with the heat of anticipation, but they made her nervous as well. What if, after all this time, she disappointed him?

"Let me wet down your feisty tufts then. I'm sure since you arranged so much privacy for us, you'd like me to do a good job."

Amaranthe took a deep breath and told herself to get on with things and not burble. He was probably getting impatient. But Sicarius appeared relaxed as he watched her watching him. Even... pleased.

She retrieved a pitcher of water to dampen his defiant locks. Once she'd flattened them as much as possible, she lifted the scissors and considered where to start. The top she supposed, to even out of all those tufts. She was about to make her first clip when he spoke.

"You've done this before?"

"Many times," Amaranthe said.

"On dolls?"

She smiled, reminded of the time she'd admitted that her wound-stitching skills had come via that route. "Yes, on dolls, but also on my father. He couldn't afford the barber, so when I was old enough, I started cutting his hair for him." She waved the scissors. "Are you ready now? Or do I need to apply for more official credentials before I can begin?"

"You may begin."

"I'm so pleased."

Though he'd granted his permission, Amaranthe started with a single snip, waiting to see if he'd object or perhaps critique. He did not. As she went on, alternating between clipping and combing, he closed his eyes. From someone else, it would mean nothing. But from him... It had taken a year, but he'd finally come to trust her fully. She wondered if it was strange that it meant more to her than a declaration of love would have from another. She dabbed away moisture gathering in her eyes.

"Tilt your head forward, please," she whispered, wanting to cut a clean line across the bottom.

He did so without comment, and she let her fingers stray again, knowing she was almost done and wanting to savor the experience. All right, she enjoyed touching that warm, sleek skin as well, following the contours of the sinews beneath. The explorations were easier with his head down, without worrying about what thoughts lay behind his eyes.

"Amaranthe," Sicarius said, "are you finished?"

"Er, almost."

She shifted to his front so she could trim his bangs. They had to be even. Aware of his face, scant inches from hers, she licked

her lips and concentrated on keeping her hands from shaking as she worked.

He watched that movement, the darting of her tongue. His eyes didn't seem so intimidating now. She recognized his intensity for urgency, yearning. How long had she experienced those same desires for him?

"Are you finished yet?" Sicarius's muscles might have been relaxed when she'd started, but they were alert now, like those of a sprinter poised at the blocks, ready to surge forward at the starter's shout.

"Almost," Amaranthe whispered. She stepped back to properly assess the evenness of the cut and noticed his hand poised in the air, as if he was merely awaiting her signal to pull her into an embrace. As eager to move on as he, she would have welcomed it, but... "Not quite." She leaned close again. "Your bangs are still a little crooked. You wouldn't want to—"

Sicarius stood suddenly and his lips covered hers, finally hushing her... burble, that's what he would call it. She might have voiced an indignant—if muffled—protest, but all thought fled from her mind as his arms wrapped about her, and their bodies molded together. Her senses came alive at the feel of those hard muscles against her chest.

The scissors clinked to the floor.

After a moment, he pulled away, a question in his eyes.

"What is it?" she asked, a little breathless.

"I did not come for the haircut," he said as if he were sharing some shameful secret.

Amaranthe kissed him on the cheek. "I figured that out."

"You... do not mind?"

His uncertainty touched her, though she hadn't expected it. That kiss they'd shared in the factory—there'd been no uncertainty in it. His time with the wizard had changed something, she sensed, reminded him that he did indeed possess human fallibility and... frailty. Amaranthe stroked his cheek with the back of her hand. She understood. Oh, yes, she understood.

"I don't mind," she whispered. "I've been waiting for you, for *this* a long time."

Relief warmed his eyes, and more... A smile touched his lips.

When she returned it—oh, how long she'd been waiting for that little gesture from him—Sicarius stepped closer again, their bodies not quite touching this time. Mirroring her, he lifted his hand to hold the side of her face and gazed into her eyes for a long moment, then let his fingers trail lower. Light as the snowflakes falling outside, they ran down the side of her neck to her collarbone, stopping at her top shirt button. Senses alight, she scarcely dared to breathe as his deft fingers made quick work of the buttons. He slipped her shirt from her shoulders, letting it fall to the floor.

A distant part of her mind protested this careless cluttering of the floor, but the warmth of his body invited her to step in instead of away to pick it up. She slid her arms around his waist and delighted in pressing her bare chest against his. Something between a growl and a rumble of pleasure reverberated in his throat, and he, too, embraced her.

His lips captured hers once more, the uncertainty replaced with surety and desire. And a willingness to please that might have brought her to tears if her body wasn't so busy responding... His lips strayed from her mouth to tease their way down the side of her neck, then to flesh far more sensitive and alive than that.

How long had she dreamed of this? She buried her face in his hair, this time not hesitating to inhale, to breathe in his scent. It had taken so much to get here; she wouldn't deny herself these simple things now.

He turned, his arms around her to keep her from falling—as if she would have let go so that could happen. Two steps and she was on the bed, the soft fur blanket against her bare back contrasting with his hard body against her chest and between her legs. Her hands roamed, delighting in what she'd never dared do before, to taste what she'd never dared taste.

Sicarius rose to his elbows, meeting her eyes again. "Do you trust me?"

The question surprised her. She'd been so pleased that *he* trusted *her*... It hadn't occurred to her that he would wonder if

she felt the same way. A monster, he'd called himself more than once. A dangerous monster. Did he wonder if she'd be afraid of being so vulnerable before him?

"Yes. With my life." She hesitated—he knew *that*—and added, "With everything."

His pushed a stray lock of hair away from her face. Their eyes held for a long time, and she decided it didn't matter if he never grew into someone who would share his every thought; if he simply looked at her like that... it was already more than she'd ever expected from him.

"Don't you think we're a little overdressed?" She glanced down. "Though I see you did find a moment to take your boots off. Was that before or after you unbuttoned my shirt?"

"After."

His hand drifted downward from her face, as did his gaze, and she stifled an embarrassed urge to drag a fur over herself. He'd seen her naked before, but she'd never been one to flaunt her body even before she'd earned the makarovi scars on her abdomen. She couldn't help but think, too, of the various beautiful women she'd seen express their attraction for him over the last year. But there was nothing disappointed in his eyes or in his hands, as their caresses drew shivers and promised there'd be more to come.

"I have," he murmured, as he helped her remove her trousers, "longed for the moment when I could openly look at you... and touch."

Yes, looking and touching were definitely more thrilling than pretending not to look when he strolled past with his shirt off after an exercise session, with his chest gleaming in the morning sun. "Oh?" she asked. "Was there un-open looking before?"

"Yes."

She was more than a little titillated at the idea of him lusting after her from afar—all this time, she hadn't known if he had any urges whatsoever, or if he sublimated them along with the rest of his feelings. She ran her hand up his arm, along his shoulder, and to the back of his neck. "What did you think of doing while you were looking?"

"Much. Often."

Amaranthe snorted softly. Terse and cryptic, as always, but it was enough to excite her imagination. She no longer felt embarrassed by his appraisal, but intrigued by it. She dug her fingers into his hair, and whispered, "Show me."

As if he'd been awaiting the command, he lowered his head for another kiss, this one less playful and more intense, his desire blatant and hungry. She opened up to him, wanting him to enjoy this as much as she was, hoping her enthusiasm would please him, as his surely did her.

She slid her fingers down his back, relishing the restrained power quivering beneath the surface, and helped him out of his trousers. He would have managed it himself eventually, she was sure, but his hands—and his lips and teeth too—were busy attending to her, sparking her own desire.

When they came together at last, it was as much a binding as a release. Oh, he'd call it something prosaic like a biological necessity being fulfilled, but his caresses, his soft kisses, the way he watched her eyes for signs of discomfort or distress, the way he smiled ever so slightly when she cried out his name... it all meant more to him than biology. She could tell, even if he didn't say a word.

Once, she'd likened Sicarius to a caged tiger, too dangerous to keep around if one didn't want people hurt. Others had called him a trained dog, ready to kill at the drop of a flag. He was neither of course. He was a human being. One scarred by life, by fate. Just like her.

Once, she'd chastised herself for being attracted to the "amoral assassin," but she'd been as much of a different person then as he had. This journey they'd survived together... it wouldn't make sense to be at the end of it with anyone else. Not the end, she decided, but the beginning.

"Tears?" he asked, lying atop her, his weight propped on his elbows, though she'd claimed him with her legs and her arms, not ready to let him withdraw.

She hadn't realized the tears were running down the sides

of her flushed face until he caught them with the backs of his fingers. He kissed her eyes, a hint of a crinkle to his brow, worry that he'd done something to hurt her. She shook her head and smiled—funny that he'd worry about that now after all the times he'd ordered another torturous lap around the obstacle course or an impossible number of chin-ups.

"What?" Amaranthe asked. "You've never had women so overcome by your tender ardor that they wept?"

His eyebrows didn't twitch, but he scrutinized her, and she imagined him calculating the appropriateness of various witty responses and rejecting all of them. "No."

"Huh. Maybe I'm odd."

His features softened. "Yes."

"Though the tales of eld often speak of women being enraptured by doting paramours eager to go along with their every word, there are times when I wouldn't mind you disagreeing with me." Doting paramours? Tales of eld? Erg. During all those times she'd dreamed of being snuggled up with Sicarius in post-coital rapture, she'd imagined much more intelligent pillow talk.

"Your chattiness implies that your breathing has returned to normal," he observed.

Amaranthe squinted at him. "You've said those words before, always during training, usually when I think we've completed our workout, only to find you have more rounds, sets, or repetitions in mind."

"You're not tired, are you?" Mischievousness lurked in his eyes.

"No," she said automatically, having long since learned that admitting to weariness would win her no leniency, only an admonition that she must improve her stamina.

"Good, I'd like to acquaint you with my tender ardor several more times before dawn."

"Acceptable," she said, mimicking his tone from earlier, though she held a hand up before he could lower his lips for a fresh kiss. "But there's one thing we simply must tend to first."

His eyebrows lifted.

Amaranthe slid to the edge of the bed and groped about, having a vague recollection of hearing a clink earlier. Ah, yes. There. She retrieved the scissors and waved them triumphantly. "It's a testament to your lovemaking skills that your crooked bangs didn't distract me earlier, but we're going to have to fix that before going another round."

* * *

Sicarius walked hand-in-hand with Amaranthe through the Emperor's Preserve toward a bier placed in a clearing made white with fresh snow. A waist-high bed of branches waited beside it, along with several of their comrades. It was a much smaller gathering of people than had appeared for the morning's public ceremony to mourn all of those who had fallen during the Time of Incertitude, as some etymology-loving journalist had tagged it.

Basilard stood, hands clasped before him, his solemn face cast downward, his head bare to the cool air. Akstyr was there, too, looking perturbed and vaguely perplexed as he muttered to himself. For once, he was dressed in clothing that fit, a black ensemble with a gray overcoat that fell to his knees. He finally looked like an adult. Maldynado, Yara, and Sespian chatted quietly a few meters away. Ridgecrest and several of Starcrest's other military allies walked up to the gathering from a steam lorry. There were also a few scholars who'd learned of Books over the last few days by studying his work. Discreetly placed guards ensured uninvited guests—such as those who might seek an opportunity to collect on bounties—would not enter the area.

Having accepted Books's death, and reacquainted himself with the notion that there was little fairness in a universe that would prematurely end the life of a professor while sparing that of a murdering assassin, Sicarius had little interest in this public sendoff. He would have preferred to spend the morning in bed with Amaranthe, though he was mollified—and pleased— that she hadn't let go of his hand during the earlier ceremony.

Though he'd admittedly been the aloof one over the last year, she'd always been quick to hide any displays of affection when the rest of the team was around, and he'd wondered if she'd simply wanted to appear professional, or if she'd been reluctant to show others that she'd fallen in love with a cold-hearted killer. This seemed not to be the case though, for she'd not let him wander far at any point that day, the handgrip an open claim for all to see.

Basilard saw them approaching and walked over to give Amaranthe a hug. He looked like he might offer the same to Sicarius, but extended his hand instead. Sicarius clasped it and let go.

"I'm sorry I haven't been around these last couple of days, Bas," Amaranthe said, though Sicarius didn't see why she felt compelled to apologize for the fact. "I've been mourning... or sulking." She shrugged. "Something of that ilk."

Basilard let his gaze fall to their clasped hands. *Oh?*

"I mean, I wasn't mourning the *whole* time. Just until last night. Someone convinced me to stop. Not that you care. Or should. Uhm." Amaranthe's blush drew a smile from Basilard.

Sometimes Sicarius found it incongruous that Amaranthe had no trouble leading men into battle and jumping into the fray herself with all manner of self-poise and confidence, but that she tripped over her tongue in abashment when the matter of her relationships and feelings came up. Of course, he had his own difficulties in that area. The night before... it hadn't mattered a speck to him if his hair were cut—more than once that morning he'd caught himself rifling his fingers through it in an attempt to find the defiant tousle again—but he hadn't possessed the courage to knock on Amaranthe's door without that pretext. Despite Starcrest's talk, and the knowledge that she should be the last person to dismiss him out of some disdainful moral superiority, he'd worried that she might change her mind in the end. Her shy stroking while she'd been tending his hair and her covert glances at his chest had relieved him. Once he'd been certain of her desire, the rest had come naturally,

though he'd wondered at one point if he was being overeager to please, having few other ways to let her know how much her loyalty—how much *she*—had meant to him this past year. But she'd never protested or teased. Indeed, the memory of her enthusiastic responses to his touch pleased him greatly. To care about the woman one shared physical intimacy with was a new and delicious experience. The memory filled him with satisfaction and... completeness. And an urge to steal off into the trees with her and to do it all again.

Basilard was watching him with an amused quirk to his lips, and Sicarius wondered if his inattention to his facade had allowed a few of these thoughts to slip out. He decided it didn't matter. With these people, he no longer worried about threats or betrayal.

"What are your plans?" Amaranthe asked Basilard. "It seems that our outlaw-mercenary efforts won't be needed here any more."

"Outlaw?" Sicarius murmured. "I thought you'd upgraded us to revolutionaries."

"True, but I'm hoping revolutionaries won't be needed any more either."

I want to return to my homeland for a time, Basilard signed. *To find my daughter and make sure she is well, and...* He glanced at Sicarius and shrugged, then gave a single nod to Amaranthe.

Sicarius had the sense of this being a follow-up to some conversation for which he hadn't been present.

"Good," Amaranthe said. "I hope your family accepts you back, but if things don't work out or if you get bored without our wit..." She tilted her head toward Maldynado, who was striding down a slope arm-in-arm with Yara, heading to a black steam carriage that was pulling up. Starcrest's conveyance presumably. "Come back to the capital, and we'll take care of you. With your culinary knack, I bet you could open an eating house or a bakery that would rival Curi's."

Perhaps so. Basilard smiled again. *Does this mean you two will stay in Stumps?*

"I... we... hadn't talked about it yet. Other than vague mentions of vacations on remote beaches far from bounty hunters." A chilly gust of wind rattled the skeletal tree branches, and Amaranthe pulled her scarf up higher. "A *warm* remote beach."

Admiral Starcrest stepped out of the steam carriage, followed by Tikaya, Mahliki, and two younger teenagers. Sicarius would have chosen to stand beneath a tree and endure this ceremony in silence, but Amaranthe still had his hand, so he perforce went where she did. It looked like she wanted to visit the Starcrests, but Maldynado had planted himself in the admiral's path, so she walked up to speak with Akstyr instead.

"Have you been well these last few days?" she asked him.

Akstyr nodded. For a while, he didn't speak, then he quietly said, "I thought he was the biggest lecturing pest, you know." He tilted his head toward the blanket that wrapped Books's body. "But he was all right. I'm going to miss him. I still don't really get why..." His shoulder twitched.

"One of the more endearing qualities to human beings is their willingness to sacrifice themselves to make someone else's life better," Amaranthe said. "My father did that for me, not by stepping in front of an arrow, of course, but in the work he chose, work that killed him far too young." She gazed toward the unlit pyre, the sadness of memory in her eyes.

Sicarius wondered if he should say or do something for her. And if so, what? He squeezed her hand, and she returned the gesture with a smile for him.

"Well, I never thought anybody would sacrifice anything for me," Akstyr said. "How do you... What do you do if you're not sure their, uhm, sacrifice... was worth it?"

"You *make* it worth it." Amaranthe looked like she might say more, but she closed her mouth, letting him figure out what her words meant.

He studied the snow at his feet. After a time, he said, "All right."

An improvement over his whatevers.

Amaranthe must have found the response acceptable, too, for she patted Akstyr's arm. "Have you heard anything about... Well, with the gangs decimated, I hope nobody will be worrying about that bounty. Do you know if your mother is still...?"

"It doesn't matter." Akstyr pulled an envelope out of his pocket. With some bemusement, Sicarius wondered when he'd stopped worrying the boy might be pulling out a weapon to use on him. Akstyr held out the envelope for Amaranthe. "Professor Komitopis gave it to me. I guess someone mentioned to her that I wanted to study the Science at the Polytechnic."

Amaranthe opened the envelope, revealing tickets for a westbound train along with a berth on an ocean liner heading to the Kyatt Islands.

"I'm leaving in two days," Akstyr said. "The professor said I could stay with her family while I study. She said her mother still cooks up piles of food for all the hands and wouldn't hardly notice if one more person showed up at the dinner table, and..." Distracted by something, his words trailed off. He was peering toward the Starcrest family, his eyes alighting not on his fifty-year-old benefactor, but on her youngest daughter.

"Two days?" Amaranthe looked at him, then toward Basilard, chagrin in her eyes. "I..." She focused on Akstyr again. "I mean, that's wonderful. I know that this is your dream, and I'm sure you'll be safe there. I heard this morning that the enforcers are already routing out the remains of the gangs. There's talk of finally renovating the old part of the city, getting it on the sewer and making sure the people living there have the same educational opportunities as everyone else."

Akstyr, having failed to catch the young woman's eyes, pulled his attention back to Amaranthe and waved dismissal. "Same educational opportunities as other Turgonians maybe, but I'm sure it'll still be forbidden to study the mental sciences."

"I wouldn't be certain about that. If Starcrest does indeed get elected to office, at least one of his children practices the mental sciences." She grimaced and rubbed her forehead at some memory; Sicarius would have to get the details of what

had happened while he'd been ensnared by the Nurian. "He might push for some reform in that area too."

"Maybe so, but the population won't be quick to accept that. Superstitious donkey lickers. I won't be in a hurry to come back here."

"Ah," Amaranthe said.

Akstyr, displaying surprising percipience for him, noticed her downcast expression. "But you could visit Kyatt, right? You don't have any reason to stay here either, do you? I could show you around." Akstyr glanced at the hand Amaranthe still had clamped around Sicarius's, then added, "Uhm, both of you," though he didn't quite meet Sicarius's eyes.

"Thank you," Amaranthe said. "I'd like that."

Akstyr, his gaze drawn back to the Starcrests again, said, "I'm going to go see how long she's—I mean they're—going to be staying and if they're going back to Kyatt for their studies..."

Amaranthe started to walk in that direction, too, and Sicarius wondered if he might talk to Starcrest while she chatted with whoever was next on her list. He could certainly make that happen if he released her hand, but he wasn't sure he wanted to yet. Later perhaps, when he'd grown used to the idea that she'd return to reclaim it if they parted.

As if she could guess his thoughts, Amaranthe paused and gazed up at him. "I'm sorry, I'm dragging you all over the place. Would you prefer to find a nice tree to lurk beside?"

"Perhaps later."

"I just want to make sure and see everyone before... Akstyr's leaving in two days. Dear ancestors, I never thought I'd miss the boy, but he's finally getting interesting."

"If that is true—" Sicarius didn't know if he'd go so far as to deem Akstyr interesting, "—then you have made him so."

Amaranthe leaned against him. "We'll see them again, right? Basilard and Akstyr? This almost feels like losing Books all over again."

Sicarius had no way of divining the future, and anything he said would be useless conjecture, so he did not speak. But he wrapped his arms loosely about her, in case that would lend comfort.

Amaranthe turned her head to rest it against his collarbone. "*You're* not leaving me anytime soon, are you?"

"No." He waited until she snuggled close to add, "Who, then, would cut my hair?"

She snorted and swatted him on the chest. "Nobody, and don't forget it. You look quite dapper today."

The crunch of footprints alerted Sicarius to others' approach long before the pair drew close—he'd noted their arrival a few minutes prior in a second steam carriage parked farther down the hill. But at the noise, Amaranthe turned.

"Good day, Deret. And Ms. Curlev. Thank you for coming."

Mancrest and the Forge woman stood as one with their arms linked, each wearing expensive fur coats snugged up to their necks. Though it seemed Mancrest had found a new love interest, Sicarius couldn't help but feel pleased that Amaranthe had taken his hand again.

"Of course, Amaranthe," Mancrest said. "I regret that there wasn't time to get to know him better. I'm pleased to hear that much of his work is being incorporated into the new constitution."

"Constitution." Curlev smiled ruefully. "There's a notion that'll take time to grow accustomed to."

"Are you finding it... if not exactly what Forge wanted, a fairer government paradigm than what we've had for the last seven hundred years?" Amaranthe asked.

"Oh, undoubtedly so," Curlev said. "I don't suppose you'll believe this, but I had very little knowledge of what was going on with Forge back here these last ten years. When we were... dreaming it up, it was to be about scholarships to empower entrepreneurs and lobbying for equality for businesses in the eyes of the law. What it became... I'll regret the loss of so many of my colleagues, of course—" she threw a quick, wary glance at Sicarius, "—but I'm not positive you did the world a disservice."

Sicarius noticed that Maldynado was still standing in front

of Starcrest, gesturing vigorously while Yara stood back and rolled her eyes toward the bare branches of a tree overhead. Squirrels ran across the boughs, no doubt hoping some of these humans had brought food.

Sicarius could guess as to the nature of the words accompanying Maldynado's gestures. A man recovering from an injury should not have to suffer such inanity. Sicarius squeezed Amaranthe's hand again before releasing it, then headed over to Starcrest.

"I'm not certain a president, having less absolute power than an emperor, should do something so megalomaniacal as having statues commissioned," Starcrest was saying when Sicarius drew near.

"What? Of course, you should," Maldynado said. "Surely, it's your prerogative to redecorate during your time in office."

"It's premature to assume I'll be the one to take that position, but what exactly would you like redecorated?"

Sicarius stopped behind Maldynado and folded his arms across his chest, trusting him to notice eventually. Starcrest had already acknowledged him with a small wave of his hand—the other hung in a sling across his torso.

"In this case, it'd be more of an *initial* decorating," Maldynado said. "We're building a new government building to replace the Barracks, right? Stumps is known for its statues, however decapitated many of them are. Don't you think the square in front of this new building will need a sculpture or two? Visitors from all over the world will stop by. You'd want the destination to reflect our culture and our veneration for the heroes of old. And new heroes as well. Perhaps even one of the heroes who helped bring down the pretender emperor. One of the more *handsome* heroes that is. After all, you wouldn't want to scare away those tourists by sticking up some dour-faced assassin."

Yara had noticed Sicarius standing there, and he thought she might warn Maldynado to sew his lips shut, but she merely smirked and waited.

"Not that anyone would think an assassin heroic enough for

a statue anyway," Maldynado said. "People would probably come up in the middle of the night and drape washout paper all over it. Now if you want someone that would invite visitors into the building with a warm smile and a noble pose..."

Maldynado propped one hand on his hip and lifted his other to his forehead as he gazed toward a distant horizon. In turning toward that horizon, he finally noticed Sicarius standing behind him. He skittered backward, and his heel caught on an icy patch. He slapped his arms down, legs coming up in an unarmed combat fall designed to protect the body from injury, but the commotion irritated one of the squirrels overhead, and it fled from its branch. Clumps of snow fell in its wake, one sizable ball landing on Maldynado's forehead.

"Oh, yes," Yara chortled. "That'll make a fine statue."

Sicarius gazed coolly down at Maldynado. "Washout paper?"

"Er. Uhm. Yes, to *polish* it of course. To make sure it stays shiny." Maldynado scrambled to his feet and offered Yara his arm. "My lady, I need to say a few words to my fallen comrade before the pyre lighter comes to free his spirit. Will you join me?"

"I better. Someone has to keep you from offending the spirits of the dead as well as the living."

"Sicarius," Starcrest said by way of a greeting when they were alone. Mostly alone. His wife and children stood nearby, talking to some of the other funeral attendees, while Akstyr lurked on the edge of the group, trying to muster the gumption to chat with the younger daughter.

"Sir." Having only intended to rescue Starcrest from Maldynado, Sicarius hadn't planned anything grand to say to the admiral. "Have you decided to take the position of president?"

"There's a vote to be held in a few days, and I understand there are other candidates who are scrambling to make cases for themselves, but the limited time frame will make it difficult for them to become suitably known by the populace."

"That is good," Sicarius said. "You are what Turgonia needs now."

"Hm. That'll remain to be seen. At least Tikaya has allowed

that a few years living here wouldn't be the worst fate in the world. Either that or she feels guilty about objecting to living in Turgonia after I spent all these years in her homeland. Not much of a sacrifice admittedly. A very pleasant island once the people get over wanting to kill you. We will have to watch the girls carefully here. Imperial men are more forthright than Kyattese men, and I don't tower so fearsomely over people here, insomuch as you can tower fearsomely once all your hair turns gray."

Sicarius did not know how to respond to this effusion of familial material. He wondered if Starcrest would like to discuss one of his texts on strategies or perhaps new work that had been published in the field. Sicarius hadn't found time to keep up to date this last year, but he'd been reading most of the publications by notable military professors and field officers before then. Would it be rude to suggest a detour in the conversation? He'd never cared about inflicting rudeness upon people before, but Starcrest was different.

"You seemed chipper at the state funeral this morning," the admiral said.

Sicarius stared. "Chipper."

"By your standards. There was an uncharacteristic springiness to your step."

This was not the new course of conversation Sicarius had had in mind. Further, he found it disheartening that others had so easily read his mood. He'd kept his face neutral, as always, but springy steps? He'd never had to worry about such betrayals from his body before.

"Do I gather that you and your lady have found yourselves, after due consideration, as compatible as you'd hoped?"

Sicarius supposed he couldn't respond with a question of his own along the lines of, "Sir, did you read Earnestcrest's paper on insurgencies and counter-insurgencies, and did it influence your decisions at all as you sought to take control of the capital?" Instead he reverted to his simple, "Yes, sir."

"Excellent," Starcrest said. "What are your plans going

forward? I regret that it may be difficult to place you in employment to the thro—presidency, if that is something you desire. At least for a time. Your work for Flintcrest, however inadvertent, did add once again to your notoriety, and the general population will not understand the concept of being under a practitioner's control."

"I understand. I had thought to take a break—" Sicarius glanced at Amaranthe, who seemed to be getting along fine with Mancrest and the Forge woman, "—a vacation regardless."

Starcrest smiled. "I thought that might be the case." With his good hand, he fished in his pocket, jangling something as he pulled it out. "Allow me to facilitate."

"Sir?" Sicarius held his hand out when Starcrest made it clear he wished to give away the item.

A set of keys dropped into his palm. "Corporal Lokdon knows where it's berthed. You'll need to requisition some supplies and remove my daughter's... collections—and please take care not to kill anything she has caged, cached, or otherwise netted up in there. There's a technical manual full of operating instructions—I have a Kyattese gentleman to thank for that, as they insist on documenting everything over there—and I'm confident that you'll be able to master them quickly. Take as long as you like out there. There's a journal penned in Tikaya's hand that points out some of our favorite spots along with their latitude and longitude. Do read the entries before deciding on one. A handful would be suitable for... vacationing, but some are favorite spots because of the archaeologically significant finds she located there, beaches full of cannibals wearing finger-bone necklaces not withstanding. Ah, but I'm rambling. You'll figure it out on your own." He patted Sicarius on the shoulder and headed toward the bier, where more people were gathering in preparation for the ceremony.

Sicarius stared at the keys in his hand, the meaning of the admiral's monologue sinking in.

"What's that?" Sespian asked, walking up.

"I believe it is... a vacation." Huh. They wouldn't even need to find a remote beach to take advantage of privacy. Simply descend ten meters in any lake or sea, and who would bother them?

"For you and Amaranthe? That's good. She could use it for sure."

Sicarius lifted his head. "Only her?"

Sespian eyed the scar at his temple. "I'd say you, too, but do you even know how to... vacation?"

"I will learn. She will help me."

"Good. Ah, how long do you think you'll be gone?"

Sicarius wondered if that meant Sespian would miss him and wanted him to return eventually. "I do not know."

"It's just that I talked to Rias, and mentioned that I'd had a position in mind for Amaranthe. That diplomatic spot."

Rias? Sespian was calling Fleet Admiral Starcrest by his first name? How much time had they spent together while Sicarius had been... unable to return?

"Do you think she'll want it?" Sespian asked. "If Starcrest is elected, he said it'd be simple enough. He has a few contemporaries in mind for positions, but agrees that some young blood would be healthy." The way Sespian smiled suggested he'd been the one to point this out.

"I do not know if she wishes to remain," Sicarius said. "We have not discussed much beyond the vacation."

"Do you actually do that?" Sespian asked.

"What?"

"Discuss. You're often... monosyllabic."

"She discusses enough for both of us."

"Ah."

"Are *you* remaining in the capital?" Sicarius asked, wondering if Sespian, too, sought a position or if he wanted a break from government. Sespian had launched a few speculative gazes toward Starcrest's oldest daughter.

"For a while," Sespian said. "It's strange though, that I don't have a place to live now. Or any money. Or a job. I hope Trog's last couple of months roaming free in the Barracks have prepared him for a life of scraps instead of choice kitchen treats."

"What happened to the money you paid us for your kidnapping?"

"Oh, Amaranthe was good about toting it around—we'd figured we might need it to buy weapons and bribe troops—and she had it stored in a safe nook in the factory. I understand the molasses flood rather thoroughly took out bedrolls, rucksacks, and suitcases of ranmyas."

"It's on the bottom of the lake?"

"Most likely," Sespian said. "And encased in a sticky goo."

Sicarius wondered how deep Starcrest's submarine could descend. He doubted Sespian cared overmuch about the money, but retrieving it might prove a good training exercise, a chance to learn the boat's capabilities.

Sespian noticed someone's wave and started walking toward the bier. The director had come with a lantern and the oil-doused lighting torch. They were ready to begin.

Sicarius thought about finding a tree to lean against, but Amaranthe, standing with Tikaya and Yara, met his eyes across the bier. There was no request or demand in them, but he thought he read a hint of vulnerability. Maybe he simply wanted her to need him. Either way, he chose to walk over and stand beside her before the pile of logs and branches arranged, as was tradition, in the shape of a shield. Bearers laid Books's body across the wood, as a fallen warrior might once have been carried off the battlefield on his shield.

Though Sicarius watched, he was also aware of Sespian coming to stand beside him. They listened in silence as the director spoke at length of Marl "Books" Mugdildor, pulling up information from his past that Sicarius hadn't known. He wondered if Amaranthe had given the history to the director, or if he'd researched independently.

"Who will speak before his spirit is sent into the next world?"

Akstyr mumbled, "He saved my life," but shifted uncomfortably under everyone's gazes and didn't say anything further.

Maldynado stepped forward, removing a sedate beaver fur

cap and pressing it to his chest. "Books was the sort to harass you with lectures, but I think it was because he was stuck in a situation where he didn't know how to interact with any of us uneducated louts, and he did the best he could. I wish he'd surviv..." Maldynado's fingers curled into a fist. "Cursed ancestors, Books, what's wrong with you? Why couldn't you have made it another night? Another *hour*? We were almost done with every—" He broke off, blinked rapidly, then brought the fist to his chest in a salute and bowed. More softly, he said, "Goodbye, Booksie."

Maldynado stepped back. Yara took his hand, and they leaned against each other.

After a silent moment, during which Amaranthe and a few others wiped their eyes, Basilard stepped forward. He nodded to Amaranthe and she translated his words for those who didn't understand the signs.

Though fate forced him down a road on which he reluctantly turned himself into a warrior, Books had the heart of a peaceful man. He would have been liked and honored among my people. Perhaps one day, Mangdoria as well as Turgonia will benefit from the documents he constructed.

When Amaranthe translated the mention of Mangdoria, Basilard lifted his head, meeting Starcrest's eyes. They must have discussed Basilard's issues at some point, for Starcrest returned the nod. The idea of the number of deals, negotiations, and overseer duties waiting for the admiral, assuming he took office, was enough to make Sicarius glad nobody would put his name on a ballot for anything. He'd rather go through the rest of his life with that bounty on his head than spend a year in charge of a nation.

Amaranthe stepped away from his side to speak at the head of the bier. "I regret that Books—Marl—didn't live to see his work adopted or the results that we as a team fought so hard for this last year. It's been a far bloodier resolution than any of us would have wished, but I have hope that the future will be a good one, one that will make our sacrifices—*his* sacrifice—worth it." She

wiped her eyes again and took a deep breath before continuing. "I wish he'd known more happiness in his life, but I hope his spirit will find a peaceful rest with the awareness that he made a difference. Losing his son always plagued his heart, and one of his biggest regrets, he once told me, was that his last words to Enis were harsh. It ate at him that he didn't get a chance to say, 'I love you' one last time before his son's loss. I hope that they'll find each other and make amends in the afterworld."

Basilard shifted his weight, a thoughtful expression on his face.

Sicarius found it odd that a people could deny the belief in deities, magic, and other mysticism, but had no trouble accepting that the human spirit was eternal and lived on in some everlasting incarnation. Perhaps the other things weren't required for the sanity of the human mind, but the idea of mortality being final was too depressing a concept to accept for those who inevitably drew closer to such an end themselves.

He noticed Sespian watching him, but when he turned to make eye contact, Sespian lowered his gaze.

"Does anyone else wish to speak?" the director asked.

Those who had not known Books that long or that well deferred. Maldynado, Amaranthe, and Basilard all looked at Sicarius though. They expected him to speak? What would he say? No words could change the fact that Books was dead, nor did he require some ceremony to accept a person's passing.

They did, though. His comrades sought something from this experience that he might never understand fully. For them, he took a step forward, though he didn't know what to say. What wouldn't be inane? What wouldn't be boorish? They probably wouldn't be impressed if he spoke of Books's progress in his training over the last year, and that it was unfortunate that chance had killed him even as he'd grown into a competent warrior.

Aware of all the gazes, of Amaranthe's and Sespian's in particular, Sicarius finally said, "In our memories he will survive."

So much for not uttering anything inane.

People nodded though, and Amaranthe gave a sad smile. "Perhaps that's where it matters most, and the history books are just... vanity of a sort."

Sicarius stepped back into the circle of bystanders, and she took his hand. As the boughs were lit beneath the body, Sespian took his other hand. It startled Sicarius, but he managed to keep from commenting or staring with incredulity.

The branches, doused with oil, caught flame quickly. The faces of those watching as the fire enveloped the body were sad, but Sicarius couldn't help but share Amaranthe's belief that the future would be better than the past. With her on one side and his son on the other, *his* future already was.

THE END

ALSO BY THE AUTHOR

The Emperor's Edge Universe

Novels
The Emperor's Edge, Book 1
Dark Currents, Book 2
Deadly Games, Book 3
Conspiracy, Book 4
Blood and Betrayal, Book 5
Forged in Blood I, Book 6
Forged in Blood II, Book 7
Encrypted
Decrypted

Short Stories And Novellas
Ice Cracker II (and other short stories)
The Assassin's Curse
Beneath the Surface

THE FLASH GOLD CHRONICLES

Flash Gold
Hunted
Peacemaker

THE GOBLIN BROTHERS ADVENTURES

5052633R00251

Printed in Germany
by Amazon Distribution
GmbH, Leipzig